THE FALL OF
LISA BELLOW

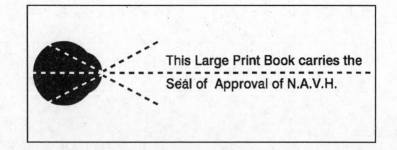

This Large Print Book carries the
Seal of Approval of N.A.V.H.

THE FALL OF
LISA BELLOW

SUSAN PERABO

THORNDIKE PRESS
A part of Gale, Cengage Learning

GALE
CENGAGE Learning·

Farmington Hills, Mich • San Francisco • New York • Waterville, Maine
Meriden, Conn • Mason, Ohio • Chicago

GALE
CENGAGE Learning®

LIBRARY OF CONGRESS CATALOGING-IN-PUBLICATION DATA

Names: Perabo, Susan, 1969– author.
Title: The fall of Lisa Bellow / by Susan Perabo.
Description: Large print edition. | Waterville, Maine : Thorndike Press, a part of Gale, Cengage Learning, 2017. | Series: Thorndike Press large print basic
Identifiers: LCCN 2017012284| ISBN 9781432840990 (hardcover) | ISBN 1432840991 (hardcover)
Subjects: LCSH: Life change events—Fiction. | School children—Fiction. | Abduction—Fiction. | Girls—Fiction. | Large type books.
Classification: LCC PS3566.E673 F35 2017b | DDC 813/.54—dc23
LC record available at https://lccn.loc.gov/2017012284

Published in 2017 by arrangement with Simon & Schuster, Inc.

Printed in the United States of America
1 2 3 4 5 6 7 21 20 19 18 17

For my mom and dad

PART ONE

1

Sometimes in the morning, while she waited for her brother to get out of the bathroom, Meredith Oliver would stand in front of her bureau mirror, lock eyes with her reflection, and say, "This is me. This is really me. Right now. This is me. This is my real life. This is me."

She would say these things to herself because she liked the moment when she suddenly became uncertain that those things she was saying were in fact true, liked the way it made her feel unmoored, the hole of doubt that opened up inside her, and the wind that blew through that hole. It was a physical sensation, as real as cresting the first incline of a roller coaster, the momentum shift from ascending to descending. It was, Meredith had decided, precisely like sucking on a giant, whole-body Mentho-Lyptus cough drop, the way it cleared her out, head to toe. And she liked equally —

not more and not less, because it was just the same sensation backward — the moment she became re-certain that those things were true — *this is me, this is really me* — when the hole closed, and the anchor caught, and she could smell the eggs her father was scrambling downstairs.

Meredith had been doing the mirror thing for as long as she could remember, on mornings both ordinary (today, for instance) and memorable (first days of school, birthdays, etc). Sometimes she went months without doing it, and then she'd resume for no reason she could name, and she did not think of it as a game or a habit or a meditation, but only her mirror thing. But even during those times when she called on it most, she didn't do it every day. She didn't want the trick to wear out. She suspected that if she overused it, it would lose its magic.

This morning the shower roared to life, the pipes humming with heat. This was encouraging, despite the fact that it would delay her from using the bathroom herself. Since Evan's injury, Meredith could read his mood, predict how the day would go, by how much of his morning bathroom routine was completed. Because the bathroom was situated between their two bedrooms, the entire routine could easily be monitored by sound alone. Some days were pill-only days, the creak of the medicine cabinet opening, the rattle of the bottle, two seconds of running water — just long enough for him to gather a handful to wash down the pill, no cup required — the creak of the cabinet closing, followed by . . . silence. No brushing of teeth, no shower, no shave. On those days he might just go back to bed, and then there would be a half hour of sitcom-worthy upstairs/downstairs, first her mother up and down, then her father up and down, then her mother again, the anxiety rising with every trip, a variety of knocks (the *breakfast-is-waiting,* the *tender-but-firm,* the *we-know-you-can-hear-us*), an assortment of appeals ("Evan, sweetie . . ." "Hey, pal . . ." "Getting late, kiddo . . ." "Evan, I'm serious . . ."). Often this was still happening when Meredith left the house to walk to school, her brother already tardy (the high school started a half hour earlier than the middle school), her parents playing out precisely the same scene they'd played out on the last pill-only day. But thankfully, Meredith thought, the pill-only days were now fewer and further between. Now most days were at least pill-and-toothbrush days, and after one round of upstairs/downstairs

Evan would appear at the kitchen table, unshaven but otherwise only marginally disheveled, his good eye flitting toward the clock every few minutes, sometimes a few lame jokes or minor complaints about the weather or the consistency of his eggs.

Meredith suspected that he got up now more often than not because he'd decided, maybe even subconsciously, that school was a better place for him to pass the day than home. Everywhere he spent any time at all — home, school, gym, hospital — was a delicate balance of distraction versus reminder, but at least at school the distractions were constant and diverse, a barrage coming at such a rapid-fire pace that sometimes he probably forgot for seconds or minutes about what had happened.

This day, Wednesday, there was brushing and showering and even the on-and-off water of a shave, which suggested not only a sulky resignation to, but perhaps actual interest in, the day, something he was looking forward to. Maybe it was the sunshine blazing through the bedroom windows. Maybe there was a party this weekend. Maybe there was a girl he wanted to talk to. Maybe his headache was just a dull pulse, an echo of pain more than the pain itself.

She didn't blame him for going back to

bed some mornings, or for his sulky resignation. She was not selfish enough to think him selfish. She liked to believe she was the only person in the world who truly understood him, so she was cautious not to judge, but just to observe. Carefully observe. The bathroom routine. The state of his bedroom. The hours spent on homework versus the hours spent on television versus the hours lying on his bed petting the tolerant cat. The tentative, jerky drives around the block. The rattle of pills tumbling out of the green bottle. The video games, some of which he could play, but most of which made his headaches worse. Smaller details: the part of his hair, reaching for his fork and missing it by half an inch, the angle of his iPhone, the *thwack* of the little rubber basketball as it bounced off the side of the mini backboard that hung over his closet door. And the thing he did with the tree by the front porch, touching the tip of a single branch with the tip of his finger. For the last couple of months he'd done this every time he left the house, and sometimes she saw him standing out there after school, doing it when he thought no one was watching.

He wore glasses now, mostly for protection of the now priceless right eye but also to obscure the view of the damage on the left. Ironically, neither lens of his black-framed glasses required any actual correction — the left lens was simply darkened, the right lens was simply glass.

In late March, just over six months ago now, Evan had been standing in the on-deck circle at baseball practice when a teammate hit a foul ball into his face. According to witnesses Evan had been maybe twenty-five feet from the plate, windmilling the bat around, stretching his shoulders, hooking the bat behind his back . . . the usual routine, the same old, same old. Meredith could picture this perfectly, had replayed the scene a million times, though she hadn't been there. The windmill, the hook, the things he'd done thousands of times, tens of thousands, loving the weight of the bat in his hand, the sun in his eyes, the confidence of knowing this one central thing about himself: he was really, really good at baseball.

When he was a sophomore, the city paper had named him the starting catcher on the all-region team, which was very rare. Their region was made up of a dozen suburban high schools west of the city, each suburb nearly a city in and of itself. Players like that, he'd told Meredith, guys who made all-region as sophomores, wound up at D1 schools, sometimes with full scholarships. It had happened abruptly; for a long time he was good, and then something changed — something physical, something in his body, something he freely, cheerfully admitted he couldn't take any credit for himself, a balance of strength and precision that elevated his skill both at and behind the plate — and suddenly he was *really* good. By that day in March he was nine games into his junior season and batting .470.

So there he was in the on-deck circle, thinking all these wonderful things about himself, or so Meredith imagined. (Sometimes, in her mind, she was watching from the stands; other times she stood no more than a foot or two away from him, so close she could hear the impact of ball on bone.) No one did anything wrong. No mistakes were made. Evan was wearing a helmet. He was standing in the appropriate spot. He wasn't goofing off. There was nobody you could point to and blame, not the kid (Matt Bowman) at the plate, not the bench coach, not the coach throwing batting practice, not Evan. It was just something that happened, a fraction of a second that you couldn't pin on anybody.

And then he was on the ground. "I never saw it coming," he'd told her months later, abruptly, bitterly, sitting on the back patio one humid July evening between surgery three and surgery four. It was the only time he'd ever talked to her about that day. "Blindsided," he'd said, scoffing. A mosquito had landed on his knee and he'd just sat there and watched it bite him, didn't even try to swat it away. *Never saw it. Not for one second.*

The doctor said that Evan's entire left eye socket was crushed beyond repair. A blowout fracture, he called it. The doctor said, "Imagine stepping on an ice cream cone." Meredith would never forget this, sitting in the hospital room, Evan sedated, she on a stiff vinyl chair looking out the window at the hospital parking lot, the doctor somberly relaying the news to her tight-lipped parents. "Imagine stepping on an ice cream cone." Why hadn't she been sent out of the room prior to this doctor-parent consultation? Why didn't her parents think to say, *"Hold on, doctor, give us a minute — Mer, honey, why don't you run down to the coffee shop and get a chocolate muffin while we talk to the doctor?"*

No, she was sitting on that hard, squeaky chair, wishing she could un-hear the sentence and un-see the image. The doctor said it was the worst baseball eye injury he'd ever encountered, that the best-case scenario was that Evan would regain some function (not "sight" — he plainly did not say "sight," but "function") in his left eye, but that he'd never play baseball competitively again.

As a catcher, Evan had been the recipient of numerous home-plate collisions, taken pitches off the shoulders and chest and knees and toes and facemask. He'd been banged up since she could remember; sometimes he seemed like one big purple bruise. Always, he recovered. But this was not like anything else.

More often than not they ate breakfast together, as a family, around the kitchen table in the sunny breakfast nook that looked out onto the backyard. Having breakfast together was a holdover from earlier years, when The Baseball Clock ruled the world, when Evan's practices or games always ran right through the evening and most dinners (except in the dead of winter) were sandwiches or one-pot pasta or French bread pizza in front of the television whenever you got hungry, or a floppy hot dog from a concession stand.

Breakfast was the meal where they could actually sit together for fifteen or twenty minutes, during which her father inevitably asked everyone to set a goal for the day. They didn't have to be serious goals — her father wasn't *that* guy — but were intended, he always said, to let everyone know something about what the others were doing as they went about their day. Meredith's stated goals were often lies having to do with academics — "I want to do well on my English test," etc. Not that this wasn't true, but her actual, pressing goals were almost always social in nature, and she didn't feel like letting on to her entire family just how shallow she really was.

"I'm going to go for a walk during lunch," her father said. Her father's response to Evan's injury had been to pursue an accelerated course of self-improvement in order that he might be better able to meet everyone's needs, whatever they might be. *Crushed eye socket? I got that!* His goals were often exercise or nutrition related, but once during the summer Meredith looked out her bedroom window and there was her father lying on the hammock in the backyard, reading the Bible, the intolerant cat grabbing at the shoelaces that hung through the netting of the hammock, her father threatening the intolerant cat by pretending to smack it with the Bible. The *Bible,* which had apparently belonged to her great-grandmother but which no one in the family, as far as Meredith could tell, had so much as glanced at since her great-grandmother's death.

"What d'ya think?" her father asked her mother now. "Care to join me?"

Her parents worked together, in the same office, the office of whirring drills and crying children, the office of the mingling smells of mint and artificial fruit flavors, the office she had adored as a child. Their practice was part of a sprawling, sparkling suburban medical park — her father referred to it as Sick City. All the buildings were identical on the outside, so patients routinely showed up at the dentist for a colonoscopy, or the orthopedist for a pap smear. But past the waiting room there was no mistaking where you were, and at the age of six or seven there was nowhere Meredith would have rather played, no amusement park more wonderful than those half-dozen chairs and the swiveling tables and the lights that dropped down from overhead like alien instruments. This was a game she and Evan especially enjoyed: Alien Examination. One of them would put on a surgical mask and the protective eyewear, the other would lie on the chair cloaked in the heavy x-ray blanket. The alien examiner would pull the light down and shine it on various parts of the specimen's face, prodding with a gloved finger at mouth, nose, eye, ear: What does this do? How does this work? What do you use this for? How lucky she and Evan had been — she knew this even (especially?) when annoyed by them now — that their parents had let them play with everything in that office, let them have the run of the place on Sunday afternoons while they caught up on paperwork. She and Evan could have broken those chairs in a hundred different ways during Alien Examination, but they never did.

"We could walk that trail in the park," her father said. Ah, the oft-mentioned wooded trail in the park adjacent to Sick City, a pretty jigsaw-puzzle image full of personal promise. It was not really for the sick; it was the place already healthy people went to get even healthier.

"Maybe," her mother said vaguely.

Perhaps, Meredith thought, it was only for Evan that they kept doing it, this pointless exercise, so things would seem normal. Her mother was standing at the counter pouring Evan a tall glass of milk. This was something he could not do for himself anymore. He could not pour a simple glass of milk. Meredith had watched him try, early on, and miss the glass entirely, as if he were actually, entirely, blind. "Some things are just a little different," he'd told her, soaking up the puddle of milk beside the glass, "but some things are impossible. Pouring — impossible. I can *see* the glass. I just don't know where it is."

"Today I will slay dragons," Evan said, taking the milk from his mother's hand. "I will dig to the center of the earth. I will reconcile warring nations. And I will learn to play the violin."

"Modest goals," her father said. "Is that it?"

"That plus a big piece of pie," he said. Then he winked at her. Meredith hated the wink now. Hated it. It bothered her that when her brother winked, he could not see at all. Why should that bother her? It was his wink, his darkness. Still, she couldn't stand it. "What d'ya think?" he asked her. "Care to join me?"

"Sure," she said. "I'll pencil it in."

At home there was Evan, and half-blind Evan was still Evan, still the safety net, whether he could actually catch her or not. At school there was no net.

The distance between home and Parkway North Middle School, a distance Meredith traveled by herself between 7:42 and 8:05 every single morning, seemed vast, a lonesome valley of suburban achievement, purring cars in driveways, crows the size of small cats milling about on rolling lawns, joggers attached to their NPR podcasts. She walked alone not because she had no friends, but because all her friends took the school bus. She lived — by some trick of fate, some ignorance of her parents when they'd purchased their dream home in their dream suburb prior to having school-aged children — in the unlucky zone just barely inside the 1.25-mile radius that required her to walk to school. Everyone who lived more than 1.25 miles from school got to take the school bus. And not that she would have loved the school bus — she knew this from friends and field trips, and, to be honest, from movies — but the school bus definitely seemed easier than walking, especially when it was rainy or cold. Her house was 1.19 miles from school, which she knew precisely because when Evan had started sixth grade, her father had driven the route twice to check to make sure the district transportation committee was right. Alas. And so she walked, alone, and at some point in the last quarter mile a giant bus barreled past her, sending her hair fluttering, and she would quicken her steps so that she could meet her friends when they disembarked, so they could enter at the glass doors as a unified front.

Numbers were essential. Solidarity was all.

It had been all downhill since fifth grade. Sometimes Meredith looked back on that golden year and felt a pang of nostalgia so keenly that she thought she might actually die. Fifth grade. Yes there were cliques, but the cliques didn't really *mean* anything in fifth grade. They were pretend distinctions between groups that rarely, if ever, translated into any real action or consequence. In fifth grade you were still friends with everyone, whether you liked it or not, because it was easier for the adults that way. Your parents didn't particularly care if you wanted to carpool with someone else to swimming lessons; it was convenient for you and Amanda Hammels to travel together, even if you never talked to each other in school, so, by god, that was the way it was going to be. Your teachers assigned you to groups with the expectation you could and should be able to work with anyone. Yes, in fifth grade there were some girls flirting with makeup and, yes, there were some girls flirting with boys, but it was all still as artificial as glittery lip gloss, all part of a world that no one yet really belonged to or understood. Plus, in fifth grade you could remember even further back, all the way back to first and second grade — you still walked down those same halls! — when some girl might have wet her pants or a boy might have cried for his mother or any number of humiliating things that held you all together, put you on an even playing field. As long as you were in that elementary school, in that physical space, everything that happened had happened equally to everyone.

But middle school? A different story. Turned out, what happened in elementary school stayed in elementary school. In sixth grade the playing field lurched to an impossible angle. How did it happen, the summer between fifth and sixth grade, how could it happen so abruptly that a level playing field could tilt so violently, tilt precisely like the *Titanic,* in a matter of mere hours the night before the first day of sixth grade? Meredith had seen the movie and this was the image she couldn't get out of her mind: everyone tumbling from the top of the ship down to the bottom, sliding, skidding, careening, frantically grabbing hold of bolted down deckchairs and stair railings. The sliders were clearly the ones who had not anticipated the tilt. Anyone who was going to get off the boat safely had gotten off already. When? In June?

Too late! The last days of August, sixth grade begins, the great slide happens, the playing field tilts, and Meredith finds herself clinging to the ship, somewhere near the middle, around the shuffleboard courts, say. She is not down at the bottom near the icy water, but she can feel the chill of it below her dangling feet, and she has no idea what's happened.

She had not gotten the memo about the iceberg.

And since then, since literally that first day of sixth grade, over two years ago, she had been trying to get her footing, trying to find her place.

Now she met her best friends Jules and Kristy at the corner of the parking lot where a herd of school buses belched and hissed. Kristy had been battling a head cold all week and had a tissue pressed to her nose, lest some shiny snot be detected by the snot police. They entered the school through the tall glass doors in the front — there was a security guard, but he was unarmed, and mostly for show. They went to their lockers. This was the most dangerous part of the day, the unstructured time at the lockers. Any social advantage that was to be gained would be gained during these precious few minutes. Of course, the opposite was also true. By the time first period started, you could feel so small, so pointless, that there'd be no chance for recovery. Meredith knew this all too well. Her locker was next to Lisa Bellow's.

Since the beginning of the school year Lisa Bellow had had a picture of a boy in her locker, taped on the inside of the door. Meredith could see it out of the corner of her eye while she unloaded her books and supplies into her own locker. In the photograph, the boy was standing on a white sandy beach. He was wearing black board shorts and sunglasses and holding a blue Frisbee. He was tan and had muscular arms, and Meredith might have suspected the picture had been cut from a magazine were it not so clearly a photograph: glossy, catching the light so that, depending on the angle of the locker door, sometimes the glare made it impossible to see the right side of the boy's body. Lisa had other things taped to her locker door — pictures of her friends, a bumper sticker from Virginia Beach, a birthday card — but the boy on the beach was at eye level, front and center, and some mornings as she turned from her own locker Meredith could not help but stare at it, her eyes drawn to it in a way she couldn't even explain. It wasn't like she'd never seen a hot guy before. It was just that everything about the photograph, every grain of sand, every crest of every wave, every finger and toe, was so *beautiful*.

Once Lisa caught Meredith staring at the picture. Meredith wasn't sure, but it was entirely possible that her mouth was open as she stared, not gaping but definitely open, and Lisa rolled her eyes and gave a tiny little huff with her nose before she slammed the locker shut and twirled away, her golden hair a perfectly silky wave of dismissal. The message was clear: not only was Meredith unworthy of looking at the picture of the beautiful boyfriend, but she was also unworthy of any actual verbal response from Lisa. This was no surprise. Despite the proximity of their lockers, Lisa had not spoken a single word to Meredith for the entire year.

Lisa Bellow and her friends had gotten the memo about the iceberg. It was possible that they had written the memo. It was even conceivable, Meredith had long ago decided, that they had somehow been responsible for the iceberg in the first place. Lisa and her pack, a half dozen girls with all-season-tanned legs and perky little boobs, had outgrown middle school boys by about November of seventh grade. Now, in eighth grade, some of them were dating boys that Evan knew, and Evan was a senior. Lisa and her friends sashayed around Parkway North Middle School, licking their lips to keep them moist and primed for the next cutting comment about somebody's stringy hair or somebody's ugly shoes. Once, the year before, Meredith had been sitting at a lunch table talking to her friends and someone called her name and she turned around and from two tables away Lisa Bellow called, "Can you please sit on the middle of your chair so your butt's not hanging over the side? We're trying to eat." Lisa's table erupted into laughter; even a few girls at Meredith's table laughed, which was the worst part. She felt herself withering inside, and instead of saying something clever just scooted toward the center of her chair and forever since made sure she was positioned correctly.

Meredith hated them. Jules and Kristy hated them. Most of the girls hated them. But then why were they the most popular girls in the school? It didn't make any sense, and Meredith and her friends had spent countless hours analyzing the data. Eventually they realized: the bitches' power came from their numbers; through some trick, two of them seemed like five, three like ten. This was partly because they clearly worked hard to be indistinguishable from one another, like Stormtroopers, Meredith often thought as she watched them cut a swath down the eighth-grade hall. Though their hair was different shades, they all wore it the same way, and they all wore too much eye makeup, and they all wore black leggings and cold-shoulder tops, and this year they all wore gold gladiator sandals, which Meredith thought were the stupidest shoes she'd ever seen. Lisa was always attached to Becca Nichols or Abby Luckett or Amanda Hammels or one of the aspirant bitches, and they stood apart and sneered at your inadequacies (those known and unknown to you) and rolled their eyes with such unabashed superiority that you really had no earthly choice but to despise them. These were girls, Meredith thought, who could only be loved by their grandparents and maybe — *maybe* — Jesus.

And yet, Meredith always thought. *And yet.* It wasn't like she herself was any great prize. She was at least ten pounds overweight, and she was forever saying something she thought was funny until the instant it passed her lips, at which point she realized it was idiotic. Also she *had* been staring at that picture in Lisa's locker, no denying that, because she stared at things — sometimes boys, but other things, too, for too long, weirdly long, until even her friends were like, *um, hello?* Also, she didn't excel at a single thing. Sometimes she lay in bed at night listing her attributes in a calculated, disinterested manner, as if she were not herself but a project she was working on for the science fair. She could say, totally objectively, that she was very good, likely in the top 5 percent, of American thirteen-year-old girls at math. And she was good, likely top 25 percent, of American thirteen-year-old girls at field hockey, clarinet, and bumper pool. Yes, there were other talents: eavesdropping, for one, a cousin to staring but less obvious to outside observers. Catching popcorn or M&M's in her mouth, especially when tossed by Evan. Picking things up off the bottom of a swimming pool with her toes. And pretending, perhaps her greatest but least useful skill — certainly less useful than retrieving a pair of sunken goggles. But she wasn't truly *exceptional* at anything. No special gift set her apart from any of the other ten million thirteen-year-olds in the world. Last year Jules had won an award for an essay about diversity; Evan had been the best catcher in the whole region; even Lisa Bellow was awesome at being a bitch. Still, Meredith always reminded herself when at her lowest, at least there were actual freaking thoughts in her brain, unlike Lisa Bellow and company. At least she wasn't just pushing out her boobs every second of the day.

Also, she regularly reminded herself, there were lots of girls who were way less popular than she was. The girls at the very bottom — like the bottom 10 percent — were staying at the very bottom, because they were there for a real and universally agreed upon reason, drugged out, silent, or just hopelessly weird. But then there were the girls who made up the huge middle — the lower-middle and the middle-middle and the higher-middle. This was 80 percent of the eighth grade class, which at their school meant about a hundred girls, and the movement within this middle group seemed to shift daily, sometimes hourly. And then of course there were the popular girls, the top 10 percent — Lisa and Abby and Becca and Amanda and the rest.

On this day, Wednesday the eighth of October, Meredith and Jules and Kristy were on the high end of the middle-middle. They had been friends for years, had stepped and been stepped on, turned and been turned on, but their friendship remained intact, despite Jules's wandering eye and Kristy's increasing, sometimes socially debilitating, shyness.

Meredith did not know exactly what she herself aspired to, socially. She only knew that she aspired.

Today was Wednesday, which meant the day started with social studies. ("Our whole freaking lives are social studies," Jules liked to say.) The class was made tolerable almost entirely by the presence of Steven Overbeck, who sat directly behind her and sometimes whispered passages from the earnest social studies textbook in funny accents. For some reason, and it wasn't only because he was cute, she found this hilarious, and it was always a trial, but a happy trial, to get through the class without bursting out laughing. "And zen," Steven whispered, "zee Haitian family must take zere clothes down to zee rivah." Steven, who had only moved to the school a year before, did other things to make her laugh. Her favorite was when he drew elaborate watches on his wrists with his blue Bic pen. Sometimes the watches were fancy and sometimes plain, sometimes studded with jewels and sometimes children's watches with cartoon characters' arms pointing to the numbers. Once he drew a watch that was broken, the springs jutting from the face, the numbers scattered across his arm. She thought Steven Overbeck was probably a genius.

Today the teacher was called away in the middle of the lesson and the room predictably erupted into chaos a split second after her departure. Steven asked if he could draw a watch on her wrist.

"Um, sure," she said, before realizing this would mean he actually had to touch her wrist — but too late, he was already scooting his chair around to the side of her desk. With his blue Bic pen he lightly drew a circle on the top of her wrist and she broke out in goose bumps on both arms. She prayed he did not notice.

"Time is it?" he asked.

She looked up at the clock. "Eight forty-five."

"No," he said. "What time is it on this watch? Just pick a time. But choose wisely."

She smiled. Her face felt weird, a little numb, and she hoped it didn't look weird. "Why choose wisely?"

"Because it's going to be that time all

day," he said. His blond bangs sprouted up in a way that looked intentional — a little boy-band-ish, even — but which she knew was totally accidental, probably the result of a fitful sleep. This added to his appeal.

"Um. Two fifteen."

"Okay. Be sure to look at it exactly at two fifteen," he said. He drew the straps and then, with only the tips of his fingers, turned her hand over and drew the buckle on the back of her wrist.

"Nice," she said. Her heart was hammering, and it continued to hammer throughout the library period. The library period was a fake period during the day, as far as she could tell, that allowed teachers to go to the teachers' lounge and drink Red Bull. Otherwise she wasn't sure what the point was. It was like study hall but with no help. It was like reading practice, so the school could announce to the community that it embraced reading.

"What is that?" Kristy asked at the circular library table, leaning halfway over Meredith to get a better look, Kleenex still anchored in place. It was Kristy who suffered the most, who was sick with worry half the time. Kristy didn't even like to pee at school. What if someone heard? What if someone said something about the sound her pee made hitting the toilet water? These were the things that weighed on her.

"Nothing," Meredith said. "I mean, just —"

"Did you draw that?"

"Steven did."

Kristy raised her eyebrows. "Oh, reeeee-ally?"

"Stop," Meredith said, hoping she wouldn't.

"So is this official?"

"Stop! It's a picture of a watch."

"Which he *drew on you*," Kristy said.

An hour later, at lunch, Jules swung in beside her.

"Did you hear?" she asked.

"I don't know," Meredith said. "Did I?"

"Becca Nichols's sister is pregnant."

"Whoa," Meredith said.

"She's *sixteen*. And she's going to have it. Six-teen. SIX-teen."

Jules spit a piece of gum into her hand and then stuck it on the bottom of the cafeteria table. "Don't tell anyone," she said. "About the gum."

"It's okay," Meredith said.

"So Becca's, like, going to be an aunt."

"That's weird," Meredith said.

"Like hoe, like hoe," Jules said. "I'll bet you fifty bucks Becca gets pregnant before she's sixteen. Can you even imagine? We'll be going off to college and she'll, like, have a three-year-old."

"A girl got pregnant in middle school four years ago," Meredith said. "She was in Evan's class. Her name was Kelly something. They were in eighth grade. She was our age."

"That's so gross," Jules said. "Oh my god, I don't even want to think about it. *Tampons* gross me out."

"I know," Meredith said.

Kristy sat down. "What's gross?"

"Everything," Jules said. "Life."

"Did you see her wrist?" Kristy asked. She grabbed Meredith's wrist and turned it for Jules to see. "Steven's mark of ownership."

"Don't get pregnant," Jules said. "Do *not* get pregnant."

In English they were reading *All Quiet on the Western Front,* which Meredith understood was supposed to be very sad, but was mostly only very boring. When she told Evan she was reading it, he said, "Spoiler alert: he dies," so now she actually liked the book more because at least there was that to look forward to — which sounded bad, but was only to say that at least she knew something was going to happen, that all the reading wasn't just going to be for nothing.

Meredith hated gym more than any other class because she did not like changing with the other girls in the locker room. She would have changed in the bathroom stalls if she could — this was what she did in the summer, at the local pool — but that was not allowed in the school gym locker room. She had tried it once in sixth grade, she and Kristy both, and the gym teacher had come through and shouted at them that the bathroom stalls were not for dressing out, that they were big girls now and could change with everybody else.

Two years later Meredith still did not feel like a big girl. She and Kristy would locate the emptiest corner of the locker room and serve as each other's shields — the changer's body bent, the shielder's eyes averted. Meredith regarded with a mixture of awe and disgust the girls who stood casually naked before their lockers. Of course Lisa and her pack were among this group, but there were others, too, people she actually *liked*. She did not understand how they could speak to each other with ease, as if their pubic hair was invisible, as if their breasts were no more to be hidden than their arms. They were like another species to her, obscene in their nonchalance.

The day ended with math. This was her

wheelhouse, and thank god it came at the end of the day, in the nick of time, because math she *got*. When they did problems on the white board she wrote with confidence, sometimes even a cheereful, uncharacteristic arrogance. She was in Algebra II with only a handful of other students, working well ahead of the rest of the eighth grade. Today they had a test on rational functions. She had studied last night. She was well prepared. "Problem 1: Does the following table represent an inverse variation function? If so, find the missing value." She was flying, acing it, sailing through the asymptotes and the x-and y-intercepts. With five minutes left in class and only one problem to go, her pencil point broke, and she stupidly had not brought a backup, so she had to get up and rush to the sharpener. Then the pencil got stuck in the sharpener and she had to wrestle with it and the class looked up at her, unhappily as one, and Mrs. Adolphson's massive brow furrowed.

Meredith looked at her wrist and realized she had forgotten to check her "watch" at the appointed hour. She knew it was now well past 2:15. She looked at the clock on the wall. It was 2:40. In just a few minutes she would be headed home. Maybe she would stop at the Deli Barn on the way.

Maybe she would reward herself with a large root beer. The promise of this gave her a burst of strength, and with one last violent, class-distracting grind, she was able to twist her battered pencil free.

2

When Meredith was a toddler, her big brother Evan was a jubilant first-grader. Young Evan was so jubilant that the first criticism ever leveled at him by a teacher was that he literally whistled while he worked. This had come in kindergarten, just after he'd mastered the skill and was determined to share it with the world. He sat in his miniature chair at his miniature desk in his cheerful sunlit classroom, coloring numbers and letters and dinosaurs and trees and trains. And whistling. He couldn't stop whistling. His closest neighbors, the others in the rectangle cluster of miniature chairs at their miniature desks, could not concentrate. How to stay in the lines while the boy beside you whistles his way through the entire *Lion King* soundtrack?

Claire and Mark had laughed over this after the initial report at the parent/teacher conference. "We've clearly failed!" they said.

"Our child is too happy!" In spirit only, they exchanged exuberant high-fives for having co-created a perfect child . . . and look, there was another co-creation, four years younger than the first and every bit as perfect!

But one afternoon the next year, when Claire went to collect Evan from school, the first-grade teacher pulled her aside in the main lobby and reported in a hushed voice that some of the other boys in class had been teasing Evan about his weight.

"His weight?" Claire shifted two-year-old Meredith to her other hip; Meredith was a squirrely toddler (squirrely but perfect!), rarely content to be in one position for more than about fifteen seconds. Claire knew if she put Meredith down in the school lobby, chaos would ensue. "What about his weight?"

It had never occurred to Claire that Evan's weight might make him a target, because she had never considered him fat. She had seen plenty of fat kids in her exam rooms; most of them had a mouthful of cavities to go with their rolling stomachs. Evan was nothing like that. Evan was big, like Mark. He'd been a big baby and a big toddler and now he was a big six-year-old, more round than straight. It wasn't his diet; it was his body type. Mark had looked the same in childhood photos, darling, thriving, not *fat*. Evan didn't eat candy or drink soda and he was always running around and —

"One of the boys called him a porker," the teacher whispered. She was a new teacher, no more than a year from under-grad, and she actually blushed when she said the word. It did sound obscene, Claire thought, especially coming out of the mouth of an adult, like it couldn't help but have a sexual connotation, but the fact that it didn't in this context made it seem some-how even more revolting. "Then it caught on and a few boys started doing it. Has he been upset at home?"

Claire put Meredith down but kept a firm grip on her hand. "When would he have been upset at home? When did this hap-pen?"

The teacher smiled (a pity smile, Claire recognized) at the bouncing Evan, who was leaping from red square to black square on the lobby's gleaming tiled floor, much to the amusement of his sister, who was at-tempting to twist her sweaty hand free from Claire's fingers so that she could join her brother. "Ebben," she said. She said this one thousand times every day. "Ebben. Eb-ben." The halls were empty now and the slap of his sneakers echoed in the stairwells above.

"It started last week," the teacher said. "I've spoken to the boys about it privately, but there's one in particular who won't let it drop."

"Last week?" Claire said. She let Meredith go. It was like letting a puppy off a leash, her daughter around the corner and down a hall-way and out of sight in seconds, Evan trailing behind. "It started last week and you're just telling me now?"

"We try to let the kids work these things out on their own," the teacher said, standing a little straighter. "If we involve the parents every time someone gets called a name . . ." She trailed off, leaving Claire to assume the rest of the sentence, in which she and every other attentive parent in the world was tried and convicted. Claire realized that in the space of two minutes she had unwittingly become *that kind of parent* — and it wasn't even fair; she'd asked only a single question, expressed in an entirely justifiable moment of surprise, and now she imagined she was flagged, probably forever, before she'd even had a chance to decide what kind of parent she wanted to be in this new world with these new rules.

"Really, I just wanted you to be *aware,*"

the teacher said. "Generally we believe in awareness, not intervention."

Hey, great motto! Claire thought. *Students, teachers, parents, please take note: Awareness is now sufficient. An actual response is not necessary. Why act on what you know, when knowing is considered enough?*

Meredith and Evan had wound their way back around to the front doors, so Claire took the opportunity for escape, muttered a thank-you to the teacher over her shoulder as she caught up with her children.

In the parking lot, in the minivan, she held out for about forty-five seconds before asking Evan about the situation.

"Don't worry about it," he said. He was sitting in a booster seat beside Meredith, who was strapped into her car seat and beaming at him, fresh off her puppy run, basking in the glorious light cast by her big brother. This was the way it always was, and Claire had tried to accept the fact that except for when Meredith was looking at Evan, for whom she had always saved her very best smiles, *happy* had never been Meredith's default emotion. Baby Evan had usually had a smile on his face, but baby Meredith's go-to expression had normally been one of consternation and/or suspicion. Creased forehead. Narrowed eyes. Pursed lips. It was if she were always waiting to be put down in her crib, anticipating it, whereas with Evan it had been a daily surprise: *This place? Again?*

"Honey —" she said to her son.

"Really, don't worry about it," he said again. He was playing a handheld video game — a car-only treat — and he didn't even bother to look up from the screen.

"Of course I'm going to worry about it," she said, watching him in the rearview mirror. "It's not nice. Does it make you feel bad?"

"Yeah," he said absently, still not raising his head. "But it's okay."

The game beeped and buzzed. Did he even know what he was saying? Was he even part of this conversation? He adored his electronic games. If they'd let him, he might have played all day. But they didn't let him, of course He exercised regularly. He played baseball with the neighborhood kids practically every afternoon. He was an active child. A porker? Ha. Hardly. She'd show those kids a porker. She'd seen a kid in the grocery store last week stuffing his face with free samples while his mother (incidentally, also a porker) stood by and watched with a big fat smile on her face. She'd bring that kid in for fat show-and-tell. "You want to see a real porker?" she'd ask the class.

She was going thirty-eight miles per hour in a school zone. Okay, Jesus. Jesus, what was wrong with her? She took a breath, eased off the accelerator. She was shocked by her own capacity for cruelty — the little boy in the grocery store had a name, a story, she reminded herself. She was ashamed, and didn't even know where the rage had come from, so suddenly. Of course it wasn't the fact that Evan was not really a porker that made the bullying unacceptable. It was terrible to call someone fat if they were actually fat. And yet to call someone fat who wasn't . . . she somehow couldn't get past this particular element of the injustice. It just seemed wrong on a whole other level.

"Evan," she said. "It's not okay, honey. It's not okay at all. It's mean and awful to call people names. I think I should talk to someone about it."

"What? No!" he exclaimed, horrified enough to look up from his game and meet her eyes in the mirror. "Don't worry about it, okay? There's nothing you can do!"

Full stop. It was a good thing, perhaps, that their eyes only met in the mirror, that it was only his reflection that spoke, that she was not looking into her child's face directly when he said this. Her eyes slipped

46

back to the street in front of her just as something crawled over her skin, something unfamiliar, something slimy and cold that surely belonged at the bottom of the ocean. In less than a second it had her covered from head to toe, and then it started squeezing. So this was the world that existed for her six-year-old son. This was it. A place where things could make him feel bad and absolutely nothing could be done about it. A place where she was powerless to protect him. At six he had somehow already reached the conclusion, independently, somewhere within the walls of that elementary school — that elementary school where he had whistled just last year! — while she at home and at the office had cheerfully and blindly persisted in her belief that she had at least a modicum of control over the things in the world that could harm him. She wasn't a fool, but really, was a modicum too much to ask?

Meredith was clamoring for his attention. He was looking at his game. The game had swallowed him. Meredith was dying for attention — "Ebben, Ebben, Ebben," frantically, smacking her hand on the side of her car seat. A group of kids darted out from behind some parked cars and Claire braked hard, probably harder than she needed to, and she and Evan and Meredith lurched forward. "Sorry!" one of the kids yelled, looking back guiltily, but another was laughing. A dog was barking in a nearby yard.

"Ebben! Ebben! Ebben!" Meredith insisted.

"Evan, for god's sake, acknowledge your sister!" Claire shouted.

In all the ways that Claire knew mattered most, she had lived a charmed life. She was fortunate, and she'd been taught from a young age to appreciate that good fortune. She was not one who went blithely through childhood and adolescence taking everything for granted, forgetting that it was a luxury to have three square meals and a room of her own and a shiny bicycle in the garage. She was an only child, and her parents — who had both been in their mid thirties when she was born — had constructed their middle age around her. They were both teachers — her father taught high school English, her mother middle school social studies — until Claire was born, and then her mother left full-time work and became a substitute teacher so that she could be a full-time mother. Home had always been a safe zone. And if her father occasionally drank too much, and if her mother sunk low and occasionally spent the morning in bed after Claire left for school, it was all forgiven and forgotten between them when she walked through the door in the afternoon.

"You were the glue," her mother told her a couple of months before she died. "You have always been the glue."

Claire wasn't sure how she felt about this. "Glue" in the sense of simply being a force that tightly bonds, or "glue" in the sense of the necessary element in fixing something broken? It seemed too late to ask her mother this question, unfair to bring up something, anything, that couldn't be satisfactorily resolved in a half an hour. That went against all the unwritten conventions of conversing with the dying. No one wanted to end on a sour note. The final days lingered on for months; every conversation might have been their last conversation but wasn't. Until it finally was.

It was cancer that killed her mother, when Claire was twenty-seven, before Evan and Meredith were born. It was the same year her marriage ran into trouble (she knew this was unfairly euphemistic, designed to not assign blame, where in truth the only one to blame was herself), so all those emotions were tangled up together. Her father remarried quickly, just over a year after her mother died, and she recalled being struck by the injustice of this, that a replacement wife could be attained so quickly and with relative ease, while a replacement mother was not even an option. Of course she knew this wasn't fair and that her mother was irreplaceable as a person, as a *proper noun,* but she clearly wasn't irreplaceable as a common noun — her father once again had a wife, whereas she would never again have a mother.

She kept her promise to little Evan. She did not call the first grade teacher and demand names. She did not deluge the principal with frantic emails, in part to prove to them that they had been wrong about her, but also because she genuinely believed that to intervene — at *that* level — would only make Evan's life worse. She very much did not want him to be the porker who, by the way, needed his mommy to helicopter in and fight his battles for him. But she was ill with fear every time she dropped him off in front of that two-story brick building with the sloping lawn. A few months before the place had seemed warm and welcoming and full of light, and now it was as if she were pitching him headlong into a jungle whose predators she could not even begin to imagine. And he — her sweet and beautiful Evan, who had been the center of her world, her only child for so long — was defenseless against them. She began to look at all the other children in his class with suspicion. That little blonde with the shirts that said "Daddy's Girl" and "Princess in Training." The lanky kid, tall as a fourth-grader, who flung himself down the front stairs, limbs flailing. The redhead with the Eagles backpack who always ignored, and then sneered at, the crossing guard.

"Who's *that*?" she'd asked Evan one day, a couple weeks after the porker incident, as they were driving home from school.

"Logan Boone," he'd mumbled. "He gets his name on the board every day."

"For what?"

"Name-calling," Evan said.

She watched seven-year-old Logan Boone swagger down the sidewalk, his backpack slung loosely around one shoulder. Even his gait was reckless, thoughtless; he shared the sidewalk with no one, perhaps not out of malice, she thought, but worse, out of the belief that his space was the only space that mattered. Wasn't that the very definition of a sociopath? He could imagine the world through no eyes but his own. And he believed himself invincible, Claire was sure of it. So his name was on the board. So what? Big deal! It would not give him a moment of pause, not sneery Logan Boone. Of course he was the one who had first called Evan the name. She was right beside him now in the minivan, and she had the urge to roll down her window and shout something obscene at him. *"Hey, you piece of shit!"* she would shout. Wait — no. *"Asshole, bastard, piece of shit!"* It felt good to even think the words, a rush of adrenaline, a moment of euphoria, a parental climax. He was not so powerful, this cruel ignorant child, this ugly boy who didn't deserve to stand beside her son, never mind —

God, what was *wrong* with her? She was losing her mind. *I am losing my mind,* she said to herself in her head, because she knew that if she really had been losing her mind, she wouldn't be able to have the thought with such clarity . . . although she had never really been sure this was true. But the rage she felt for him was immense: god, that *sneer.* She thought of the phrase "wipe that look off your face," and understood it completely for the first time. She wanted to leap out of the car and wipe that look off his face with her fingernails. But she was helpless. He couldn't have been any uglier, this boy now receding in her side-view mirror, receding back into the place where he could do anything he wanted, where she could not touch him.

"Some kids are just assholes," had been Mark's predictable response, when she'd told him she'd positively identified the "porker" culprit. "Wasn't anybody ever mean to you?"

"Not in first grade," she said. "They're not supposed to be horrible to each other already. Isn't that what middle school's for?"

"It's a different world," Mark said, shrugging. "Everything's changed. Our kids are going to have cell phones when they're ten."

"Our kids are *not* going to have cell phones when they're ten. Absolutely not."

"All I'm saying is that everything happens sooner," Mark said. "The clock's sped up. But maybe that means it'll be over sooner, too. Maybe by the time they're fifteen they've already lived through all the crap we had to deal with until we were nineteen."

"Do you really think so?"

"I don't know," he'd said. "We can hope."

He could hope, that was the thing. Mark could *always* hope. It was a permanent condition, like freckles, or lupus. Mr. Glass Half-Full, she sometimes called him, though they both knew that 90 percent of the time she did not mean it as a term of endearment. Everyone loved Mark. And why not? He was lovable. What you saw was what you got. Nothing lurked under the surface. She knew some people thought he was a phony — her own mother had thought that for a long time — that his endless chattering away to patients was an act, his friendliness to strangers insincere. But it was all maddeningly genuine, every bit of it. Blessed with impeccable chemical balance, Mark took pleasure in things without questioning why he was taking pleasure in them.

On weekends, when the kids were little, she and Mark would have their friends over, other couples with young children, and the men would set up Mark's movie projector and sit in lounge chairs in the backyard, drinking beer and watching James Bond movies on the side of the garden shed, while the women sat on the patio talking about their babies and their jobs and complaining about those men in the lounge chairs.

And inevitably one of the women (they were all divorced now, every single one of those couples, a 100-percent divorce rate among those early friends) would say, "But then there's Mark." This was always followed by resigned sighs, then several minutes of tipsy, joking-not-joking envy, and then finally a group PowerPoint-presentation-minus-slides detailing several Great Things About Mark. (He separates whites and colors! He took the kids to the doctor without her! He compliments her new haircut!) And later, after the friends had all left, Claire would look at him through their eyes, swept up in his star power, thrilled anew that she possessed him, and the night would inevitably end with them wrapped together in bed and him saying, "We should definitely have those people over more often."

So he was great, yes. In all sorts of ways. But his fathering motto — "We can hope!" — had never been much help, and in fact was becoming increasingly useless with every passing year. It was, to Claire, once the wolves were at the door, nothing short of infuriating.

Would her mother have been useful then, after the honeymoon period of Evan whistling and baby Meredith beaming at, utterly entranced by, her whistling brother? Would her mother have had wisdom to impart? Her mother had always had an uncanny, sturdy sense of perspective — not a judgment that diminished you for what you were feeling, but just the right questions to rack the world into a clearer focus long enough for you to see your issue in its proper place.

Sometimes she tried to conjure up her mother and imagine what she would say — certainly she would not applaud Claire's hysterical rage. But Claire did not have her mother's gift for perspective, and so she couldn't recreate what her mother would say — or at least not how she would say it — and bring herself any clarity or relief. Her mother had become a shadowy figure to her, by then almost a decade gone; the list of things her mother had missed was as long as the list of things she had not missed, and the listing was too sad, the conjuring not only unhelpful but also depressing, so Claire put those thoughts aside.

She had to focus on her children. She had to change the game. She had been spoiled by her own happiness, by Evan's happiness, by the family's happiness, allowed herself to believe that raising children would be more pleasure than pain. She had simply been going along, foolishly thinking she under-stood the rules. She and Mark had provided for the children. They had a lovely home and roomy van and a reliable second car. They watched movies and played games and sang songs, and her heart was full and she had imagined that this would suffice, but she had not counted on the world. How could she have forgotten about the world? Was she so stupid? So naive?

If she hoped to survive this — this *motherhood* (the word now felt just a tiny bit sinister when she heard it in her head) — she would have to change her tactics.

Two months after the "porker" incident, after everyone but her had forgotten it (or at the very least moved on from it), she walked into exam room 3 on a dreary Tuesday afternoon to find Logan Boone supine in the chair, the blue paper bib chained around his neck. She actually did a bit of a double-take. She had seen him so often swaggering down the sidewalk that this was the image of him that had burned itself into her mind, so much so that even in her little indulgent fantasies of confrontation it was always that school street sidewalk where she faced him down. He looked small in the chair — everyone did, flattened out like that, bug on its back — but even horizontal there were angles in his body that seemed consciously intended to illustrate his superiority.

"Everything looks okay," the tech said, handing Claire the chart.

"I'll just take a peek, then," Claire said.

This was the way it worked. For the standard checkup, the tech did 95 percent of the work, then Claire or Mark came in at the tail end to confirm that all was well. People expected to see the dentist, if only for a couple minutes at the end of the appointment. They'd paid a hundred bucks — or their insurance company had — and they needed face time with someone with a "Dr." in front of his or her name.

Claire sat down on the stool beside Logan Boone, looked at her tray of instruments, and picked up the scaler.

"Open," she said, and he did, without looking at her. She was certain Logan Boone had no idea who she was. His gums were bright pink from cleaning, his teeth smooth and well spaced. He'd already lost six of his baby teeth; Evan had only lost one.

She located the spot where the most recent baby tooth had vacated — it looked like only several days before — and poked the point of the scaler into his tender pink gum.

"Ayyyy," Logan said, his face twisting.

"Be still," she said. She readjusted herself on the stool. "There's just a little something here."

"Wha'?" Logan asked.

She twisted the point into the gum where

the new adult tooth was forming and Logan gasped in pain. His eyes, for a moment, lost their hardness and there was fear in them. No, Claire thought, it went deeper than that — it was the pleading look: astonishment, confusion, betrayal. Claire often thought that it was precisely this expression that made so many dentists so miserable, a look regularly given to dentists but almost never to doctors, a frantic look born of pure pain and irrationality: Why are you doing this to me?

She saw it all the time, midprocedure, not only from children but from adults, people who understood full well the necessity of the work being done on them, being done *to* them. This, of course, what she was doing to Logan right now, was a different kind of necessity.

"Got it," she said, looking Logan straight in the eye, just to see if she could. His eyes were thick with tears and his lips were quivering. *You big baby,* she thought. *You pathetic, horrible crybaby.* "Rinse out," she said.

She slept better that night. The pit in her stomach subsided. There were things that could be done. Perhaps her children were defenseless, her boy just seven, her girl nearly three. But she was ready to enter a new phase of parenting. The joy was ending, and the battle beginning. At least she, the dentist, had some decent tools with which to fight for them.

3

When she reached the door of the Chestnut Street Deli Barn and saw that bitch Lisa Bellow posing at the counter inside, Meredith nearly turned on her heel and headed home. Forget the soda. She didn't need it. Yes, its promise had propelled her through that final problem on the algebra test. Yes, its promise had helped dispel the nagging disappointment that she had not had enough time to graph the asymptotes on that final problem and thus would at best only get half credit for it (and only if Mrs. Adolphson was feeling in an extremely generous mood). But it wasn't like she was desperate for a soda, like going without one would kill her.

There was no one in the Deli Barn besides Lisa and the curly-haired guy who made the subs — "Sandwich Farmer," his shirt proclaimed — so Meredith would have to say something upon entering in order to not look like a total whack job, and she didn't particularly want to have to think up something to say to Lisa that was at once fiercely clever and totally nonchalant. She had done enough thinking today, thank you very much. Often after school she felt as if she'd just spent seven hours and fifteen minutes *on stage,* with two brief intermissions during which she sat on a stone-cold toilet in a tiny stall cursing herself for all the missed cues and blown lines. Now, after curtain, all she wanted from the remainder of the afternoon was a large root beer and a peaceful 1.19-mile walk home in the dwindling warmth of early October. But of course there was Lisa Bellow to screw things up, Lisa Bellow who had taken so much from Meredith already, Lisa Bellow, taking again, this time a root beer.

Lisa glanced up in the direction of the door and the girls' eyes touched for a moment through the glass. There was nothing extraordinary in the eye contact, really only the merest shade of recognition, but now Meredith was trapped; a hasty retreat, witnessed by the enemy, would be just another heap of coal in the furnace that powered their operation, further proof that Lisa and her friends controlled not only the middle school itself, but also the quiet streets, small businesses, and suburban neighborhoods that lay just beyond it.

Meredith took an instant to gather herself then casually pushed open the jingling door — there were bells attached that looked like Christmas bells, though they were there year-round — and setting her head at a disinterested angle, muttered "hey" in the general direction of Lisa and the sandwich farmer. Then she went to the potato-chip rack and began studying the nutrition information on the back of a bag of Doritos while Lisa ordered her sandwiches.

Meredith thought back to the summer between third and fourth grade, approximately a hundred and seventy-five thousand years before, when she and Lisa Bellow had both taken tennis lessons with about thirty other grade school kids at the community park. This was long before anyone was a bitch — before anyone was anything, come to think of it — and one sweltering morning Lisa Bellow had been smacked in the face with a recklessly swung Venus Williams junior racquet and her bottom lip had burst open and the instructor told Meredith (who was close enough to the incident to receive a shower of Lisa's blood on her white shorts) to take the injured girl to the Snak Shed for some ice. Meredith and Lisa wound up spending the remainder of the morning eating snow cones in the blissful rectangle of shade thrown by the Shed, watching all the other kids getting yelled at for sloppy footwork and poor follow-through. Meredith was 98 percent certain that Lisa had no recollection of this event, that she had blocked it out, or perhaps even rewritten it with Meredith in the role of the clingy flunky sent for ice. But Meredith was sure there had been no flunky on that day, because she recalled vividly the surprise she'd felt when Lisa Bellow, her fingers green with lime snow-cone syrup, had brushed a wayward strand of hair from her face and said, "This is the best day of my whole summer."

Not that it mattered what she'd said, what either of them had said or done, what either of them remembered. They'd been babies then, nine years old, and nothing that happened when you were nine counted for anything anymore. You certainly couldn't collect on it now. Not that she would have wanted to anyway.

Lisa was ordering two sandwiches. One was turkey and provolone with light mayonnaise and the other a foot-long club with pickles and green peppers and extra onions. Meredith guessed that the sandwich with all the onions was for the boy in the picture in Lisa's locker, the tan boy on the beach with the Frisbee. Lisa was probably headed to his place right now. He'd probably texted her — *pick me up a sandwich* — on his way home from the high school. A girlfriend and a sandwich delivery service in one! His parents at work, his man cave thick with the funk of Phoenix-scented Axe body spray (she knew this smell well, from her own bathroom), the boy with the Frisbee would devour his sandwich right before he climbed on top of Lisa and stuck his thick oniony tongue halfway down her throat.

"Just one stripe of mayo," Lisa was telling the sandwich farmer. Meredith noticed that she had her iPhone in her hand. It was the newest iPhone, naturally, and the biggest, large enough to contain Lisa's large life. Meredith's phone was Evan's hand-me-down and the screen had been cracked for over a month, ever since she'd dropped it out the car window while trying to take a picture of a rainbow. Lisa was wearing the usual uniform: black leggings and a white, cold-shoulder peasant top, its straps just barely wide enough to pass the school district's two-finger rule.

"Not a big glob," Lisa said. "Just one little stripe."

Meredith had had this exact exchange with various sandwich farmers before, but she was sure she hadn't sounded so nasty when she said it, like it was this guy's entire purpose in life to measure out mayonnaise, like this was what he'd gone to school for, to differentiate between a stripe and a glob to make this eighth-grade bitch the perfect sandwich.

The front door jingled open and Meredith turned and saw a man stride purposefully into the Deli Barn. The man had on a black ski mask — not the kind with the eyeholes cut out, but the kind that only covered the bottom half of his face, so she could see his dark eyes and pale blond eyebrows. He wore a gray hoodie that was too long — it went nearly to his thighs — and jeans and big brown hiking boots. The door closed behind him and the Christmas bells rang for a moment in Meredith's mind even after they were still. The man was holding a gun.

Meredith had never seen a gun in real life before, except for maybe in a policeman's holster, but this thing in the man's hand looked exactly like every single gun she had ever seen on television, so she didn't doubt that it was real. The man pointed the real gun at the sandwich farmer and said, "Open the register, fat ass," which didn't make sense because the sandwich farmer wasn't even fat. Lisa Bellow let out a little squawk, and the man's head swung toward the girls.

"Get on the floor," the man said. His voice was muffled by the mask, so it sounded more like "Gone the four." It also wasn't clear who he was talking to, so Meredith only crouched down slightly until she saw Lisa Bellow getting on her hands and knees and then she did it, too, and felt — astonishingly — a stab of embarrassment that she had not been able or willing to do it herself initially and instead was following the lead of Lisa Bellow. What was wrong with her? This was a robbery. The Deli Barn was being robbed. The Deli Barn was being robbed and that was all and she didn't have to worry and there was nothing wrong with her.

As she lay down she caught a fleeting glimpse of her left wrist, Steven Overbeck's drawn-on watch buckle, blue ink already fading, joined at her pounding pulse. Her backpack was still on her back and it was incredibly heavy — her Algebra II book alone must have weighed five pounds — and it shifted and settled awkwardly across her upper back once she was flat on her stomach, its weight suddenly immense, like the weight of a whole person with his foot pressed into her shoulder blade.

Because she had been at the bread station, and Lisa a few feet ahead at the condiment station, when Meredith lay down she and Lisa were face-to-face, though their feet were pointing in opposite directions, Lisa's toward the front door, and Meredith's toward the potato-chip rack. The floor was cold and smelled like dishwasher detergent. Meredith could hear the sandwich farmer breathing and the jiggling of the cash register drawer.

"You know the safe combination?" the man with the gun asked.

"There's no safe," the sandwich farmer said.

"You wanna die in this shithole?" the man said. "Is that what you want?"

The sandwich farmer started crying, or at least it sounded like crying, or maybe hyperventilating. Meredith wasn't sure because she couldn't see anything except for Lisa. Lisa was crying, too. Her lips were trembling and slimy with spit, and thick teardrops slid down her cheeks and puddled on the floor about six inches from Meredith's nose. Meredith could feel Lisa's breath as it came out in hot little puffs. Meredith wasn't crying. Her eyes felt dry and sore, like she'd been staring at a movie screen for a long time without blinking. In her mind she saw a picture of her and her brother sitting on Santa Claus's lap at the Parkway Mall. She was two or three years old, and her hair was clipped back in green barrettes that were shaped like Christmas trees.

"Swear to god," the sandwich farmer said. "I swear to god there's no safe."

"Show me," the man said. "You show me."

Meredith heard them walking into the back room. Somebody's shoes were squeaking (sneakers), and somebody's thunking (hiking boots). Now it would be okay. There was a door back there, to the outside — Meredith had seen sandwich farmers smoking by that door before — and the man with the too-long hoodie would see there was no safe to open and then he would run out that back door with the money he'd taken from the cash register and he would go far away, first to another state and then probably to another country, and no one would ever hear anything from him again. It would be a clean getaway. That's how it would be described in the newspaper tomorrow: a clean getaway. Vividly, as vividly as anything in the Deli Barn, Meredith could see her family sitting around the breakfast table, her mother reading aloud from the newspaper article: "It was a clean getaway."

Meredith licked her dry lips. "It's okay," she whispered to Lisa Bellow. She couldn't remember a time she'd been so close to someone else's face for so long. And it was especially weird because their eyes were almost perfectly in line but the rest of Lisa was upside down. "It's okay now. It's okay."

Lisa's mouth opened like a word was going to come out, but only a little wet pop came from between her lips. Thick black mascara lines connected her eyes to the floor. Meredith thought of the scorching tennis court that summer morning, all those years ago, Lisa's lip gashed, the blood spattered on her white Nike tennis shirt. Had Lisa cried then, there on the court, or after, walking across the dry brown grass to the Snak Shed? Meredith didn't think so. But back then there was no makeup to ruin, no face to distort so colorfully, so maybe she had, a little. Maybe, their backs propped against the Shed, Lisa had held the Baggie of ice to her face and in doing so shielded Meredith from the brimming tears in her eyes.

The thunking feet, the hiking boots, returned. The steps were heavy and unhurried. No squeaking accompanied the boots. The boots were alone. Meredith couldn't see him, but when the thunking stopped she was pretty sure the man, the robber, was standing right behind her head, between her and the counter. He had come back without the sandwich farmer. Meredith had heard no gunshot, but something had happened in the back room and now it was just the man with the too-long hoodie and her and Lisa. And now Meredith was absolutely certain of something, as certain as she'd ever been of anything in her whole life, and that thing was as far from what she had just said to Lisa as a thing could be:

It was definitely *not* okay.

It was definitely definitely definitely definitely not okay. It was not okay now, not anymore, not ever again, because the man was going to kill her. He was going to shoot her in the head as she lay on this floor. This spot, this very spot, was where she was going to die. She would never see her mother or her father or her brother or her cats or her room or her toothbrush again. In a moment she was going to be dead. Now she was completely alive but in an instant she would be completely dead and she wouldn't even know it, it would just be over, and she wouldn't even know it was over because she herself would be over, and all the stuff in her brain — all the thoughts in her brain right now, right this second — would just be a big sticky mess on the floor of the Deli Barn. And it was now — now — now. It was this instant — no, this instant — this instant — this —

— *this is me. This is really me. This is my real life.*

She realized her eyes were closed, bracing for the impact of the bullet, and she wanted to see the world one more time — even if it was just a crappy old Deli Barn — so she opened her eyes and there was Lisa Bellow staring right at her.

"Don't worry, Meredith," Lisa said. "It'll be okay." She didn't even whisper it. She said it in a normal voice, as if nothing were wrong, or even out of the ordinary. She had stopped crying. Her cheeks were dry. Something in her face made Meredith think she was about to smile.

"You," the man said. "Get up."

Meredith knew from the startled look on Lisa's face that the man was talking to Lisa. He must have touched her leg with his boot, maybe given her a nudge. Or maybe not. Maybe Lisa Bellow just knew the man was talking to her because, given the choice between the two girls lying facedown on the floor, of course the man was talking to her.

And Meredith knew this, too, and did not move.

Lisa got to her feet. She stood still for a moment and Meredith (though she could see only Lisa's sparkly gladiator sandals) had the sense she was composing herself, maybe brushing a wayward strand of hair from her face, adjusting the straps of her peasant top, slipping her Vera Bradley backpack over one shoulder. Meredith did not dare move. She didn't even want to move her eyes. She had an idea that if she lay completely still with her eyes fixed straight ahead that she would be invisible. This was called something but she couldn't remember what. Scared possum? What even *was* a possum? Was it like a porcupine without the points? The left cuff of Lisa's black leggings had a small white mark on them, something from the floor probably, and would require washing. And her gladiator sandals were — but then they were nothing, or rather they were gone, still something but gone, out of Meredith's sight, no longer her concern, only a recollection hovering among the settling molecules in the space they'd just occupied. Then the door opened and the Christmas bells jingled and there was a little burst of air in the restaurant, like a quick breath of October inhaling, and then a car door slammed, and then an engine rumbled, and then acceleration, and then silence.

Meredith Oliver lay alone on the floor of the Chestnut Street Deli Barn for eleven glorious minutes. It was the most wonderful place Meredith Oliver had ever been, more comfortable than any bed, warmer than summer sand, safer than her brother's famous polar bear hug. The tile was smooth and cool on her face and she could see dull stains from spilled sodas under the counter and her body slowly and resolutely attached itself to the floor as if the floor were mud or glue. Meredith thought about her algebra test. She went over every problem in her mind. She thought again how Mrs. Adolphson would probably only give her half credit for the last problem because she hadn't graphed the asymptotes. **Find the vertical & horizontal asymptotes. Find x- and y-intercepts. State the Domain and Range in interval notation.** She had run out of time; that was all. She knew what they were. She just hadn't had time to graph them.

$$y = \frac{x+4}{x-2}$$

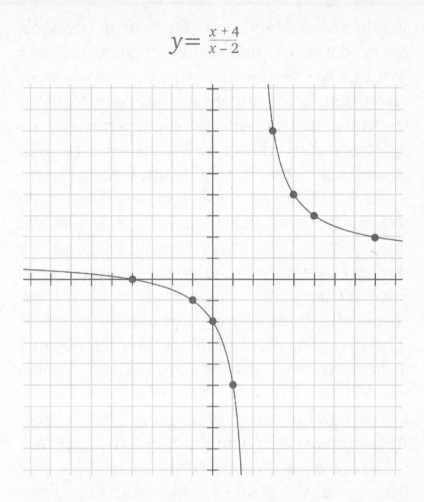

If she hadn't had to get up and walk across the room to sharpen her pencil, between problems 14 and 15, she would have had time to graph the asymptotes. Next time there was a test she would remember to bring two sharpened pencils to class. This would be her goal on the morning of the next test. On the morning of the next test she would write herself a note. She would use a black pen. There was probably a black pen by the cash register. The note would say: "Remember to bring two sharpened pencils to algebra." She would write the note on her hand so there would be no question but that she would see it. She would use a black pen. There was probably a black pen by the cash register. She would definitely use a black pen. As soon as she got up from this floor she would write it on her hand. This would (vertical asymptote: $x=2$) be her goal. The best way to remember something was to write it on your hand. There was probably a black pen (horizontal asymptote: $y=1$) by the cash register. People needed pens to sign their credit card slips. On her hand she would write: "Remember to bring two sharpened pencils to algebra."

Later, after a customer came in and discovered the scene — Meredith facedown on the floor beside the counter, the sandwich farmer unconscious in the doorway to the back room, the register drawer ajar — and called the police, the paramedics tried to coax her to her feet, but she would not budge. When they attempted, as a group, to lift her, Meredith shrieked and thrashed and dug her fingernails into the neck of the EMT who knelt beside her. Finally it took a needle full of Thorazine to peel her from her cherished spot.

4

Claire had long since resigned herself to the question, "What made you go into dentistry?" The question — regardless of the asker — was almost always delicately posed with a cautious, falsely friendly tone that was obviously meant to very clearly state, *I'm not passing judgment, but . . .*

It went without saying that no one ever asked this question of a medical doctor, except possibly podiatrists, the only group that regularly fell below dentists in the general public's unwritten pecking order of respected health professionals. Feet and mouths no one could understand, a knee-jerk underestimation of the importance of each, Claire felt, a remnant from the seven-year-old mentality that mouths and feet were icky. Hearts and brains, of course — she could give them that. It was natural that those should be at the top of the list. They were the heavy hitters, the prestige organs.

(What parent had not dreamed of the words, "And this is my son . . . the brain surgeon"?) But what about ENTs or rheumatologists? What about orthopedists or gynecologists? Why did no one suspect that *they* had settled, that some flaw had prevented them from reaching their potential, that somehow — intellectually? emotionally? — they just hadn't been able to cut it?

In dental school the majority of their friends admitted they had decided on dentistry for the money. The pay was good — sometimes outstanding — and there was job security and a steady paycheck (teeth were never *not* going to be a problem), and unlike most of the med students they knew, they would all be able to go home at the end of the day and not go back to work until the next morning. Many of them were already planning on a four-day work week. So now in addition to settling and/or failing, they were also greedy and/or lazy.

It was an impossible situation, one that infuriated Claire because it just wasn't fair. No one accused bankers of being lazy, or plumbers of being greedy. How could you begrudge someone for choosing a lucrative career? And yet there was a sense particular to dentists that they had simultaneously succeeded and failed, that they had sold out, that their moral obligation to help their fellow man in a more significant, meaningful way had been first acknowledged and then, poof, dismissed. Sure, I *could* be a doctor, but I *choose* to be a dentist. Why? Because it's easier.

Well, she was done thinking about it. She had been done thinking about it, officially, for almost twenty years. She was not going to apologize or make excuses for having a steady job in which she helped people, contributing to society in a way that was desperately needed. Wasn't that supposed to be what you did in life? Fill a need, and make a wage doing it? Yes, she was done thinking about it. No one was going to make her feel bad about it. She was free to make her own choices, and she had.

Except that, in truth, she had been somewhat talked into it.

Mark's father had been a dentist. He preached dentistry like a religion. He was *called* to dentistry; it was his professional duty and personal joy. Neither settling nor greedy nor lazy, he loved his work and believed in it absolutely. "The teeth are the unsung heroes of the human body," he was fond of saying, to whatever unsuspecting partygoer he managed to corner to talk about it. She and Mark used to laugh at this. For years they said it to each other at least once a week as a private joke, usually to lighten the mood when one of them was feeling down about something. She'd said it to him when it rained throughout their honeymoon, he to her when she broke her ankle on their icy front steps. It was the secret phrase that instantly improved every situation. *The teeth are the unsung heroes of the human body.*

When they met as college juniors, both bio majors, she still did not know what she was going to do, what path to follow. She had always pictured herself in an operating room — yes, probably at work on the prestige organs –with classical music playing in the background, a nurse laying a glittering scalpel in her gloved hand. It sounded strangely peaceful, and she imagined herself feeling totally in control of the situation, the conductor, the scalpel her baton, always certain of what note, what incision, was to come next.

Senior year, spring break. They'd been together for eighteen months. They were on a community service trip, helping rebuild houses in a little town in Oklahoma that had been all but wiped out by a tornado. At the end of the day they sat on the floor in an empty second-story bedroom, passing one beer between them, and Mark — maybe inspired by the promise of the house going up around him? — had said, "Listen, we could open our own practice. We could run the show. We just pick a place we like and move there and be our own bosses and set our own hours."

And it wasn't as if she didn't like the idea — she did. If she had had more than the vaguest notion of another direction, it might have been different. But she was open to suggestion, and he suggested, and now here they were twenty-five years later, being their own bosses and setting their own hours, a busy office in Sick City, both of them well respected in their community of dentists, and with enough money to do almost anything they wanted. And yes, she was the conductor of sorts, only her theater was noisier than the operating theater she had imagined, and you couldn't hear classical music over the hum of the drill.

Here was the thing: they relieved pain. She liked relieving pain, especially for people who were older, patients in their sixties and seventies who were spending an awful lot of time going from office to office in Sick City. She liked giving people something they could rely on, something that could be fixed, even as the rest of their bodies failed.

Dentistry had its disadvantages, to be sure — that devastating look of betrayal chief among them — but there was something that made dentistry more fulfilling than other medical pursuits: you could almost always fix a tooth, and when you couldn't, you could take it out and put in something that was just as good, or better. She liked to be able to say, "Mrs. Elscott, you don't need to worry about this anymore. This will not fail you. Yes, your heart might stop or your brain might stroke (she did not say this part), but those teeth in your mouth — provided you continue your stellar record of yearly visits to the dentist! — are not going to turn on you."

They are, in fact, the unsung heroes of the human body.

After his retirement from private practice, Mark's father (and his mother, as his assistant) moved to Honduras to work at a free clinic, providing dental care to people who would never live a single minute of their lives like the fourteen hundred and forty minutes Claire lived every day. Mark's parents resided in a small apartment above the clinic and were often awakened by pebbles tossed against their bedroom window by their first patients of the day, children who came to have cavities filled before walking miles to school. They occasionally talked of returning to the States, but Mark did not believe this would ever happen. "They'll die there," he told Claire. "Right in the middle of a root canal."

Sometimes she thought Mark's favorite part of being a dentist was rolling around on stools. Sundays when the kids were little, Mark would race them down the office corridors, stool versus stool, a contest that normally ended with him on the floor and his stool upside down, its wheels spinning. He also occasionally liked looking at the dental hygienists. He was not an ogler, but she could slide something into the space between an "eyes passing over" moment and the amount of time that his eyes actually lingered.

"You're such a cliché," she often told him.

"I know," he'd say. "But I'm your cliché."

The thing was that, like her, he did not like messy. They dealt with it in different ways, but shared the aversion, which got deeper with time. Because of this, she did not fear those occasional lingering glances. Yet another of the Great Things About Mark: he looked, but he did not touch.

It was one of the hygienists — Debbie — who came to fetch her on Wednesday afternoon. Claire was in exam room 4, with her last patient of the day, filling a tooth.

"Dr. Oliver? There's a phone call for you?"

She lifted her eyes. Not for nothing would they bother her in the middle of a procedure. Evan. He'd skipped school. He'd gotten into a fight. He'd disappeared. He'd crashed the car.

"Coming," she said.

They had called last year, Friday, the twenty-ninth of March. The call had come from the coach. The ambulance was en route to the hospital, he'd said. Evan was talking as they loaded him into the ambulance, the coach had said. He was talking. He was moving. He was conscious. (This was all code for *he's not almost dead. You're not going to get to the hospital and find out he's dead.*)

Where was Mark? In her panic she had been unable to recall, and the phone line was suddenly lifeless, the coach's voice silenced, and she was there alone with this information. The receptionist had to remind her: Hillsboro. Their mobile dentistry. Once a month one of them went to the Hillsboro Home and saw patients who were too old to leave, too weak to be moved, but required dental care. They traded months; it was terrible work, but they felt too guilty, too

85

necessary, to give it up. That was where he was. That was why he couldn't be reached. That was why she was suddenly in her car — having somehow gotten herself into it, and driving, and halfway to the hospital before she realized she was still wearing her rubber gloves, and it seemed she had not breathed nor had a thought since she'd heard the coach's voice.

It was the call she had been waiting for, the bookend — not even to Logan Boone and the porker incident — she saw that clearly during that drive to the hospital — but to a moment in the eighth month of her first pregnancy when she had put her hand on her belly and thought, *Stay there.* By the ninth month she was not having these thoughts anymore, but she remembered it with such clarity now, a feeling she could not understand nor name but which she felt so strongly (and later attributed to the roller coaster of hormones): *stay there.*

His eye had been crushed. When she saw him in the emergency room, she knew at once the bloody mass would not see again — how could it? — but in the moment she hadn't cared about that. She only wanted the MRI. She wanted to know if his brain was bleeding. His brain could be bleeding. While they waited, while she gripped his fingers, his brain could be bleeding, the blood flooding the things (goddamn prestige organs) he most needed to survive. It was only a few minutes but terrible things often only took a few minutes. She had said this to her children, naggingly, "Sometimes a single minute makes a difference." How she hated that stupid nagger now, wanted to throttle that nagger, because it had always been about homework or being on time for school or getting the trash rolled to the curb before the truck rumbled down the street.

He'd been shaking, her beautiful, terrified boy, those giant powerful hands trembling in hers. She had waited for something to come from her mouth, something useful, something comforting. She had waited and waited and nothing had come.

"Where's Dad?" Evan had asked, because Dad was better at this, let's face it, Dad would act rather than standing there in the ER muted and stunned.

"He's coming, honey."

And he did come, there he was, soon after — seconds? minutes? hours? — and she could have wept just that he was there and she did not have to carry the burden alone anymore. If she could have physically picked up Evan and dumped him into Mark's arms in that moment she would have done it.

"Take this," she would have said. "Take this. Carry this."

Over the years there had been things that had almost split them up. She had nearly left him ages ago, before the kids were even born. Soon after her mother had fallen ill she had fallen, too — someone she knew in high school, someone who had recently returned to their hometown, a brilliant but aimless emotional vagrant who occasionally met her for coffee at the hospital when she flew home on weekends to be with her mother, who touched her hand and said things to her like "Are you sure this is really the life you want?" and "You're only twenty-six. Nothing's set in stone" — the worst kinds of things to hear in the days when you are newly married and your mother is dying and you are contemplating your own mortality.

There had been no affair, per se, but there had been long letters and whispered phone calls and panic and indecision. He offered repeatedly to come pick her up at her home in the middle of the night and just drive away. To where? Who knew? For how long? Maybe a month, maybe fifty years. The affair — or whatever it was, she didn't even know what to call it; it was really just hands and words — lasted through her mother's illness and continued after her death, and when she found she could not decide for herself what to do, which man to choose, which life to pursue, she told Mark about it in the hopes that he would decide for her, that he would be furious and leave her or forgive her and fight for her. But he misunderstood his role. He was furious and did not leave her. He neither forgave her nor fought for her. Instead, after a day of fuming, he turned it — the admission, the decision — back on her. "Do what you want," he'd said, "but for God's sake do something." That was the night he grew up, she thought now, the night he really stopped being a boy, his ego crushed, his clear vision of the future shaken, his boyish heart hardened, and then, impressively at twenty-seven, his grown-up resolve: "For God's sake, do something." Even then she felt sad for the boy she killed that day, in part because she never got to say good-bye to him.

She did something. She made a decision. She decided she would wait and see what happened. She would stop writing the letters and making the phone calls and would see how she felt about things and then after a little while she would decide once and for all what to do. So she waited to see what she would decide. And while she waited, she and Mark went on with their life together and after a couple months she woke up one morning and realized that, in not deciding, she had made her decision. She had not called for the midnight getaway car, had not triggered the escape hatch. She was lying next to Mark, so apparently that was her choice. And so they did not split up.

And then there was Logan Boone, the first-grader whose bright pink gum she had dug into with the point of her scaler, intentionally, to cause him pain, to punish him for mistreating Evan. When she revisited the moment in her mind in the months that followed the incident, she never felt remorse, but rather some delicious satisfaction that was perhaps more damning than the act itself. When she saw Logan Boone outside the elementary school, brushing past the crossing guard, she convinced herself that his strut was less confident, that he'd been taken down a peg or two, that she had won. Yes, *won.* She had taught the aggressor a lesson, overpowered the powerful, and in doing so had eradicated, permanently, one unmistakable danger from her children's lives.

Why in the world had she thought Mark

would understand? Mark, of all people? Maybe she didn't, not really. Maybe, as with the non-affair affair, she wanted to tell him so that the feeling of delicious satisfaction would stop. Maybe she needed someone to remind her of the thing Mark had always seemed best about reminding her: "You're better than that."

It came up to begin with because he — Mr. Nice Guy! — was complaining about an annoying teenage girl who'd been in for a cleaning that day.

"She wouldn't stop bitching about the chair," he said. "She said we should get new chairs because the ones we have are uncomfortable. I swear, I thought about leaving her there with the bite wing in her cheek and going for coffee."

"You should have," she said. "Sometimes, well, we need to, you know —"

"Teach zem a lesson?" he said, pretending to crack his knuckles.

Well, there was her opening. "Seriously, honey, listen," she said. "Okay, there's this kid. He's been picking on Evan for years. And so one time I gave him a little extra poke with the scaler." She smiled coyly. "Just, you know, a leetle poke."

They were in the file room, finishing up some patient notes. It was the end of the day. Everyone had gone home. He had just knelt down to tie his shoe and now he looked up at her.

"What?" he said.

"I just tapped him a little bit. You know." She held her thumb and index finger a half inch apart. "A leetle."

He stood up, his shoe still untied. There was no expression whatsoever on his face, which was probably the most frightening expression she had ever seen. "You're kidding."

Rewind, she thought. *Rewind.* She actually almost prayed this word: *rewind.* She'd been fooled into thinking she could tell him anything, lured by a connection that in that moment — despite the fact she'd kept this secret for three years — seemed not only could withstand a little honesty but maybe even flourish because of it. Okay, well, obviously an error had been made. *Rewind.* Obviously she had misjudged the situation. *Rewind.* The non-expression on his face made this very clear.

"I'm kidding," she said, so utterly unconvincingly that if they'd been onstage an audience would have roared with laughter. "Of course I'm kidding."

"You're not!" he'd shouted, loudly enough that she took a step back. "You're not kidding! Jesus Christ! You're telling me you stuck a kid in the gum because he was mean to your son? Are you really telling me that?"

"It was one time," she said. She was still trying to smile. "Mark, really, it was like literally for one second."

"But you did it! You did it. You thought about doing it and then you actually did it."

"I — I know. I thought — I don't even know what I thought. I wasn't thinking." *Appeal to fatherly instincts. Must appeal to fatherly instincts.* "I was, maybe, I don't know, maybe I felt like I was protecting Evan or something."

"Protecting him?" He yelled this. He never yelled. Actually, once he'd yelled at three-year-old Meredith when she'd rushed into the street in front of Independence Hall, and the entire city had screeched to a halt. "Protecting him? What the hell? How does that protect him?"

"I know it sounds crazy," she said. "It was just —"

"That's not protection, Claire," he said. "That's *revenge.* Those are two very different things."

"It wasn't *revenge,*" she said. "It wasn't even . . ."

"What?"

"I already told you, I didn't really even

93

think about it," she said. "It just happened. You know how things just sometimes happen. Don't things ever just sometimes happen to you?"

He didn't answer. He just stared at her. The contempt, the utter disgust, that she had felt for Logan Boone was being reflected back at her. She wasn't sure anyone had ever been disgusted by her before, but here it was, here was how it looked and here was how it felt. And yet, even as she stood there among the patient files, withering under her husband's appalled gaze, she did not regret what she had done. She only regretted telling.

She was walking down the carpeted corridor, past the tooth posters, full of friendly reminders to practice responsible dental care. Sometimes she wanted to make a poster that said, FOR CHRIST SAKES, JUST BRUSH YOUR TEETH.

Maybe it wasn't Evan that the phone call was about. Maybe it was her father. Maybe he'd had a heart attack. She had pictured this many times, her father keeling over, because, though nearly eighty, he insisted upon pushing a hundred-pound wheelbarrow around his yard and putting Christmas lights on his roof. So this was how it would be: swift. The good-bye with her mother had been endless; with her father there would be no such torture. DOA. Nancy on the phone (technically her step-mother, though it felt odd to say this about a woman she'd never had as a mother, so only Nancy), tears, etc. She'd have to cancel everything, clear the appointment calendar, get the kids out of school. Two days before the funeral, then the funeral, then a day after — four days away for certain, maybe more for her. Why this lack of emotion? It wasn't as if she did not love her father, only that the details were —

"It's a police detective," the receptionist said.

"What?"

They were sitting behind the desk, three of them, in a row, silently. The one holding the phone held it out to her.

"It's the police," she said.

After she'd spilled the beans about Logan Boone, Mark didn't speak to her for two days. It was the week before Christmas. They were supposed to drive halfway across the country to see her father and Nancy. They had always loved car trips, taken them whenever they had the chance, first when it was just the two of them, then with just the three of them, then with the four of them. They'd never understood people who flew around the country, friends who complained about a ten- or twelve- or sixteen-hour car trip, who said their kids couldn't stand being cooped up for more than a couple hours, or that *they* couldn't stand being cooped up for more than a couple hours with their kids. It was pathetic, really. Together Claire and Mark believed: if you raised your kids on car trips, your kids loved car trips. And if you really didn't want to spend several hours in close proximity with your family, maybe your issue didn't have anything to do with cars, or trips.

Oh, life had been so much simpler when they were better than everyone else! Now, with Mark not even speaking to her, it was difficult to imagine they would be going anywhere together ever again, in any mode of transportation. But he packed his bags and the kids' bags and paid the cat sitter and stopped the paper and watered the plants, all without speaking a single word directly to her. And then as they were loading the luggage into the back of the minivan, he turned to her. He was wearing a T-shirt and basketball shorts, even though it was twenty-five degrees outside, because this was what he liked to drive in, regardless of season. She loved that about him, as stupid as it was, as ridiculous as he always looked in his long black shorts, standing in the cold, pumping gas at the turnpike service plaza as the snow fell around him. God, she *loved* him.

"Whoever you are," he said, "I forgive you."

They drove through the afternoon and into the evening and then into the night-time. Meredith was just five; by 8:30 she was asleep. For a while after dinner Mark drove and Claire and Evan tried to name all the state capitals. Then she and Mark switched off and she drove and Mark slept and Evan turned on his Nintendo DS. It was nearly 10:00 and they still had a hundred miles to get to their hotel, though Claire felt she could easily drive all night, watch the hotel disappear behind her, cross one state line, then another. She watched her son in the rearview mirror, his gentle face lit by the faint, flickering light of Mario Kart. Beside her, her husband slept; behind her, her daughter slept. They were in the dark, in their minivan, with their things inside. They were safe, protected by a half-dozen air bags, stability control, traction control, safety locks, side impact beams, and antilock brakes. These were the features they had paid for, the equipment they could rely on. This was what they had worked for. In the van, on the highway, on the edge of Ohio, there was nothing that could hurt them. If only she could keep driving, keep them all here together in the dark van, nothing could hurt them ever again.

She drove on.

5

For just a moment, when Meredith woke up in the hospital, she thought her parents were dead. She had never seen a dead body in real life, but her mother and father looked like TV murder victims, both slumped on a stiff green couch in the corner of the room, half-sitting and half-lying, their heads titled awkwardly back against the cushions, their eyes closed, their lips slightly parted. She lay quietly, her thoughts coming sluggishly, and regarded them with a strange, dreamy curiosity until she understood that they were merely sleeping. The heavy blinds in the room were open and it was dark outside, though the lights from the parking lot were bright and cast dull shadows around the room she lay in.

She knew she was in a hospital, though she had no memory of arriving. The last thing she remembered clearly was the cool air on her forehead as the Deli Barn door *whoosh*ed closed and the sound of the car rumbling out of the parking lot. Drowsily she wondered if perhaps Lisa Bellow had opened the door of the car as it sped away, tumbled out onto the unforgiving pavement of Chestnut Street, ripping skin from her knees, maybe breaking her arm, certainly screaming bloody murder, and was now lying in the bed beside her on the other side of the hospital room, applying eyeliner or texting her friends or flipping through some piece-of-crap magazine. Meredith slowly turned her head to look. There was no bed beside her. It was a single room.

The spring before, when Evan had suffered his horrible injury, he'd been in the hospital for almost a week and shared a room with an eighty-year-old man who every so often would bellow, "Goddammit, are you kidding me?" to no one but his own pain. They had had enough of hospitals, all four of them. And now here they were again. No wonder her parents looked dead.

She rubbed her hand hard over her eyes. Her face throbbed and her head seemed to be full of wet sand. She was so sleepy she could feel individual sections of her brain shutting down, like a night watchman was walking through her head turning off lights, one by one. She was closing her eyes to sleep again just as Evan came into the room, carrying a fountain drink and a bag of Cheetos. The straw was in his mouth, and when he saw her half-open eyes he froze for a moment, then pulled the straw from his lips.

"Hey," he whispered.

"Hey," she whispered back. The word was thick and strange in her throat, her brother little more than shadow in the muted light.

"How's it going?"

She tried to shrug, but wasn't sure if she'd succeeded. " 'kay."

He nodded toward their parents. "Check them out. Where's the camera when you need it?"

She smiled groggily. She wanted to tell him not to wake them, but she couldn't get the words to form. But it didn't matter — he knew what she wanted (he almost always did), and made no move to rouse them from their sleep. He sat down beside her on the bed and set the bag of Cheetos at her feet. He smelled like a cafeteria, like french fries.

"Sleepy," she said.

It seemed like almost everything was better, easier, when it was just the two of them. Their parents were forever complicating matters by inserting some practical, know-it-all point of view into a situation. Objectively she recognized that this was their job, to be parental, but that didn't make it any less annoying.

For years she had imagined this alternate reality — a family of two — especially before Evan had gotten hurt. She loved books and movies where the parents were MIA (detained, missing, conveniently deceased) and the kids had to take care of themselves — the older sibling doing all the boring parental necessities (laundry, bills, etc.) while still effortlessly retaining his carefree pre-tragedy personality, the younger sibling making grilled cheese for dinner every night, the two working together to cleverly dodge authorities and stay out of foster care. Or better yet, the stories where the siblings were alone and in some sort of dire situation — shipwrecked, captured by terrorists, surrounded by lions — and had to rely on each other to survive. Her talents would complement his; their sense of humor would ease the tension; their cunning would get them out of endless impossible circumstances. Yes, if only it weren't for her parents, keeping the lions at bay to begin with. She always knew she and Evan would excel at peril, given the chance.

"Cops . . ." he was saying.

"What?"

"Okay?" he said. "Do you . . . ?"

"What?"

"You're asleep," he said, smiling. "Don't —"

She tried to shake her head, but nothing moved.

The spring before, she'd sat on the edge of his hospital bed, trying, failing, to get the sour look off his face, cracking jokes and telling stories, all the while trying to not make eye contact with him. His left eye had been bandaged, and she did not like him looking at her with only one eye. She didn't say this, of course — she wasn't that insensitive — but it creeped her out, that single right eye. It was wrong, imbalanced, and when it darted around the room it seemed frantic in its searching. When the bandage came off and they all got a look at what remained of his left eye — not much of use, as it turned out — she still preferred its milky drifting to the lone, darting eye from the hospital.

"All right?"

She felt her eyelids droop. "Evan," she said.

"The cops," he said. "They want . . ."

She couldn't catch the end of this. She tried to keep her eyes open, to look at him squarely, but he was fuzzy and each time she let her eyes close it became harder to open them again. Had she figured out the vertical asymptote? Had she graphed it?

"Lisa?" she asked.

"They don't know," he said. "They thought —"

Wait . . . *there* she was. Meredith, her eyes closed, breathed a sigh of relief. She could see it all clearly, as if she were standing right outside a glass door, just like the one she'd looked through before going into the Deli Barn. There was Lisa Bellow, sitting on a tattered brown couch in the living room of a small apartment, holding a little white dog on her lap. It was a very little dog, like a Chihuahua but not quite, and its name was Annie. It had a stubby tail and pointy ears and a thin red collar, no bigger than a bracelet. Lisa was scratching Annie behind the ears, and Annie was twisting her head back happily the way dogs do when you scratch them in just the right place. Lisa's face was still stained from all the makeup she'd cried off, and Meredith thought she looked a little bit like a child who had tried to make herself up like a circus clown.

The man with the too-long gray hoodie came into the room where Lisa and Annie sat, but he wasn't wearing his hoodie any-more. Of course, he wasn't wearing his black ski mask either, because this was his apartment, but Meredith knew it was the same man because of his dark eyes and his blond eyebrows. Behind him Meredith could see a little kitchen. There was a silver trash can with a foot pedal. There was a blender on the counter. There were photos magneted onto the refrigerator, and there were people in the photos, but because she was outside the door, Meredith couldn't make out any of the faces. The man wore jeans and a navy-blue T-shirt. He had a mustache she had not seen before, and a face with a lot of little dents and grooves. He looked at the girl on the couch.

"That's my dog," he said. Meredith could hear him clearly, and she looked and realized the glass door was open a few inches, though she'd heard no bells to announce her arrival. "That's Annie."

"She's sweet," Lisa said quietly.

Something had already transpired between them, Meredith realized, some information exchanged or understanding reached, because Lisa wasn't trying to run for the door or scream for help or even ask the man what was happening. Lisa didn't even seem all that upset. She seemed content to be petting the dog, and the dog was content being petted, and Meredith was content because, of all the terrible things that might have happened to Lisa Bellow, here she was sitting on a couch petting a cute little dog, and maybe it wasn't so bad after all, what had happened to Lisa.

Someone touched her arm and Meredith turned from the glass door and there was a man she didn't recognize, a handsome young man with black hair. He wore a blue button-down shirt and a white jacket.

"How're you feeling?" the man asked.

Meredith turned around to see Lisa again, but there was nowhere to turn. She was on her back. She was in a bed. The sheets were itchy on her bare shins. She was in the hospital and the man with the black hair and the white coat was, well . . . duh.

"Okay," she said. "Fine."

"The police need to talk with you," the handsome doctor said. "I'll be back in a few minutes, but the police need to speak with you now."

The doctor looked exactly like a doctor on a soap opera her grandmother watched. Was he real? Again she tried to turn to catch a glimpse of Lisa. Which part of this was real? Now there were other people she had never seen before, a black woman with round glasses and a tall bald man, the woman seated beside her on her right side and the man standing at the end of the bed.

"Where's Evan?" she asked.

"He'll be back soon." This from yet another voice, another woman seated beside her, on the left, with her hand resting on Meredith's shoulder. She turned to look at this woman. This woman was her mother.

It was important, the black woman said, it was imperative to get her story as soon as possible, so that they would have the best chance of finding Lisa safe and sound. That's what the woman — the police detective — said: "safe and sound." The detective spoke slowly. She chose her words carefully, it seemed to Meredith. Her name was Detective Waller. She was a small compact woman, young, maybe thirty, with efficient hair and mannerisms. She spent a lot of time adjusting her glasses. The other detective, a tall bald man with a black mustache, stood at the end of the bed and wrote things down in a notepad. Her mother sat on the opposite side of the bed from Detective Waller and remained completely still as Meredith relayed the story of what had happened in the Deli Barn.

She told them about the Christmas bells. She told them about the gunman calling the sandwich artist a fat ass. She described the man (the kidnapper, she thought, but she could not quite form this word) as best she could — his too-long hoodie and his ski mask and his hiking boots and his pale eyebrows and about how tall he was and about how much he might have weighed. She guessed he was about the same weight as her father and the detectives' heads swiveled in unison toward where her father sat on the stiff couch, as if he might be the black-masked bandit. She told them how the kidnapper's boots thunked and that his voice was not deep and that he had said that Lisa had to go with him and so Lisa did.

She did not tell them quite everything. She did not tell them what Lisa had said in that moment when she, Meredith, had lost all hope. She did not tell them that Lisa had told her it was going to be okay. It didn't make any difference to the investigation, she was sure, and somehow this thing that Lisa had said to her was like a coin already deep, deep in her pocket and she did not want to dig it out and hand it over. She wanted it in her pocket — she didn't even want it to see the light of day — because once it was out it would not really belong to her anymore.

She asked the detectives about the sandwich farmer. He'd been hit in the head, they said, but he would be fine. They had already talked to him and gotten his statement, and now that they had hers they had a better chance of finding the perpetrator.

"But you were there the whole time," Detective Waller said. "So your story is very important. Most important. Because you were there when they left."

"Yeah," Meredith said. "But I didn't see his car or anything."

"Do you have any idea how long you were there after they left, before Mr. Fulton found you?"

"Mr. Fulton? The custodian?"

"That's right," Detective Waller said. "He's the man who came in and found you and called the police."

"That's so weird," Meredith said. Mr. Fulton was forever giving them hand sanitizer. That seemed to be his entire job, to stand in the main hall squirting out hand sanitizer to germy children. She didn't know anything about him except that he was black, and someone, probably one of Lisa Bellow's group, had started a rumor that he had spent twenty years in prison for murder. Of course this rumor made the rounds about every single black male who worked at the school, including the principal.

"How long would you say you were there,

after the man left with Lisa, and before Mr. Fulton came in?" the tall Detective asked.

"I don't know," Meredith said. "I don't even remember it. I don't remember Mr. Fulton coming in."

"She clearly didn't remember Mr. Fulton coming in," her mother said. "You just told her and she was obviously surprised."

"Ma'am," Detective Waller said.

Meredith looked at her mother. She'd seen the look on her face before. Years ago Evan had dubbed this look "the constipated rhino." Oh, that had been hilarious. How many years had they laughed over this?

"Did he tell you to stay still for a certain amount of time?" Detective Waller asked. "Did he tell you not to get up?"

"No," Meredith said. "Why?"

"Did he threaten you?" the tall detective asked.

She shook her head.

"The man had a gun," her father said from the other side of the room. "I think that —"

"Of course," Detective Waller said in her clipped way, though she didn't stop looking at Meredith. "That in itself is a threat. It must have been very scary."

It wasn't until this moment that Meredith realized what this conversation was about, and why it was important how long she had lain on the floor, and why it mattered that she'd been so out of it or crazy or whatever it was that was making her not remember Mr. Fulton and not even remember the ambulance or getting to the hospital or any of it. Now she understood. If she had leaped up the moment the car pulled away, if she had called 911 right then from her cell phone, then the man with Lisa wouldn't have had such a big head start. If she had even sat up and looked out the door she would have seen the car, would know at least its size and color, and maybe if she'd been on the ball, maybe even what kind of car it was and maybe even some numbers from its license plate.

And worse, just dawning on her now — how long had it taken before someone had realized that a kidnapping had even occurred? It would have just looked like a simple robbery; there was no trace of Lisa, just an unconscious sandwich farmer and one flipped-out teenager, no one to say Lisa had ever been there, no reason for anyone to suspect a third person had been involved. For all Mr. Fulton or the cops or anyone knew, there were only two victims, and they were both lying on the floor of the Deli Barn.

What time was it now? She could see light behind the curtains. How long had the sandwich farmer been unconscious? How many hours until, maybe in the middle of the night, being interviewed as she was now, had he said, "Then the girls laid on the floor" and Detective Waller jerked her head up and said, "Girls?" and then the pieces had started falling together — yes, in fact, a girl's mother had called the switchboard in the evening, somebody Bellow, her daughter had never come home from school, she thought she was at a friend's house, but now it was late, and . . .

So while she and the sandwich farmer slept, the man in the car was getting farther and farther away, and Lisa was getting farther and farther away, and no one knew the clock was ticking, no one knew to shake them awake in their hospital beds, wake them up for Christ sakes, there were *three* people in that store, three people, three victims, not two.

Why had she lain on the floor so long? What had she even been thinking about? Maybe the man had said something. Maybe he had said, *"Lie there for an hour and don't move. Lie there for an hour or I'll come back and kill you. Lie there for an hour or I'll kill her"* — yes, maybe that was it. Maybe she'd forgotten that because she'd forgotten everything else. All she knew was what people told her about what happened, and there was no one here who could tell her this. Maybe she was just following instructions.

"The last thing I remember is them leaving," she said. "I don't remember anything after that until I woke up here."

"Do you think he could have hit her?" her mother asked. "She might have been unconscious."

"Doctor said no bodily trauma," the tall detective said.

Meredith felt her mother take hold of her hand, not squeezing it, but wrapping her fingers carefully, like you'd hold something fragile that might be blown from your grasp.

"More likely you were in shock," Detective Waller said. She smiled gently. She wasn't unfriendly. She wasn't accusing anyone of anything. She was just doing her job. "It's understandable," she said. "It happens. You did what you could."

Which was nothing, Meredith thought. *What I could do was exactly nothing.*

"We have a good description and a clear time frame. We know you and Lisa went to the restaurant after school, and we know that Mr. Fulton arrived at the restaurant about three twenty-five. We just don't know precisely when they left. But we're working on it. We just wanted to talk with you as soon as we possibly could, so we have the best chance of finding Lisa."

Meredith wanted to tell them that Lisa was safe, at least for the time being, that Lisa was in the man's apartment, on the man's couch, petting the man's little white dog. But she knew how this would sound, and she wasn't sure she believed it herself, though she knew the dog's name, and she knew about the blender and the silver wastebasket with the foot pedal, and that had to mean something, didn't it?

"One more thing," Detective Waller said. "The man. Did he seem familiar to you? At all?"

"No," Meredith said. "But his face was —"

"His voice sound at all familiar?"

"No," she said. "I don't think so."

"Why would he be familiar?" her mother asked.

"We're just exploring all the possibilities," Detective Waller said. "Meredith, do you think he could have been younger than you thought? Do you think he could have been a teenager?"

"I don't think so," Meredith said. "He

didn't really sound like a teenager."

"And you don't think you'd ever encountered him anywhere before?"

"No."

"Do you think Lisa recognized him?"

"No," Meredith said. "I mean, she didn't act like she did."

"How did she act?" Detective Waller asked.

"She already told you," her mother said. "She —"

"She cried," Meredith said. "And then she stopped. And then . . . then she left."

"Do you think Lisa might have known him?" her mother asked Detective Waller.

"I don't think anything yet," Detective Waller said, standing. "But we have to consider everything. Many people who are abducted have some connection to their abductor. That may not be the case here. But we just don't know yet."

Meredith was relieved when they were gone, but only momentarily, because then her father stood up. He didn't come over to the bed. He just stood in his spot and looked at them expectantly, an actor waiting for his cue. Her mother's hand was ice cold. Meredith couldn't even remember the last time she'd held her mother's hand, but this hand was not something you'd go out of your way to grasp for comfort. In addition to being oddly freezing — it wasn't cold in the room at all — her mother's fingers were narrow and hard. It felt like they were made of metal, like they themselves were dental instruments.

"The doctor said you can come home tomorrow," her mother said.

"Okay," Meredith said.

"We'll fold out the couch in the family room and you can watch movies."

"Like a sick day," Meredith said. "Dad can bring me comic books."

"Great!" her father exclaimed. "I'm on it."

She was kidding, but the joke was completely lost on her father, who of course lived to provide material satisfaction — even the briefest, shallowest happiness — for anyone at any level of discomfort. From the time they were little kids, whenever she or Evan were sick, her father would come home from work with a bag full of comics, handheld pinball games, baseball cards, invisible ink trivia books, a dozen varieties of Jell-O, six-packs of 7Up.

"It is a sick day," her mother said, squeezing Meredith's fingers with her dental instruments. "You can have a sick week if you want. Whatever you want, Meredith —"

Her voice wavered and she did not finish her sentence. God, where was Evan? Meredith wondered. He'd abandoned her here, with emotional parents and no buffer. She had sat in the room last spring and listened to the ice cream cone diagnosis while he was *unconscious.* He owed her this. He owed her his presence.

"You want something from the café?" her father asked. "A soda? Maybe a juice box?"

It had been at least five years since she'd stabbed a straw into a juice box. "No thanks," she said.

"You hungry? You want some chips or a candy bar or something?"

"I'm really okay."

He was looking slightly desperate, like a robot who'd been given contradictory instructions. She played the only card she had. She yawned. It was a fake yawn at first, but after the initial intake of air it turned into an authentic one, so she didn't feel too guilty about it.

"We should let you sleep," her mother said. She turned to her father, relieved. "We should let her sleep."

"Sleep is the best thing," her father said.

On this they could all agree.

In Meredith's half sleep, one thing was for

sure: Lisa Bellow would definitely not be allowed to accompany the man to walk Annie the dog, not out in broad daylight, in the apartment courtyard, where any well-meaning citizen could instantly recognize her instantly recognizable face and call the police. Her story, no doubt, was all over the television. Not that Meredith had seen any news. . . . the TV in her room had been conspicuously dark all day, the remote control nowhere to be seen. Lisa's photograph, Meredith assumed, would be her seventh-grade yearbook picture, the one in the Parkway North Middle School *Pioneer,* which Meredith was ashamed to admit she could conjure in her mind on cue. Meredith and Jules and Kristy had spent an embarrassing (even by their own lax standards) amount of time looking at the seventh-grade section of the yearbook, flipped through it nearly every day over the summer until its pages were limp, categorizing, defining, ranking. Plus, due to some annoying trick of fate and a refusal to alphabetize, Lisa Bellow's picture was directly above Meredith's, so there was no *not* comparing them, Lisa with her perfectly timed smile, Meredith caught off guard (was that really the best shot they had?) in a lopsided grin, looking like the idiot cousin.

But of course the dog — Annie — would have to be walked. It was inevitable. Annie was not one of those genius dogs featured on Animal Planet that could use the toilet. At least a few times a day the man would have to take her outside, even if only for a minute or two, even if only a couple steps outside the front door of the apartment building to pee beside the concrete planter with the cigarette butts stuck in the soil. (In her half sleep, the image could not have been clearer; the concrete planter's base was chipped; one of the cigarette butts was ringed with lipstick.)

For this minute or two of dog peeing, Lisa would be alone in the apartment, unguarded. How would the man keep her from making a phone call, or walking out the door and sprinting to the parking lot, where surely there were people who could help her? He would have to put her in the bathroom. This would avoid the time and energy of tying her up, which — time and energy aside — Meredith was certain he didn't even really want to do anyway. Probably he couldn't lock the bathroom door from the outside, but he could push something against it, something heavy, like a dresser or a trunk. Maybe his old trunk from the army, which he'd held on to and dragged around with him from apartment to apartment for the last dozen years. All that was inside were blankets and towels and a winter coat, but if he turned it longways it wedged perfectly between the bathroom door and the hall wall, so there was no chance of it budging, nowhere she could go. Of course she could pound on the door, scream her head off, try to alert the neighbors. Yes, he would have to tell her something to keep her from doing this. He would have to offer her something meaningful in return for her good behavior.

Maybe, Meredith decided, he would say she could have whatever she wanted for dinner, as long as she didn't make any noise.

"What're you thinking about?" Evan asked her.

"Nothing," she said quickly. She had been turning over this question: What would Lisa choose for dinner? "My algebra test."

"Your algebra test?" He raised a doubting eyebrow at her. "Really? You just became the single most dedicated student in the history of algebra."

They were walking down the hall, doctor's orders. No reason to lie in bed all day, the handsome doctor had said. Go for a walk with your brother, take a spin around the floor, see the sights! He was one of those doctors, eager to prove he was cool by saying everything in a slightly mocking tone, lest you think he took himself too seriously. Walking beside Evan, Meredith peered into rooms along the hallway, watching people struggling with dinner trays. Until last year, when Evan got hurt, the most experience she'd had with hospitals was her favorite children's book, *Curious George Goes to the Hospital.* Not that she really expected it to be the way it was in the book — monkey puppet shows, sick but gleeful children — but those were the colorful images she had in her head the evening she first came to see her battered-faced brother, and those were the colorful images she left behind forever when she and her mother drove home that night.

But strangely, over the week Evan was a patient, she found a new version of the hospital that was no less pleasing, that was perhaps even more pleasing, than a monkey in a wheelchair. Over that week Meredith came to appreciate the orderliness of hospitals, because it was exactly the opposite of middle school. In a hospital, even in times of urgency — maybe especially in times of urgency — there was a clear plan of action. Things happened in a certain way; there were procedures to be followed, and everyone knew their assigned role. Patients wore robes and pajamas and slippers. They were vulnerable, and the people dressed in white were charged with caring for those who were vulnerable. Things were clear: there were the caring and the cared for. And you always knew who you were. All you had to do was look down and see if you had on pajamas.

"Mom said you get to come home tomorrow."

"Yeah," she said.

"So that's good."

"Yeah," she said. "I guess."

"It's weird that no one knows."

"You mean —"

"Yeah. That it was you."

No information about Meredith had been released. Not her name, not her age, not her condition. Her parents had told her this earlier. At the press conference the police had stated that Another Customer had been present in the Deli Barn at the time of the abduction. For all anyone knew — anyone besides her family and the police and the doctors and the sandwich farmer and Mr. Fulton the janitor — Another Customer had been an adult. For all anyone else knew — even her friends — she had walked straight home that day, passed by the Deli Barn without even glancing inside, continued down Chestnut Street, made the left on Duncan, then the cut across the edge of the park, then the right on Glenside, then into her house, a snack from the fridge, her phone, the television, the computer, same old, same old.

"I don't think it'll last," she said. "Somebody'll find out."

"It is middle school, after all," Evan said.

They reached the end of the hall and turned around. She realized she was shuffling a little, and wasn't sure if there was anything actually wrong with her or if it just seemed like at least one of them should be shuffling. Inside the corner room a baby was crying and someone was trying to hush it.

"Do you know her boyfriend?" she asked.

"No," he said. "He's a freshman, I think. Somebody told me he's a dick."

"I'm sure," she said. But then she didn't really feel like saying anything bad about Lisa, not with Lisa sitting on the edge of the tub in that bathroom, waiting for Annie to pee by the concrete planter, thinking about what she wanted for dinner. It was possible that Lisa was a little scared, even though nothing all that scary had happened. It was possible that —

"He plays lacrosse," Evan confirmed. For this was how people were defined at the high school, at least the people who mattered.

In her mind, Meredith left Lisa in the bathroom and made herself think instead about Evan, Evan who didn't play anything anymore. Evan was undefined. Evan was floating. Actually, Meredith thought, Evan was hovering, bobbing in the air like a parade balloon, untethered but too heavy, too burdened with ropes, to drift away. He was supposed to be looking at colleges, she knew — it was October, and she knew some of his friends had already applied places for early decision — but she wasn't sure he had done more than take the letters and catalogs from the mailbox and toss them into the recycling bin. A year ago he'd had a box — not a shoebox, either, but a box from the grocery store that said DOLE BANANAS on the side — full of recruiting letters from programs that wanted him to consider them. Just *consider* them. Now that he was no longer a baseball player, there were no more personal letters, only standard junk mail that every high school senior got. The banana box was gone, broken down, put out with ordinary pizza boxes. Evan wasn't anyone special anymore, just another kid with a decent GPA.

Part of her wished she had seen it, really seen it and not just imagined it. She did not like to think that his life had changed so utterly while she was unaware, probably over at Kristy's watching YouTube videos on her computer, probably laughing at some asinine thing while Evan stood there in the batter's box, windmilling his bat around. He'd had three bats and they all had names, like boats. She didn't even know where the bats were now. Probably her parents had whisked them away: out of sight, out of mind! She hoped they had not gotten rid of them. She hoped that, wherever they were, they did not yet belong to someone else.

The windmill. Then maybe he starts to turn his head. Maybe — she'd seen the moment ten thousand times — he's going to yell something at the batter, nothing special, just some routine chatter. And then, just like that, he's on the ground — maybe on his stomach, like she'd been, looking at those Coke stains under the Deli Barn counter. But Evan's in the dirt. Evan's unconscious. And the baseball that hit him is still rolling, and it rolls and rolls and understandably no one pays any attention to it, that ball, so that when they go back to find it afterward, they cannot distinguish it from the other batting practice balls.

When they took the bandages off he was not completely blind in the eye, as they'd feared. He could see some light, some shape. He had one surgery, then another, then another, to repair the fracture. It was delicate, tedious, endless, in and out of the hospital, his pain constant. Some more light came through, some shapes grew edges. There was cautious hope. Part of her believed — part of all of them, she suspected — that he was the one in a million, that his sight would be fully restored. But by July it had leveled off. Most likely, the doctor said, that was it: it was as good as it was ever going to get.

"They'll find her," Evan said, in answer to a question she had not asked. "She'll just show up. Today, probably. She'll wander up to a gas station and just start laying into some guy pumping his gas."

"Maybe," she said, though she doubted it, not with the army trunk wedged against the door.

"She'll be like, give me your cell and make it snappy. Then she'll call the lax bro and he'll go get her in his dad's Porsche. But first he'll go through Starbucks and get her a skinny latte."

They had reached her room. Her parents

were talking in hushed tones to someone inside. Evan leaned against the doorway. "And before they go to the cops she'll make him take her to the mall so she can get an outfit to wear for the press conference. And then she'll be like, drive smoother so I can paint my nails."

Her legs were heavy. She felt like she'd just walked ten miles in the sand. She looked up at her brother, her very best friend, the love of her life, her co-conspirator, with his uncombed hair and his hidden, milky, useless eye.

"Can you not?" she said.

6

"Words cannot express," was the phrase Claire couldn't get out of her mind. People had said it to her about her own losses (her mother all those years ago, her son's perfect vision the previous spring), and she had used it herself in comforting others, but now she felt ashamed at having called on it so cavalierly. She lay in bed with her back to Mark, whom she was almost certain was also not asleep, and they were silent.

They had lain like this, back to back, for over an hour — it was past 1:00 a.m. — and she literally could not think of how to frame a single thing she was feeling into words. Surely there would be some solace, at the very least some relief, in talking, in rolling over and beginning a sentence, fumbling through some explanation of her state of mind, however inadequate. But there were simply no words. It wasn't that she couldn't bring herself to say them; it was that she didn't have them.

They had brought Meredith home in the afternoon, set her up in the family room on the foldout couch with her favorite magazines and an assortment of snacks. Meredith had sat cross-legged on the bed for about an hour, staring vaguely at the television, the cat across her lap, and then after dinner had said she'd really rather sleep in her room than on the foldout. And she'd taken the cat (the tolerant cat, who allowed himself to be cradled like a baby) and gone up to her room, and Claire had thought to herself that she would give her a few minutes, give her a little space, and then go up and sit on the edge of her bed and talk about it. *Really* talk about it.

A psychiatrist had spoken to them in the hospital room while Meredith and Evan were out walking the halls. This psychiatrist specialized in trauma, they'd been told by the medical doctor. Trauma was *his thing*. The psychiatrist had said of course it was impossible to predict precisely how someone would react to a situation like this, to an event so unimaginable, so distressing, that each person would handle it differently, with different types of coping mechanisms.

"Like what?" Claire had asked.

"She might be terrified?" the psychiatrist

said. His name was Dr. Moon. He was very thin and had silver hair, so perfectly silver that Claire was certain that friends had sung "By the Light of the Silvery Moon" to him at his fiftieth birthday party. Claire already didn't like him — though, to be fair, she did not like psychiatrists in general. She had seen a psychiatrist in college, to combat test anxiety, and plunged into a deep depression after a half-dozen sessions. "She might have nightmares? She might be afraid to leave the house?"

"Understandably," Mark said.

"Understandably," Dr. Moon agreed. "Or she might be angry? She might be angry at you, that you let this happen to her? She might feel like she can't trust you? She might look to her brother for support, or she might shut him out? She's bringing her own personality into this, so you might have some idea of how she'll react. You *know* her. But she's also grappling with something entirely new, so she may also act completely out of character? She may be needy or she may be reserved? She may feel frightened or she may feel emboldened? She may feel relieved or she may feel guilty? Or she may feel all of those things?"

"Thank you, doctor," Mark said, and Claire had nearly laughed out loud. *Thank you, doctor? Really? For a hundred questions and no answers?*

"So you really can't tell us anything," Claire said.

Dr. Moon raised his hands in the universal symbol for being useless. "Keep the lines of communication open," he said. "That's really all you can do at this point. I'll be available if you need me."

"We can do that," Mark said. He nodded at her resolutely. "We can definitely do that."

He turned back expectantly to Dr. Moon, and Claire realized with equal parts despair and affection that her husband was apparently so pleased to have been given something concrete to focus on that he failed to realize that the lines of communication were not literal *lines of communication* and that Dr. Moon would not, in fact, be handing them a telephone or a walkie-talkie or even pair of tin cans connected by a string. She could read the disappointment on Mark's face as Dr. Moon excused himself and pushed open the door, revealing Meredith and Evan standing just on the other side, in the gleaming white hall, an odd space between them large enough for the psychiatrist to walk through with ease.

Oh yes, it had sounded very simple in the hospital room, and the truth was that even she had nodded understandingly at Dr. Moon. Of course The Lines Of Communication would be open! Of course! But now here they were, ten hours out of the hospital, and Meredith seemed to be *underwater,* in some kind of tank that separated her from the rest of them, like Harry Houdini on a stage inside one of those giant tanks wound with heavy chains and those huge, ancient padlocks. How the hell could The Lines of Communication be open when someone was on a stage inside a giant tank?

Ascending the stairs, Claire steeled herself against the wall she was about to face, determined to break through. This was her child. Her baby girl. She would do anything for her. But when she cracked open Meredith's door she found the room dark and Meredith and the tolerant cat sound asleep. Not pretend asleep, either, and not fitful sleep — Claire stood there long enough to make sure — but just normal, another-ho-hum-night-of-my-life sleep. And she had been enormously relieved — thank god! off the hook! conversation postponed! — and then embarrassed and disgusted by her relief.

Then she went to find Evan, but he had retreated to his room as well — she could hear him watching something on his computer, something with gunshots — and she told herself lies she knew were lies to justify not knocking on his door, and so then by 9:00 p.m. it was just her and Mark, and then Mark went to the grocery store, because that was what he did, and so she stood in the kitchen by herself and drank two beers and ate an entire bag of sour-cream-and-onion potato chips, listening to the house settle. And now here they were lying in bed, she with a beer-and-sour-cream lump in her stomach and a taste in her mouth no toothpaste could combat. Here they were, lying in bed, and no one in her family was talking about anything, no one was even making a *sound,* despite the fact that her daughter had been through an unimaginable trauma and should be screaming and pulling out her hair while her family held her and wept with her and raged.

But.

But.

Yes, but.

She was in her room.

Her daughter was in her room, in her pajamas, under her blankets, under her roof, in the light of her nightlight, in the sight of her cat, nine steps from her brother, fifteen steps from her mother, her clothes in her closet, her shoes on her floor.

She was in her room. Meredith was in her room.

So how much rage was fair? How many tears were justified? There was a part of Claire — a big part, honestly, the majority of her — that felt like *dancing,* a pure joy that took her breath away every few minutes. This, as much as anything, was the part she could not put into words, this absolute contradiction of emotions. Shouldn't they be celebrating? Shouldn't they be on their knees, weeping not with grief but with gratitude? *Thank god.* Not only was her daughter alive and unharmed, but she was right down the hall, wrapped around her cat. She was safe. Two days before there had been two girls lying on that floor and one had been chosen and it had not been Meredith. Fifty-fifty, heads or tails, long straw, short straw — her daughter had won, had been left there on the floor shaken but safe, while the other girl —

Well, they hadn't found her yet. Now it had been over forty-eight hours. On television they said the window of opportunity was closing. There were leads but nothing more. There were no suspects. There were no persons of interest. The girl's cell phone had been found by the side of the road three blocks from the Deli Barn. But they hadn't found anything else. Most notably, they hadn't found a body. That was a good thing, right? That had to be a good thing. As long as there was no body then there was a chance she was alive.

But when she thought these things — even about a *body,* finding a person's *body,* finding a girl's *body,* for Christ sakes — Claire felt no quickening in her chest. The girl, Lisa Bellow, was nothing to her in this moment. Nothing! She had heard her name kicked around in carpools and at parties — she knew only that she was one of those popular girls Meredith and her friends hated — but that had no bearing whatsoever on Claire's lack of anxiety for her. Lisa Bellow could have been the nicest girl on the planet. She could have been their next-door neighbor. She could have been Meredith's closest friend. No, she didn't care one bit who Lisa Bellow was; the only important thing about Lisa Bellow, to Claire, was that she, not Meredith, was the girl who was taken. Certainly it would be better if she were found alive, better for Meredith, but all that really mattered was that Meredith was alive. Meredith was safe. Meredith, her baby, her baby girl, was down the hall.

"They didn't have those mini Tater Tots," Mark said.

She was startled by the sound of a human voice. She flipped over to face him. "What?"

He propped himself up on his elbow. "Sorry. Were you asleep?"

"No," she said. "I was — what Tater Tots?"

"You know she likes those little ones, the minis, instead of the fat ones. They didn't have them in the freezer. I know I've gotten them there before. So I tracked down the manager and he said they didn't carry them anymore. He said he wasn't even sure they made them anymore. But I'm gonna call around tomorrow and see what I can find out."

"Okay," she said.

They had taken off the last two days, canceled all their appointments. The receptionists had called every patient — "family emergency, need to reschedule" — and theirs was the kind of practice where some of their patients might say, "Oh, I hope everything's okay" but no one would lose any sleep over it. Tomorrow was Saturday. On Monday they would go back to work. They would go back to their lives.

"I went ahead and got the big ones," he said. "I thought that'd be better than nothing."

"Sure," she said. "I'm sure they'll be fine."

He was quiet for a moment — had he

finally settled this to his satisfaction? — then added: "I can always have them for backup if we find the little ones."

"Honey, it's fine."

"I know," he said. "I just wanted to tell you."

She loved him. That was just a fact. You turned on the radio and there was music playing. You turned on the tap and water came out. That was all there was to it. They had been married twenty-three years and they had survived everything and here they were, lying in bed talking about Tater Tots. As absurd as it was, there was no one else in the world she would have rather had this conversation with. She turned her pillow over and rested her head on the cool side and closed her eyes.

"They have them at Stop and Shop," she said. "That's where I got them last time."

"Okay," he said. "I'll go there tomorrow. First thing."

It would have been easy to pretend that their bond, their mother-daughter closeness, had been shattered by what had happened at the Deli Barn — by the man and the gun and the missing Lisa Bellow. But the truth was that, for Claire, looking at her daughter for the last year or two had been something like looking at the flat face of a mountain range and being told to scale it, without ropes, without safety equipment, and without a canteen and PowerBars. To make the flat face worse, Claire could see some footholds near the bottom, but then, the higher the mountain rose, the flatter it became, until really it was only a solid sheet as unblemished as glass, a mountain only a superhero could scale, a task that would require not determination, skill, fortitude, attitude, or training, but magic.

With Evan she had never seen anything coming. Before Evan, she had always considered herself a person who prepared carefully, allowing her to adjust her external and internal responses in anticipation of any eventuality. But beginning with childbirth, everything with Evan was a shock, everything astonishing, both the highs and the lows. Pregnancy she could handle. Sometimes in those months she felt sick and uncertain, but the cause of the sickness and uncertainty was still inside, still a part of her, and as such completely dependent on her. She was still, in the ways that were most important to her, in control.

But beginning with the unimaginable act of childbirth — truly unimaginable, despite the billions of women who had done it before her — everything took her by surprise. She learned that any preparations or assumptions she might make were meaningless, a lesson driven home with the final, inevitable nail of the porker incident, her sweet, wise, ruined first-grader in the backseat, telling her in no uncertain terms: "There's nothing you can do."

So, with the second born, different. She was now armed with the necessary information . . . or at least with the necessary *lack* of information. Thank god — now at least she knew more or less what was coming. *This time,* she told herself, *I will be prepared to not be prepared. This time I will expect the unexpected, anticipate the pointlessness of anticipation. This time I will give in sooner to my powerlessness. This time I will not try to fight a battle that is already over.*

Thus, when that flat wall appeared, Claire accepted the impossibility of the task that lay before her, took one long look up at the face of that mountain and quietly, and not without some real sense of relief, and under the cover of a very busy schedule, returned to her base camp.

7

Everyone knew that men thought about sex all the time. Young men and old men and married men and single men and rich men and poor men and black men and white men and gay men and straight men and rock stars and bank tellers and crossing guards and presidents and lacrosse players and math teachers and brothers and fathers and kidnappers. So Meredith wasn't going to be a baby about it and try to pretend that Lisa Bellow wasn't getting raped.

She lay in bed and listened to morning things downstairs: the gurgling of the coffeemaker, the ringing of cereal hitting bowl, the bump of the front door being opened (intolerant cat out) and closed (newspaper in). Meredith thought about sex a fair amount as well, not every nine seconds like guys did — according to the internet — but maybe every nine minutes. She and Kristy and Jules often lay awake during sleepovers talking about things that were going to happen to them, sex they were going to have, and with whom, but in all these fantasies Meredith was always nineteen or twenty, a sexy and confident college student who bore almost no resemblance to her current self. Her sexual partner, often the adorable and funny drawer of watches Steven Overbeck, was also a sexy and confident college student in her fantasy, with muscles and sometimes a mustache. So although she could very vividly imagine herself having sex with Steven Overbeck, and was aroused by the thought, the self she imagined in the throes of passion was an entirely different version than the self that lay in this bed now listening to morning happening downstairs.

It was possible that Lisa had already had sex with the freshman lacrosse player, the boy on the beach, the orderer of the oniony sandwich. It wasn't common (which is to say usual, which is to say ordinary, which is to say normal) in eighth grade, but it happened; Meredith had heard stories. But it was also very possible that Lisa had thus far limited herself to hand jobs and blow jobs, possible that Lisa was holding out, hanging on to the one valuable property she still held, already understanding her own sexual power, already knowing about things like being "used goods," saving herself not as a moral choice but out of a desire to have something — anything — left for high school.

Regardless. Today, Saturday, October 11, sixtysomething hours post–Deli Barn, the queen of the eighth grade was definitely no longer a virgin.

It was a good thing for Lisa that there was the dog, Meredith thought. Right? At least there was little Annie, who might stand idly by while the sex was happening, chewing her Nylabone and minding her own business, but who afterward would definitely leap up onto the blankets covering Lisa and curl up in a ball beside her while the man stood by the bed pulling up his pants.

And maybe the sex itself wouldn't have been *that* bad, not *too* bad, not really awful but rather just sort of awful, just something to get through, like a long school assembly or your grandparents' anniversary dinner. This thought was enough to buoy Meredith into an upright position. Having sex with the kidnapper — really she wasn't even going to think of it as rape, because maybe it wasn't quite exactly rape, not like someone jumping out of the bushes and tearing your clothes off — was unpleasant, to be sure, but it probably wasn't *horrible*. Maybe Lisa even thought the kidnapper was sort of cute. Maybe he *was* sort of cute. Maybe, in a certain light, he looked a little bit like the mustached, grown-up version of Steven Overbeck.

She stood up and clenched her toes into the thick carpet of her bedroom. She knew she had to go downstairs eventually. A check of the clock told her it would not be long before they came up and did a gentle *tap-tap-tap* on her three-quarters-closed door, the door opening a little farther with each tap, then a face in the space between door and frame. They did not come into her room often. She and Evan, children of two working parents, were expected to take care of their own spaces. They made their beds and straightened their desks and every night put their clothes in the laundry hamper in the bathroom. Meredith did not understand people who left clothes lying all over their bedroom floors, though some of her friends did this, just kicked aside piles to make more piles, until at some point a mother intervened and picked everything up and put it in the washing machine and then folded it and replaced it in drawers and closets and then the whole thing started over again. She liked that her mother did not have to do this for her, liked that her room felt more like an apartment, a place that was truly her own. One time at Jules's house, Jules's mother had come into Jules's bedroom and flopped down across the bed, and Meredith had to conceal the distaste she felt spreading over her face.

It was possible they would send Evan to fetch her, and Evan was always welcome in her room, and sometimes he would just come in and sit down on the floor and start playing with the battling animals. They had a vast collection of these figures, wild animals who walked upright and carried swords and clubs and axes — and they would set them up around her room and have battles, and there was no sense that any time had passed. He could have been seven and she three; he could have been twelve and she eight. She didn't play with the animals with anyone else, because it wouldn't have been any fun. They had belonged first to Evan, and then they had each had several, and divided them into defined teams, bitterly opposed (Croc/ Rhino/Lion/etc. vs. Tiger/ Ram/Octopus/ etc.). Now they all lived in her room, the whole collection, but it was understood that they all belonged to both of them.

She got dressed and went downstairs. As anticipated, her parents were instantly intolerable. Before a single word was spoken, she could see that they were doing their best to appear friendly but parental, caring yet not overbearing. They were failing on nearly every count. Her father was a flashing yellow light in the middle of the kitchen; her mother's smile looked like she'd drawn it on her face after consulting an illustrated encyclopedia of expressions.

"I made pancakes," her mother said.

"Thanks," she said. "Where's Evan?"

"Still sleeping, I think. Should we wake him?"

"I'll go get him," her father said, lurching into motion.

"No," Meredith said. "It's fine."

She sat down at the kitchen table. Her parents, who had apparently already eaten, sat down across from her.

"Well, that's a little formal, isn't it?" her father said, and he scooched his chair to the corner of the table so that it looked a little less like an interrogation, but now felt weirder for the anti-interrogation effort having been made.

"Did you sleep okay?" her mother asked.

"Yeah."

"You seemed to sleep well," her mother said, which was her mother's way of telling her that she'd come to look in on her in the night. How many times? Meredith wondered. Three? Thirty?

"I did," she said. "Really well." She took a bite of the pancake, which was undercooked, even on the edges, promising a goopy middle. Her mother had no patience when it came to pancakes, yet continued to make them, and they never got any better, and she always wound up throwing half of them away before they even made it to the table. These were worse than usual.

"Meredith," her mother said.

She studied her pancake. "Yeah?"

Of course Meredith knew exactly what was coming. She and Evan had overheard the end of their parents' conversation with the psychiatrist, Dr. Moon. She knew all about the Lines of Communication and how important they were. She'd gotten away with silence yesterday, but she knew it wouldn't last.

"What happened to you," her mother said. "I can't even. I don't even. I can't even."

A for effort, Meredith thought, then immediately felt guilty for being so mean. Her mother was *trying.* Everyone was *trying.*

"It's okay," she said. "I'm all right."

"What your mother's saying," her father said, "is that we are here. For you. We are here."

Like this was always a good thing. Like all anybody ever wanted was their parents *here,* two feet away and ready to pounce.

"I know," she said. "Thanks."

"If you want to talk," her mother said. "If you want to tell us. Something. Anything. Feelings. Things. Emotions. Tricky emotions. Anytime. If you want to say something. You can say anything."

Meredith made herself look up from her pancake. Her mother was smiling, but her eyes were drowning eyes, pleading eyes. Meredith could have swum in her mother's failure. She could have launched a boat into it, a battleship, an aircraft carrier. When Evan got hurt she'd felt sorry for her mother. The night after Evan's second surgery, which had been endless and especially frightening, Meredith had gotten up to go to the bathroom and heard the kettle on downstairs and come down to the kitchen and her mother was sitting at the kitchen table and there were tears just rolling down her face onto the table. It was the weirdest crying Meredith had ever seen, soundless and motionless but for the tears themselves, spilling onto the table.

"It's all right," Meredith said. "Okay? Really."

She knew she had to throw them a bone,

so she looked back and forth between them, made actual eye contact, and added, "I mean it's really weird and probably it hasn't quite hit me yet, you know? And so maybe a little later I'll want to talk about it — but for right now I just kind of want things to go back to normal as much as possible."

"Normal?" her mother said, like she didn't quite believe in the word, but she wanted to grab onto it like a life preserver — Meredith congratulated herself for rescuing both her mother and herself simultaneously.

Her father put both hands palms down on the table, to indicate the conversation had reached a satisfactory conclusion. "Who would like some Tater Tots?" he asked.

"It's breakfast," Meredith said, looking down at her inedible pancake.

"Who says Tater Tots are not for breakfast? I went out first thing this morning and got those teeny-tiny ones. They're like breakfast potatoes. They don't call them breakfast potatoes but that's exactly what they are. They are exactly, precisely, a hundred percent breakfast potatoes."

"Okay," she said.

Her mother had layers; she had always known this, known it well before the silent crying over Evan's eye, known it well before she, Meredith, had reached the age to be embarrassed or even annoyed by her mother. Her mother had layers and secrets and dark spaces where she kept god knows what. Her father had no such dark spaces. Her father was transparent, which is not to say he was shallow or stupid or even uninteresting. He just was what he was. Sad things made him sad and happy things made him happy. His emotions were fine-tuned. And he was almost never angry at people. He got angry at *things,* particularly things that didn't work — she had once seen him punch a closet door that he was trying to repair, strike it with such fury, such personal hostility, that she'd backed out of the room and later, when she'd seen a bandage on his hand, hadn't asked about it.

Evan shuffled into the kitchen.

"Nobody ever made me Tater Tots for breakfast," he said. He sat down at the table and looked at Meredith's plate. "How're the pancakes?" he asked.

Or Lisa could be dead, Meredith thought.

But no, it wasn't even a thought. It was more like a near miss. She heard the sound of the thought missing her, heard it whistle by like a foul ball, like the ball that struck Evan would have sounded to him if he'd been standing six inches closer to the dugout. Yet somehow she knew what the thought was — strangers talking, a snippet of conversation, a voice overheard, an adjoining room — without it having actually made an appearance in her brain. Then, over the blank space in her brain where the thought did not appear,

"I need some new shoes," she said.

She didn't know where it came from, but she knew once she'd said it that it was 100 percent true, that she needed new shoes, that new shoes were precisely what she was lacking. It was the first thing she'd asked for in three days, and the pleasure it brought to her parents was obvious and immense. Maybe that was partly why she had said it, to give a gift to her struggling parents.

"My shoes are too small," she clarified. "I need some new ones."

"There's a plan," her father said. "The shoe plan. The plan of shoes. Why don't we hit the mall after breakfast?"

"What kind of shoes, sister?" Evan asked mock suspiciously.

"Clown shoes," she said. "Red ones."

"With tufts?"

"Yes. Yellow tufts," she said.

"I see," he said. He pretended to write on his paper napkin. "Yellow tufts. Yes. Yes, interesting, I see where this is going."

"Evan can take me," she said. "He knows

what I'm looking for."

"We'll all go," her mother said cheerfully. "There's something I need from there, too."

"Yeah," Evan said. "She needs, um, what was it, let me see, oh yeah, a baby monkey. With a, uh, golden rattle. A baby monkey with a golden rattle. It's the baby monkey with a golden rattle plan."

"The plan of the baby monkey with the golden rattle," Meredith said.

"They just keep on dishin' it out and I just keep on takin' it," her father said, popping a Tater Tot into his mouth. He couldn't have been happier, she knew, his children smiling, his family brought together, safe in their home with their jokes, with a plan.

If Lisa Bellow was the queen of eighth grade and the middle school was her castle, then the Parkway Mall was the country village where she deigned to mingle with the town folk. This was in large part why Meredith wanted to go there to buy new shoes. (What shoes? She would just have to figure that out when she got there.) Meredith had spent many Saturday afternoons at the mall with her friends, but there were the girls who went to the mall and the girls who ruled the mall, and it was easy to tell them apart. There was apparently no occasion too mundane, and no place too commonplace, for Lisa and her besties to take a selfie. They were forever squeezing into the frame — Lisa and Becca and Amanda and Abby — with their skinny vanilla lattes at Starbucks or beside the nearly pornographic mannequins at Victoria's Secret or cuddled together in the leather chairs in front of Hollister. For what purpose? Meredith and Jules and Kristy often wondered. Just to show that they had been there . . . again? Another corner of the mall conquered . . . again? Meredith sometimes wondered if they ever even looked back on those selfies. Or was it just about the taking, and not the remembering? Meredith recalled seeing the iPhone in Lisa's hand the moment before the door opened at Deli Barn. If only there had been occasion for a selfie moment then, perhaps the man, or even his car, would have been captured in the background.

She could not explain why she wanted to see the country village without Lisa in it, only that she wanted to experience a world without Lisa before she went back to school on Monday, a trial run, a test. Normally she wouldn't be caught dead in the mall with her parents, especially not on a Saturday. After the age of eleven, the weekend duties of parents primarily involved transportation. But she knew they would not let her out of their sight. Too many things could happen to girls without their parents.

But those girls, the selfie girls, Lisa's friends, were not at the mall. There was no eighth-grade pack. In fact there seemed to be no middle school pack at all, and very few teenagers but for the stray one with a parent attached, and Meredith wondered if it was they or their parents who were keeping them at home on a Saturday afternoon, whether it was grief or fear at work.

Was there a danger to the public? The police had not said so specifically. They had not said be careful, watch yourself, pay attention. In the three days that had passed it had not occurred to Meredith that what happened at the Deli Barn might be anything other than an isolated incident, but the thin crowds at the Parkway Mall suggested that this thought had occurred to others. Many others.

She went with Evan and her parents into a shoe store. It was ridiculous, the four of them shopping together. She could not remember the last time this had happened — surely it had been four or five years. Evan stood beside her and her parents hung back, scoping out the place for kidnappers.

"Those," she said to the saleslady, pointing at the shoes she had last seen seventy-two hours before, the golden gladiator sandals on the feet in front of her face, right before the feet had disappeared. She liked those shoes after all. Jules had been trying to convince her to buy a pair but she had never wanted them before, because she thought they were stupid and phony — "Are we gladiators? I don't think so!" — but now that she had seen them close up she realized they actually were kind of cute.

"Cute," her father agreed, not that he wouldn't have said that about anything she'd decided to put on her feet, including six-inch slut heels. She walked around to get the feel of them. They felt different from her old shoes. They were not so tight. Her feet felt more like feet. She looked in the mirror. It was just the same old her but the shoes looked good.

"They're you," the saleslady said. "And they're very trendy. This is our last pair. End of the season."

"I'll take them," Meredith said.

Lisa was missing the mall. Meredith closed her eyes on the car ride home and could see Lisa sitting on the couch in the apartment, watching TV, the dog on her lap, pretty much okay except for missing the mall.

Missing being a bitch at the mall, Meredith thought. God, what would it feel like to walk through a space like that knowing that you owned it, to have that confidence that anything you wore was the right thing to wear and anything you said was the right thing to say and anything you did . . .

But Lisa was probably missing her friends a bit, too. Mostly she was thinking about bossing them around, but also maybe she was thinking about how Becca always got the cinnamon pretzel with extra sugar and Abby always got the pretzel bites because they weren't as greasy as the classic pretzel and her mom was totally going to kill her if she ruined another skirt with pretzel grease.

And speaking of Abby's mom, and moms in general, Lisa might also be remembering the way her own mom always waited until the last possible minute to use the hair dryer in the morning, and how she was always busting into the bathroom shouting at her mom, "It's time to go!" and her mom was always like, "What? What?" over the high-pitched whine of the hair dryer, and how Lisa would mouth, *Time to go,* and her mother would be like, "What?" and Lisa would stab her finger on the time on her iPhone and her mother would be like "What? What?" And how it took her, Lisa, forever to realize that her mother knew perfectly well what she was saying but said "What?" anyway because she thought it was funny to prolong the moment, because it was their thing, the thing they'd always done and no one else knew anything about it, and so she, Lisa, kept doing it, too. Parents, right? You never knew what dumb thing they'd think was hilarious.

She missed that, the wail of the hair dryer, her mother's long hair flying in wispy curtains, the steamy bathroom . . . though the little white dog was warm on her lap, and the day had been mostly quiet and peaceful, and maybe she wouldn't be there forever, in the apartment, with the man.

There wasn't any decent reason she could think of why he couldn't let her go.

"What's all this?" Evan asked.

Meredith opened her eyes. They were driving through the main square in town, the intersection with the town hall and the courthouse and the two old churches. In the courtyard outside the town hall, where there was a farmers' market on Wednesdays and where on other days the homeless man sat on the nicest bench and everyone made a wide berth around him, a few hundred people were milling around.

"Pull over," Meredith said, realizing what "all this" was, recognizing half the kids in the eighth grade. This was the reason they weren't at the mall.

Her father pulled the van into the bike lane and turned around in his seat. "You want —"

She slid open her door.

"Meredith —" her mother said.

But she was already out of the van, her feet on the sidewalk, walking into the midst of it. Someone she didn't know, a heavyset woman with huge glasses, thrust a yellow flyer into her hand. Here's what all those selfies were good for. Lisa Bellow, bright eyes, all smiles, laid out in black and white across the 8 1/2 ×11 that read MISSING.

Someone grabbed her arm. It was Evan.

"What're you doing? They're flipping out. You can't —"

A horrible screech interrupted him. There was a man with a megaphone on the town hall steps.

"If you're going door-to-door, please go as a team," the man said. "We have as many flyers as you need. We're trying to get one to every house in the county. But please go as a team. Do not go alone."

She looked back down at the flyer.

TAKEN FROM CHESTNUT STREET DELI

BARN ON WEDNESDAY OCTOBER 8. 5'5",
110 LBS. BLOND HAIR, HAZEL EYES. LAST
SEEN WEARING BLACK LEGGINGS, WHITE
BLOUSE, AND GOLD SANDALS.

"If you are part of a search party please coordinate with the police so that we can cover as much ground as possible," the man with the megaphone said. "This is a police investigation. They appreciate all the community support but we need to let them do their work."

Who was this man? Meredith wondered. The mayor? Was this what county mayors did? She pushed through some people to get to the front of the crowd, though she didn't know what she was going to do when she got there.

There were clots of her classmates and clots of parents and clots of teachers. It was a cool fall afternoon and the courtyard was lined with pumpkins and if you didn't know what was happening you might imagine these people had all gathered for a Halloween parade, a fall festival, something celebratory.

Lisa's best friend Becca Nichols was sitting on the bottom step of the town hall with a tall stack of yellow flyers beside her. There must have been a thousand of them, secured with a stone on top.

"Hey," Meredith said. "Um . . ."

Becca looked up. "Flyers?" Becca was in her algebra class. They saw each other every day, but in her eyes and her tone there was no acknowledgment that she even knew Meredith.

"Sure," Meredith said. "Yeah."

Becca slid a stack from under the stone. "Don't go alone," she said flatly.

"I won't," Meredith said. "I . . . my brother . . ." She looked around but couldn't locate Evan. The crowd was thick; it had closed behind her and she could no longer see the street where she'd hopped from the van. It wasn't a few hundred people, she realized. It was way more. One huge mass of bodies. She wondered if Evan could have gotten lost in a crowd so large. Would it be harder to find her with one eye? Where were her parents? Had they sent him after her and then gone to park? She was stupid to have leaped out of the van like that. A crowd like this — five hundred? seven hundred? — you could disappear into and it might be hours before anyone even knew you were missing.

Becca handed her the stack of flyers, which fluttered in the breeze as they passed from hand to hand, and Meredith turned from the steps. She saw the homeless man at the edge of the crowd. He was wearing a gray hoodie that was stained on the chest with something brown . . . coffee, it looked like from far off. She took a step toward him. Or maybe it wasn't brown. Also, maybe it wasn't a hoodie. The stain might have been red and the hoodie might have been a sweater. The homeless man had a black wool coat on over it so it was hard to tell. This was the black coat he always wore. Last winter, when it was in the single digits for two weeks straight, her father had gotten out of the car at the courthouse intersection and given the homeless man his green North Face winter jacket. They'd been on their way out to dinner, and Meredith had watched from the car as her father held the jacket out to the man, and the man had taken it warily from her father's hand. But the next time they saw the man, a few days later, he was still in his black coat. "He probably sold your jacket," her mother had said. "He probably traded it for drugs."

Some people started singing "Amazing Grace." A group of women. Who knew who they were or if they even knew Lisa. A few more people started singing, including some of her classmates and their parents. Out of the corner of her eye Meredith saw Becca stand up.

"Jesus," Becca said. "Not again."

Meredith turned from the steps and bumped into a man. He was tall and blond and smelled of cigarettes. He was too young to be anybody's father.

"Easy, girl," he said, laying his hand on her shoulder. She pulled away and turned left and there was Evan, his phone at his ear, shouting over the singing, "I've got her! I've got her!"

He slipped the phone in his pocket and smiled at her.

"Heart attacks all around," he said.

She wanted to hug him but resisted. But she did not resist when he took her hand and led her through the singing crowd and back to the minivan.

"I've been trying to call you," Jules said. "Your mom said you were sick."

"Kind of," Meredith said.

It was Saturday night. She was sitting in her room, on her bed. The new shoes were on the floor beside the bed, looking up at her. The stack of yellow flyers was on her desk. What was she supposed to do with them? Why had she even taken them from Becca Nichols? It wasn't like she was going to go door-to-door herself, looking for Lisa. But it seemed horrible to throw them away

161

or even put them in the recycling bin, so she'd just set them on her desk until she could figure out what to do with them.

Downstairs, her parents were watching something on television; they'd muted it as she'd passed, asked her if everything was okay, could they get her anything, blah blah blah.

"Oh my god, at school yesterday, oh my god," Jules was saying. "People were freaking out all over the place. We had an assembly where they told us not to freak out, but the whole time it was totally obvious that everyone was freaking out, including the people telling us not to freak out. Only like half the school was even there because everybody's parents are like oh my god, no way are you leaving this house."

"Jules," she said. "Listen."

"Did your parents make you stay home? Or were you really sick?"

"Listen," Meredith said. "I'm trying to tell you something."

It wasn't Jules she should have called. It was Kristy. Kristy was her better friend, probably her best friend. And Kristy was quieter, less dramatic, always more willing to listen without interruption. But had anything that had ever happened to her been more worthy of drama?

"It was me," she said.

"What was you?"

"I was the other person in the Deli Barn. I'm the Other Customer."

There was a long silence. Then:

"What do you mean?"

"I mean I was there. It was me. I was there with Lisa, and the . . . person. I wasn't in school Thursday or yesterday because I was in the hospital."

"You're in the hospital?"

"Not anymore. I was, but now I'm home."

"You were there? You saw it?"

Meredith drew her knees to her chest. It felt like she was talking about something she'd seen on television, like she was relaying someone else's story. It didn't really make her *feel* anything to tell Jules this, nothing but the rush that came from the act of telling, of having news, of sharing a secret. It wasn't a happy rush, but it wasn't a sad rush either.

"Yeah," she said. "I saw it."

"Jesus. Jesus, Meredith."

"I know, right?"

There was a long silence, then another, "Jesus. What'd your parents do? Are they flipping? What'd Evan do? Oh my god, I can't even believe —"

"Nobody knows," Meredith said. "I mean,

except the police and my parents and Evan, obviously. And now you."

"So what happened? Can you tell me the story? Are you allowed to tell me the story?"

"There's no story, really. I was just getting a root beer. And then the guy came in and then he took the money and then he took Lisa and that was it."

"What did you do?"

"What do you mean?"

"What were you doing while all that was happening?"

"Lying on the floor," she said. "He told us to lie on the floor."

"Jesus."

"You can't tell anyone, okay?" Meredith said. "I'm going back to school on Monday and you can't tell anyone."

"Don't you think people are going to find out eventually? Isn't there going to be like a trial or something?"

"For who?"

"Okay, that was stupid. I just mean, it seems like this is the kind of thing people find out about."

"Just keep it to yourself, okay?" Meredith said. "For now? Okay?"

She knew that Jules would tell. She wouldn't tell everyone — she wasn't going to post it on Facebook or anything — but she would tell at least Kristy and probably two or three other people, because Jules liked to know things first but, more importantly, Jules liked to *tell* things first. It wasn't like letting out the intolerant cat, exactly, but rather like leaving the door open to see what the intolerant cat would do.

Meredith hung up and lay down on her bed. You could never tell for certain, 100 percent, what a cat would do. But Meredith knew that Lisa knew what the dog, Annie, would do. The dog would wait until everything in the bed was over. Then the dog would leap up onto the bed and form a barrier between Lisa's body and the other body.

Meredith knew that Lisa could count on this. She was sure of it. It was all she could count on.

8

Claire knew Meredith was on the phone and she knew it was Jules whom she would call first, because Jules's personality was stronger and she would say things that would make Meredith feel better. Concrete things. Definitive things. Jules was just dumb enough to be sure of herself, to offer proclamations and advice without any waffling, unlike Kristy who had always been wise enough to waffle. That said, Claire had heard all of them — not just Jules, but Kristy, and Meredith, too — say things about other girls that had shocked her. The predictable antics of Lisa Bellow and her clique of mean girls often paled in comparison to the cruel judgment of the supposed nice girls in the back of her minivan — their slut shaming, their collective contempt, their insistence that the most popular girls were "stupid hos." Every carpool, entire lives were being dismissed with the wave of a hand.

Maybe they were all bitches, Claire thought. Maybe that was all there was to be in eighth grade. Maybe you didn't have any choice. Maybe your only choice was figuring out what kind of bitch you wanted to be.

She could never say something like that to Mark. It wouldn't be as bad as willfully injuring a child with a dental instrument, but it was in the same ballpark, lumping every eighth-grade girl into that one ugly category. She knew that when he looked at Meredith and her friends the girls he saw were still eight or nine, still only playing at being teenagers, their giggles about kisses instead of blow jobs, their whispered conversations some version of the Mystery Date board game they had played years ago, where the luckiest girl always wound up with the dark-haired singer from the boy band. Claire knew that Mark not only *imagined* the girls that way, but that was what he really *saw* when he looked at them, the way an anorexic girl really *saw* a fat girl in the mirror, despite all the physical evidence to the contrary.

Not that Claire was any expert on teenage girls, or even (or, okay, especially) her own teenage girl. She listened to them in the car as she drove them to the mall or a movie or a birthday party, and sometimes she stood outside Meredith's room and listened to her talk on the phone, or listened to the three of them late on a Friday night during slumber parties, their voices clear as day until they dropped to whispers when a romantic bombshell was coming. She was not the mother who sat around chatting with the girls about who was going out with whom and what the popular shoes were.

(The shoes. Mark had called them cute, those awful gold sandals, but had there ever, ever been any more ridiculous shoe? She had seen them on the feet of some of her young patients and sighed inwardly, amazed again by the power of peer pressure. Only when under the hypnotic power of someone else, or someone elses, would a person believe that the shoe, last embraced by a hot, sandy society approximately two thousand years ago, was actually attractive. Still, Claire knew that there was some compelling reason Meredith had picked those shoes on this day, and so she was not going to say anything about it. If Meredith had picked out those shoes on a normal day, at the end of a week where she had not almost been abducted, strapped them on and wobbled absurdly around the shoe store like she had this afternoon, primed for the colosseum, Claire would have said *no way*.)

Claire had not turned on the news, or read the news online, or listened to the car radio, or even read the updates that rolled across her iPhone. If there was any news any of them needed to hear — if Lisa Bellow was found, however she was found, or if there was a suspect and it was necessary for Meredith to become involved, Claire was certain they would hear from the police. After Meredith's abrupt departure from the van at the crowded town square and her re-appearance ten minutes later, hand in hand with her brother, Claire wanted to believe that their part in the drama was finished, and believed it so much that for a few hours on Saturday evening she forgot the story that was whirling around out there, the work that was being done, the leads that were being followed. "I just want things to go back to normal," Meredith had said at breakfast. She had said those exact words, of her own accord, not been fed them by anyone, had thought and spoken them herself. So that's what they would strive for: normality. All day Saturday they'd heard nothing from the police. But on Sunday the police detective, the woman, called and said they'd like for Meredith to look at some pictures.

"We can come to you," Detective Waller told Claire. "To your house. But we're at a point where we do need her help."

"You have a suspect?" Claire asked.

"We're at a point where we need her help," Detective Waller repeated.

It was not Detective Waller who arrived at the house but the other detective — the tall man with the mustache. His name was Detective Thorn. He appeared with five thick books, photo albums of suspects. On each page there were four pictures, hundreds of men in all, maybe thousands. Could all of these men possibly be suspects in Lisa Bellow's abduction? It seemed to Claire that perhaps they should just take a picture of every man on the planet and get these giant books out whenever anything happened. Maybe that *was* what they did? Everywhere the police went, everyone they talked to, maybe they automatically brought the books of men who might take you.

Meredith sat at the dining-room table and flipped through the books slowly. She looked at every man. Claire sat beside her. They were mug shots, mostly, and a lot of the men looked defiant and a lot of them looked broken and a lot of them looked, well, normal. And then there were a few who looked unhinged, sporting the crazy psychotic smiles you imagined when you heard a sound at night, alone in a house. And a few more who looked like they just didn't care, the Logan Boones of the world, their names on the board still meaning nothing to them, their walk still the easy swagger of the superior. She imagined in jail that would come to an end. She imagined that a week in prison was not unlike having a dentist hurt you with her tools.

"If you see anyone that even looks a little bit familiar," Detective Thorn said, "we can get another picture."

"I hardly saw him," Meredith said. "The mask . . ."

"I know," the detective said. "But it's worth a try. Try to imagine him some other place, not at the Deli Barn. Imagine you see him across the street when you're walking somewhere. It's cold out so he's wearing a ski mask. He's just a man taking his kids sledding."

Detective Thorn turned to Claire. "That helps sometimes. Distance it from the event. Take the anxiety out."

Claire thought this idea — imagining the kidnapper, on the sidewalk, taking children sledding — would likely cause more anxiety rather than less, but she didn't say so.

Meredith's face was blank. She turned another page, then another, and all the men looked back at her. It could be any one of them, Claire thought. She could be looking right at him and not even know it. What was she supposed to recognize?

Meredith closed the last book.

"Sorry," she said.

"No apologies necessary," he said. "We've got some more books. One more today and then maybe another couple tomorrow. If you're up to it."

"Sure," Meredith said.

Detective Thorn reached into his bag and took out the Parkway Senior High School yearbook. "I'd like you to take a look through this. Just in case."

"That's a yearbook," Meredith said.

"It is," Detective Thorn said. "You remember at the hospital, what we told you? Most people are abducted by someone they know. We don't know if that's the case here, but we have to look at every possibility."

"This isn't even our yearbook," Meredith said. "This is the high school yearbook. The middle school yearbook is —"

"We know Lisa spent time with high school kids," Detective Thorn said.

"And he had a car," Claire said. "The . . .

the . . ." she fumbled, forgetting what to call him. "The . . . abductor." She was relieved, absurdly, to realize that the abductor could not be an eighth-grader because he had to be at least old enough to drive.

"Her boyfriend's in high school," Meredith said.

"That's right," Detective Thorn said. "Do you know him?"

"No. I know he plays lacrosse."

"It sounds like she interacted with several people at the high school. So we thought a look at the yearbook couldn't hurt." He cast a glance at Claire. "Kids, you know . . ." he said sadly. He shook his head.

Know *what*? she wondered. Know that kids sometimes abducted each other? What message was the detective trying to send her? Did they suspect something and weren't letting on? Did they think this could be a joke of some kind, a senior prank gone wrong? It didn't make any sense. What about the unconscious employee? The safe? The gun?

The detective had bookmarked the yearbook so that Meredith was able to skip all the candids and go straight to the headshots. As she flipped through Claire recognized boys from the baseball team, boys that had been Evan's classmates for years. Meredith stopped on the *O*'s in Evan's class.

"That's my brother," she said to Detective Thorn.

Claire looked at the photo, taken a few months before the injury. Her son looking confidently with both eyes toward the future. Meredith flipped the page and Claire looked away. All these boys, not yet the men in the official books of suspects, but fixed forever now in their own book of suspects, the preface to the ongoing series of men who might take you.

Meredith closed the book. "Sorry," she said again.

"We'll keep trying," he said.

"Can I go now?"

"Sure. We might do it again tomorrow."

"Okay." She left the room and went slowly up the stairs, dragging her hand along the banister. Claire wondered if she had paused partway up to listen, sat down soundlessly on what they called the Christmas Step, the spot where the stairs turned and there was a mini landing large enough for two kids to wait until they were summoned downstairs to see what Santa had brought them.

"Are there any leads at all?" Claire asked.

Detective Thorn frowned. "Lots of tips. People call the line, say they saw a man driving with a teenager. Most of the time it ends up being a girl and her dad. But that's how we do it, how we find people. We follow every tip."

"Do you really think it might be a student?"

"We have a lot of ideas."

"But nothing solid."

"Not yet," he said. "But someone will see something eventually. We're fortunate. Lot of people are invested in this. Lot of community support. Social media. Posters. People putting together search groups and the like. Ribbons. Fund-raisers."

"Fund-raisers for what?"

"Help out her mom," the detective said. "Single mom, not a lot of resources. Just people want to lend a hand." He cleared his throat. "Speaking of her, I think she'd like to speak to you."

"Who-what?" Claire asked.

"Lisa's mom," he said. "Colleen's her name. I think she'd like to speak with you."

"Why?" Claire asked quickly, then considered, too late, how it might look to ask why, to question anything. She was the mother who had won; Lisa Bellow's mother was the mother who'd lost.

"She's distraught," he said flatly.

"Of course," she said. "Of course she is."

"I think she thought she might find some

comfort in speaking with you. And in speaking with Meredith. I've told her that you all and Meredith are working with us, helping us in whatever way you all can. But I think this is more of an emotional question than a practical one. If you see what I'm saying."

"Of course," Claire said. Claire did not want Colleen Bellow in her living room or on her couch or at her dining-room table, did not want her reclining against her throw pillows or drinking out of her glasses, did not want her washing her hands in her bathroom sink, did not want her home and family polluted by that degree of agony. If she was being honest with herself — and there was no reason not to be — she would appreciate it if Colleen Bellow would keep her own tragedy off their doorstep. They — Meredith, the whole family — had dodged the bullet. It was a gruesome, awful bullet, but they had dodged it, goddammit. Could they not simply dust themselves off, breathe a sigh of relief, and move on? Did they have to become *involved?* She could not say any of this to the detective, of course. If she was going to be a terrible person, she was going to have to be a terrible person in private. This was something she had learned long ago.

"So it would be all right if someone

brought her by later? You'll talk to Meredith and make sure that's okay? I think it would be a nice thing for Mrs. — Ms. — Bellow. I'm not sure she's had one minute of sleep since Wednesday."

"Anything we can do," Claire said, because what other option did she have?

"Her mother?" Meredith said. Claire thought she looked more appalled than distressed. "Here?"

"We can tell them no," Mark said. "If you're not up to it."

"We can't really tell them no," Claire said.

Mark gave her a pointed look. The look plainly said: *You want to rethink that one? Because I'm pretty sure you want to rethink that one.*

"Well, I'm sorry, but I don't feel we can say no," Claire said. "The woman has lost her daughter. She would like to speak with Meredith. Meredith was the last person to speak with her. Her daughter —"

"You say that like —" Mark started.

"— before she was taken. The last person to speak with her before she was taken."

"I'm not saying she doesn't *ever* have to talk with her," Mark said in his super-enunciated voice, normally reserved for elderly patients. "I'm saying that she doesn't

177

have to do it *today*."

"Her daughter," Claire said, "is missing."

"It's okay," Meredith said, her game face on. "It's okay. I can do it."

Strangely, Claire had not fully understood the origin of Meredith's game face until the day she'd caught the exact same expression in her own reflection in a car window. It was the determination and deliberate detachment made necessary by a difficult situation. Sometimes Claire imagined that one day, when Meredith was her age and she was diagnosed with pancreatic cancer, or Alzheimer's, or whatever was going to kill her, she and Meredith might just stare at each other with their game faces on until Claire died. This frightened and heartened her simultaneously.

She arrived a little after 4:00 on Sunday afternoon. It was Detective Waller who brought her, the detective they'd seen at the hospital the morning Meredith woke up. Claire was certain she would recognize Colleen Bellow from school, that she'd remember her face from a band concert or open house, but the woman she saw bore no resemblance to anyone she knew. She seemed much too young to be the mother of a middle-schooler, looked closer in age to an eighth-grader than to a mother of one. She was shorter than Claire and had long straight blond hair, the kind (Claire always thought) that women who were not quite willing to grow up clung to as long as possible, especially if they had daughters. She was cute and dressed like the dental hygienists at the office, in clothes that came from stores Claire hadn't set foot in for at least ten years.

Claire had also expected Colleen Bellow to look more like a wreck than she did. She'd imagined a crazy-woman with bloodshot eyes and tangled hair and splotchy skin — all the earmarks of a *stricken* woman — but Colleen Bellow did not look all that bad. She looked, in fact, better than Claire felt.

"Thanks for letting me come over," she said to Mark, shaking his hand, identifying him quickly, as everyone always did, as the welcoming one, despite the fact that he'd been the one to try to rescind the invitation. "I can't tell you how nice it is to be in a house."

Claire thought it was an odd thing to say (surely Colleen Bellow lived in a house?), but she tried to smile warmly as she shook the woman's hand. The hand was surprisingly strong, the grasp firm. Her daughter was missing but her grip was full of resolve.

"What can we do for you?" Claire asked. "Can we get you anything? Coffee?"

"I can't stand another cup of coffee," Colleen said. Her eyes moved to the staircase. "Is Meredith here? Is she in her room? Can I talk to her?"

The plan had been that she and Mark would talk to Colleen for a few minutes, evaluate her mental state, see if they thought talking to her was something Meredith was up for, before they brought her into it. They wanted to control the situation. They did not want to give Meredith more than she could handle.

"She's . . ." Mark started. He looked to Claire for support.

Of course you wouldn't sleep, Claire thought. You wouldn't dare. What your mind would do to you in the moments before sleep, the images held at bay while you talked to people, while you kept moving, kept drinking coffee, kept answering the phone, kept making lists — they'd have nothing to keep them back if you stopped and lay down in a dark and quiet room and closed your eyes. Of course you would look like this, not stricken but driven; of course your handshake would be firm, firmer than it ever had been before, knuckle bruising if necessary. In the first days, when that window of possibility was still open, her leftovers still in the refrigerator, the smell of her still on her sheets, when you could sense the window sliding shut but still feel her breath blowing through the opening, you would do nothing but *do do do.* There was only action, forward motion.

For a moment Claire was standing in Colleen Bellow's home, their roles reversed, Meredith missing, Lisa left behind, and Claire was looking hopefully up the Bellows' stairs in the direction of Lisa's room and asking to speak with her, while just on the other side of the window in her mind was the horror of what might be happening to her daughter in this moment, this exact moment, and thus the need to go back to the last moment, the last moment that could possibly be accounted for. . . .

"I'll go get her," Claire said. "She's just upstairs. I'll be right back."

Her children were sitting on the floor of Meredith's bedroom quietly playing with what they called the battling animals. They weren't even really *playing* with them; they were setting them up, which always seemed to them to be more fun than the actual playing, the placing of each one in its strategic position in order that it might have the greatest advantage in the battle, when and if that battle was finally waged. The bull with the ball and chain was on the desk chair; the alligator with the sword on the overturned trashcan. Claire stood in the doorway and watched them for a moment. They weren't speaking to each other, but they were making little mumbly animal growls as they arranged their toys, and anyone who did not know them would think that they both suffered from some sort of terrible disability.

"Meredith," she said.

"Grrrr," Evan said. "Who dares interrupt our preparations?"

"Honey," she said. "Mrs. Bellow is downstairs."

"I know," Meredith said. "I heard her."

"So you need to come now, okay?"

Meredith looked at Evan. He raised his eyebrows. Was he asking her if she wanted him to come, too? Claire did not know. She was not, nor had ever been, privy to the meaning of their gestures. She imagined they could have an entire conversation, with the help of the battling animals, and she would not know a single thing that had been said.

"Okay," Meredith said. She lay her animals down on the battlefield. Claire walked down the stairs behind her and on the bottom stair gave her what was intended to be a comforting touch on the back but which wound up, somehow, maybe because Meredith slowed, to seem like a shove. They both felt it, the shover and the shoved, and Meredith tensed up in that moment and walked stiffly into the living room where Mark and Colleen Bellow were sitting on the edges of their chairs, not talking, and Claire wondered if they'd said a word in her absence aside from Mark's increasingly desperate offers to get her something from the kitchen.

Colleen stood up when Meredith came into the room.

"Meredith," she said. She said it warmly and with great relief, as if they were old friends who had been separated for years. Claire could see that Colleen Bellow wanted to hug her daughter, and could also see that Meredith was going to do everything possible with her body — arms crossed, legs pressed against the end table — to prevent it.

"Hi," Meredith said.

"It's so good to see you again. You probably don't recognize me, but I know you and Lisa have known each other for years. Isn't your locker next to hers?"

Claire saw her daughter struck by this

comment.

"Uh, yeah," Meredith said.

"She's mentioned you a bunch of times," Colleen said. She looked at Claire. "She's mentioned her," she said.

"Yes," Claire said. "I think they've been in several classes together."

"I remember a birthday party," Colleen said. "A roller-skating birthday party. I think it was for Mary Berger. It was at the community center. I remember that you and Lisa were both really good at limbo. I was so impressed that anyone could think about limbo and roller-skating at the same time."

"Hmmmm," Meredith said.

"Do you remember that party?"

"Sort of," Meredith said. "I think it was a while ago."

"I'll never forget that," Colleen said. She turned to Claire. "They were both so good, and they were the last two, and the bar just kept getting lower and lower and they kept doing it. Do you remember that?"

"It rings a bell," Claire said, though it rung not the slightest, faintest of bells, and she was sure that even if such a birthday party had ever happened that, one, she had not been there and, two, that Colleen Bellow was confusing Meredith with someone else, some other girl Lisa vaguely disdained, because Meredith had inherited her poor flexibility, and was terrible on roller skates, and would never in one million years have been a finalist in a limbo roller-skating competition.

"I bet Mark remembers it," Colleen said.

"I do," Mark said, always the hero. "I remember it well."

Meredith sat down on the hearth. Colleen looked at her and smiled.

"Lisa just had a birthday," she said. "Two weeks ago. When's your birthday?"

"Not till March," Meredith said.

"What do you want for your birthday?" Colleen said.

"I don't know," Meredith said. "I mean . . . it's still a long way off."

"Your parents are really lucky to have you," Colleen said.

"We feel very lucky," Claire said, then wished it back, lest it seem like they were flaunting their luck, speaking not just of the general good fortune of having nice children (which is obviously how she'd intended it), but of this very specific moment of good luck that their child was the one sitting on the hearth in this living room and Lisa Bellow was — Claire thought with a sudden, vivid shock — lifeless, bruised, and tangled in some brush by the side of the interstate.

"You know we will help in whatever way we can," Mark said. "Anything we can do."

Colleen turned to Meredith. "I know you've talked to the police," she said. "But if there's anything you forgot to tell them about what happened, any more you can remember . . ."

Detective Waller had been standing silently in the archway between the foyer and the living room, but now she straightened up.

"Sometimes just the smallest detail can help," she added.

"She was ordering a sandwich," Meredith said. "Two sandwiches."

"Two?" Colleen said.

"One foot-long and one six-inch," Meredith said.

"What was on the foot-long?" Colleen asked.

"Like, a lot of onions, I think. That's the only thing I really remember."

"That's my sandwich!" Colleen said, turning to the detective. "That's the one she was getting for me."

Now she turned to Claire. "I usually don't get off work until seven, and so sometimes she gets me a sandwich and puts it in the fridge so I have something to eat when I get home, so I don't have to cook."

"It sounds like she was —" Claire started, then swallowed what was to follow, "a wonderful girl," and was able to quickly replace it with, "getting you your sandwich."

"Yes," Colleen said. "She was. That was *my* sandwich. It was for me."

"What kind of sandwich was it again?" the detective asked, uncapping her pen.

Claire was sweating. In some way she couldn't explain, the discussion of the sandwich was actually worse than the image of the bruised body tangled in the brush. She never wanted to talk about sandwiches again. She hated sandwiches, period. Sandwiches were dead to her. (And here, now, the wildly inappropriate impulse to giggle.)

Meredith told the rest of her story. She told the same story she'd told before, now ten, a dozen times, no new details, all she remembered. Claire did not like to imagine Meredith lying on that floor so she stopped listening near the end.

"And then she got up and they walked out," Meredith finished.

Colleen frowned. She was not going to cry, Claire realized. Maybe she hadn't cried yet. Maybe she was never going to cry. Maybe crying was as bad as sleeping. Maybe, until there was something definite to cry over, something physical, not an idea or a possibility of even a probability, but a body, there would be, could be, no tears. There was only *do do do.*

"I don't understand how there can be such a good description, but still no one knows who this man is," Colleen said to the detective. "Meredith's done an awesome job."

"She has," Detective Waller agreed.

"Meredith," Colleen said. "Do you think maybe you saw the car even a little bit? Because I was thinking, the door, the door at the Deli Barn, it's all glass. All the way down to the bottom. So even while you were lying there you might have seen it. After Lisa got up, you might have seen it. You were looking that way."

Colleen Bellow glanced over at Claire. "She was looking that way," she said.

"Sort of," Meredith said. "I mean I was looking sort of that way. But I —"

"She doesn't remember," Claire said. "She didn't see the car and she doesn't remember."

"Those are two different things," Detective Waller said. She didn't say it critically, Claire noticed, only like a point of fact.

"They may be two different things," Claire said. "But they're both true."

"I never saw the parking lot," Meredith

said. "I never saw the car. I know that. I heard the car but I never saw it."

"Why didn't you look when you heard it start up?" Colleen asked softly, kindly, even.

Meredith shook her head. "I don't know," she said.

Because she's thirteen, Claire thought. *Because a man had a gun pointed at her head. Because she thought she was going to die. Because her mind was frozen. Because the rules of common sense did not apply. Because how could she know that the simplest thing could be the most important?*

She wished she could go back in time for one second — she wasn't greedy, wasn't asking for much, just one second to take Meredith's head, tilt it in the right direction. *"Look outside,"* she'd say. *"Meredith, Meredith, please, look."*

"That was horrible," Mark said, later, in the kitchen, while they were doing the dinner dishes. "Horrible. I know it sounds selfish, but I don't want to do that again. I don't care what they say. There's no reason to —"

"I hope that poor girl is already dead," Claire said.

He turned off the water. "What?"

"I hope she's already dead."

"How can you say that?"

"It's not going to end well," Claire said. "It's been four days. Imagine those four days if she's still alive. Imagine. It's not going to end well so the best everyone can hope for is that it ends soon. For everyone. The girl included."

"Did Meredith even know her?"

"Meredith hated her. Don't you ever listen to anything? She was horrible. She was awful."

"And now you hope she's dead."

"Oh, come on," she said. "For god's sake, you know I didn't mean —"

"I'm sorry," he said, and he looked sorry, and he should be sorry, she thought. "I'm sorry. That was horrible, sitting there with that woman, talking about goddamn Deli Barn sandwiches."

"Did someone mention Deli Barn sandwiches?" Evan said, appearing in the doorway. "Because I'm starving."

"Stop it," Mark said. "Just don't, okay? People are in pain. You don't even know the kind of pain that was in our living room this afternoon."

It was not at all like him to talk this way, certainly not to Evan. He was rattled, and he was bad at being rattled, and Evan stood there silently in the doorway waiting for his father to apologize, which, Claire suspected, would take no more than five seconds.

"I'm sorry I blew up," Mark said, on the count of four. "This is not about you."

Evan continued his punishing silence.

"Okay?" Mark said. "Okay? Everything's crazy. Everybody's crazy."

More silence. Her son's face was a mask of granite disinterest. He knew how to hurt them. He had the weapons, and he wasn't afraid to use them.

He had been drifting around the house like a ghost for months, his dreams in shambles. Not that they were very good dreams to begin with, and not that in some ways this wasn't for the best. She'd told herself this a thousand times. The upside to Evan's partial blindness was that there would be no horrible disappointment in the future with regards to baseball. He was very good, but he would have hit the wall eventually, likely as soon as he got to college when he was no longer the best, when every boy in the dugout had been the star of the high school team, a hometown hero. Evan was not going to play professional baseball, and she'd already been dreading that slow realization, the gradual resignation, the prolonged agony. Now that was all erased in one quick stroke. At least the stroke itself was quick, if not the aftermath. Losing the eye was terrible. The dream itself was no great loss.

"You want to do something?" Mark asked. "You want to play cards or something? You want to play rummy?"

Evan shook his head slowly.

Mark looked at her. "I'm going to take a shower," he said. "For like two hours. Or until the hot water runs out."

"Okay," she said.

When it was just her and Evan, Claire said, "He's very stressed out."

"No shit," Evan said. "Who isn't?"

He sat down at the kitchen table and took off his glasses and pressed the heel of his hand over his blind eye. This was something he did. She knew he was in pain, though they no longer spoke of it. She knew he still took a pill every morning. Sometimes after he left for school she went into their bathroom and counted the pills, and some days — not most days, but some days — there were more gone than the prescription allowed.

"Are you all right?" she asked, sitting down across from him.

"It's fine."

"Are you sure?"

"It's not *awful*," he said.

"Has she said anything to you? About

anything? Do you know the girl?"

"I know who she is," he said. "One of those eighth-grade hoes."

"Don't say that."

"Why not? I'm not making a judgment, I'm just saying. You asked who she is and I'm telling you: one of the eighth-grade hoes. Maybe the leader of the eight-grade hoes. I'm sure Meredith hated her guts."

"It doesn't matter if —"

"It does matter. Of *course* it matters. I'm not saying she's not freaking out. Maybe you'd freak out more if it's someone you hate, because maybe part of you doesn't really care, or maybe even part of you is glad. And what does that say about you? Are you a monster? No, you're just a normal thirteen-year-old human being. But you're too stupid to know that. Why? Because you're just a normal thirteen-year-old human being."

She loved that he could be so blunt and still remain so utterly likable. Was he a little crueler now than he'd been a year ago? Probably. And yet he could not shake that sweetness, her whistling boy.

"Will you talk to her?"

"About what?"

"About anything. About everything. Will you try to talk to her? It's going to be hard, going back to school . . ."

It wasn't as if she was asking him to do her job, only that he would do it better, have a better chance of doing it right, of making some difference.

"I'm not going to make her talk. That's not what she needs."

"What do you think she needs?"

"How should I know? I've never almost been kidnapped before."

"But you know her. And you know what it's like to . . ."

"To what? Get hit in the face? She didn't get hit in the face, Mom. She got out of the way."

"Evan," she said. He was on the other side of the kitchen table and she could have reached out and touched him, almost, but the table was too big. She would have had to practically lay herself across the table to do it because he was leaning back in his chair, in his defensive position now, and what was she supposed to do, flatten herself across the tabletop just to reach him with the tips of her fingers?

"She trusts you," she said. "Anything you can say to her, anything will help. Even just being funny. That will help. She just needs to know you're there for her."

"Well, obviously," he said. "Where else would I be?"

9

Meredith hadn't looked very long at the books, but now, in her bed, it seemed like she could vividly recall every page, every face. How could there be so many suspects? How could it be that so many men might have taken Lisa? Surely if that were true then people were being taken all the time, every day, all over the country, girls brought to their feet inside a hundred Deli Barns, walked briskly to unidentified cars, bells ringing in their wakes.

But probably most of those men were not real criminals. Right? Probably they were potheads or deadbeat dads or petty thieves — the ones who broke into minivans left unlocked in driveways, who fished change out of unused ashtrays. Probably there were not so many men (were all of those men from around here? was that a *local* book?) who were capable of real crimes, serious crimes, crimes where detectives came to your house and laid books across your dining-room table, the table where a long time ago, before baseball, you ate dinner, and sometimes still did. Probably good, too, that she did not recognize any of those faces as the half face glimpsed in that moment when she'd first looked up from the counter and realized what was happening. She had seen enough movies to know what happened next, what happened when you could positively identify the criminal.

What happened was that the criminal came back for you.

She rolled over and looked at the clock. It was 5:15. No one else was awake. Except maybe the intolerant cat, who sometimes moved about in the night, when there was no one to bother him, and sometimes made noises that sounded like a window sliding open, or footsteps on the stairs, or the creak of a door.

Lisa could sleep late, which was nice for her. There would be no one hassling her to get out of bed so she could catch the bus, no one asking her if she'd finished her homework or if the field trip form had been turned in, or reminding her to pick up a sandwich on the way home. That was weird, right? Getting your mother a sandwich at Deli Barn? Of course Meredith understood it was nice, it was thoughtful, but it was also kind of weird, like your mother couldn't stop on her own way home to pick up a sandwich? Because by the time she got home after work that sandwich would have been in the fridge for like four hours and the bread would be cold and hard, and there was almost nothing worse in the world than cold, hard bread.

So not for the boyfriend, the lacrosse player, the boy on the beach, not for him those onions, but for her mother. Her mother who remembered some party from like three years ago, some party where not only had she not even talked to Lisa but also definitely had not participated in any stupid limbo contest. And her mother knew, somehow, that their lockers were beside each other this year? What had Lisa said: *"Hey, Mom, can you see if you can get me a new locker, because I'm next to Meredith Oliver who is a total loser"?* Her mother looked like a grown-up version of Lisa, like the kind of mother who was dying to be confused for an older sister. Not that she, Meredith, should be a jerk about it because, after all, Mrs. Bellow's house was completely empty now, and there was no one to bring her a sandwich.

He'd gotten Lisa some clothes, almost

definitely. Right? She was not still wearing the same clothes from Wednesday, the cold-shoulder peasant top and the black leggings. Certainly, he'd picked up something for her — most likely some sweats she wouldn't be caught dead in in public, but what else would she need, she'd have her sweats and her couch and her daytime television. And probably a bag of chips or something. It was sort of blissful, when you thought about it, that part at least, although probably there was a little part of Lisa this morning that was wishing she were going to school, despite all the hassle and pain in the ass of it, wished she were sliding her folders into her Vera Bradley backpack and strapping on the gladiator sandals, wished she could glide through the halls on those sandals like she always had instead of sitting on the couch, all alone.

But she wasn't all alone, Meredith reminded herself. Of course not. Where was little Annie? She listened hard for the jingle of Annie's collar. And then there she was, right on cue, jingling into Lisa's lap.

Lisa smiled. Meredith smiled. The house was quiet. She went back to sleep.

"We'll give you a ride," her father said as they were finishing their breakfast. "It's on our way."

"That's okay," Meredith said.

"It's on our way," her mother repeated, both of them determined not to acknowledge the fact that in three years of middle school — six, actually, if you counted Evan's years — it had never once been on their way to drop a child off. "And we'll pick you up after."

"Okay," she said. "Whatever."

"And it's still okay to not go," her father said. "You can come to the office with us. You can hang out there for the day."

"No," she said. "I'm good. It's not like anyone knows about me, anyway."

"Just drop me off at the corner," she said, when she saw Kristy and Jules standing there, waiting for her.

"You sure?"

"Yes, I'm sure."

Her father pulled up to the girls and waved at them and they waved back. Meredith could instantly tell that Jules had told Kristy everything.

"Call us if you want," her mother said. "It's fine. We can come get you."

"I'll be okay," she said. "See ya."

She slammed the door and turned to Jules before Kristy could say anything, Kristy who was just standing there with an open mouth anyway.

"I can't believe you told her," she said.

"I didn't tell her, and everybody knows," Jules said.

Meredith turned to Kristy for confirmation on both these points. "Everybody," Kristy said. "Every single person on the bus was talking about it. About you."

It was a slo-mo moment, turning toward the school, a moment from one of those movies she sometimes watched on Saturday mornings with Evan, the old zombie movies, where you turn to sneak a quick look and all the zombies are staring at you. The crowd in front of the school was facing her as one unified wall, or at least it felt that way.

"How'd they find out?" she asked.

"Who knows?" Jules said. "But they know."

Of course no one said anything, not in that initial zombie-moment. They looked at her sideways and there was a little bit of whispering, but mostly as she walked toward them, they just cleared a neat path leading to the main doors. Perhaps this was how Lisa felt sometimes, the path cleared before her, the sea of students parting to let her through, a path that led all the way up to her locker, next to which Lisa was not. In Lisa's place were hundreds of tiny green ribbons, taped or glue-sticked to her locker, plus some messages on colorful Post-it notes — LOVE U, MISS U, COME HOME — as if Lisa might see these and be buoyed up, as if Post-its could somehow *help*. Meredith focused intently on her own locker, on its dull contents, and was surprised when she turned and there was Mr. Fulton, the custodian, standing at Lisa's locker.

"Morning," he said. He was a big man, bulky. All those times he had squirted hand sanitizer onto her hands, he hadn't seemed so large. But standing by her now, in Lisa's place, she felt tiny beside him.

"Hi," she said.

"Looks like you and me are famous." He smiled warmly. "How you doing anyway? You feelin' all right?" He had a wide, expressive mouth that had before seemed friendly when it smiled. Probably this was the same smile he had always smiled. Probably it was the same wide smile he smiled at his own kids. But Meredith had a sudden thought, standing here at her locker, that Mr. Fulton could eat her.

"Okay," she said. "I mean . . . I just got here."

She had never spoken to him before. She didn't know anything about him. He was in his fifties, maybe early sixties, older than her parents but not ancient, his mustache and beard sprinkled with gray.

He gave Lisa's locker a little tap with his knuckles. "Went through it last week," he said. "I opened it up for the police. Thought there might be a clue in there, in case she knew him, the man who snatched her."

"Was there?" she asked quietly.

"A clue? No. Just what you'd expect. Same as yours or anybody else's."

How did he know what was in her locker? Or anybody else's? Did he have keys to everything? The bell rang and people started streaming past her on their way to class. Someone bumped her from behind and she stumbled toward Mr. Fulton. He held up his hands to catch her but she caught herself, only grazed his open hands.

"I gotta go," she said, closing her locker.

"Strange," he said. "You being right next to each other here, and then being in the same spot when it happened. You all don't run in the same crowds though, do you?"

"Not really," she said. She thought it was weird that Mr. Fulton had some under-standing of what crowds people ran in, the social structure of the school. But maybe that was all he did, while he swept with his giant flat broom and squirted out hand sanitizer. Maybe he knew everything. Maybe he had a big book that explained it all, a book with lines that connected people. Maybe he was keeping score.

"I knew when I saw you lying there on the floor," he said. "I knew it was bad. I didn't know how bad, but —"

"Yeah," she said. "Thanks." Humiliating, that he had seen her on the floor. She couldn't remember any of it, and now again the unpleasant thought: Why had she lain there for so long? What had she been doing, flat on her stomach, not moving, long after the danger had passed? God knows what he'd seen when he'd walked into the Deli Barn. God knows what she was doing or saying.

"You take care today," he said.

"Thanks," she said again. He had found her there on the floor. Maybe he had comforted her before the ambulance arrived. She managed to look him in the face for an instant, to make eye contact, to be polite. Was his face in the book? How many men had been in that book that looked just like Mr. Fulton, old men with wide mouths and little to lose?

■ ■ ■ ■

Abby Luckett slid up beside her in the lunch line.

"You have to sit with us," she said. "We need you."

"What?" Meredith asked. She literally almost turned around to see if Abby was talking to someone behind her.

"We need to talk to you. It's about Lisa."

"Um, okay."

There was a vacant seat at their table. The seat was sacred ground, an empty throne, and Meredith was apparently going to be the only one allowed to fill it. There were five other girls at the table. Before she sat down she looked across the lunchroom and saw Kristy and Jules watching her. Meredith felt like a spy. She had never wanted to sit at this table. Except maybe once or twice, just to see how it felt. And now she knew.

"We're solving this, okay?" Abby Luckett announced as Meredith scooched her chair in. "We, the people at this table. We're going to find her. Everyone else isn't doing shit. We have to do something."

Amanda Hammels turned to Meredith. "The cops are idiots," she said. "They're shit. Have you met them? They don't know anything. They don't even know where to start."

"Um . . ." Meredith said.

"She had guys following her all the time," Abby said. "There were like three guys stalking her on Instagram. And one of them she said she'd meet up with. The guy is like thirty. She talked to him practically every day for the past month."

"Did you tell the police about him?" Meredith asked.

"They're not listening to us," Abby said, scowling. "They look at us like we're retards. They said they'd look into it, but I don't think they're really doing anything. They're acting like it was some random thing."

For a second Meredith thought about telling them about paging through the high school yearbook, that it didn't seem to her like the cops thought it was necessarily random. Was that confidential? Was it against the law to tell them what the police had asked her?

"It wasn't random," Amanda Hammels said. "It was that skeeze from Instagram."

"There are like twenty guys who are totally in love with her," Abby said. "It could have been any one of them."

"It did seem kind of random," Meredith said. "It was a robbery. He asked for money.

He was looking for the safe." She glanced across the table at Becca Nichols. Becca was almost certainly Lisa's best friend, and so far she hadn't said a word. She was looking at her food but not eating it. Meredith recalled what Kristy had told her last week (possible? only last week?) about Becca's older sister being pregnant. Well, when it rained it poured. What did that even mean?

"Did he look at her funny when he came in?"

"I don't know," Meredith said. "It was hard to —"

"Did he actually *say* it was random?" Amanda asked. "When he was in there, did he say it?"

"Christ, Amanda," Becca exploded. "Who would walk in there and say, 'Nobody move. This is a random robbery'? Seriously, are you even listening to yourself?"

"She's trying to help," Abby said, "which is more than I can say for you."

"He just said he wanted the money," Meredith said. "That was all he said."

"Right," Abby said. "Of course that's what he *said*. That's his cover. He makes it look like a robbery so no one will know he's been like stalking her for two months. Nobody is going to solve this mystery but us, Meredith."

"For her mom," Amanda said. "For Colleen, we have to find her. And for us, too. For the whole school. For everybody. We need her. People are starting to say she's dead. That's not fair. That's not cool. She's not dead."

"I don't think so either," Meredith said. "I think he's keeping her somewhere."

"Who?"

"The guy. Whoever he is." She knew she was on thin ice. Maybe it was all pretend anyway, what she knew, what she thought she knew. "What do you know about him?" she asked. "The Instagram guy? Do you know anything?"

"He's from Pittsburgh," Abby said. "He said he was a hockey coach. He said he'd show her his big stick."

"Wow," Meredith said. "What did the cops say when you told them that?"

"The cops are shit," Abby said. "They don't care. Will you help us?"

"Sure," Meredith said. "But I don't think there's really very much I can do."

"We can only do so much, but there is so much we can do," Amanda said. "That was our mission trip motto last year." She bent over to retrieve her Vera Bradley backpack. When she sat up again she was smiling.

"Oh my god," she said to Meredith. "I

love your shoes."

Steven Overbeck was not interested in engaging with her in social studies. Despite his sweetness, or perhaps because of it, he was clearly out of his depth, and her fantasy, college-Steven-Overbeck would have to suffice for comfort. Without his banter behind her, she thought about what Abby had said, about the hockey coach from Instagram, but she didn't think there was anything to it. She was fairly certain that the man who came into the Deli Barn had decided only *after* the robbery was a bust that he would take Lisa.

Why? Why would a robber become a kidnapper?

Because he needed money. Because he thought that maybe if he kidnapped her he could ask for a ransom, and if he lost his nerve or if it wasn't worth it he could just let her go. Because he wanted to take something. Because there was only a couple hundred bucks in the register and there was no safe (where the hell *was* the money anyway?) and he had risked everything, every single thing he had, going into that store with that gun, and by god he was not going to risk everything and then leave with two hundred and eleven dollars. Meredith knew that all this had gone through his mind while he'd stood there looking down at them, all this in the space of four or five seconds, and then he had noticed her hair, Lisa's hair, and then those slim bare shoulders courtesy of her cold-shoulder top, and then the fleshy gap at her lower back between her leggings and where her top had ridden up, then the firm slope of her leggings, and then her sandals. And then his eyes moved to the other girl, the one with the brown hair who was at least fifteen pounds heavier. Perhaps it wasn't just about good looks: Which one could he carry, if there needed to be carrying? And the fatter one was wearing flats instead of heels, so she could run like hell, couldn't she, run for her life in those sensible shoes, whereas no one could ever hope to run for her life in those golden sandals.

No. Meredith called bullshit on herself. Lisa was hotter. And that was why. There could be no doubt. He'd taken the pretty one. Everything Lisa had ever done, every stroke of the brush, every meal not eaten, every afternoon of shopping in every dressing room, everything had led her to this moment, to this choice. Years of reading her mother's *Cosmo* had finally paid off. She'd won. The man had stood there wanting something, and then what he wanted was that. *That.* He could figure out the rest later. And that's what he was doing right now, while Lisa sat on the couch, watching TV with Annie the dog, and Meredith sat at her desk in social studies with silent Steven Overbeck dutifully taking notes behind her, the scratch of his pencil the soundtrack of Lisa's endless morning.

He was figuring out the rest.

"What did they say?" Jules wanted to know during library period. "What did they want?"

They were sitting in the back corner of the library in the beanbag chairs. There were only three beanbag chairs and you had to ask to use them during library period, and usually the answer was no, but Meredith could tell by the look on the librarian's face that she, Meredith, might very well get the beanbag chairs every day for the rest of the year.

"They just wanted to know what happened," Meredith said. "They think it was some stalker guy from Instagram."

"I heard that," Kristy said. Her voice dropped to a whisper. "Someone from the governor's office."

"What?" Jules asked. "The governor?"

"Somebody from his *office,*" Kristy said. "That's what people were saying on Friday."

"My mom thinks it was a setup," Jules said. "That she just made it *look* like a kidnapping."

"I heard that, too," Kristy said. "I heard that's what the police think."

"What do you mean, a setup?" Meredith asked. "Like how?"

"Like she just wanted to run away with some guy," Jules said. "But she didn't want to get in trouble, so she made it look like a kidnapping. *They* made it look like a kidnapping, she and the guy, whoever he is, to throw everybody off. But it was all a fakeout."

"Why would you go to all that trouble?" Meredith asked. "And so where are they now?"

"A beach," Jules said. "You know, in like Guadalajara or something."

"You don't even know where Guadalajara is," Meredith said. She was surprised by the edge in her voice, so added, gently, "She's not in Guadalajara, okay?"

"How do you know?"

"It was a robbery," Meredith said. "I'm telling you. I was *there.* It was just a robbery. And then he took her, just . . . I don't know. Just . . . because."

"If that's true, you are so lucky," Kristy said. "Oh my god, it totally could have been —"

"I know," Meredith said.

"Or maybe it wasn't luck," Jules said, shifting onto her side on the beanbag chair, redefining its shape. "Maybe it was just all that bad karma catching up with her."

"That's mean," Kristy said.

"Don't tell me you haven't thought it," Jules said. "Because I know you have. He couldn't have picked a bigger bitch. Years of treating people like shit, and now, well . . ."

Don't say, "Serves her right," Meredith thought. *Don't put those words out there. Once they're out there . . .*

"I'm just glad it wasn't you," Kristy said. "It would be horrible if it was you. I mean, it's horrible no matter what . . . just not *as* horrible."

"So are you like friends with them now or what?" Jules asked.

"I don't think so," Meredith said.

"What else did they talk about?" Kristy asked.

"Nothing," Meredith said. "I mean, nothing really. It was all about Lisa."

"Are you sitting with them tomorrow?"

"I don't know," Meredith said. "We didn't . . . I mean, nobody said anything about tomorrow. So probably not?"

"You're popular," Jules said. "I can't believe it. Of all of us, I didn't think it would be you first."

"That's messed up," Kristy said. "She's not popular. She's just . . ."

"Popular," Jules said.

Lisa was taking a nap on the couch. He had given her some sheets and a blanket and gone to work and she fell asleep watching television, the dog tucked in the crook of her arm, its little paws jerking with rabbit dreams. In Lisa's dreams all the stores in the Parkway Mall were open twenty-four hours and she was moving from store to store and taking anything she wanted.

After school Becca Nichols came up behind her at her locker.

"My friends are crazy," she said. "They don't know anything. They just wish they knew something."

"Sure," Meredith said. "It's understandable. I mean . . ."

"Are you walking home?" Becca said.

Except for their brief interaction on the town square, and the occasional forced exchange in math, Becca Nichols had never actually spoken to her before. She had moved to the area in sixth grade and immediately allied with Lisa and her group. She was prettier than Lisa, had long straight hair that was so dark brown it was almost black. It went to the small of her back and shimmered. Meredith knew this because in seventh grade she'd sat behind Becca in Algebra I and spent a long time staring at her back trying to figure out how someone's hair could shimmer, if it was something Becca put in it or if it was just her natural good luck that made it look that way.

"My parents are picking me up," Meredith said.

"They must be freaking out," Becca said.

"Kind of." Meredith closed her locker. "In their own way."

She turned toward the door and Becca turned with her. They walked past the rows of lockers and Meredith could feel people watching her, watching them. They pushed out the front doors and stood on the pavement outside the school. It was a sunny day and didn't feel like October, though it was only two weeks until Halloween. Kids were boarding the buses. Did Becca ride the bus? Meredith didn't know.

"Lisa's dead," Becca said abruptly. "I haven't said so to anybody else, but since you guys weren't friends I can say it to you. I'm pretty sure he killed her. I think he killed her right away."

Meredith felt something break in her, a crack as real as bone, something that made her want to strike Becca, the way her father had struck that closet door last summer.

"She's not dead," Meredith said.

"How do you know?"

"I just . . . she's not. She's not dead," Meredith said.

"I think he killed her," Becca said flatly. "That day. That afternoon." Meredith could tell she'd been saying these things to herself all weekend. They sounded rehearsed, almost. "I think he raped her and then he killed her. I think they're going to find her body somewhere. In a Dumpster or —"

"I have to go," Meredith said. She could see their minivan in the lot, parked illegally, idling behind the buses. But she would have fled regardless. She would have gotten into any car in the world to get away from Becca. She would have gotten into a car with a total stranger. She would have gotten into the car with the kidnapper. She walked quickly toward the van and swung into the front seat, dropping her backpack at her feet. Her father was driving.

"Well?" he asked.

"Fine," she said. She sat on her trembling hands. "It was fine."

"Yeah? Good."

She could see the Deli Barn from the school driveway. There were two cars in the parking lot and someone standing on the sidewalk out front. It was a block away so she couldn't be sure, but it looked like Mrs. Bellow, Lisa's mom. But maybe not. Maybe it was just some lady, popping in for a ham and Swiss. Her father turned the car the other way, even though it would be shorter to go by the Deli Barn.

"So I take it everybody knows," he said.

"Yeah," she said. "How —"

"We've gotten a lot of calls. Nice calls, I mean. Support. I guess you can't keep something like that under wraps for very long. Was it okay?"

"It was okay," she said.

"Do you want anything? You want to stop anywhere? You hungry?"

"No," she said. "I just want to go home."

"Then home it is," he said.

Lisa was watching television. This is what she did. This is what you did when you were kidnapped. When you were a kidnap victim. When you were a victim of kidnapping. You were neither free nor dead and so you lived in the suspended animation of television watching. What else was there to do, you in the sweatpants and T-shirt and the un-washed hair tangled from the bed and smelling like a man you didn't know? You watched television was what you did.

Except Lisa wasn't exactly watching the television. She was sitting on the couch facing the television and the television was on, but she wasn't watching it. She was just pushing the up arrow on the channel button on the remote and the channels changed and she did not stop. She went all the way up and after a hundred and something it was just black but there were still numbers in the corner and so she kept going up and up and then finally at seven hundred and something it flipped around to zero again and she started over. And again she didn't stop on anything, not even for a second, and it was just flashes of people that she saw, and some she recognized but most she did not, but even if she did she just kept going and then it was past the channels and then it was three hundred and then it was four hundred and seventy-four and she just kept clicking, sitting by herself on the couch and Meredith, watching her through the glass door, wanted to run into the room and take the remote from her hand and — what? Hit her with it? Knock her out cold? Or just settle on a channel already, on *Meerkat*

Manor or *Cupcake Wars* or *SpongeBob,* just anything, just stop anywhere, somewhere, please, and then shove the remote under a couch cushion like she and Evan used to do so that no one could find it and change the channel. Lisa with the hair, that blond hair from the yearbook Meredith had rubbed at with her thumb, hoping to diminish but not destroy it, and it was now hanging like weeds from Lisa's head.

She was sitting on the floor of her bedroom. She was not going to do her homework. No one would care if she did her homework. She set up the battling animals and Evan came into the room and sat on the floor but he didn't pick up the animals.

"The first day will be the worst," he said.

"It was okay."

"It'll get better," he said, because the lie was so obvious. "In a couple weeks it will feel normal at school. People will start forgetting. There'll be something else."

"Not something else like this," she said. For years she had been comforted by Evan's confidence, his bold predictions, his cavalier superiority; now she suddenly found it irritating. "There's nothing else *like this.*"

"Doesn't matter. It doesn't matter what it is. Something else is something else. There always has to be something else because the collective attention span of any group of teenagers is only a few weeks. Trust me: something new will take its place. In June they'll give her the last page of the yearbook with an inspirational quote from Maya Angelou and that'll be that."

"Jesus," she said. "Stop. Jesus, what's wrong with you?"

"I didn't say it wasn't awful, Mer. I just said that's the way it would happen." He picked up the lion, who was doubly armed: a long ax in one hand, a sword in the other.

"The queen is dead; long live the queen!" Evan said in the lion's voice.

She snatched the lion from him. "Stop it," she said. "Get out. Stop messing with my stuff."

He raised his eyebrows. "*Your* stuff?"

She could not stand him sitting here on her floor. All she wanted was to be left alone.

"I'm sorry," he said. "Listen, really, I am sorry. All I'm trying to say is, life at Parkway North marches on. The world keeps spinning."

Spinning, yes. That was an accurate description of her current state. For thirteen years she'd never felt the motion of the earth, and now suddenly she couldn't stop feeling it. And this earth, this new earth, was rotating her through two worlds simultaneously, spinning her so fast that she was no longer certain where one world ended and the other began.

"Let's watch a movie," Evan said. "Let's watch something funny. Something stupid."

"I'm tired," she said. "I'm gonna go to bed."

He stood up, stretched. Sometimes he seemed massive, ten feet tall. "C'mon, Mer. Something mindless. Good for the soul."

"I don't —" she started.

"I'm gonna carry you," he said.

"No."

He grinned. "You know I'll do it."

Would he? He used to all the time, before the injury, trap her in the polar bear hug and then in one swift motion swing her off the ground and into the cradle of his arms, like a bride or a baby. Long after her parents had stopped picking her up, Evan was still doing it. Sometimes when he put her down he'd flex his muscles and kiss his biceps. She had imagined those days were over.

"My only concern is the stairs," he said. He paused a moment, put a finger to his chin in mock consideration. "Probably we won't fall. Probably."

"Okay," she said. "Stop. Okay. I'm coming."

■ ■ ■ ■

Meredith closed her eyes. Lisa was still on the couch and the man was in the bathroom. What was he doing in the bathroom? He'd been in there a really long time. Something was amiss. Lisa was sitting cross-legged on the couch. Something was missing. Something was — Annie. She was not on the couch. The television was turned off and the remote was on the table and Lisa was just sitting there by herself looking at the black television.

Meredith listened for the jingle.

Lisa stood up and went into the kitchen and opened the refrigerator. It was nearly empty. There were some Baggies of shredded cheese and an almost empty jar of black olives; the few olives inside bobbed around in the juice like little shrunken heads. Annie was not in the kitchen. More alarming to Meredith was the fact that Annie's bowls were not on the kitchen floor. Where the bowls had been there was a little rickety table with a bunch of brown bananas on it. On top of the refrigerator, where Annie's box of Milk Bones had been yesterday, there was an old radio.

Maybe he was giving Annie a bath in the

bathtub and he had taken her Milk Bones in there to give her as treats and her bowls were in the dishwasher. But there were no sounds coming from the bathroom. Lisa went past the bathroom door and into the bedroom. The door was only partially open, but Meredith could see there were clothes lying on the bed and the sheets were askew. Annie was not curled on the pillow, not stretched out at the end. There was no sign that Annie was there, or had ever been there.

The door clicked open and the man came out of the bathroom. He was wearing black boxer shorts and nothing else. Lisa was sitting on the edge of the bed. She looked up wearily.

"There's my girl," the man said. He went into the bedroom and closed the door.

Where the hell was Annie? Meredith was in the apartment now. Actually in the apartment, for the first time. She could see everything. She could walk from room to room regardless of where Lisa was. She had stopped spinning. She was not going to walk into the bedroom because she already knew what was happening the bedroom, but she was going to find Annie because she wanted Annie to be there when it was over and she was going to pick up Annie and set her in front of the bedroom door. But maybe Annie had run away. Maybe that was it. Maybe he'd opened the door and she'd dashed out. Meredith looked at the hook by the door. There was no leash there. There was a baseball hat hanging on it. She went and sat down on the couch. She licked her index finger and dragged it along the brown suede cushions. Crumbs. Ashes. No fur.

He hadn't given her away. She hadn't run off. Annie wasn't just gone. It was way worse than that. It was this: there was no Annie.

There never had been any Annie.

Meredith opened her eyes. She was in her own family room. Outside the window it was dark. The dishwasher was running in the kitchen. On television a bride and groom were sprinting away from a church. Her brother was next to her on the couch. He was smiling at the movie.

"There's no dog," she said. At first she wasn't sure if she'd said it aloud, but he looked over at her.

"What?" he said, still smiling. Then he saw her face and he stopped smiling. "What?"

It felt like someone had taken hold of her lungs, one in each huge hand, and was squeezing.

"There's no dog," she said.

10

"There's no dog?" Mark asked. "What does that even mean?"

"It means we need to call the psychiatrist," Claire said.

They were standing in the kitchen, Claire and Mark and Evan. Meredith had gone to bed. According to Evan, she'd stood up from the couch after making the comment about the dog and gone upstairs without another word. By the time Evan had reported what she'd said — it took him a few minutes, he explained, because he wasn't sure if it was "reportable behavior" — and Claire had gone upstairs to check on her, she was asleep.

"I think it's obviously reportable," Claire said. "Since we've never had a dog."

"I don't even know if it was about us," Evan said. He was sitting backward on the kitchen chair. Claire realized that, darkened lens aside, he looked more like his old self than he had in months. Something had changed in him in the past week. Maybe all he'd needed was distraction. Maybe this was her son, again, still. Maybe his own tragedy had come to an end, replaced by his sister's.

"It was like the thought had just occurred to her," he continued. "Like it was something she'd just figured out, like a math problem or something."

"A math problem with a dog?" Claire asked.

"Maybe it was one of those logic problems," Mark said. "Like a boy and his father are horribly injured in a car crash, and when they get to the emergency room the doctor comes in and takes one look at the boy and says, 'I can't treat this boy — he's my son!' And, you know, you have to figure out how this could possibly be."

"Because the doctor's his mother?" Claire asked.

"Okay," Mark said. "That's obviously an outdated example. My point is that maybe it's one of those."

"Right," Evan said. "So in this case the doctor comes into the emergency room and says, 'I can't treat this boy — there's no dog!'"

"Not every single thing is joke worthy," Mark said.

"You're telling me?" Evan said. "Almost *nothing* is joke worthy, okay? Lesson learned. But you're not even listening to me. I said it was *like* a math problem."

"Fine," Mark said. "Just, let's . . . just let's figure this out."

Claire could see Mark trying to hold himself together. It was a whole new thing this week, this fatherhood. He had crossed some line; his old standbys were failing him. Even after Evan's injury, he'd held it together, but now something in him had cracked. Maybe it was the invisibility of the damage. Mark liked to *see* damage. He liked it obvious. This was true even with mouths; he preferred patients coming in with chipped teeth, oozing abscesses.

Evan stood up. "Do you want my help or not? Mom asked me to help. I'm trying to help."

Mark turned to Claire. "You asked him to help?"

"I'd ask everyone in the world to help if I could," Claire said. "Don't make it sound like —"

"So I'm basically the same as everyone in the world?" Evan asked.

"You know that's not what I mean," she said. "I'm trying to —" *Handle your father* is what she wanted to say. There was no way she could win the battle on both fronts simultaneously, and no way she could ally herself with either faction without ruining her chances with the other. (Faction? What was wrong with her? This was her husband. This was her son. She didn't even know what they were arguing about.)

"Everybody just calm down," she said.

"You're the one freaking out," Evan said. He stood up from the table and went to the refrigerator and took out a carton of milk, then pulled a short, wide glass from the cabinet. "Maybe she was just dreaming, you know? Maybe she was trying to break into a junkyard and she was happy because there was no dog."

Slowly, very slowly, he filled his glass with milk and then returned the carton to the fridge. She watched him do this curious thing but, somehow, in the moment, could not figure out why it was so curious.

"Evan . . ." she started.

"Was she upset?" Mark asked.

"I don't know!" he exploded. "I wasn't even looking at her. We were just watching TV. Where were you guys anyway? Maybe if you'd been there you might have done a better job than I did."

"Nobody said you did a bad job," Mark said. "But you're right. It's not your job.

You are not her parent."

He looked at Claire when he said this, not too subtly. Claire felt Mark was getting a little liberal with his expressions of displeasure in front of Evan. He really was coming unglued. It seemed to her as if the adrenaline of the last five days was wearing off and the reality setting in, the what-ifs, the images Mark had somehow managed to slyly dodge over the weekend were suddenly filling his mind. He'd been a wreck at work that day, useless, and finally Claire had sent him home, but first sent him to pick up Meredith from school. They had planned to do that together, but Mark had fallen so far behind schedule and someone had to pick up the slack, didn't someone?

"So there was no dog," Mark said. "Where does that leave us?"

"With the psychiatrist," Claire said. She steeled herself. More doctors. More appointments. More paperwork. "Have you ever suffered from . . . ? Has anyone in your family ever suffered from . . . ? Has anyone in your family ever suffered, period?" Unbelievably, there'd been this question on Evan's neurologist's form: "Has anyone in your family ever died for no apparent reason?" And she'd sat there in the waiting room with Evan slumped in the chair beside her, thinking, *Good Christ, who* hasn't *died for no apparent reason?* Yes, more waiting rooms. More distant, inoffensive music. More weathered magazines. More sliding windows, more cheerful receptionists, more informational videos on TVs you couldn't turn off. These things didn't bother her when she was the doctor. They didn't even particularly bother her when she was the patient. But when she was the mother . . .

"Dr. Moon," Mark said.

"Tell me that's not really his name," Evan said.

"He's an expert," Mark said. "A trauma expert."

"Trauma is *his thing,*" Claire said wryly.

"No fair," Evan said. "Trauma is *our thing.*"

Claire loved her office. She loved every room, every chair, every tray, every instrument. Some mornings she arrived before anyone else and would walk through, turning on the lights and loving the office and the things in it like she loved a person. All of these things were hers, and they were beautiful.

She loved her office less when it was populated by patients. That was just the fact, and one she had reconciled herself to

230

long ago. Patients disrupted the order, although most were on their best behavior, polite with simmering anxiety. There was polite and there was crying. There was not much in between.

Mark chatted nonstop with his patients. He could talk about absolutely anything with enthusiasm, keep up both ends of a conversation with someone whose full mouth prevented much more than a few grunts and nods. Claire had made herself a weather expert. She had thirty conversations a day about weather.

"Lunch?" he asked, surprising her in the small office where they wrote up their notes. He had a hand on either side of the doorway and leaned in over her, hovering inches from her head, like a horsefly.

"I'm behind," she said. "We're behind."

He looked at his watch. "I don't think so. It's just —"

"In general," she said. "I need to go over some —"

"Did you call Dr. Moon?"

"Yes," she said. "He can see her Friday."

He sat down on a wheely stool in front of her. "You okay?" he said.

"Sure, yes, no. I mean, are you okay?"

"Maybe we should take some time off," he said. "Maybe they should, too. Maybe we should all take some time off and go somewhere."

"I'm not sure a vacation is —"

"I don't even mean a vacation," he said. "More like a break. We could go an hour away and stay at a hotel and just chill out. Just have some time for us."

It sounded awful. The four of them in a hotel? Doing what, exactly? Maybe if the children were ten years old and the hotel had a swimming pool? It was a terrible idea.

"I'm not saying it's a terrible idea," she said. "I'm just wondering what we would do."

"We could go for walks. We could find a place that's pretty."

No one wanted to go for walks. Why did he persist in the notion that they were a family that went for walks, despite all evidence to the contrary? Even he didn't want to go for walks.

"We can ask the kids," she said. She knew this was a safe bet. "Maybe they'll have some ideas."

There was little chance to introduce the topic of the fake-cation. Five minutes into the meal, Meredith excused herself and went upstairs.

"Someone should talk to her," Claire said.

"Did she say anything about school today?"

"She said it was fine," Mark said.

"Well, there you have it," Evan said. "All's well."

"Evan, will you?" Claire asked. "She'll talk to you."

Evan pushed his chair back and went upstairs. A moment later he returned.

"It sounds like she's throwing up," he said.

And this, obviously, was a mother's job. She had seen Mark literally run from vomit, both at work and at home. He'd drive a thousand miles for a bottle of ginger ale but was unable to put a barf-soaked towel into the washing machine.

She went upstairs. Meredith was in her bedroom. She knocked softly and pushed the door open. Meredith was in bed. She had not undressed.

"You okay?" Claire asked.

"I threw up," Meredith said quietly, not opening her eyes. "But I think it's over."

"You stay home tomorrow." Already Claire was racking her brain, thinking of all the cancellations. She could work faster than Mark. "Your father can stay with you."

"Okay," Meredith said. Still, she did not open her eyes. Claire stood beside the bed, uncertain if she should stay or go. If Meredith had been younger, much younger,

Claire would have put her lips to her daughter's forehead to check for fever. But Meredith and Evan had vetoed this method long ago. Maybe she should get a thermometer from the bathroom. Maybe she should get some medicine of some kind. But she did not want to be a bother. She wasn't sure if Meredith was even still awake.

"Meredith," she whispered.

Meredith opened her eyes.

After her mother's first round of chemo, Claire had visited and found her mother sitting on the couch, eyes closed, with three comforters on top of her. Claire had sat down gently on the chair beside the couch and her mother opened her eyes and Claire knew at once that her mother had seen something previously unseeable, witnessed something that clarified in very real terms precisely what was to come. Her mother knew she was going to die. Her mother knew that death was simply a bodily function, the result of her cancer, no more remarkable or mysterious or dramatic than tears being a result of chopping onions.

Those eyes, her mother's eyes, were Meredith's now.

Her mother's eyes had held that look for two days, and then they lost it, and it never returned, not even at the very end. So maybe the look only came once, only the first time you understood. Or maybe you could only bear to see it once in someone else's eyes, but that didn't mean it wasn't still there.

But also maybe she was overanalyzing this. These eyes — Meredith's eyes — were the eyes of someone who had just thrown up. Her mother, too, had of course been horribly ill from the chemo. Maybe it was not death they'd faced but simply the grueling act of vomiting.

"Can I get you anything?"

"No."

"Sweetheart, I think —"

She stopped herself, for it seemed Meredith's eyes were already returning to normal, her face once again the flat face of the mountain, impenetrable.

"What?" Meredith asked.

Claire made herself smile. "Call me if you need me?"

"Okay," Meredith said.

She called Dr. Moon.

"I know you're talking to her at the end of the week," she said, "but we're at a loss. We have no idea what to do."

"She'll find ways to comfort herself," he said. "Those ways might not make any sense to you or me. But that doesn't mean they're not working."

"Working?" she asked. "What does that even mean? What's she working toward?"

"She has to process what's happened," Dr. Moon said. "She has to figure out a way to fold it into her life. It's part of her now. She has to find a place for it. That's what she's trying to do. She just doesn't know it."

"And what are we supposed to do in the meantime?"

"You're supposed to wait. And you're supposed to be there for her when she's ready. Obviously it's a fluid situation."

"How will I know when she's ready?"

"You've been protecting her your whole life," he said. "You'll know."

But he was wrong. Protecting her? Psychiatrists were stupid. Psychiatrists, in fact, were complete morons. She could not protect her daughter. She could not protect her from the stomach flu. She could not protect her from cancer or AIDS or the common cold. She could not protect her from the mean girls. She could not protect her from her friends. She could not protect her from her own thoughts. She could not protect her from men who took girls from the line at the Deli Barn and killed them.

She could not protect her son. She could

not protect him from bullies. She could not protect him from pill bottles. She could not protect him from girls who would break his heart. She could not protect him from drunk drivers. She could not protect him from crazy people with guns. She could not protect him from baseballs.

She could vaccinate them and make them wear seat belts and batting helmets. She could give them cell phones with emergency numbers on speed dial. She could give them straight-talk books and scared straight DVDs and a solid, honest, pitch-perfect piece of advice every single morning on their way out the door. But in the end there was no intervention.

There was only awareness.

11

"Just one stripe of mayo," Lisa was telling the sandwich farmer. Meredith noticed that she had her iPhone in her hand. It was the newest iPhone, naturally, and the biggest, large enough to contain Lisa's large life. Meredith's phone was Evan's hand-me-down and the screen had been cracked for over a month, ever since she'd dropped it out the car window while trying to take a picture of a rainbow. Lisa was wearing the usual uniform: black leggings and a white, cold-shoulder peasant top, its straps just barely wide enough to pass the school district's two-finger rule.

"Not a big glob," Lisa said. "Just one little stripe."

Meredith had had this exact exchange with various sandwich farmers before, but she was sure she hadn't sounded so nasty when she said it, like it was this guy's entire purpose in life to measure out mayonnaise, like this was what he'd gone to school for, to differentiate between a stripe and a glob to make this eighth-grade bitch the perfect sandwich.

The front door jingled open and Meredith turned and saw a man stride purposefully into the Deli Barn. The man had on a black ski mask — not the kind with the eyeholes cut out, but the kind that only covered the bottom half of his face, so she could see his dark eyes and pale blond eyebrows. He wore a gray hoodie that was too long — it went nearly to his thighs — and jeans and big brown hiking boots. The door closed behind him and the Christmas bells rang for a moment in Meredith's mind even after they were still. The man was holding a gun.

Meredith had never seen a gun in real life before, except for maybe in a policeman's holster, but this thing in the man's hand looked exactly like every single gun she had ever seen on television, so she didn't doubt that it was real. The man pointed the real gun at the sandwich farmer and said, "Open the register, fat ass," which didn't make sense because the sandwich farmer wasn't even fat. Lisa Bellow let out a little squawk, and the man's head swung toward the girls.

"Get on the floor," the man said. His voice was muffled by the mask, so it sounded more like "Gone the four." It also wasn't clear who he was talking to, so Meredith only crouched down slightly until she saw Lisa Bellow getting on her hands and knees and then she did it, too, and felt — astonishingly — a stab of embarrassment that she had not been able or willing to do it herself initially and instead was following the lead of Lisa Bellow. What was wrong with her? This was a robbery. The Deli Barn was being robbed. The Deli Barn was being robbed and that was all and she didn't have to worry and there was nothing wrong with her.

As she lay down she caught a fleeting glimpse of her left wrist, Steven Overbeck's drawn-on watch buckle, blue ink already fading, joined at her pounding pulse. Her backpack was still on her back and it was incredibly heavy — her Algebra II book alone must have weighed five pounds — and it shifted and settled awkwardly across her upper back once she was flat on her stomach, its weight suddenly immense, like the weight of a whole person with his foot pressed into her shoulder blade.

Because she had been at the bread station, and Lisa a few feet ahead at the condiment station, when Meredith lay down she and Lisa were face-to-face, though their feet were pointing in opposite directions, Lisa's toward the front door, and Meredith's toward the potato-chip rack. The floor was cold and smelled like dishwasher detergent. Meredith could hear the sandwich farmer breathing and the jiggling of the cash register drawer.

"You know the safe combination?" the man with the gun asked.

"There's no safe," the sandwich farmer said.

"You wanna die in this shit hole?" the man said. "Is that what you want?"

The sandwich farmer started crying, or at least it sounded like crying, or maybe hyperventilating. Meredith wasn't sure because she couldn't see anything except for Lisa. Lisa was crying, too. Her lips were trembling and slimy with spit, and thick teardrops slid down her cheeks and puddled on the floor about six inches from Meredith's nose. Meredith could feel Lisa's breath as it came out in hot little puffs. Meredith wasn't crying. Her eyes felt dry and sore, like she'd been staring at a movie screen for a long time without blinking. In her mind she saw a picture of her and her brother sitting on Santa Claus's lap at the Parkway Mall. She was two or three years old, and her hair was clipped back in green barrettes that were shaped like Christmas trees.

"Swear to god," the sandwich farmer said. "I swear to god there's no safe."

"Show me," the man said. "You show me."

Meredith heard them walking into the back room. Somebody's shoes were squeaking (sneakers), and somebody's thunking (hiking boots). Now it would be okay. There was a door back there, to the outside — Meredith had seen sandwich farmers smoking by that door before — and the man with the too-long hoodie would see there was no safe to open and then he would run out that back door with the money he'd taken from the cash register and he would go far away, first to another state and then probably to another country, and no one would ever hear anything from him again. It would be a clean getaway. That's how it would be described in the newspaper tomorrow: a clean getaway. Vividly, as vividly as anything in the Deli Barn, Meredith could see her family sitting around the breakfast table, her mother reading aloud from the newspaper article: "It was a clean getaway."

Meredith licked her dry lips. "It's okay," she whispered to Lisa Bellow. She couldn't remember a time she'd been so close to someone else's face for so long. And it was especially weird because their eyes were almost perfectly in line but the rest of Lisa was upside down. "It's okay now. It's okay."

Lisa's mouth opened like a word was going to come out, but only a little wet pop came from between her lips. Thick black mascara lines connected her eyes to the floor. Meredith thought of the scorching tennis court that summer morning, all those years ago, Lisa's lip gashed, the blood spattered on her white Nike tennis shirt. Had Lisa cried then, there on the court, or after, walking across the dry brown grass to the Snak Shed? Meredith didn't think so. But back then there was no makeup to ruin, no face to distort so colorfully, so maybe she had, a little. Maybe, their backs propped against the Shed, Lisa had held the baggie of ice to her face and in doing so shielded Meredith from the brimming tears in her eyes.

The thunking feet, the hiking boots, returned. The steps were heavy and unhurried. No squeaking accompanied the boots. The boots were alone. Meredith couldn't see him, but when the thunking stopped she was pretty sure the man, the robber, was standing right behind her head, between her and the counter. He had come back without the sandwich farmer. Meredith had heard no gunshot, but something had happened in the back room and now it was just the man with the too-long hoodie and her and Lisa. And now Meredith was absolutely certain of something, as certain as she'd ever been of anything in her whole life, and that thing was as far from what she had just said to Lisa as a thing could be:

It was definitely *not* okay.

It was definitely definitely definitely definitely not okay. It was not okay now, not anymore, not ever again, because the man was going to kill her. He was going to shoot her in the head as she lay on this floor. This spot, this very spot, was where she was going to die. She would never see her mother or her father or her brother or her cats or her room or her toothbrush again. In a moment she was going to be dead. Now she was completely alive but in an instant she would be completely dead and she wouldn't even know it, it would just be over, and she wouldn't even know it was over because she herself would be over, and all the stuff in her brain — all the thoughts in her brain right now, right this second — would just be a big sticky mess on the floor of the Deli Barn. And it was now — now — now. It was this instant — no, this instant — this instant — this —

— this is me. This is really me. This is my
real life.

She realized her eyes were closed, bracing
for the impact of the bullet, and she wanted
to see the world one more time — even if it
was just a crappy old Deli Barn — so she
opened her eyes and there was Lisa Bellow
staring right at her.

"Don't worry, Meredith," Lisa said. "It'll
be okay." She didn't even whisper it. She
said it in a normal voice, as if nothing were
wrong, or even out of the ordinary. She had
stopped crying. Her cheeks were dry. Something in her face made Meredith think she
was about to smile.

"You two," the man said. "Get up."

There were candy wrappers all over the
inside of the car. It looked like a family car
the morning after Halloween, the way they
were littered everywhere, the floor, the seats,
and all different kinds: Snickers, Kit Kats,
Butterfingers, M&M's. She and Lisa sat still
in the backseat while he walked around to
the driver's side of the car, not holding the
gun out in the open but his hand tense
under his jacket, watching them through
the windows every step he took, making
sure they knew he was not taking his eyes
off them. He got in the car and pulled the

ski mask off his head and turned around. His face was flushed pink from the mask but besides that he was ugly. His eyes were squinchy. He had a knobby chin and a mustache that drooped around the sides of his small mouth. It was the kind of face that had always looked older than it really was. Probably he was in his late twenties but he could have been forty. He was a little man who had been made fun of in eighth grade by girls just like Lisa.

"I'll shoot you if you try to get out of the car. Got it?"

Meredith was shaking from the inside, which she didn't even know was possible. The shaking started in her heart and lungs and spread out to her sides and legs and arms, and her fingers were trembling and she wanted to put them in her mouth and bite down on them to stop the trembling. It was the only thing she could think to do, the only thing she felt like might make things better, sticking her fingers in her mouth and biting down, hard. She raised her hand to her mouth.

"Got it?" the man said again, and she froze where she was and then lay her hand back on her lap.

A minivan drove haltingly by the Deli Barn parking lot, and inside the van Meredith could see a mother turned halfway around trying to hand something to the kid in the backseat. The van couldn't have been more than twenty feet away from them. If both she and Lisa screamed bloody murder, the mother in the minivan might hear them. If they opened the back doors and leaped out, the van would surely screech to a halt. If they did it together, maybe only one of them would be shot. And maybe he was full of crap anyway. Maybe he wouldn't really shoot but would just tear off, his tires squealing. Maybe. But Meredith didn't even have time to pass this idea on to Lisa, not even with a look. The minivan turned the corner, and the man started the car.

"You *suck*," Lisa said. She leaned forward until she was practically right behind the driver's right ear. "Do you hear me?" She was screeching. "You *suck*. You asshole!"

Meredith turned to her, horrified. Lisa looked furious, possessed. There was spittle on her lips from screaming.

"Shut up," the driver said, throwing the car in gear. "Shut your mouth. Shut it. Shut it."

"You shut *your* mouth," Lisa said savagely. "You stupid fuck."

The driver shut his mouth. Lisa turned and gave Meredith a triumphant little smile.

Meredith had seen that smile on Lisa many times before — in the cafeteria, the locker room, the library, every chaotic hall of Parkway North Middle School. It was the smile of the person in control of the situation. It was the smile of the person in charge.

Meredith couldn't feel her face. She had the sense that her mouth was hanging open but she didn't feel like she had the ability to close it. Her whole body was numb. The man pulled out of the lot and turned right onto Chestnut, then made a left onto Willow. Lisa was smirking and rubbing her fingers together.

"I got this," Lisa whispered. "I *got* this."

The apartment complex was sprawling. It seemed to go for blocks and blocks, and from the outside all the apartments were identical. Meredith had never seen the complex before, or if she had she didn't remember it, for there was nothing memorable about it. It had taken them only fifteen minutes to get there from the school, but part of that was on the highway, at least two or three exits, so she wasn't exactly sure where they were. His was a ground-floor apartment with an outdoor entrance; they passed two other drab brown doors on the way to his drab brown door. His hand was tucked in his jacket. He pushed them inside.

It had dawned on Meredith way too late that she and Lisa had broken one of the cardinal rules of abduction by allowing themselves to be taken to a second location. She knew this was a rule because one afternoon the spring before she'd spent a harrowing two hours reading every single pamphlet in the hospital lobby. The pamphlets, hundreds of them on a wide array of subjects, were all distributed by the same company, so essentially the same cartoon people faced hardship after hardship, with a very limited number of facial expressions. By the end of that afternoon Meredith knew about every terrible thing that might possibly ever happen to her and suggestions on how to go about avoiding the terrible thing (or, if unavoidable, like acne or menopause, at least how to gracefully manage it). She got the cartoon lowdown on cervical cancer, meth addiction, miscarriage, colonoscopies, cystic fibrosis, tinnitus, STDs, domestic abuse, and athlete's foot. And abduction. She actually remembered the drawing that accompanied the second-location rule, a stick man and stick woman standing beside a car, and a big X drawn through the car. Once you got to a second location, the pamphlet informed her, your chances of survival dropped by over 50 percent. But who could stop and think of that in the moment, when the flow of events (not to mention a gun) was propelling you across a parking lot? And what were the other rules? There had been at least five more, perhaps as many as ten. But Meredith could not recall what they were. Would she only remember each one as it lay broken behind her?

They shuffled into the apartment and the man closed and locked the door behind them.

"Sit on the couch," the man said, pointing at the couch with his gun. "Just sit there and let me think."

Meredith sat. Lisa did not.

"Let us go," Lisa said, riding high on her triumph from the car. "Let us go right now. Just open the door and we'll walk out and you'll never hear anything from either of us again."

"Shut up," he said. He seemed to have remembered that he was the one in charge. Maybe because he was in his own home. "You shut up now."

"Make me," Lisa said.

The man punched Lisa in the face. The sound reminded Meredith of leaping from the monkey bars onto the playground sand — some smack, some give. Lisa fell backward over the arm of the couch and landed on top of Meredith.

"Now you just sit there and shut up," he yelled. "Do you understand me?"

"Yes," Meredith said. She winced as Lisa's elbow dug into her stomach. "We understand you."

Lisa rolled off Meredith and into a kneeling position on the floor beside the couch, holding her face. There was blood seeping through her fingers. There was blood on her white blouse and on the couch and on Meredith's leggings. The man sat down at a chair at a little table and set the gun down in front of him. He closed his eyes and took some deep breaths and rubbed his mustache with his left index finger, rubbed it hard, like he was trying to make sure it was firmly attached. Meredith could tell he was thinking. He was trying to decide what to do. Things had not gone as planned. He had told them to get up — a split-second decision, the disappointment of so little money — and now here they all were in his apartment, the snotty one already covered in blood. In thirty seconds he'd gone from armed robbery to two counts of kidnapping, and now here they all were and he was going to have to figure out what to do with them. And he was going to have to figure it out fast. And the first thing he was going to have to figure out was just how far he was willing to go.

Crushed ice would have been better, but at least it was something — big cubes with sharp edges that Meredith wrapped in the cuff of her sweater sleeve to hold on Lisa's swollen face. Lisa hadn't said anything for a half hour, only tensing up when Meredith moved the ice. The whole bottom half of her face was purple and swollen. Looking at it, Meredith was now more afraid of getting punched than getting shot. She wondered if something in Lisa's face could be broken.

The man was sitting at the table again. He'd given them the ice and then he'd gone into the bathroom. He hadn't closed the door and she heard him peeing and then the water in the sink ran for a long time. Then he'd come out and gone into another room and changed his clothes. Now he was back at the table with the gun still in front of him. He fingered it absently and appeared lost in thought. If he had wanted to kill them, really wanted to, maybe he would have done it already, Meredith thought. Maybe he would have killed them in the car instead of going to the trouble of bringing them back here. Maybe thinking about things was a good sign.

Outside it was dark. It must have been after 7:00. Her parents would be frantic by now, would have called the police. It made her stomach hurt to think of her parents. She was sorry she had caused them this trouble. They did not deserve this, first Evan, and now this.

Yes, Evan. What she needed was Evan, precisely, always her imagined partner in this kind of scenario. Lisa was a shit partner because she had no experience with peril. She thought she could boss this guy around like he was one of her Parkway North bitches, and it had worked, incredibly, for a couple minutes, until the guy remembered that she was the *hostage,* and now it wasn't going to work again. Ever. But Evan would know what to do. He would not have made the mouthy mistake, not have started things off on that note. She needed him to inter-vene, to rescue her (well, them), and not in any showoff-y Superman way, not bursting in here and wrestling the gun away and beating the guy to a bloody pulp, but something clever, something no one else would think of. He would come dressed as a pizza delivery guy. He would appear to be no threat, due to his dark lens. It would be the dark lens that would gain him access into the apartment, just a foot in, six inches, one step, just enough to catch sight of them out of the corner of his good eye. And then — what? He'd send her some sort of message, somehow. Maybe with the pizza?

"I'm hungry," Meredith said softly.

"Shut up," the man said.

And then it was like that for a long time, him at the table, thinking, and she and Lisa on the couch. The ice had all melted but she did not dare ask for more. Her sleeve was wet and the couch cushion between them was wet, too, and some of the wetness was blood. The moisture had soaked through her leggings but she did not try to move away from it. On the other side of the stain, Lisa sat motionless, so motionless that every so often Meredith cut her eyes toward her to make sure she was not unconscious.

The clock on the cable box was flashing 12:08, so she had no idea what time it really was. She was pretty sure that in a nearby apartment someone was watching TV, because although she couldn't make out any voices, every once in a while there would be the canned murmur of a laugh track. But after a while even that seemed to stop and then it was only silent, as if no one else lived in these apartments, or no one else lived anywhere.

"I have to pee," Lisa said.

"Do you?" he said.

"Yes," she said flatly, no nasty comeback even on her radar judging from the tone of her voice.

"You sure?"

He was trying to pick a fight, Meredith saw. Maybe he missed the girl who had talked back to him.

"Yes."

"Fine. Actually, yeah, fine. You want to go to the bathroom, why don't you both go to the bathroom?" He stood and picked up the gun. "Both of you, in the bathroom. You go in there and you stay in there until I come for you. You got that? And I don't want to hear a single word."

They must have been sitting a long time because Meredith's legs ached when she stood, maybe from tensing them for so long. She limped on her way to the bathroom.

"What's wrong with you?" he asked. "Something wrong with you?"

"No," she said softly.

"You sure?"

She had the feeling he would kill her if there were something wrong with her. "I'm sure," she said.

He pushed them both into the tiny bath-room.

"Quiet," he said. He put his finger to his lips. Then he closed the door. She could hear something being dragged in front of it. Something heavier than a chair. A trunk, maybe. An army trunk.

The bathroom had a tub and a toilet and a small basin but had not been designed to hold any actual people, much less two. There was about one square yard of floor space between the three appliances. Lisa peed while Meredith washed the blood from her hands. Then Lisa wetted a wad of toilet paper and wiped the blood from her face and her neck. They stood for a minute, awkwardly suspended in each other's space, and then Meredith realized they could sit in the bathtub. She gestured to it with her head and then got in and sat down. Lisa climbed in quietly and sat down on the other side of the tub. It was a small tub and even sitting cross-legged their feet and knees touched. It was like they were on a small boat — no, not a boat, but a raft. They were bobbing in the water.

Then they heard his voice. At first Meredith thought there was actually someone else in the apartment, but after a few seconds she realized he was on the phone. She couldn't hear what he was saying but she didn't think he was ordering a pizza: there was a desperate whine to his voice that was clear even when the words were not. He was telling someone what he had done. He was calling to ask for help.

"Are you okay?" she whispered to Lisa, as quietly as she could, not a slumber party whisper or even a library whisper but more like a funeral whisper. Some of the words weren't even words, just the movement of lips and eyes.

"I think so," Lisa whispered back. "Just hurts."

"Cold water?"

Lisa shook her head.

Out in the apartment the voice continued to rise and fall. Every so often a recognizable word or words: "she," "tomorrow," "Jason," "I know!"

"Who do you think?" Lisa whispered.

Meredith shrugged. "Friend?"

"Girlfriend?"

Girlfriend. It was an encouraging thought, a wonderful-sounding word, in fact, a thousand times better than simply "friend." He'd called someone for advice. And a girlfriend would definitely tell him to let the girls go, as soon as possible. A girlfriend would be, finally, a girl. One of *them. "Jesus Christ,"* she would say. *"And now they're in your bathroom? Seriously? What were you thinking?"* She might worry about what would happen to him, but this too could work in their favor: *"Let them go right now,"* the girlfriend would say. *"And then we'll leave town. We'll just clear out of here. We'll go far away."*

A friend, a male friend, might have other ideas, ones that would not work in their favor. A male friend might make different kinds of suggestions. Maybe a male friend would even offer to help implement those suggestions. Suddenly it was very easy to divide the world in this way, even though Meredith knew it wasn't fair to do this, not fair to her brother or her father or Steven Overbeck. Fair didn't matter. The fact of the moment was this: everything depended on whether the person on the other end of the phone was male or female.

Lisa leaned forward. "Do you think he killed him?" she asked. Again, it was as much mouthing as speaking, the words just hints of words.

"Who?"

"Deli Barn. Do you think he killed him?"

Meredith leaned in so that their foreheads were almost touching. "He didn't shoot him," Meredith said. "No gunshot. So prob-ably not."

"He doesn't look like he'd kill someone," Lisa said. "He doesn't look that bad."

"He's scared," Meredith agreed. "He just wants it to be over. It's easier if he lets us go."

They quieted as they realized the talking out in the apartment had ceased. Had he hung up? Had he heard them whispering? Was he standing in the hall with his ear pressed to the door? It was impossible to tell. They both sat listening. What if he had left? How long before they should stand up?

"Hey."

He was on the other side of the door. "You hear me? Say yes if you hear me."

"Yes," they both said.

"You're gonna hear the door close. I'm just going out to my car. I'm not going to be more than fifty steps from you. If you scream, I'll hear you. If you try to go through the window, I'll see you. You got that?"

"Yes."

His car. Why would he go to his car?

The apartment door closed, then locked.

"He's gonna wipe it," Lisa said, still whispering but with a little more sound behind it.

"What?"

"He's gonna wipe it clean. Our fingerpints are all over it. That's what the person on the phone was doing, telling him how to get rid of the evidence."

"Maybe he's going for cigarettes or something."

Lisa frowned and leaned back. "Shit. My backpack's in the car."

"Mine, too."

"I bet he's throwing them in the Dumpster."

Meredith thought of all her school books, of all the threats the teachers made at the beginning of the year about what would happen to you if you lost a book, how much money your parents would have to pay. Surely there were exceptions.

"What time do you think it is?" Lisa asked.

"I don't know. Late."

Lisa looked up at the ceiling.

"My mother probably doesn't even know yet," she said.

Meredith didn't say anything. She didn't know anything about Lisa Bellow's mother or family or where she lived.

"She works till seven, and then she probably thought I was at somebody's house. She might still think that. Would your parents know?"

"Know what?"

"If you didn't come home after school. Would they know it was something bad?"

"Yeah," Meredith said. "I mean, not right away. They work. They get home at like five thirty, though. They'd know by now."

"My mother's all alone," Lisa said. "When she finds out, she won't have anybody."

"I'm sure she has some friends or something," Meredith said. "They'll help her out. They'll bring food."

"I left her sandwich at the Deli Barn," Lisa said. "It's still sitting there on the board."

"It's probably not very good anymore," Meredith said.

Lisa smiled. "It's probably *fine.* It's the Deli Barn, right? It's probably exactly the same as it was six hours ago. What were you getting?"

"Just a root beer. I promised myself a root beer at the end of my algebra test."

"I hate algebra," Lisa said. "Oh my god, I hate algebra and I hate Mr. Kane. Are you in my class?"

"I'm in Algebra two."

"What do you do in there? Is it really hard?"

Meredith closed her eyes. She could see the problem in her head, still, all these hours later. Stupid broken pencil. She had not had time to complete the graph.

"You know what an asymptote is?"

"Um . . . some bullshit word you made up?"

"No," Meredith said. "It's a real thing. You'll find out next year."

"Oh my god, I can't wait to go to high school," Lisa said. "I literally can't wait. In high school you get *choices.* About everything. You actually get to *choose* what you want."

"My brother's at the high school. He hates it."

"Isn't your brother blind or something?"

"He's not blind," Meredith said. "He's mostly blind in one eye. He got hit with a baseball."

"That sucks," Lisa said. "He must be so pissed. I bet that's why he hates high school."

"Yeah. Probably."

"I'd love high school even if I was blind," Lisa said. "You don't even have to eat in the cafeteria. Did you know that? You can take your lunch anywhere. You can eat outside at the picnic tables. Even in the winter."

"Why would you want to eat outside in the winter?"

"It's just an example," Lisa said. "Of what

you *can* do. Without someone tearing —"

The door closed. They heard his footsteps. Then the bathroom door opened.

"You," he said to Lisa. "Get out here."

Maybe the quiet was the worst part. Meredith could have anchored herself to sound, followed the act moment by moment, and some moments would have been less horrible than others, and at least she would have known when it was over. But there was only silence — stark, utter, silence — and so there was no sequence of events, only the worst moments happening again and again and again in a never-ending loop, no release, no relief at the conclusion. Her back was killing her — how long had she been sitting in the tub? — and finally she slid down flat and rolled onto her side and hugged her knees and waited.

In the morning she awoke to the click of the bathroom door. He came in and peed and she didn't move, just lay very still in the tub in the hopes that he would forget she was even there. He must have been sorry she was. He must have been thinking how foolish it was to have taken them both, the disadvantages of two girls far outweighing any advantages — the work, the complications, the mess of it all.

"There's food in the kitchen," he said, and then he was gone. Still, she waited a minute or two before rolling over. The bathroom door was ajar. She slowly stood and stepped carefully out of the tub. Every part of her ached, but nothing more than her right side, on which she'd slept for who knew how long on the hard porcelain. She took two steps into the hallway. There was no sign of him, and no sign of Lisa either. She looked toward the bedroom. The door was halfway closed and she could not see the bed. There was no sound coming from in there and for a moment she was certain that Lisa was dead, sprawled across the bed, the air choked out of her, her eyes still open, her body twisted from the struggle. She could see it vividly and knew it was there, just as she imagined it, just on the other side of the door.

She tiptoed into the kitchen. There was a box of Rice Krispies on the counter and part of a loaf of white bread. On the rickety little table there were several brown bananas. Magneted to the refrigerator with a Liberty Bell magnet was a photograph of a little dog on a beach. The dog had a tiny blue Frisbee in its mouth. The dog was Annie.

"What're you looking at?" the man asked.

She turned, startled. He was standing in the doorway wearing black boxers and a gray T-shirt.

"Nothing," she said. "Just . . . the fridge."

He stepped forward so that he was standing right next to her. She could smell him, a sour smell, overpowering, causing her stomach to lurch. He slid the photo from underneath the magnet and held it in his hand and smiled at it. Most of his smile was lost inside his mustache. She wondered if he knew that.

"She was great," he said. "She liked to swim. You shoulda seen her. Out there paddling. Dog paddling."

She had no idea how to respond. She should just say something nice. She should say only nice things, from here on out until the end. She shouldn't be weird or angry or morose or quiet. She should just be nice. Didn't the abduction instruction booklet say that? Or was it exactly the opposite?

"She's cute," she said softly.

"Yeah," he said. "She was the best."

He slid the picture back under the Liberty Bell magnet. There was something about the magnet that made it seem ancient, its loopy font like something you'd find at an old lady's garage sale.

"You don't have to be afraid," he said. "I don't want to hurt you. I think you're great. I think you're doing a real great job."

"Thanks," she said. Had she really said this? Jesus Christ, here at the end, her last act, thanking this man because she was too chicken-shit to do anything else. She was pathetic.

He put his hand on the middle of her back. It was a teacherly gesture, a fatherly gesture, at the very least a big-brotherly gesture. There was no sex in it but it was gruesome, like some heavy dead wet thing had been laid on her.

"You believe me?" he asked.

She had to will herself not to squirm away from his touch. "Yeah," she said.

"You don't sound real sure."

She took a deep breath. At the end of the breath she found something, something totally unexpected, something she hadn't even been looking for, but there it was for the taking, like turning a blind corner and bumping smack into the one thing that could save you.

Resolve.

Yes. Yes. She could feel it in her bones. Something had changed. She was in charge now. She was in control. What happened to Lisa from here on out — it was all on her.

There was nothing outside this apartment, or nothing that mattered anyway. There was only this. And this was everything.

"Where's Lisa?" she asked, turning to face him. His hand fell from her back, one dead thing sliding off another dead thing. But no. No. Not dead. Not yet. She knew now that there was only one way she was going to have any chance of surviving this, and it was by knowing that Lisa was here in the apartment with her, still, always, not dead yet either. And she knew, too, that this was the only way Lisa would survive. It was imperative that they remain together. Their very existence depended upon it. There was no other way. And if he wanted to kill her for asking . . .

"She's asleep," he said. "I didn't want to wake her up."

"I'm going to make her some breakfast," she said. "And then I'm going to take it to her."

"There's not much," he said, nodding to the counter.

"It'll do," she said.

"That's real nice," he said. Then, after a pause, "It's funny."

"What?" she said.

"I didn't take you all for friends."

■ ■ ■ ■

When she turned from the counter with the bowl of cereal Lisa was sitting on the couch in the living room. She had dragged a blanket with her from the bed and had it on a pile on her lap. Meredith went and sat down on the couch.

"You should eat something," Meredith said. She held out the bowl. "Eat some cereal."

Lisa stared at her dumbly. Her chin was black from the blow from yesterday, and around her mouth was purple. She also had a mark on her neck.

"Seriously," Meredith said.

"You were in my tennis group," Lisa said softly. "Do you remember that? That summer tennis camp. There was that mean coach who called everybody names."

"I remember. At Eaton Park."

"One day Brianne Kirk hit me in the face with her racquet. And you had to walk me to that concession stand to get ice. Do you remember that?"

"Yeah," Meredith said.

"Really?" Lisa said. "Do you really remember it? Are you just saying that?"

"No," Meredith said. "I really remember

it. I never forgot it. I was thinking about it just . . . just yesterday."

Lisa closed her eyes for a moment. All her makeup had worn away and her hair was a tangled mess. The girl from the yearbook was gone. This was another girl.

Lisa opened her eyes. "That was such a great day," she said. "That was the best snow cone I ever had in my life."

"It was lime," Meredith said.

"It was," Lisa said. "It was lime. Your face was green."

"*Your* face was green."

Meredith looked out the window. It was raining and the branches of the trees were swaying in the wind. Yesterday it had been sunny and you could believe in an Indian summer. Today it was rainy and the leaves were falling from the trees and summer was over.

"Meredith," Lisa said.

"What?"

Lisa lay back until her head rested on the arm of the couch.

"What?" Meredith said again.

Lisa took a little bite of her bottom lip. "I don't think we're ever getting out of here."

PART TWO

12

The sound coming from below her, in the garage, did not surprise Claire. Not at first. It had been the soundtrack to their lives for so long, the background noise of so many early mornings, that when she woke to it she did not think of all the months that had passed without it. It was so familiar that she couldn't have said, in that first moment of being awake, if it had been six hours or six months since she'd last heard it, the *ping* of aluminum on leather.

She rolled over to face Mark's side of the bed. He was awake, looking up at the ceiling. "You hear it?" he asked.

As if there were any not hearing it. When Evan had first started his routine, the summer before his freshman year, they had looked into putting extra insulation in the garage, which sat directly under the western hemisphere of their bedroom. Or maybe, they suggested, he could take his swings just a little later in the morning. Or after school? But he was thirteen and he cared about something, cared about it intensely. He had a routine. He stuck to it. He was disciplined. It felt wrong to discourage him, even if it was a little annoying. Wasn't this precisely what you wanted from a boy approaching fourteen? Passion? Commitment? Practice?

So they got used to it, like the sound of traffic, or crickets, or lapping waves. There was a rhythm to it. *Ping.* Beat (ball from bucket). Beat (ball on tee). Beat (stance). *Ping.* Beat (ball from bucket). Beat (ball on tee). Beat (stance). *Ping.*

She looked at the clock. 5:55. Even the traditional time. Half hour of swings before a shower, alone in the garage with his tee and a net and his big, beat-up white bucket of weathered balls, no sound but the contact, no distraction, no chance of distraction, everyone else still in bed. How many hundreds of hours had he spent there, how many swings, how many balls launched into the soft net? After that first summer the garage had become Evan's personal training facility, in and out of season. Sometimes his teammates came over on winter evenings and there would be a group of three or four down there, their voices echoing against the metal door, laughter, *ping*-beat-beat-beat-

ping, music playing from someone's phone, jeering, the voices of boys now, suddenly, the voices of men. But mostly it was Evan's alone, his sanctuary. Often she'd be in the kitchen making the coffee when he finished at 6:20, and they'd exchange smiles as he passed. He never seemed more comfortable in his own skin, more sure of himself, than that moment he crossed from the garage into the kitchen. Not even when he was actually playing in a game.

After the injury she and Mark, together, had zipped the bats into the black bat bag and hung it up beside the rakes and snow shovels. They'd pushed the net back into a corner, laid the tee on its side, put the cover on the ball bucket, little by little erasing what had been, or if not erasing, at least obscuring. But they'd never put the cars back in the garage. The cars had remained in the driveway, throughout the spring and summer and into fall. Maybe they would have put them in come winter, at the first frost. But now, October, there was this.

"God, I missed that sound," Mark said. "I didn't know it until now."

His eyes were closed and he was smiling, the way you closed your eyes and smiled while you listened to your favorite song. But even as she watched him smile Claire felt the dread begin to seep under her skin. The sound could only mean one thing.

"He can't do it," she said to Mark. The whole sentence came out as a sustained groan.

"What?"

"He can't play baseball."

He turned and propped himself up on his elbow, head in palm. "He's just hitting the ball off the tee. Imagine how good that must feel. God, after all these months. Just imagine."

This was Mark, always wanting to return to the way things had been before. Everything fixable. Nothing ever truly out of reach. Everything open to regain, renew, restore. There was a card game they'd played all the time when the kids were younger — she couldn't recall the name — in which the rules changed frequently, but every so often you drew a card that said, "Throw out all new rules. Return to basic rules." Mark was always so relieved to get that card. The kids loved the new rules, but he'd play that card the second he got it. *Return to basic rules.* And here he was, back at his basic rules: 5:55, *ping*-beat-beat-beat-*ping.*

"This is bad," she said. "It's —"

"Don't do that," he said. "Please. Don't

do what you're —"

"How can you not see that this is bad?"

He sat up. "For Christ sakes, he's been lying on the couch for six months and finally he —"

"It's because he wants to play. He thinks he can just rejoin the team. He thinks he —"

"First," he said, pointing his finger a little too close to her face — she was still lying down — "you don't know that. And second, what if he does? Who's to say he can't?"

She pushed his hand out of her way and sat up. "The doctor," she said. "Remember? The eye doctor? The expert?"

"He didn't say he couldn't play. He never said that he *could not* play. He said he wouldn't be able to hit a ball. But listen! Listen! He's hitting a ball."

"Off a tee," she said. "Let's not get carried away."

"Oh no," Mark said. He flipped the covers off and got out of bed. "That's the last thing we'd want to do, isn't it? We definitely wouldn't want to get *carried away*. We definitely wouldn't want him to get off the goddamn couch and start thinking maybe he could have his life back. Wouldn't want that. Oh no."

"That's not —"

"He hits twenty balls off the tee and you've already lived through the disappointment of the next year, mapped it all —"

"I'm not. I'm —"

"I can see it in your face. You've planned it out already, for all of us, stop by stop, every dashed hope along the road. *Whoosh,* seen it all. No need to live it. Just shut it down right now, close up shop. Why not? You already know what's coming."

"You're screaming at me," she said. "You are screaming at me. Meredith can hear —"

"Meredith can't hear *anything,*" he spat from across the bed. "She's hardly even looked at me for two weeks. She's so far away from us I don't even know how we can still see her. But he" — he nodded in the direction of the *ping* — "he's coming back. Don't you dare screw that up."

She wanted to hit him. She imagined getting out of bed and walking over to him and punching him in the face, and when that was not enough she imagined picking up the alarm clock and smashing him over the head with it. "Don't you dare screw that up." There was no way to read that other than the way it was so obviously intended, the accusation that screwing things up was always what she did, that only due to the emergency intervention of others was she able to *not* screw up every single thing she touched.

"You're being horrible to me," she said, her voice shaking in a way she absolutely despised, a pathetic, wronged-housewife whine.

"Well, I'm sick of it," he said. "I get to be horrible. Maybe for like a month, okay? I get to be horrible for one fricking month. I'm sick of being the nice one. I want my children back. I want my children."

"Your children are gone," she said. She swung her legs out of bed and spoke with her back to him. "They're gone. They grew up. Accept it. Things happened to them. Terrible things. And now they're gone. And they're not coming back."

"They're still here, Claire," he said. She couldn't see him but she knew the expression on his face. He had faith in what he loved. His face always said so, in a boyish, earnest way. It was part of what everyone who barely knew him adored about him. "Believe it or not," he said. "Like it or not. They are still in this house."

"Barely," she said, scoffing. It was an ugly sound, uglier than she thought she was capable of, made even uglier by its juxtaposition with his conviction.

"They are still. In. This house," he said

again. Then he went into the bathroom and closed the door.

One thing he'd said was true, the thing about Meredith. Something had happened to her that night, the night she'd said the mysterious thing to Evan: "There's no dog." Meredith had vanished in a way that Claire could not specify. She was going to school. She was doing her homework. She talked on the phone. She ate and slept and showered. But there was something essential missing, some profoundly blank space.

Several years ago, before the tolerant cat and the intolerant cat, they'd owned a cat that had absolutely no interest in them, in a way that far surpassed the normal, expected indifference of cats. The cat actually did not seem to understand that there were other sentient beings living in the house. It became a great family joke, just how aloof this cat could be. The children became desperate to befriend it, not because they especially loved it, but because they wanted to defeat its indifference. The cat walked across their feet while they stood in the hallway, walked across their bodies on the couch as if they were merely part of the furniture, material objects to be crossed or scaled. One day after they'd had him a year or so, the cat walked down the long back-yard — Claire saw it go from the kitchen window — and never returned, and the children never missed the cat because he'd never really been their cat to begin with.

Meredith walked around the house like that cat. It was like she couldn't even see them. Or when she did see them, what she saw was something else.

But maybe that was just what happened to you when something happened to you. Meredith had been to two appointments with the psychiatrist in the last ten days, and each time, after fifty minutes with Meredith, Dr. Moon had sent her back to the waiting room and called Claire and Mark into the office and without inviting them to sit down told them the same thing he'd told Claire over the phone:

"She's processing. Still processing. Be patient. It's a process."

So maybe all there was to do was to wait and see if Meredith wanted to say something. Say *anything.* Processing was a process, yes. You couldn't expect things to get better overnight. You had to be patient, like Dr. Moon said. Maybe all there was to do was stand back and wait for the processing to be complete, the way you waited for X-rays to develop, for the images to rise out of the black pool. It had always been so satisfying for Claire, that moment, her instincts confirmed: Yes — yes! There was the problem, the damaged root. And now that the problem has been revealed, the solution must surely be at hand. But there was no rushing the image. To rush, in fact, was to ruin.

"Goal of the day," Mark said.

Her goal of the day was to not smash him over the head with the alarm clock. She poured Evan's milk and set it down in front of him.

"I'm going to go for a run this afternoon," Evan said.

Sometimes Claire held her hand over her left eye and tried to do things, simple things: walk down the stairs, plug in her phone, put a stamp on a letter. She knew from the specialist that this wasn't truly seeing the world as Evan saw it — that covering an eye couldn't really replicate monocular vision, that it was not just Evan's eye that had changed but also his brain — but it made her feel better anyway. A run was fine, right? Unless something came at him from his blind side, something fast, a Frisbee, a speeding car.

"On the track?" she asked.

"Probably just around here," he said.

"The track would —"

"— be smooth, yes," he finished. "Even. No surprises."

"I just thought for a first time," she said.

"It's not the first time, Mom," he said.

It was nearly the end of October. What was he thinking? That he would be in shape by February, for the preseason? That he'd be crouching behind the plate by the first of March, his senior season excavated from the earth like some pristine fossil, perfectly intact, only in need of a dusting? And when exactly had he decided this, and in consultation with whom? His coaches? His teammates? His father? Maybe he needed a psychiatrist as well (maybe Dr. Moon offered some sort of two-for-one, multichild, multitrauma offer?), someone to speak sensibly, someone who did not just seem like a wet freaking blanket, someone who could nudge him into reality with simple common sense. He could not see out of his left eye. *He could not see out of his left eye.*

Competitive baseball was over. He was not going to play in college. He just needed to apply to college. Just apply. Just somewhere. Application deadlines were rapidly approaching. In another couple months, community college was going to be his only option. He was better than that, smarter than that. But that wasn't even the point (she reminded herself . . . again). The point was he was not going to be a baseball player. Not anymore.

"I'm going to take a half hour and read," Mark said. "Over lunch. I'm just going to find a quiet spot and read a book."

"What book?" Evan asked.

"I don't know. Maybe it won't be a book. Maybe it will be the newspaper."

"You could just read *People* in the waiting room," Evan said.

"It is absolutely true that I could do that," Mark said. "Meredith?"

She looked up from her cereal. "Can I go to a Halloween party this weekend?"

"Is that a goal or a question?" Evan asked.

"A question," she said.

And there it was, Claire thought. There was the difference. Normally an answer to Evan would have had more bite to it, a joke attached, at the very least a facial expression.

"Whose party?" Claire asked, as lightly and cheerfully as she could. "Jules's?"

"I don't think she's doing one this year," Meredith the detached cat said. "It's somebody else. I don't think you know her."

"I know her," Evan said. "I went to her house once. She's awesome."

Meredith manufactured a smile for her brother. It was deliberate and evasive, a professional job.

"What's your goal?" Mark asked her. He, too, wore a manufactured smile. They could open a factory. The new family business.

After Evan left for school Claire went to Meredith's room. Meredith was sitting on her bed, putting on her golden shoes. How long until it was too cold to wear those sandals? Would that day ever come? Would she wear them in the snow?

"Can we talk?" she asked. "I could drive you." She stood in the doorway.

"I don't mind walking," Meredith said.

"I know," Claire said. "It's just . . . your father said something that made me think."

"There's a first," Meredith said.

Claire didn't know whether to smile or be offended, so she did neither, instead leaned against the doorframe with what she hoped seemed a casual, friendly lean.

"What's going on at school?" she asked.

"Same as always."

"I don't see how that can be."

"You wouldn't," Meredith said, looking at her phone before slipping it into her purse. "So you just have to trust me."

"It's not that I don't trust you. It's

just . . ."

Just what? Even she didn't know. What did people do with their children after they were not kidnapped? How were you supposed to help the girl not taken? There was no group for this. No best practices. Did she even need your help? Or did she just need you to leave her alone?

"I have to go," Meredith said. "I'm going to walk. I meet people on the way. I walk with them."

"What people?"

"Just people."

She left then. Feet on the stairs. Door closed, then across the yard like the cat. Never to return?

There was a clothes hanger, overlooked, jutting out from under the bed. Claire picked it up and went to Meredith's closet, opened it. The inside of the closet door was covered with yellow flyers. MISSING. There must have been forty of them, four across and ten down, like wallpaper, Scotch taped to the door, neatly, so that instead of forty individual posters it seemed like one big poster with forty Lisas. TAKEN FROM CHESTNUT STREET DELI BARN ON WEDNESDAY OCTOBER 8. Claire walked out of Meredith's room and into the upstairs hallway. She wanted to show this to someone. She could hear the water running in the master bath — Mark in the shower. Evan was long gone, already sitting in a classroom. Who else was there? She went back into Meredith's room. She realized she was tiptoeing. Gently, as gently as she could, she closed the closet door.

Her cell was buzzing in her coat pocket. Until recently she had not carried it with her while she was with patients. But now she felt better having it on her, just the buzz against her hip, not the sound itself, in case something happened. (What could happen that had not happened? Imagine if she had three children! Or four!) She stepped behind the patient's head and looked at the phone. The number was one she did not recognize, which was more alarming than not. The police. The school. Anyone, anything. She backed out of the room and into the corridor.

"Hello?"

"Is this Claire?"

"It is. Who's this?"

"It's Colleen," the voice said. "Colleen Bellow."

For a split second she thought Colleen had called to tell her that Lisa had been found. And then instantly she knew that the last thing Colleen Bellow would be doing, if Lisa had been found, was to be on the telephone calling anyone.

"Hello," Claire said. "How —"

"I know you're probably at work but I just wanted to tell you that the girls are here with me."

"Okay . . ." Claire said, carefully, because it sounded like something a crazy person might say, and the fact that Colleen had called an almost total stranger to say it made it seem even crazier. "So . . . what girls?" she ventured.

"Meredith and some of Lisa's other friends. The whole gang. They came over after school. They're hanging out, having a snack. They just got here but I thought you'd want to know. I'm sure you worry if . . ."

Claire was trying to process this. She glanced at her watch. It was 3:45. Meredith was supposed to go straight home after school, where Evan would be waiting to meet her. She had been walking for the past week, had told them she did not want to be picked up anymore. "I like the walk," she had said. "It's peaceful." And so she and Mark had relented (again), returned to their old routine — return to basic rules! — where they got home around 5:15 and the kids were doing homework or watching TV or staring into their phones.

"I thought you might want to come by and have a coffee," Colleen said. "On your way home. You could pick her up."

"Um, yes. Sure."

Mark was walking down the corridor toward her. He slowed, raised his eyebrows in question. She nodded — all was well. Well, well-ish. No one was dead or maimed or abducted.

"Yes. Okay. Um, yes. I'll come."

She realized how she must have sounded, wanted to explain that she wasn't resistant, only caught off guard.

"If this isn't a good time . . ."

"No, no," Claire said. "I'll be leaving the office in a bit. Give me your address. I can come. I — that would, yes, that would be lovely."

Had she really said that? *Lovely?* Had she ever said to anyone, about anything, *that would be lovely*? Wasn't that what you said at a funeral — it was a lovely service, that was a lovely tribute, they did a lovely job with your mother's hair. (Her mother had so little left, such a modest amount to work with, that the funeral home had suggested a wig when her father said he wanted the casket open, and she had said, "Dad, no,

289

come on, no wig, she wouldn't want that," and so they had styled her hair as best they could, and when she saw it she'd thought, okay, maybe a wig would have been the way to go; maybe these people know what they're talking about; maybe her mother was dead and so who cared what she would have wanted, and/or maybe what she would have wanted was for her hair to not look so thin and sad that everyone approaching the casket did a little double-take because except for the hair her mother looked as spectacular as a dead body could look, if absolutely nothing like herself. But it was too late by that point, and of course everyone was lovely about it.)

"I'll be there soon," she said to Colleen.

She had always liked the neighborhood. They had looked at a house here, twenty years before, and she had loved the way the streets wound around themselves and how that made the houses near the center seem so far from the main road when they were really just nestled into the middle of three or four spiraling streets. There was a creek, too, which explained the wind of the street, because it followed the wind of the creek, and most of the driveways were partly little bridges over the shallow creek. The houses themselves were small, which is why she and Mark had looked elsewhere. They had lived in an apartment for a year while they'd set up their practice. Once the practice had taken off, they could already afford something bigger than what the cozy street offered, even though it was still just the two of them.

The Bellows' house was a split-level — many of them in the neighborhood were — and looked its age in every other way as well. Colleen Bellow opened the front door and Claire was accosted by two twirly-tailed black Labradors.

"Let me put them out back," Colleen said, and she was gone for a moment and Claire looked around. There was a two-sided fireplace that connected the living room and the kitchen, and a little tunnel under it where Claire knew Lisa must have played as a toddler, if they'd lived here then.

At least she had the dogs, Claire thought, listening to them bark in protest as they were shut outside. At least there was that. "Stop now," Colleen was saying in the manner of people who regularly talked to dogs. "Stop it. You're fine. You're both fine."

Did the dogs know Lisa was gone? Did they sleep in her room? Did they nap by the front door, waiting, their ears perking every time an acorn hit the front walk?

"I hope I didn't bother you," Colleen said, coming back into the living room. "Calling you at work. I just thought you might like to know she was here."

"Of course," Claire said. "Where . . . ?"

"They're in Lisa's room. They wanted to be up there, I could tell. They said they'd stay down here with me and I said, go on up. When they're up there I can imagine she's there, too. So that's something."

"Yes," Claire said. "I would think. I think. Yes."

There were two full cups of coffee already sitting on the coffee table. Claire sat down on the chair, despite it being farther away from the table than the couch, so that Colleen would not be able to sit directly next to her. (It was settled: she was a horrible person.) She picked up one of the cups and took a sip — lukewarm — and then rested it on her knee.

"I'm sure this hasn't been easy on Meredith," Colleen said. "It's good that she's at school and with friends. Is she well?"

"Mostly," Claire said. "She had a little bug right when she went back. We don't know — it may have been her nerves. She was out a couple days. But since then she's been okay."

"Lisa used to get sick like that," Colleen said. "First day of school, every year, all through elementary school. She was wound up so tight."

"That's hard," Claire said. "It's hard to know . . . hard to know what to do for them."

Laughter from upstairs. Footsteps, a creaking floor. Claire tried to imagine Lisa's room. The room of a princess surely, a canopy bed — oh, how she'd wanted one herself, at ten — and lots of frilly pillows, posters of boys and kittens, a mirror lined with pictures of grinning friends with arms around one another. She doubted there were any battling animals, preparing for offensives along the base of the desk. How had Meredith wound up here? Claire was dying to hear the story, get the sequence of events that had led her to this house, and at the same moment she was sure that she would not, that Meredith would have nothing to offer but monosyllables.

"It's nice to have people in the house," Colleen said. "It's been really quiet. I mean, some neighbors have stopped by." She snorted a laugh. "The fridge is full, you know? But no one stays long. I might go back to work just so I can talk to people."

"It's good they've given you the time off,"

Claire said.

"I've used up all my vacation time," Colleen said. "Like for the next five years. Vacation, right?" She gestured around the room.

"Do you have family in town? Does Lisa . . . ?"

"Her dad's not in the picture," Colleen said. "Just her and me. Always has been."

Claire tried to imagine what life would be like if it were just her and Meredith. No Mark. No Evan. She couldn't even begin to get her head around it. But then she and Meredith were very different people than Colleen and Lisa Bellow. She and Meredith were . . . well, they were different people. That was all.

"My boyfriend has two kids," Colleen said. "They come on weekends. We got out a bunch of Lisa's old stuff, brought it up from the basement. I thought I was saving it for grandchildren. Now I have a boyfriend with two little kids. Lisa's really good with them, especially Cara. She's seven. Of course she thinks Lisa's a queen."

All the children, all the little girls, aspiring to be Lisa Bellow. More laughter from upstairs. Should they be laughing? They should. What were the options? Sit around Lisa's room and cry, or mope, or worry? It was a good thing, good for this woman sitting across from her, who could probably almost hear her daughter's laugh in the mix.

"Of course they don't understand any of this," Colleen said. "How do you explain to a seven-year-old that something like this could happen, that someone can just —"

"I don't know," Claire said. "It's inexplicable. It is. Is there any? Have you —"

"You know they found her phone," Colleen said. "Cracked on the side of the road. Thrown out the car window, they think. Last text a little before three, to Becca. She said she was going to the Deli Barn. And that was it. The police came and took our computer, took my phone, took her old iPod — she hasn't touched it in years. They said they needed to check everything. So they're checking everything. They talked to my boyfriend. They interviewed him at the police station. They asked him where he was at the time of the robbery. Can you imagine?"

"That's terrible," Claire said, thinking that, if she were the police, she would have interviewed the boyfriend, too. Those were the stories you heard, the creepy boyfriend, the teenage daughter. Maybe he looked at them sometimes — the mother and the daughter — and was not able to tell them apart, with their matching hair and clothes, their matching bodies. How old *was* Colleen Bellow? If she'd had Lisa at eighteen or nineteen . . .

"Peter almost cried, he couldn't believe it. They interrogated him, like he was a suspect."

"I guess they have to ask everyone."

"They don't know anything," Colleen said. "Fifteen days and nobody knows anything."

"Someone has to," Claire said. "Someone has to know someone who —"

"I'd kill him with my own hands," Colleen said. She set her coffee down on the table; her hands looked steady but Claire noticed that the coffee itself was trembling. The girls had turned on a song upstairs but she couldn't hear the words, only the beat, a dull, music-less *thunk*ing. "I told Peter that, and you know what he said? He said that kind of thinking didn't help. Like I could just turn it off because it's not helping anyone. Like that's the point. Like helping is the point of thinking."

"It's . . ." Claire desperately search for a word. ". . . hard. So hard. I'm sure it's . . ."

"I can't turn it off. No matter what I do, I can't turn it off. All I can think is, if I ever have the chance, I'll kill that piece of shit with my bare hands. Sometimes that's the only way I can go to sleep, you know?" Colleen looked at her hands lying in her lap. Her nails were painted but Claire could see there were little chips in the paint. "I imagine my hands around his neck. I imagine that until I fall asleep. It's the last thing I see."

Claire saw that her own coffee was trembling. "I understand."

Colleen looked up at her abruptly. "I don't think you do."

There were winners and there were losers. There were people in big houses and people in small houses. There were people who drew X's through entire sections of school forms and people who had a name for every box. There were people whom others spoke to with respect, and people who others looked past. There were people who had choices and people who did not. Why was this, again?

A rush of voices, then footsteps. She tried to compose herself. Two girls she'd never seen before appeared at the foot of the stairs, then Meredith, then another girl she recognized from a swimming lesson carpool years before — Amanda something. Meredith blushed when she saw her and dropped her gaze to the floor. She was obviously embarrassed Claire was here, as if she'd shown up uninvited, as if coming here was a choice.

"Hey, we were talking," said one of the girls she didn't know. "And we were thinking we could maybe make some sort of bracelet that people could wear, something that Lisa would have picked, instead of just those green ribbons."

"Not that the ribbons aren't nice," the Amanda girl said. "But this could be like something people could keep."

"A keepsake," another of the girls said. "Silver. Like the one she always wore. Wears."

Meredith was still looking at the floor.

"Sounds great," Colleen said.

"We're going to look online and see if we can find a place that will do them cheap. Like silver plated or whatever."

"Perfect," Colleen said. "You girls want more soda? Plenty in the fridge."

The girls filed into the kitchen. Claire stood up and through the glass doors of the fireplace watched them sit around the kitchen table filling up their glasses. Meredith smiled and laughed at something one of the other girls said, then said something herself, and they all laughed.

"I wait every second for the phone to ring," Colleen said quietly behind her. "It's like holding in a scream. It's horrible if it rings and it's horrible if it doesn't ring. It's like the rest of everything is on the other side of the ring."

Claire turned to her. There were winners and there were losers. There were people with sterling silver bracelets and people whose silver flaked away and left their wrists stained green. There were people whose children were taken. And there were people whose children were spared.

Once, many years before, a police detective had called them at the office, requesting the dental records of a man whom they suspected had died in a house fire in the city. The police were merely confirming the man's identity — the house was rented in his name, and his car was parked on the street out front. But there were suspicious circumstances surrounding the fire, and they wanted to make sure that the corpse they had found, little more than bones and teeth in the rubble, according to the detective, was in fact the man they thought it was.

"Shall I look at them?" she'd asked the detective over the phone.

"We have people who do that," he'd said. "If you could just track them down and leave them at the desk, we'll send someone over."

She'd found the file herself rather than asking the secretary to pull it. And then she had looked at the X-rays anyway, despite what the detective had said. They both had, she and Mark, over lunch that day, laid the panorex gently on the light box (often they just slapped them up there, but that seemed wrong), and flipped the switch.

"You remember him?" Mark had asked. The date listed on the panorex was six years earlier, and the patient's records showed he hadn't been seen at their office since. How had the police even tracked them down? A wife? A magnet melted to the fridge? One of their personalized toothbrushes, smoldering in the bathroom, their names still visible?

"No," she said. "You?"

"No," he said.

A crown on the upper-right first premolar. The lower left canine blocked out. A left condylar fracture, several years old. She and Mark stood there in the white light of the dead man's teeth. Neither wanted to be the one to turn off the box. Finally, she stepped forward and flipped the switch.

Who knew when they would find Lisa, if they would ever find her. Teeth, the unsung heroes of the body, so vulnerable to Dr Pepper and Jolly Ranchers and complex carbohydrates, so often victims to human stupidity and shortsightedness. But once the human failings ceased, those same teeth proved immune to the manner of decay brought about by water and earth, the natural degeneration of the body that destroyed almost everything but was no match for the stalwart tooth. Who knew how many weeks would pass, how many months, before what was left of Lisa Bellow washed up along a riverbank, or was unearthed in some remote field. A dentist would be called to confirm the suspicion. Who but a dentist would recognize her?

13

For almost her whole life, there was no place Meredith had loved more than the middle row of seats of the family minivan. Every June, and sometimes at Christmas, they took the two-day trek halfway across the country, deep into the endless Midwest, to see her grandparents, she and Evan in the middle row, the back row folded down and crammed with suitcases, pillows, stuffed animals, baseball gloves, swim stuff (summers), presents (Christmas), and the twelve-cup coffeemaker her mother insisted on bringing every time because her grandparents didn't own one. Wedged between her seat and Evan's was an enormous box of car stuff: trivia cards, playing cards, baseball cards, comic books, coloring books, Yes & Know invisible ink books, toy catalogs, Etch A Sketches, flashlights, dice, calculators, maps, stickers, license plate magnets, Power Rangers, My Little Ponies, car bingo, priceless "gems" in tiny suede bags. All four of them could have been stranded in the car for months and never run out of things to do.

Her friends always complained about family car trips. How could they be so stupid? There was nowhere in the world better than the middle row of a minivan, flying along a long flat stretch of highway, cornfields flashing by your window. And there was no better time than the two hours after dinner, pushing on an extra hundred miles to that hotel in eastern Indiana, darkness falling, the murmur of her parents' voices in the front seat, the glow of Evan's Nintendo DS, then iPod, then iPad, then iPhone.

But there were few places that Meredith loved less than the *passenger* seat of the family minivan. The middle row was her world, *their* world — hers and Evan's — its connection to the front row sporadic and almost always voluntary, whereas the passenger seat was squarely adult territory, and as such there were certain expectations for those who sat in it. Like speaking. Like talking. Like answering questions.

As her mother pulled away from the Bellows' house, Meredith steeled herself for the coming onslaught. Why was she hanging out with Lisa's friends? Were they spending time together at school? Were they eating lunch together? How did they wind up at the Bellows' house? Did they walk or did they take the bus? Had she ever been to the Bellows' house before? Was it strange to be in Lisa's room? Which one of the girls had invited her? Had she wanted to say no? Had part of her wanted to go and part of her not wanted to go? What did they talk about? Did they ask her about what happened? Did she even like those girls? Were they nice to her? Did she feel uncomfortable? Did she feel like herself? Did she feel like someone else?

"Do you still like that chicken casserole?" her mother asked.

"What?"

"The chicken casserole I used to make. With the mushrooms and the rice. I feel like we haven't had that in a long time."

"Um, sure," Meredith said. "That sounds good."

Then: nothing. Then, a moment later: the radio. Meredith didn't trust it, her mother's silence, the music, but that didn't mean she wasn't going to enjoy it, for as long as it lasted.

She could not explain what had happened to her, or how she had come to be in the place, or places, that she was. She only knew that in all the universe there was only one spot where she was truly safe right now, today, and it wasn't in a minivan or in her bedroom or in the Bellows' kitchen or in a psychiatrist's office or in algebra class. It was instead in an apartment off the highway, an apartment with a concrete planter out front where cigarettes were ashed, an apartment with a ratty couch and a big TV and a kitchen wastebasket with a foot pedal and a bedroom door that was only ever slightly ajar and a small bathroom with a cold bathtub where she could sit with Lisa. The apartment was in close proximity to everywhere, at the end of every off-ramp and every thought, around every corner and every conversation, tucked inside silences and empty spaces, and the more silences and empty spaces there were, the easier it was to get to the place where Lisa was.

Meredith could not explain it, but even if she could have, she would not have wanted to. Who would she tell? Evan? Becca? Her mother, this woman sitting silently beside her in the minivan, this woman who seemed to believe in nothing? What would she even say? Surely, anyone she told would think she was crazy. Maybe she *was* crazy. But more than that, Meredith knew that if she revealed this place to anyone, she would risk destroying it. And if it were destroyed, how was she supposed to save Lisa?

She looked out the van window. She sort of liked this street, Lisa's street. Her own street, that she'd lived on her whole life, was geometrically pleasing and user friendly, rectangular lawns that were ideal for lawn tractors, impossibly smooth sidewalks for no-bounce scootering, wide and straight for as far as the eye could see, all of it utterly predictable. Lisa's street wound around haphazardly, following the path of a little rocky creek. There were no sidewalks. Meredith liked that most of the driveways were bridges, if only for a few yards. She imagined Lisa and the other kids in the neighborhood had played under those bridges when they were younger, building dams in the creek, constructing forts with stones and branches, hiding as cars rumbled overhead, fathers coming home from work — not her father, not Lisa's father, but some other neighborhood father who might come out with Popsicles for the whole gang, toss them into the gulch, to their waiting hands, and then go back to his beer.

"I never even saw a picture of my father," Lisa said, "until I was like ten. Then I found my mom's high school yearbook in my grandparents' house. I was sitting on the couch flipping through it and my grandfather sits down next to me and points to this guy and goes, 'You know who that is?' And then he got a funny look, like he totally realized he was doing something he shouldn't. And I go, 'No,' and he whispers, 'That's your dad.' Then he looks around the room to see if anybody's there, and then he goes, *'shhhhhhhhh.'*"

Lisa put her finger to her lips and arched her eyebrows comically.

"*Shhhhhhh.* Like, who's he shushing, right? Like he just *told* the person that the shush was for. He's actually mentally ill, my grandfather. You know, diagnosed or whatever. By a doctor."

They were in the bathtub. It was really Lisa who had chosen the spot, proclaimed it their own. Even when the couch was free, even though the couch was warmer and obviously twenty times more comfortable, even though on the couch they could watch TV, even though on the couch there was a slice of sunlight in the afternoons and you could see the outside, or at least a sliver of it, through the gap in the curtains. Even with all that, Lisa wanted to sit in the bathtub, so that's where they sat and talked. Of course Lisa always sat on the end without

307

the hardware, the smooth end where she could lie back unimpeded, her legs stretched out in front of her. Meredith got the bad end, though she'd found a position that wasn't awful, scooched in the corner and her arm draped over the rusty spigot. She was stretched out as well, her legs entangled with Lisa's, so that sometimes, if she just looked at the four knees, Meredith forgot whose legs were whose, because they were both wearing black leggings.

"Did you ever tell your mom?" Meredith asked. "About seeing the picture?"

"Are you kidding? No way. But I took the yearbook. It's on the bookshelf in my room and she's never even noticed it."

"You could look him up," Meredith said. "You could google him. If you know his name?"

"Why would I want to look him up?" Lisa said. "It's not like he ever looked me up."

Meredith could not imagine having a father out there, knowing his name and even what he looked like but never having seen him in person. Wouldn't you wonder about him? Wouldn't you wonder if he laughed like you, or hated cantaloupe like you, or couldn't hold a tune like you? Wouldn't you wonder if he wondered about you?

"Do you ever miss him?" she asked Lisa.

"What's to miss?" Lisa asked. She was inspecting her thumbnail. Some of her perfectly painted nails were chipped. From a struggle? Meredith pushed this thought away.

"He could be anywhere," she said.

"Sure," Lisa said. "But I probably wouldn't even recognize him if he walked up to me. He probably doesn't have that cheesy yearbook smile anymore."

But wouldn't you always, always be looking for him? Meredith thought. At the mall or the movies or walking down the street? Maybe Lisa's father's picture was in the police book, too, in addition to the yearbook. Maybe he was a suspect in something. Maybe, due to his prolonged absence, he was a suspect in everything.

Evan was in the kitchen eating a banana in that way he had of eating a banana. He peeled the whole thing, broke the banana in two, and then put one half entirely in his mouth, swallowed it seemingly without a single chew, and then as soon as his throat was clear did the same thing with the other half. It was like one of those YouTube videos of a snake swallowing a squirrel whole, where you could see the outline of the squirrel as it slid down the snake's gullet. Did a snake even have a gullet? Wasn't a snake all gullet? In any case, that was how Evan was eating his banana, leaning against the kitchen counter, his elbow resting on the microwave, and that was how she knew he was playing baseball again. He hadn't eaten a banana like that in six months. Her mother went upstairs to change; she could hear her father watching television in the family room.

"So," Evan said, swallowing his squirrel. "Hanging out with the cool kids, eh?"

"How do you even know that?"

"Dad told me. Mom told him. Is there a secret handshake? Or whatever girls do? A secret giggle?"

"We're doing a project," she said. "A service project. We're trying to help her mom. Who cares anyway, who I hang out with?"

"You know what people are saying now? They're saying the whole thing was a setup. She and some guy she met online faked the whole thing. Made it look like a kidnapping."

"That's not new," she said. "Some people said that from the beginning."

"Well, now lots of people are saying it. It makes some sense. Disappearing without a trace? And no ransom note . . ."

"That's stupid," she said. "Ransom notes are in movies. This isn't a movie."

He shrugged. "I'm just sayin'. It's a theory."

"What about the sandwich guy?"

"How hurt was that guy, really? Bump on the head. Just enough to make it look like a real crime."

"She was *crying,*" Meredith said. "She was scared."

"Maybe," he said. "Or maybe she was *acting.*"

He was in his sweats and black Under Armour shirt. The official uniform of breaking your mother's heart. There was a paunch in the Under Armour, courtesy of months of Chester Cheetah and the family room couch. But he still looked about three-quarters like his old self.

"Are you playing baseball?" she asked. She was not interested in hearing any more of his theories.

"Maybe," he said. "Maybe not."

"Mom'll kill you."

"I'm seventeen years old."

"You can kill someone who's seventeen."

He grinned. There was something in him, standing there in the kitchen with his elbow propped on the microwave, his head set at a slight angle, a little stinky from his run, that was very clearly not miserable. Something had changed over the last few weeks. He had ownership over himself; he was the master of his fate; he had resolve. The darkened left lens in his glasses was an afterthought.

She'd hardly talked to him in at least a week. What was the point? Perhaps the miserable Evan would have understood what was happening to her. But this Evan, this banana-swallowing, Under-Armoured Evan, would be little help. He was not her safe space anymore. She'd woken and heard him hitting down in the garage and understood at once that that was his place now. He had his place, and she had hers, and they did not overlap. He was abruptly so gone that she didn't even miss him.

She had stopped waiting for Jules and Kristy at the corner of the parking lot. Jules and Kristy, it needed to be said, had become more than a little bit irritating, Jules with her pathetic insistence that she did not want to be popular while simultaneously doing everything she possibly could to be popular, and Kristy with her whiny, sixth grade–holdover insecurity. Plus it was just *easier* to be with Lisa's friends. They weren't her friends, not exactly, but they were nice enough, and the distance between them and the bathroom where Lisa waited for her was infinitesimal, no more than a blink. With Jules and Kristy there was history, and baggage, and expectation. With Lisa's friends, the only expectation was that she mourn the absence of their friend.

She went straight into the building and to her locker as soon as she arrived at school. There were still little green ribbons covering Lisa's locker, but every morning some would have fallen down overnight, scattered like tiny leaves, and she would pick them up and toss them into the bottom of her own locker. How long would they let that locker, 64C, sit there, unused? How long did missing-person ribbons stay up? Was there an expiration date, some point where they officially became irrelevant, a day when the fall of Lisa Bellow became the winter of someone else, as Evan had predicted from the start? She imagined Mr. Fulton brushing the ribbons away with a few heavy swipes of his large hand. Yes, maybe after Christmas they'd give the locker to a new kid, some guy from far away who transferred in and was none the wiser, who would fill the back of the locker door with his own life.

Or maybe not. Maybe in a week Lisa

would be standing at her locker again, found, freed, the criminal arrested, the mystery solved. Maybe everything would revert to the way it had been. And if Lisa were beside her here in this hall, would Lisa be ignoring her? In some ways this thought was as troubling as Lisa's continued absence.

"Return to basic rules," like in Fluxx, the game they'd played endlessly that one summer. Her father's favorite card. She and Evan, and even her mom, were always making things crazier — draw four, play your whole hand, switch hands with the player across from you, take six cards randomly from the discard pile — but her dad, god, the look of relief on his face when he drew it: "Return to basic rules." They all laughed at him. Not in a mean way. Just in that way you were allowed to laugh at your father because you knew he would laugh along with you.

Something was thrust in front of her face.

"Look. At. This." It was Amanda Hammels. The thing in front of her face was a catalog. The page in the catalog showed a silver chain bracelet, ten or twelve ovals looped together to make the whole.

"It's like the chain of life. Like the chain of friends. Like the chain of support."

"Cool," Meredith said.

"It's perfect," Amanda said. "Abby is freaking out, it's so perfect. Her mom already emailed the company and they can get them special order, like super fast, so we can have them at the Halloween party."

"That's great," Meredith said.

"It's the chain of giving," Amanda said. "It's the chain of love. The love chain. Or is that weird? Maybe that's too kinky. We don't want it to be all sexed up or anything. Oh my god, that would be really bad." She snorted out a laugh. "Lisa would think that was funny."

"It's probably not a great idea, calling it that," Meredith agreed.

"Yeah. We'll work on it. We'll figure it out at lunch. I just wanted everybody to see it ASAP. Have you seen Becca?"

"No. I just got here."

"Okay. I'll find her."

She skipped off. Amanda had never been as mean as Lisa, always been a background giggler, not smart enough to come up with a comment or facial expression that could actually wound you. You got the feeling that you could turn Amanda in any direction and push the go button and she would go in a straight line until someone thought to turn her in another direction, or until she bumped into a wall and just kept butting into it for eternity, a wind-up toy with no off switch.

"It's not like we don't know what you think of us," Lisa said.

"Who?" she asked. "What?"

"You and your smarty friends. It's not like we don't know what you're saying about us behind our backs."

"That's pretty hilarious, coming from you."

"I'm not actually any meaner than you," Lisa said. "I'm just way more popular."

"That right there is meaner than anything I would say."

"It's not mean," Lisa said. "It's just the truth."

Meredith thought about the awful thing Lisa had said in seventh grade, about her butt hanging off the chair in the cafeteria, but she was too embarrassed that she even remembered it to mention it now.

"She is stupid," Lisa said. "Amanda. I mean, you're right. But she has a lot of good qualities. Have you ever seen her *braid*? She's like some kind of braiding genius."

"Well it's good she has that to fall back on," Meredith said.

"See?" Lisa said. "You're a bitch. Just like

me. See?"

Lisa slipped a Sharpie out from under her leg and wrote bitch on the tile wall of the shower in big, thick green letters. Meredith gasped.

"Where'd you get that?"

"What?"

"That marker."

"It was in the bedroom," Lisa said. "In a drawer. I stole it. I thought I might need it."

"For what?"

"For this," Lisa said, then underlined BITCH.

Lisa did not talk about what happened in the bedroom. Meredith realized that this may in fact have been the first time she'd even mentioned the word "bedroom." It wasn't every night. It was sometimes. He would come home — from where? from work? — a couple hours after dark, and maybe they'd be watching TV but more than likely they'd be in the tub. He would come in with a greasy bag from somewhere — usually Burger King but sometimes Taco Bell and sometimes KFC and once it was the plain brown paper bag from Deli Barn, which was funny for about five seconds. He'd toss the bag into the bathroom, the way you'd fling slop to pigs, and then she and Lisa would spread out the bag like a picnic blanket between them, dump all the fries into a pile, and dig in. If he was going to take a shower, then they'd go sit on the couch and watch *CSI* and eat and then later, back to the tub, except sometimes he came for Lisa.

It wasn't even very scary, not anymore. (Had it ever been? Meredith could no longer recall those first days. Had it been a week yet? A month?) He'd just come into the bathroom and go, "You, get up" — just like he had that afternoon, at the Deli Barn — and Lisa would stand up and Meredith would lie down on her side and the bedroom door would click shut and then Meredith would fall asleep. And then the next day it was the same thing all over again. They had their routine, all three of them.

"What about Becca?" Meredith asked.

"What *about* Becca?"

"She's not dumb."

"Becca is the only friend I have who can actually have a conversation," Lisa said. "That's why I wanted her in our group, when she moved here."

"To help with homework?"

"No." Lisa made a tally mark under bitch. "But, okay, yes, sometimes. But no — she's just, you know. She just sees things smart. Smartly. She has perspective."

"She's in my algebra class," Meredith said. She smiled. "She knows what an asymptote is. So you can ask her next year."

"Ha, yeah, she knows it's made up. Asymptote. Buttymptote."

"It's not made up," Meredith said. "It's a real thing. It's just . . ." She paused for dramatic effect, then waved her hands like an illusionist. *"Invisible."*

"Invisible algebra? Great."

"It's an invisible line that you can't cross. A curve gets right up next to it but it can't cross it. It just *almost* touches it, to infinity."

"Yeah, well, if it's so invisible, how does the curve even know where it is?" Lisa smiled triumphantly, the way she had in the car that first day when she'd told the kidnapper to shut his mouth. "I'd like to see them explain that."

"I guess you'll just have to ask Becca," Meredith said.

Lisa and Becca. Becca and Lisa. The gruesome twosome, Jules had called them. Or the twin bitches. Slut squared. Had she thought of that one herself? Maybe she had. But Lisa and Becca had deserved it — they'd made each other meaner, the two of them together some kind of weird, indefinable force, making everyone around them feel small, sometimes without a single word. Or, now that she thought about it, *often* without a single word. In fact, Meredith had to admit she could not recall a specific instance of Becca Nichols actually being mean to her directly, but rather an indistinct montage of superior looks and eye rolls and silent snubs.

Once, she'd been in the car with Jules and Kristy and they were complaining about Lisa and Becca. "Those bitches think they rule the world," Jules had said, and Jules's mother had commented, "Just so you know, they're definitely peaking now." Meredith had instantly recognized this as one of those things parents said to make unpopular children feel better. But surprisingly it had worked, and she and Jules and Kristy had spent a pleasant evening coming up with all the particular ways in which Lisa and her friends would be total losers as soon as next year, and then probably pregnant and divorced and poor — maybe even homeless, and certainly humiliated — right around the time they themselves were graduating from college and marrying gorgeous men.

"She's probably my best friend," Lisa said. "Becca. She's definitely the person least likely to screw me over. Most of my other friends would stab me in the back in a second if they could."

"Why are you friends with people who would stab you in the back?"

"Everyone's friends with people who would stab them in the back," Lisa said. "Hello? Otherwise you'd only have like one friend."

"That's really sad," Meredith said.

"That's the difference between people like you and people like me. You think everything's sad. Because all you do is *think* about stuff all the time. If you only think about stuff like half the time you're way less sad."

"What do you do the other half of the time? When you're not thinking?"

"Uh, I don't know, maybe have a *life*?"

"It's not like I don't have a life," Meredith said.

Lisa looked at her. There was the look. This was why everyone hated her. This was why middle school girls had stomachaches when they woke up in the morning. This was why girls were afraid to read the next text, or turn the corner into the cafeteria. This was why Jules could think, why they all could think, all the girls who were not her friends, why they could all secretly think:

Good riddance.

There was a police car parked in front of

their house. Meredith slowed almost to a stop when she saw it from a block away. A police car could mean a lot of things, and none of them were good. At Lisa's house that day, Mrs. Bellow had told them that she was always waiting for the phone to ring, but that whenever it rang she was afraid to answer it. Now Meredith understood why Mrs. Bellow didn't want to answer the phone.

Detective Waller and Detective Thorn were standing on her front porch. It looked like they had just rung the bell. As she approached she could see that Detective Thorn was holding a slim manila folder. On television, slim manila folders held photos of corpses. Sometimes the photo was just a pale face, other times a whole body, in whatever position and condition it had been discovered.

"Hi," she said.

"There you are," Detective Waller said, turning. "We were just ringing the bell."

"Nobody's home," she said.

"Where are your parents?" Detective Thorn asked.

"At work."

"You come home alone?"

"Usually," she said.

They exchanged looks, as if this might be

important information. In truth, Evan was supposed to be home where she got here, and normally was. Since he'd started working out again, she'd beaten him home a couple times.

"We've got something we want you to look at," Detective Thorn said. He slid a photo out of his folder. "You know we've got Lisa's phone. We've identified everyone in her pictures, except one person. Nobody seems to know who he is."

Meredith looked at the photo. It was a selfie: Lisa and a smiling man, maybe in his midtwenties. He had blond hair and a neatly trimmed beard.

"It was taken last month," Detective Waller said. "Date stamp of September twenty-ninth."

"Did you ask Becca?" Meredith said.

"We did," Detective Thorn said. "And several others. Like I said, nobody recognized him. Is he familiar to you at all?"

"Did they tell you they take selfies all the time? Literally all the time. Lisa and her friends? I'd see them at the mall taking selfies with strangers."

"So you don't recognize him?"

"I didn't see the man who took her," she said. "I couldn't see him. He was wearing a mask."

"Okay," Detective Waller said. "Okay. So you said."

So you said. Maybe she hadn't meant it to come out like that, but there it was on the porch between them. What did they think, that she had lied about the mask? That she had seen the man's face? That she knew him?

"He was wearing a mask," she said again. "I know he was. Didn't the sandwich farmer say that, too?"

"Who?"

"The Deli Barn guy. Whatever his name is."

What *was* his name? Had she ever known? She had forgotten about him, nearly. It was as if he'd been in the back room, unconscious, all this time. She thought of what Evan had said: "Bump on the head. Just enough to —"

"We have his statement," Detective Thorn said.

"He's been very useful," added Detective Waller.

Why were they being so cagey? Across the street, Mrs. Reed walked out her front door, saw the police car, and went back inside.

"You haven't gotten any unusual texts lately, have you?" Detective Waller asked.

"What do you mean?" Meredith asked.

"What time will your parents be home?" Detective Thorn asked.

"Soon," she said, though this was not true. Evan would be here soon. But she felt if she said her parents would be here soon then the detectives were more likely to leave. Something had happened. They knew something. And now she was acting all weird — snotty, guilty even. She imagined the mental notes they were taking. *Agitated. Defensive.*

"We'll check back with you in a couple days," Detective Thorn said. "But I'd like for you to let us know if you see or hear anything unusual."

She went into the house and locked the door. She slid off her backpack and stood with her back pressed against the door. They were still out there, on the porch. They weren't talking but she could tell they were still there. What were they doing? What were they waiting for?

Evan didn't get home until her parents had been home for over an hour. He rolled in, sweaty and swaggery, and stood at the kitchen counter eating his banana, even though the three of them were sitting at the kitchen table clearly eating dinner.

"We started without you," her father said.

"We didn't know where you were," her

mother said. "It's almost seven o'clock."

"I was with some of the guys," Evan said.

"What guys?" her mother asked tightly, like the answer might be mobsters or heroin addicts.

"The *guys,*" Evan said. "My friends. Do I stink too bad? Do you want me to shower or can I sit and eat? Mer, do I stink?"

"No," she said, without bothering to take a whiff. More people at the table meant less attention on her. That was simple arithmetic.

Evan filled a plate at the stove and sat down at the table.

"How is everyone?" he asked.

"Your mother wants to know if you're going to play baseball this spring," her father asked.

Her mother made a scoffing sound, with a little furious yelp at the end. "Really?" she said. "That's how you're going to ask that question?"

"It's true, isn't it?" her father said. "That's the question. Is that or is that not the question?"

"What your father meant to say," she said, "is that he and I would like to know if you're thinking about playing baseball."

"I'm not thinking about playing baseball," Evan said. "I am playing baseball."

"Evan," her mother said. "The doctor . . ."

"The doctor, yes. I know what the doctor said. But the doctor isn't in my head. The doctor doesn't see what I see. Every injury is different. He said that, right? I'm not making that up. Every injury is unique. He said that, didn't he, Dad?"

"He did," her father said. When her mother scowled he turned to her and shrugged. "He did. He said it. The man said that."

"Right," Evan said. "So here's the thing. I didn't think I'd be able to see the ball well enough to play. But my *brain* knows where the ball is. The ball moves in a straight line. The ball is always the same size and shape. My brain gets it because the ball hasn't changed. My brain doesn't get a balloon. You could throw a balloon to me twenty times and I'd be lucky to catch it twice. But a pitch follows a line. And my brain knows the line because it's seen the same line a million times. I can catch. And I can hit. And I can run. That's all I need to be able to do. I'm not saying I'm gonna be in the Hall of Fame. I'm saying maybe I can play with my team for one more season."

"You can hardly pour a glass of milk," her mother said.

"You haven't been paying attention," he

said. "I can pour a glass of milk. And I can hit a fastball. I hit one today at the cages. I hit a hundred of 'em, actually."

"Really?" her father asked. "How fast?"

"The eighty cage. I was a little rusty because I'm out of shape. But, Dad, other than that, it's just the same. I know the line of the ball. My brain knows where the ball is, even if my eye doesn't."

"That's incredible," her father said. "I can't even —"

"I know, right? It is incredible. But it's true." He looked at her mother. He was right on the edge of a smile, a real smile. Meredith could see it coming. "Mom, I swear, it's true."

Her mother set down her fork. "What about pop-ups?" she asked.

"Jesus, Claire . . ."

"What?" she said. "Don't *Jesus* me. It's a reasonable question."

"Some things are harder than others," Evan said. The expression that was almost a smile faded. "Some things are going to take longer to get right. No question. But . . . yeah, okay, of course. Some things are harder than others."

"I'm very proud of you for getting back out there," her father said. He put his hand on Evan's forearm. "Whatever happens. I'm very proud of you."

"Honey, Evan, I'm proud of you, too," her mother blurted out. "I'm not saying I'm not proud. I'm only saying —"

"She's only saying what about pop-ups," Meredith said. "What about pop-ups? What about pop-ups? What about pop-ups?"

They all stared at her in silence. Part of her wanted to keep saying it. She felt like she could say it forever, say it until they had to take her to a hospital, say it until they had to give her the Thorazine again, say it until Lisa came home.

"Really, Evan, honey," she said, turning it from crazy-town to nasty-town, doing her best, cruelest imitation of her mother's voice. "What about pop-ups?"

Why did she want to hurt her mother, side with the boys? Her mother was right, after all: What *about* pop-ups? Her brother and her father were idiots, buoyed by a common dream. Any five-year-old on any pathetic T-ball team knew that baseballs didn't always travel in straight lines, didn't always rip mound to plate, or hand to glove, or bat to eye. What *about* pop-ups, those towering ones straight above the plate, a hundred feet in the air, the ones she'd seen Evan park under, his mask thrown aside, waving his arms, calling off the pitcher and the third baseman as the ball spun and wavered in the breeze, sometimes changing direction at the last second so that he had to lunge, throw that flat mitt out to snag it inches from the ground. Yes, what about those?

Her mother was absolutely right. Her mother who thought she could just sit in the Bellows' living room drinking the Bellows' coffee out of the Bellows' mug acting like she knew every goddamn thing in the entire world. Her mother who always had an answer for everything, a reason why whatever it was you wanted to do wouldn't work unless you did it her way. Her mother, always judging everyone, always knowing what was best for everyone. Why had her mother asked her about the stupid casserole? Driving home from the Bellows', why hadn't her mother asked her why the hell she was there to begin with?

The next day she walked into the PE locker room with Amanda and Becca, and instead of veering off to her usual spot in the corner found herself swept along into their aisle of lockers, the popular aisle, the one in the center of everything. Before she knew what was happening she was pulling her clothes out of her gym bag and opening a locker beside Becca's. She glanced over to her

330

normal area, the corner where she and Kristy had for almost three years now served as each other's human dressing shield. Kristy was sitting on the bench with her back to them. Meredith turned to her new friends and found herself face-to-face with Amanda, who was naked except for her underpants.

"Want me to braid your hair real quick?" Amanda asked.

"That's okay," Meredith said. She sat down on the bench and stared straight ahead and slowly took off her shoes and socks. If she was slow enough, maybe they would go on into the gym without her. On her left, Amanda was wrestling herself into her sports bra. On her right, Becca, topless, bent over to slip on her shoes. Did they not know there was an order to things? Shoes off, socks off, leggings slid down and in one seamless move shorts slid up, shirt off, bra off with oncoming gym shirt as partial blocker, sports bra over breasts, sports bra strap adjustment, gym shirt on, socks and shoes on.

She peeled off her leggings without standing.

"Oh my god I love that birthmark," Amanda said, plopping down on the bench beside her and putting her index finger on

Meredith's thigh. "Oh my god, that's so cute."

It wasn't much, really, just a little sideways squiggle on her upper left thigh, although Meredith liked to believe it looked a little bit like a tiny dark bird in flight. No one had ever looked at this part of her body long enough to notice it.

"Let me see," Becca said, squeezing in between Meredith and the row of lockers and crouching down. She traced the bird with her finger.

"I have one, too," she said. "Birthmark. It's not as cool." She bent back and shifted her left breast and Meredith could see a small horseshoe.

"Ooh, some man's going to love that," Amanda said.

"What's this?" Becca asked. She touched Meredith's bare right knee. "Is that another one?"

"I don't think so," Meredith said. "I think that's just a freckle."

"It's not a freckle." Becca rubbed it with her thumb, then inexplicably blew on Meredith's knee, as if the spot were an ash that might be swept away by a breath. The chill of Becca's breath on her knee gave Meredith goose bumps up and down her arms, the same goose bumps she'd gotten when

Steven Overbeck had drawn the watch on her wrist, and she hoped that no one could see them.

"You should probably have that looked at," Becca said.

Amanda bent over to inspect it more closely. "That is kinda weird," she said. "That's how my aunt's skin cancer started. With one spot."

Meredith could not help herself — she glanced over at Kristy, who was already dressed (they could change in twenty seconds flat) and sitting on the bench tying her sneakers, watching the show. Amanda's hand was on her left thigh and Becca's thumb on her right knee. Alien examination, all the fun drained away.

The bell rang and Amanda and Becca threw on their clothes and ran out with their shoes still untied. Kristy continued to sit on the bench looking at Meredith.

"What?" Meredith said.

"Are you okay?" Kristy asked softly. Meredith had known Kristy practically her whole life, and she had never wanted to smack her more than she did in this moment. She couldn't stand the look on her face.

"What do you mean?"

"I mean . . . are you *okay*?"

"Do I look not okay? Do I look like there's

something wrong with me?"

"I just —"

"Jesus, Kristy, it's not like they raped me."

She didn't even know why she said it. The word hung between them for a moment and then Kristy got up and walked past her and into the gym. Meredith sat on the bench, still in her underwear, her heart pounding. She could feel their hands and their breath on her. From the gym came the throbbing of basketballs, five, then ten, then twenty, then thirty. She wanted to take a shower. She wanted to put on a winter coat. She wanted to wrap up in a blanket and sit on a couch. Or in a bathtub.

14

For years, watching Little League baseball had always bored Claire in precisely the same way that watching children run around a playground bored her. It wasn't awful. It wasn't a *hardship* to sit there on the bleachers and watch. If the day was pretty and she was sitting beside someone whose company she enjoyed, it could be a perfectly pleasant way to pass a spring or summer afternoon. But the game itself, the action on the field (if it could even be called *action*) could not hold her attention. When Evan came to bat, of course she watched and clapped her hands and cheered when he hit the ball hard or far, and also when he didn't. But when the other boys were up to bat, or when Evan's team was in the field and she couldn't even see his face behind the chunky catcher's mask, she did her best to appear engaged but she couldn't have ever said, without looking at the scoreboard, who was winning, or by how much, or what inning it even was — only that it always seemed like it was the top of the third *forever.*

By the time the boys were ten or eleven, this lack of interest set her apart from almost every other parent in the stands, including her own husband, who perched for three hours on his row of bleacher as if he might at any moment have to spring over the backstop and join the game. She could not understand it when parents yelled at the umpire — almost always the same skinny, acne-faced teen who looked like he'd agreed to be an umpire with a gun held to his temple — nor when the parents made terse comments under their breaths about who should be batting cleanup or why the coach continued putting that boy at first base even though he always took his foot off the bag. *"They're ten,"* she always wanted to say. *"Who cares?"*

But then something happened, something that surprised everyone. Or maybe not everyone. Mark, she had to admit, had anticipated it for years, claimed to see something in Evan, some great promise in his build, his hand/eye coordination, some secret baseball recipe — though she'd just always attributed the prediction to Mark's usual optimism. But Mark was right. What happened was that Evan suddenly got good. Really, really good. Claire had seen his body change over the winter of his seventh-grade year, his shoulders and chest broaden, the belly that had once earned him the unmentionable nickname transform into muscle, the mustache darkening on his upper lip. (Really? So soon? She had not steeled herself properly for that darkness, had to stop her double-take the morning she first noticed it.) But she had never considered how puberty might translate on the field. Always one of the better players, at the age of thirteen Evan was abruptly and undeniably the best, hitting the ball with power that made parents lingering at practice look up from their phones and say *whoa.* He hit screaming line drives that other boys, instead of trying to catch, leaped away from. And she did not blame them. And suddenly, though she was ashamed to admit it, she turned from an apathetic baseball parent to the foam fingered #1 fan in the space of — well, really, there was no space. She was one, and then abruptly she was the other.

Claire loved going to his high school games, loved that Evan was the star, because she loved watching him excel, in the same way she'd loved, when we was two, watching him put the shaped blocks into the correctly shaped holes. It seemed to come to him just that easily. But it was more than that. It was something about *her,* too. She had always sat back and judged the other parents a little bit, how seriously they took everything, but now she was one of the crowd, automatically included: somehow Evan's success was her ticket past the gates of her own judgment. She and Mark were *popular.* At the games they were Evan Oliver's parents, a single unit of accomplishment. They held hands on the bleachers while they cheered the boy who had made them popular and modestly accepted the accolades from those around them, the mothers with their big sunhats and Dunkin' Donuts iced teas, the fathers with their Phillies caps and hypertension. It was a mortifying cliché, but nonetheless true: Claire was actually warmed, inside, by the glow of her son's towering home runs.

The mothers — a few of them she'd gotten to know well enough to look forward to their company — had called often after Evan was hurt, called over the spring and summer, and then eventually stopped trying when she did not return their calls.

Claire had long been friendly with many people but had no close friends. After what she and Mark always referred to half-jokingly (ha-ha-ha) as the Season of Divorce, when the three couples they had been best friends with split up, she had had a difficult time making connections with people that were based on anything other than convenience. She was too busy and too old to make new friends. Not that she could no longer be friends with the divorced couples. She was — she and Mark both were. They had made a somber vow that they would not be side choosers, but ironically it was that vow that wound up making the individual friendships difficult to sustain. You could say all you wanted that you would not choose sides, but the fact was that of remaining good friends with half the divorced people, they became acquaintances with all of them. Sometimes the men came over for movies in the yard, but their lives were different now, and everyone could feel it. And sometimes the women came over for drinks, but Claire grew tired of the variation on the theme from years before: you wouldn't understand; you have Mark.

Still, this was not something that had particularly bothered her, and it was only after Evan stopped playing baseball that she realized that those people, the women in the stands with the iced teas and sunhats, had become her closest friends without her even realizing it. And then they, too, were gone, in the course of one afternoon, in the path of one foul ball.

"Do you give out toothbrushes at your house?" a young patient asked Claire on Halloween.

"We're just dentists," she said. "We're not monsters."

In fact she had always loved Halloween, and they had the perfect Halloween neighborhood — no porch lights dared dim on their street, the long lawns dotted with gravestones and giant inflatable spiders. She would stay on the porch swing with her cauldron of candy while Mark walked the kids around one square block, and then they'd switch places and she'd take them on the second loop of the figure eight. They would not have given it up, either of them, the sight of their children bathed in the light of someone else's front porch, the looks on their faces when they turned from the door and started back toward the sidewalk, their pumpkin buckets swinging, Evan holding Meredith's hand so she would not trip on a darkened stair or stone. Claire mourned the loss of those moments even as they were happening. And now here she was, those moments ghosts.

The days of trick-or-treating had long passed for Evan and Meredith. Now it was parties — music, costumes (either bloody or ironic, extra points for both), possibly pranks, probably alcohol. This year, with Halloween on a Friday — *there should be some sort of law preventing this,* Claire thought — both kids would be god knows where and she and Mark would sit on their porch swing with their cauldron of Kit Kats for two hours and feel ancient. And it wasn't as if they could even feel ancient together. Tonight, she was fairly certain, they would feel ancient alone.

It was true that sometimes Claire went months without thinking of that man all those years ago, her escape hatch, and then other times she thought of him almost every day. She knew the danger zones — god knows they were clearly marked — and recognized all the signs of her mounting vulnerability. She knew she was in a dangerous place now. What fool would not want the escape hatch at this moment?

She was mature enough to acknowledge that the man himself did not even exist anymore. It had been twenty years and she could hardly conjure his face. He wasn't on any social media — this meant he hadn't changed. Unless it meant he was dead. But more than likely he just turned his nose up at that kind of thing. More than likely he was tending to Syrian refugees. But no, there she went again, creating a hero from the sketchy outline in her head. Maybe he was just being a selfish bastard somewhere. He'd had that capacity, that was for sure. Maybe that had been part of his appeal. Mark had never been a selfish bastard. He wouldn't have known how to be a selfish bastard if his life depended on it. She hated that about him.

"We're coming for you at ten o'clock," she said to Meredith during dinner.

Meredith set down her fork. "Ten o'clock? Seriously? That's when most people will be getting there."

"Probably true," Evan said.

Evan was now her number-one enemy, if one had to think in those terms, looking around the kitchen table at the three people she loved most in the world.

"I don't even know this girl," Claire said. "Who is it again?"

"Abby Luckett. And just because you don't know her doesn't mean she's bad," Meredith said. "All it means is you don't know her."

You were held at gunpoint twenty-three days

ago, Claire thought. *You were lying on the floor of a restaurant and a man had a gun pointed at your head. Do not talk to me as if that didn't happen. Do not talk to me like a typical snotty teenager.*

"How about ten thirty?" Mark said.

"Whatever," Meredith said. She lifted her fork as if it weighed seventy-five pounds, then began morosely stirring her vegetables. "Maybe I won't even go. I'll just . . . whatever."

Claire watched Mark fall headlong into this obvious trap and did nothing to prevent it, which was, in a way, falling headlong into the trap herself.

"We didn't say we don't want you to go," Mark said. "We want you to go, honey. We think it's great that you're going. We just don't want you to stay super late. What time does the party end?"

"It's not a birthday party, Dad. There is not an *end time.* It's just over when everybody leaves, which will probably be at like midnight."

"Eleven," he said. "We'll come at eleven."

"It's a good offer," Evan said. "At thirteen. It's a fair offer. I'd take that offer."

"Where are you going?" Claire asked him.

"Nowhere," he said. "Just to Zack's or whatever."

Zack was the shortstop.

"Are you driving?"

Night driving was trickier than day driving. She knew this. Headlights complicated matters. And on Halloween, kids darting out from between cars, kids in dark costumes, Darth Vaders, Hogwarts robes. It was like a shooting gallery with cars as bullets, kids as ducks, difficult enough for someone with perfect eyesight.

"I'm taking the stilts," Evan said. "And there's nothing you can do to stop me."

"I'm serious," Claire said.

"Sam's picking me up," Evan said. "We may just crash at Zack's."

Sam was the first baseman. The shortstop and the first baseman and the catcher. She hadn't seen those boys in — how long? Weeks? Or was it months? She should be happy for her son. She was happy for him. She was.

"What're you guys going to do?" she asked.

"We're gonna play baseball in the dark," he said. "We're gonna get drunk and throw baseballs at each other's heads. Stuff like that."

"Just as long as you have a plan," Mark said.

Claire sat on the front porch swing with her giant cauldron of candy. It was a mild night, clear and moonlit, ideal Halloween weather. So where was everyone? Had she inflated the numbers from the past, swept up in her nostalgia, or were there actually fewer trick-or-treaters this year? Had the suburbs been spooked? Maybe it was in bad taste to trick-or-treat when girls were being taken from Deli Barns. Maybe it was wrong to pretend to be scary, or scared.

Lisa Bellow had fallen off the edge of the news. For the first week she had been the top story, of course, every night, when a break seemed imminent. Then for the ten days following, they recapped, because there were no updates. Each story began, "Police continue to follow leads in the abduction of —" but there was never any new information. "Officials encourage anyone with knowledge," etc., etc., etc. The same picture of Lisa, a new plea from Colleen, a shot of the Deli Barn, the sign on the middle school lawn studded with green ribbons. It was the same story now, every night on the 11:00 local news, every morning when she lay in bed and read the news on her iPhone, every sentence of non-news punctuated by a *ping* from the garage.

Of course there were glimmers of hope, because there was always an exception to the rule, always someone who beat the odds, always some incredible story shouted as far and wide as the internet could reach. (And wasn't this why Evan believed he could play baseball? Because there was always someone who did something extraordinary, and that was always the someone you heard about? Because who wanted to make a TV movie about all the people who tried to do something extraordinary and failed?) There was the girl who had been kidnapped out of her bedroom and been missing for how long? A year? And then one day on the street someone spots her and she's reunited with her family and yes, god knows it was awful, terrifying, life altering, but now she's home safe. And those women in Ohio, kept in a house for a decade or more, long enough to have children fathered by their rapist, somehow kept there by one single maniac until the day they finally believed they could kick the door out and make a run for it? These were the stories you had in the back of your mind. No one mentioned them. To mention them would risk a jinx. But everyone knew them, and surely these were the stories Colleen Bellow reminded herself of every day so that she could get out of bed.

MISSING. She looked at those yellow flyers on Meredith's closet door almost every morning, and once in the middle of the night while Meredith slept behind her and the tolerant cat rolled its back against her shins. She kept hoping she would open the closet to find them gone. 5'5", 110 LBS. BLOND HAIR. HAZEL EYES. Claire desperately wanted to take them down, get them out of Meredith's room. She could hardly bear the thought of Meredith looking at them every morning, every night, like a lover or a stalker or . . . or a what? She didn't even know. She just knew that she wanted to hide them away, the way they'd hidden Evan's bats after his first surgery. She wanted to zip them up in that bat bag in the corner of the garage, tuck them away in the place that held all the things you couldn't bear to look at, all the things you couldn't bear to love anymore. But that had failed. Evan had found the bats, found his way back to them, even with only one eye.

The van pulled into the driveway and Mark got out. He swung the keys around his finger and came and sat with her on the swing.

"Busy?"

"Only four or five," she said. "Two groups. Three Princess Elsas. How was the party?"

"I only stayed for the Jell-O shots," he said.

"Did you see any of her friends? Was Kristy there?"

"No idea. They all looked exactly alike. Same makeup. Bunch of zombies standing around in the yard."

"High school kids, too?"

"Seriously, no idea. Maybe you should have gone."

"I'll pick her up," she said.

He rested his hand on hers, between them on the swing, and she looked at him. He was wearing his dumb puffy white sweater that was about nine sizes too big. He smiled.

"Nice to see you," he said.

She might have cried right then had the voices not reached them from a couple houses down, kids whooping. A moment later a battalion of Stormtroopers appeared on the sidewalk, marching in their direction, led by an Irish setter.

"You want a beer?" he asked.

"I want ten beers," she said.

"Let's start with one."

Two hours later it was 10:15 and they were on their backs in the front yard, looking up at the stars. The last of the trick-or-treaters had been gone for hours. She'd had five beers and at least as many Kit Kats. Her only solace was that she now knew she could still enjoy getting drunk with her husband and that she genuinely no longer wanted to kill him.

"Go inside," she said. "Go to bed. You don't want to fall asleep out here."

He was notorious for this, going from pleasantly drunk to sound asleep in a matter of seconds. In dental school he'd fallen asleep on the couch of every single person they knew, often while the party continued around him, and on two embarrassing occasions he had fallen asleep with his head on the table at a restaurant.

"Two-minute warning," she said, because she knew all the signs. "Trust me. You don't want to sleep in the yard. For so many reasons."

"I really don't," he said. "I really, really don't. But you —"

"I'm fine," she said. "I still have a little time. I'll have some coffee. I'll be fine."

"Are you sure? I could call a cab or something."

"Terrific. We'll show up to pick her up in a taxi. She'd love that."

They had a deal, an unwritten agreement,

more binding than their marriage vows. They were not reckless people. They did not do reckless things. The list was short but absolute. Among the terms: they did not drink and drive.

"Okay," he said. He stood unsteadily in the grass, took a few deep breaths. "Okay. I can do this. I'm going to bed. I'm going to walk into the house and go to bed."

"In the bed," she said. "You're going to bed in the bed. Our bed."

"In our bed," he confirmed. "But wake me up if you don't think you can drive. Seriously. Wake me up and we'll figure something out."

"It's fine," she said. "I'm fine."

Which was almost the case, a cup of coffee later. She sat behind the wheel of the minivan and took a long deep breath. She was fine. She backed out of the driveway. The thing was, she was *tired.* There was no law against driving tired, although probably there should be. She had read once that more accidents were caused by tired sober adults than drunk teenagers. What about drunk mothers? Not that she was a drunk mother. She was, at the very most, a mother who had been tipsy a half hour before but was now fine but tired. Better than Evan, surely, and they let him drive.

She put a hand over her left eye. He might be out driving right now. He might be driving Sam's car. She might crash into him at the next intersection. He'd get out of the car and say, *"What the hell, Mom?"* And she, still with her hand over her eye, would say, *"I was just trying to understand how you see the world. Is that so wrong?"*

It was possible that she smelled a little bit like beer. Or maybe it was just the car that smelled like beer, which might have been worse. On a Friday Halloween there would be roadblocks everywhere. It was nearly as bad as New Year's or the Fourth of July. An officer would walk slowly up to the van and she'd roll down the window and the stench of beer would erupt from the interior. And the cop would say — she'd seen this many times on TV, so she knew — *"Ma'am, would you please step out of the car?"* and she would say, would have to say, *"My daughter was almost kidnapped earlier this month."*

She had driven herself to the Deli Barn by the middle school. She was sitting in the parking lot of the Deli Barn. She had come here for coffee, without thinking about it, or at least without being aware of thinking about it. She had stopped here before for coffee once or twice, and for sandwiches many times, but of course all that was before everything, and of course she had not forgotten, but rather used "forgetting" as an excuse to finally come here, a place she had avoided even driving by in the last weeks.

There were three teenagers sitting at one of the tables, and a man and a little boy who was dressed as Buzz Lightyear (Evan had worshipped Buzz Lightyear) and when she walked through the door some bells jingled and the little boy laughed, although probably not at the bells.

There was a huge bearded guy behind the counter with bulging, tattooed muscles. He was not the injured sandwich farmer, whose picture she knew from the newspaper. This guy was in his thirties and looked like he could snap a masked kidnapper in two. Perhaps he had been hired expressly for this purpose.

"Do you have coffee?" she asked.

This was it. This was the spot. Claire was seized with the urge to take off her shoes. Socks, too. She wanted to be barefoot on this floor, on this cold and sticky slab. This was where her daughter had lain down, her cheek flattened against the chill, where Lisa had lain down, where the two girls had stared at each other before one was taken. This was where her daughter had believed she was going to die, had thought . . . what? Claire had never asked. How could you ask? Wouldn't it be cruel to ask, to force her to relive that moment, rethink those thoughts?

"Black, yes," she said.

Had the girls said anything at all, in those minutes (how many? three? four?) leading up to Lisa's abduction? She had heard Meredith's story of that afternoon repeated to the police at least a half dozen times, and there had never been mention of any talking, though surely even if they had not spoken, something, some message, some understanding, must have passed in that narrow gap between them, those few inches that separated their faces, that space — this space she inhabited now — that a thousand ankles had breached since. A look. A gesture.

She was standing where the man had stood. She looked down at her own feet, saw the floor from his perspective, imagined this thought: *I will pick something up from this floor. I will pick something.*

"Thank you," she said, taking the cup that was handed to her.

She got back into van and tried to sip the coffee but it was too hot. It was a few minutes past 11:00. She would let Meredith have a little extra time, sit here for a couple minutes and allow the car to fill up with the smell of coffee. Maybe she should have gotten something else, something that smelled stronger, a sandwich with extra onions — wasn't that was Lisa had ordered for her mother that day? Some kind of club sandwich with extra onions? Maybe she should start picking up that club sandwich for Colleen Bellow on her way home from work. Maybe she would leave it at her front door so she wouldn't have to have the conversation, the one where she was told again and again that no, she did not understand. Or perhaps Colleen Bellow had only said this once but the echo of it had continued unabated.

After a few minutes Claire pulled from the lot. The coffee was still undrinkably hot but it definitely smelled good, potent, and she almost felt like she was drinking it even though she was only smelling it.

She pulled up in front of the assigned house and was aware of bumping over the sloped curve onto the grass of the front yard, but only a tiny bit, a few inches at most, and it was the kind of thing that might have been intentional, a courtesy to passing traffic. There was no one standing around the yard anymore, and she walked to the front porch where two high school boys sat on white wicker chairs, looking at their phones. One of the boys was short and blond and had a cigarette. The other boy was Logan Boone. She had not seem him in at least five years but there was no mistaking him, his shock of ginger hair. She stood at the bottom of the porch stairs — there were only seven or eight steps, but there might as well have been a thousand. She was one-hundred-percent certain her legs would not support her bid for the top.

"Is this the eighth-grade party?" she asked, her head titled up at the boys. She was startled by the sound of her own voice, which sounded louder and more judgmental than she had intended.

"Yeah," the blond boy said, not looking up from his phone. "They're all inside. We're protecting them from zombies."

Logan Boone laughed and set his phone on the table between them. "We're the hired help," he said. His voice was very deep. He didn't look like a teenager, not like Evan and his friends. He looked like a man. He looked sturdy. He looked like a man who would fix her car or check her electric meter. What did that even mean? She had no idea. Was she drunk? Or was she just surprised? Her heart was hammering.

She did not think he recognized her.

"Who's your daughter?" the blond boy asked. "I can go get her."

"Meredith," she said. "Oliver."

"Meredith Oliver, princess of darkness."

"That's the one," she said.

"They're all that one," Logan said.

The blond boy stood and stepped on his cigarette and went inside the house. Was she not allowed inside the house? What was happening inside the house? She stayed at the bottom of the stairs, silent.

"They're watching scary movies in the dark," Logan said. Had she asked her question aloud? "There're about fifty of 'em all over the floor. Believe me, you don't want to go in there. Can't see a thing."

"Okay," she said. "Thanks for the tip."

She thought she might sit down on the porch steps to wait, but then she would have to turn her back to him and that seemed rude. Then he stood up. He was tall, well over six feet. He walked slowly down the stairs. "I think you were my dentist," he said, reaching the bottom step. "A long time ago."

"Is that right?" she asked. "Well, it's certainly possible." He smelled like cigarettes and she recalled vividly the smell of cigarettes in an embrace, her nose pressed against the white cotton shirt of a smoker.

What smoker? When? College? High school? She took her phone out of her purse. "I think I'll just text her and tell her I'm out here."

She started through her contact list and the phone slipped from her fingers and landed on the stone walk. It broke apart and the battery went flying into the dark lawn.

"Oh no," she said. "Oh, wow. Oh, no."

"I'll find it," Logan said. He crouched down and started brushing through the tall grass. "Happens to me all the time. Every time I drop it the battery goes flying somewhere. Once in a pool."

"Was it ruined?"

"Oh yeah. Big time."

He was on his knees in the grass, sweeping his arm across the dark blades in wide arcs, and then he crawled away from her into the blackness and vanished. Somehow he was just gone, abruptly, into a place where the porch light could not reach. She felt weak. She felt like something terrible was about to happen to her, like he might not return from the darkness, and then she might never get home. She was Meredith with her cheek pressed to the cold floor and the man standing over her. And then she was Lisa Bellow, kneeling, standing, walking, stepping from the restaurant into the afternoon, and then into the car, and then, and then, and then.

"Here you go," Logan said, on his feet now, materializing ghost-like from the dark yard and back into the glow from the porch. *Only a step from total darkness into light,* she thought. *Only one step. Only half a step. Only an inch. Only a millimeter.* He held out his hand and she took the battery from him.

"Thank you," she said.

"Are you okay?" he asked.

"I'm fine," she said. "I'm just really tired. I've had a long day."

He smiled. "Halloween must be a tough day for dentists."

"Oh, you know it," she said, forcing a smile in return.

"Well let me know if you need a ride home," he said. "We're here to help out."

"Are you a babysitter or something?"

"Abby's my cousin," he said. "I'm just helping look after everyone, keep everybody out of trouble."

"The adults, too," she said. "Apparently."

"Sure," he said. "I mean, whoever."

The door opened and the blond boy emerged with a girl who might have been Meredith. The girl had a white face and bright red lips and a bloody tear on her cheek. "I found her," the blond boy said. "One princess of darkness, only slightly traumatized."

"Thanks," Claire said.

The girl who might have been Meredith was walking down the stairs toward her. How would she know if she'd gotten the right girl, the one she'd come for? Would Logan know?

"See ya, Meredith," Logan said.

"See ya, Logan," Meredith said.

"Thank you," Claire said to him. "Thank you for fixing my phone. Or for finding it. Or, you know."

She and Meredith walked to the car in silence. She tried to walk carefully but not too carefully, evenly but not too evenly. The last thing she wanted was to stumble, but she also didn't want to look like she was trying not to stumble. By the time she got in on the driver's side Meredith was already seat-belted in and had her head leaning against the window, looking back at the house. Claire turned the car on, then promptly turned it off again. She rolled down her window and took a deep breath. She would sit for a few minutes in the fresh air. She would sit and enjoy her cup of coffee from the Deli Barn. She would —

"What are you doing?" Meredith asked.

"It's nice out. I thought we might just sit for a minute." She picked up the coffee and took a sip. "How was the party?"

Meredith stared at her. The bloody tear on her cheek was smudged, and some of the white face paint beside it partially rubbed away. Had someone touched her face?

"Your face is smudged," Claire said.

Meredith reached up to flip open the mirror on the sun visor. Something jangled on her wrist. It was a silver chain bracelet. Claire reached out for it and Meredith snatched her hand away.

"It's pretty," Claire said. "I just wanted to see."

"You can buy one," Meredith said. "They're five dollars. You can buy your own. It all goes to charity."

"What charity?"

"Mrs. Bellow."

Claire took another sip of the coffee. She was fine. Everything was fine.

"Mrs. Bellow isn't a charity," she said.

"She is now," Meredith said.

15

It was supposed to be an eighth-grade party, exclusively, but it wasn't like Abby Luckett's parents were paying attention to every single person who showed up in their front yard, so there were a handful of high school kids there, some invited, some not. Abby's brother and cousin, the one her mother had looked ready to plant a wet kiss on for fixing her phone, were in high school, obviously, but they were the ones who were supposedly in charge while Abby's parents sat in their bedroom watching porn and fooling around. Or at least that was what Abby said they were doing. But there were other high school kids, too, mostly freshman boys who'd come for the rumor of smuggled-in beer and eager girls, and including the lax bro who Meredith found in a corner of the stuffy, noisy basement with Becca, passing a tall skinny can of beer between them.

"Want some?" the lax bro said, holding it

out to her.

"I'm okay," she said. This was a Life Lesson from Evan, something he'd taught her last year but which she had not had occasion to use until tonight. When someone asked her to do something she didn't want to do, for whatever reason, she should say "I'm okay." Not "No thanks" or "I'm not really into that" or, god forbid, "My parents won't let me," or anything else suggesting fear or naiveté. Just plain and simple, "I'm okay." Evan claimed this would get her through 75 percent of awkward teenage situations.

"More for us," the lax bro said, passing the can to Becca.

"This is Jeremy," Becca said. "Jeremy, Meredith."

"The famous Meredith," Jeremy said. "How does it feel to be famous? Have you sold your movie rights yet?"

"Jeremy is Lisa's boyfriend," Becca explained, which Meredith already knew because she'd seen his picture in Lisa's locker and also in Lisa's room. He looked smaller in person than in his pictures, and considerably less gorgeous than his beach Frisbee photo. He wore no costume or makeup. Most of the kids had a bloody scar or two on their faces and a couple of the boys had masks or fangs. Meredith had gone for the all-white face paint, bright red lipstick, and a single bloody teardrop, because that's what Becca and Amanda and Abby were doing. Zombie chic, they called it.

"*Was* Lisa's boyfriend," Jeremy said, his words sliding together, connected like cursive. He looked squarely at Meredith. "We know she's dead. Me and Becca know. Everybody else is pretending. Coming up with these crazy shit stories. Making themselves feel better, I guess. What do you do to make yourself feel better?"

"I don't know," she said. "Nothing."

He leaned into her. "You must do something," he said. She felt his breath hot on her face and she thought of Lisa, her quivering lips, her panting. "You tell yourself any crazy stories, Meredith?"

He was drunk, or something like it. The embarrassing truth was she didn't really know what a drunk person looked and sounded like. Once, at a family wedding, her parents were on the dance floor flinging their bodies around like total maniacs to the song "Footloose," and her mother had kicked off her high heels so wildly that one had flown into someone's table and shattered a wineglass and her father had actually fallen onto the dance floor laughing. She still wasn't sure, looking back on that night, if they'd been drunk or just really, really happy. But she knew she had never, except on TV, heard someone slur their words like Jeremy was doing right now. There was a part of it that seemed fake, like he, too, had only seen drunk people on TV.

"Nobody ever comes back after this long," Jeremy said, slouching into his chosen corner. "Cops are desperate. They show you that picture? The mystery dude nobody recognized? Turns out that guy was some guy from Starbucks. Just some guy she talked to one day. She'd talk to anybody."

"Anybody'd talk to her, more like it," Becca said.

"Cops are pathetic," Jeremy said. "Searched my room. Searched my fucking locker. Why don't they just start digging?"

"Where, genius?" Becca asked. "You can't dig up the whole world. She could be anywhere."

They were very matter-of-fact about it, Meredith thought, especially considering they were the people who were supposedly closest to Lisa. What would Lisa say to them, these two? What would Lisa say, sitting in her bathtub, to know that they had given up on her?

"Meredith was the last person to see her alive," Becca said. "Except for the guy who did it."

"That's so weird," Jeremy said. He stared at her. "Meredith, isn't that weird? You were the last person to ever see her. The last person. Ever."

"Except the guy," Becca said again. "He was the very last."

"You were the last friendly face she saw," Jeremy said wistfully. He studied the beer can in his hand for a moment, then looked again at her. "Are you sure you don't want some of this?"

"I'm okay," she said.

He shrugged, apparently shrugging off his melancholy as well. "You know what she'd want? Do you girls know what she'd want? She'd want us all to have a good time. She wouldn't want us sitting around feeling sorry for ourselves. She'd say, 'Go on and live a little.' "

He detached himself from the corner and wobbled off into the party.

"That's totally not what she'd want," Becca said, rolling her eyes. "He didn't know her very well."

"How long did they go out?" Meredith asked.

"Since last spring. He's such a dick. She

was about to break up with him. They were about half broken up already. It's not like he needs an excuse to get drunk. He just likes to add some drama to it. He's very tortured."

"I can see that," Meredith said. Across the room Jeremy was talking to Missy Carmody, a *seventh*-grader, a well-known desperate wannabe. Missy took the beer can from Jeremy and smelled the opening before taking a swallow. The outlook was bleak for Missy Carmody.

Meredith turned to Becca. "What would she want?"

"What?"

"You said it wasn't what Lisa would want. What do you think she'd want?"

"Oh, she'd want some moping," Becca said. She was quiet for a minute. Then she said, "I don't mean that in a bad way. I think most people would want some moping. Wouldn't you?"

"Sure," Meredith said. She imagined herself gone. Really gone. Body and spirit. Her desk vacant, her bed empty. How long would the moping last? Who would mourn her most?

"There was this thing we used to do," Becca said. "Lisa and me. We'd take her dogs out really late, like after midnight. We'd

walk around her neighborhood and everywhere there were lights on we'd try to guess
what the people were doing inside. Sometimes it was obvious because you could see
the TV, and once we saw shadows of people
making out. But usually you couldn't see
anything, just the light behind the curtains,
and so we'd make up stories. Lisa was really
good at it. Her stories were *crazy.*"

"That sounds fun," Meredith said.

"It was," Becca said, and for the first time
Meredith thought, *She was her friend, her
best friend. She was . . .*

"It was fun," Becca said. "But it was also
kind of sad sometimes. You know? 'Cause
it . . ." She trailed off, her eyes moving to
the basement stairs. "Loser alert," she said,
smirking. "Who invited them?"

It was a group of five or six nerdy eighth-
grade boys, including Steven Overbeck, who
despite what Meredith thought were good
looks were not good enough looks to overcome his nerdy status. At the end of the day
even the handsomest nerd ranked lower
than a boy who was ugly but cool. At the
end of the day, for the guys, physical appearance had almost nothing to do with
popularity.

"I'm surprised they stay up this late,"
Becca said.

"I'm surprised they're not trick-or-treating," Meredith said.

Becca laughed. The boys were lingering around the Ping-Pong table, cheering on a ninth-grade match, trying to look like they fit in. Meredith accidentally caught Steven's eye and he smiled and nodded at her, raised his Sprite in greeting.

"Do you know him?" Becca asked.

"He sits behind me in social studies," Meredith said.

"He's like nine," Becca said. "Once in English last year he asked if he could draw a watch on me. A watch. Is that the weirdest thing you've ever heard?"

Which watch? Meredith wondered. The watch with the springs sticking out? The one with monkey paws for hands?

"It's pretty weird," she said.

"Can you move your legs?" Lisa said. Even though it was a question, she didn't ask it. It was the kind of question your mother said: "Can you set the table." "Will you get the door."

Meredith pulled up and sat with her legs crossed. She actually liked sitting like this under normal circumstances, often sat in this position (*Indian* style, her father called it, until she informed him this was offensive)

368

on the floor while playing battling animals with Evan or hanging out with her friends. Of course the bathtub wasn't as comfortable as her bedroom floor, not nearly wide enough for crisscross-applesauce, so her knees were both pressed against the porcelain sides, and since she was sitting a little cockamamie already so as to avoid the spigot . . .

"I'm *tired,*" Lisa said, drawing out the word so that it sounded like a sickness. "Are you tired?"

"What time is it?"

"What time isn't it?" Lisa asked.

"It isn't time for social studies," Meredith said. "It isn't time for English. It isn't time for —"

Lisa drew another hash mark on the shower wall under the word BITCH.

"For what?" Meredith asked.

"For you being a bitch. All I asked was what time isn't it?"

"I don't think that's worthy of a bitch mark."

"What are you even *doing* here?" Lisa asked abruptly, a sour look on her face.

"What do you mean, what am I *doing* here?"

"I mean what are you *doing* here? In this place. It's not like he needs you for anything.

It's not like —" She stopped midsentence. She rubbed at her nose and then her eyes. She looked like she was getting a cold.

"What?" Meredith asked.

"Nothing." Lisa closed her eyes and rubbed a spot between them, like she had a sinus headache. "Forget it. Never mind."

"No, what? It's not like *what*?"

"I'm sorry, but I just don't understand the purpose of you," Lisa said, her eyes still shut, her lips twisted into a grimace. "What's the *purpose* of you?"

"I don't know. I guess . . . company?"

Lisa stopped rubbing the spot and opened her eyes. She stared at Meredith for five long seconds. Then she made another mark on the wall.

"What?" Meredith asked. "What was that for?"

"For company . . ." Lisa said, mocking her. It wasn't how Meredith had said it at all. She couldn't understand how Lisa could have heard it that way.

"I just —" she started.

"Look, it's my pen, so I get to make the marks."

What did the man think of the marks on the shower wall? It was a Sharpie — a permanent marker — that Lisa was using. Why had Meredith not considered this before? It wasn't like those marks were ever going to go away. They couldn't just wipe them off with a towel. How long had it been since the man had taken a shower anyway? Was it possible there was another shower in the house? Or maybe that he showered at work?

"What do you think his job is?" she asked Lisa.

"Who?"

As if there were any other *his*, any other *who*.

"His." A gesture with her head toward the rest of the apartment.

"Oh, he works at a store," Lisa said. "He works at Best Buy."

"How do you know?"

Lisa sneezed. She didn't have one of those cute, tiny, guinea-pig sneezes. She sneezed like an adult, a full body affair.

"Gimme me some toilet paper," she said.

Meredith pulled some off the roll that was sitting on the edge of the tub. Long ago they'd dispensed with putting it on the roller. They used it as napkins and Kleenex.

"So how do you know?" Meredith asked.

Lisa wiped her nose and tossed the wad of toilet paper in the direction of the wastebasket. "Know what?"

"That he works at Best Buy."

"Oh, he told me. He told me he could maybe get us a TV for in here."

"For in here? Where could we even put a TV?"

"We could mount it," Lisa said, annoyed. "We could like . . . I don't know. We'll figure it out."

"Maybe he could get you a phone instead," Meredith said. "You know? Maybe you should ask for that, since he's feeling generous."

"Maybe . . ." Lisa said absently, totally missing the joke, the point. Did Lisa even want a phone? Meredith wondered. Did she even want to call for help? Or would she rather just watch television?

Lisa shifted again and kicked her in the shin. Meredith stood up.

"Don't get up," Lisa said, no longer absent.

"I have to pee."

It was weird how it was no big deal, peeing in front of Lisa. It wasn't like being in the locker room at all, or even at a sleepover. She never thought in her whole life that she'd be able to pee in front of someone else, but now she did it without even thinking, sat on the toilet without shame, as if she were by herself. She pulled up her leggings and washed her hands in the small sink. She looked at herself in the mirror and her reflection reminded her of a game she used to play at home, before . . . before this. Well not a game, really — something like a game. Something she would say to herself.

This is —

"Why'd you just lie there?" Lisa asked from behind her.

Meredith blinked at the face in the mirror. *This is?*

"Meredith. Why'd you just lie there?"

She turned. "What?"

Lisa was staring at her. They looked at each other in silence for what seemed like forever. Meredith was afraid. Of what? She couldn't figure it out. Only that it seemed like if she spoke, everything might change.

Finally Lisa spoke.

"Bring me a cup of water?" she asked. "I'm dying of thirst. I think I'm getting a cold."

"You don't look very good," Meredith said. Too late she realized this comment would surely get her a mark on the wall, but the pen was limp in Lisa's hand.

"I don't feel very good," Lisa said.

Meredith filled a Dixie cup with water and stepped back into the tub.

Upstairs, in the Lucketts' dining room,

Amanda and Abby were sitting at the head of the table selling Lisa Bellow Chain of Support bracelets for five dollars. There was a line of about twenty zombies waiting to claim theirs.

"You guys!" Abby said, when Meredith and Becca squeezed in behind them. "We've been working like dogs. Are you gonna help or what?"

"Sure," Meredith said. "Let me take a shift."

"No, it's *fine,*" Abby said. "I'll keep doing it." She smiled as she turned to her next customer.

"This is sort of gross," Becca said as they walked toward the living room. "I think they're enjoying themselves."

"They're your friends," Meredith said.

"Eh," Becca said, shrugging.

In the living room a movie was playing on the flat-screen on the wall. Bodies were splayed out on the living-room floor, some piled like puppies. How many people were even at this party? Meredith wondered. She didn't recognize half of them. She and Becca sat down in the corner. On the TV screen a man dressed as a clown was applying bright red lipstick to his eyebrows.

"It's good, though," Meredith said. "It's good to support Lisa's mom, right?"

"Lisa hated her mother," Becca said.

"She did?"

"God, yes, she was always tearing her down. She complained about her constantly, made fun of her, sometimes right to her face. Seriously, she said terrible things about her all the time."

"Don't you say terrible things about your mother?"

"My mother has enough on her plate," Becca said. "She's about to have a baby, because my sister's about to have a baby. My mother already works all day and takes care of my father. I don't think she needs me saying terrible things about her on top of all that."

Meredith looked at the TV screen. A girl was running through an empty hospital, her hair swinging behind her. She didn't have any shoes on. She was running down a dark corridor, and then she turned a corner and there was the clown, and everyone in the living room screamed as the clown thrust a barbecue skewer through the girl's throat.

"This movie sucks," Becca said.

Meredith did not look behind her. She did not like to look behind her, not anymore, not even when someone was calling her name, or when there were footsteps, or like now, this November afternoon, when she could hear clearly the sound of a car following slowly, the crunch of tires, slow moving tires, on the brittle leaves that covered the street. She gripped the straps of her backpack and increased her pace, not running, but walking as fast as she could without breaking into a trot. To look behind was to acknowledge that there was something there. The police? Her parents? A face from the books of men who might take her? They were all the same in this moment, something to be ignored, or outrun.

"Meredith?" a voice called.

Still, she did not stop, not recognizing the voice, and then the car pulled even with her and then a little bit ahead of her so there was no way to not see the face leaning out the driver's side window, the smiling, hopeful face of Mrs. Bellow.

"Hi, Meredith."

She stopped walking. She was breathless but tried to pretend otherwise.

"Hey," she said.

"Do you need a ride?"

"No," she said. "My house —" she gestured in the general direction — "just a few blocks."

"It's cold," Mrs. Bellow said. "I'm just coming from work. Let me take you?"

Meredith looked down the road. She could nearly see her street, but not quite. She looked back at Mrs. Bellow, smiling her hopeful smile. "Okay," she said. "Sure."

She walked around the front of the car and got into the passenger seat, cradling her backpack on her lap.

"I'm working mornings now," Mrs. Bellow said, turning in her seat to face Meredith, not driving nor, seemingly, preparing to drive. "So if you girls want to come over after school, I'll be there."

"Great," Meredith said. "I'll . . . I'll tell them."

"How was school today?"

"Fine," Meredith said. "You know. All right."

The car was idling. It was an old car, and the noise of the engine rose and fell as it idled, as if it didn't understand what it was supposed to do. A car passed them, then another.

"Who'd you have lunch with?" Mrs. Bellow asked.

"Becca. And Abby and Amanda."

"Good. They're nice girls. I'm glad you all are friends."

"Yeah," Meredith said.

"Did you have any tests or anything?"

"We had a test in social studies," Meredith said.

"That was Lisa's favorite," Mrs. Bellow said. "From way back. She loved learning about other places. I always felt bad that we didn't have enough money to travel in the summer. Or I was always working. Or something."

"You will," Meredith said. "I mean, someday you can travel. You and Lisa."

"I think so, too. I'm thinking Spain. Right? Get a couple cute little bikinis to wear on the beach. Find some cute guys."

"Sure." Meredith could picture this easily, Lisa and her mother and some hot guys on a sunny beach in Spain. But then she remembered what Becca had said about Lisa ripping on her mother, and so she imagined that, in Spain, Lisa and the hot guys might ditch Mrs. Bellow at the hotel and go to the beach without her.

"Do you have a boyfriend?" Mrs. Bellow asked.

"No."

"Do you like anyone? Do you have a secret crush?"

She could tell that Mrs. Bellow really, really wanted her to have a secret crush. She thought of what Lisa had said about the boy in the high school yearbook, the boy who became her father. Had that boy been her mother's secret crush once? Had she imagined their wedding, their honeymoon, their babies? Did the high school Mrs. Bellow imagine the way the boy would touch her? Meredith thought of Steven Overbeck, his watches, how his fingers had felt on the inside of her wrist, how Becca had laughed at him at the party. One day Steven Overbeck would be a boy in the high school yearbook. Would she point to his picture?

"Lisa has a boyfriend," Mrs. Bellow said. "Do you know him?"

"I've met him," Meredith said.

"I've had pretty bad luck with men," Mrs. Bellow said. "That's the truth. A couple years ago I dated this guy, a real creep. He called me last week and said he'd heard about Lisa. I didn't like the way he said it. It wasn't like he was calling to say he was sorry. It was like there was some other reason he wanted me to know that he knew. I called the police and they went to his house. They said they didn't see anything unusual. They said he just had a house full of cats." She paused. "Don't you think that's unusual? A house full of cats? It's not like he's an old lady."

"Yeah, that's kinda weird."

"Anyway. I have a great guy now. Knock

wood he doesn't take off. I don't think he will. Of course, I've thought that before." She half-smiled at Meredith, and Meredith understood why Lisa hated her, and also why Lisa always brought her a sandwich from Deli Barn and left it in the fridge.

"I have a lot of homework to do," Meredith said.

Mrs. Bellow started driving, but instead of going straight at the stop sign she turned left. Meredith didn't say anything. She wasn't sure if Mrs. Bellow was lost or if she was just taking a different way or . . . or what?

"Peter," she said. "That's the man I'm seeing." She sneaked a look over at Meredith. "He thinks Lisa might have run away. He thinks maybe she went to one of those places we always talked about going. Spain. Brazil."

"Why would she do that?"

"I don't know. I mean, I do know. She wouldn't. She wouldn't do that."

"Some other people are saying that, too," Meredith said. "But I don't think so either."

"Of course not," Mrs. Bellow said. "We know she wouldn't do that. The police asked me about it. They said they had to ask me about it because she did it once before, ran off. Just for like twenty-four hours, but I called the police, so they have a record of it. She was twelve. It was when I was with that man, the one with the cats. I got up in the morning and her bed was empty."

"Where was she?"

"A friend's house. In the city. Some girl I didn't even know. Some girl she'd met online. She told the girl's parents that I knew where she was, but I didn't. And she knew I didn't. She stayed there the whole day, too. A whole night and a whole day. She was trying to scare me. She was twelve. She was only twelve then. She wasn't very smart."

"But you don't think she ran away, right?" Meredith asked. "I mean this time."

"I know she didn't. Because when she came back that time, and she saw how I was — I was a hot mess — she promised she would never do it again. And she wouldn't. She wouldn't do that to me. She wouldn't do that to me because she knows that I would die without her. So she wouldn't do it."

"I don't think she would either," Meredith said. She looked out the window. A group of four little kids, maybe kindergarteners, were walking in a line down the sidewalk, a mother and a beagle bringing up the rear.

"You know her," Mrs. Bellow said. "That's not who she is. I'm not saying I'm perfect. I'm not saying she's perfect. I'm just saying that's not who she is."

The next day when she came home from school the house was quiet and Meredith thought she was alone. She went up to her room to change and from the window saw Evan in the backyard. He was throwing a ball underhanded up in the air and then trying to catch it. It was a game a four-year-old might play. He wasn't even throwing it that high — maybe ten or fifteen feet — but she could tell he was trying to spin it so that it didn't drop straight into his glove. She stood in the corner of the window and peered through the curtain so he wouldn't see her. He missed three in a row before he caught one. After the catch, he threw the ball up only about five feet, a couple times, and one he caught and one glanced off the heel of his glove. Then he threw one really high, circled under it, looking confident.

The ball landed about six feet to his left.

She stepped away from the window. She changed her clothes and sat down on her bed and started reading. They were finishing *All Quiet on the Western Front*. They'd been reading it all fall, it seemed. The teacher kept reminding them how young the boy was — only nineteen — but that didn't seem so young to Meredith.

Evan stuck his head into her room.

"He dies," he said.

"You mentioned that already," she said. She closed the book but kept her finger in it. "What're you doing?"

"Nothing. Working out."

"How's it going?"

"Good," he said. "It's going good."

"Good," she said.

He walked to the window. He had to know she had seen him now. He turned.

"How're the cool kids?"

"They're fine."

"You blowing off the not-cool kids?" He was pissed. He was pissed because she had seen him miss ball after ball.

"It's not like that," she said. "I —"

"What's it like, then?"

"It's like I have a life that's none of your business. Just like you have a life that is none of my business. You don't see me telling you what to do."

"You want to tell me what to do?"

"No," she said. "Not particularly."

"Sure you do," he said. "Go ahead. Go on and tell me. You think you know what I should do? You think I can't catch pop flies?

Think I should hang it up? Think I should apply to college and just forget about baseball? Or maybe I could be the trainer, or the equipment guy. Maybe I could put all the batting helmets into the dugout cubbies."

"I never said any of that."

"What is it with you? Suddenly Lisa Bellow is like your BFF just because you were almost kidnapped with her? Suddenly you're tight with her friends and chilling at her house and drinking beer with her lax bro."

"I didn't drink beer with her lax bro."

He shrugged, as if to say that was not how he had heard it.

"You don't know anything about it," she said. She wanted to say, *You know who was drunk that night? Mom.*" She wanted to say, *"The lax bro is a total asshole who didn't deserve Lisa."* She wanted to say, *"I am drowning, I am drowning, I am drowning in a bathtub."*

Instead, she said, "Why don't you go back outside and miss some more pop flies?"

He looked at her book. "Hey, guess what? George kills Lenny in *Of Mice and Men*. The Great Gatsby gets shot in his pool. Hamlet dies. Romeo and Juliet die. Christopher's father killed the dog. The dude at the end of *1984* gets eaten by rats. There's your reading for the next two years, spoiled."

"That's not spoiled," she said. "Everybody dies. That's not a spoiler."

"My mother screwed up her life a thousand ways from Sunday," Lisa said. "And she just keeps screwing it up a thousand ways more. She has this boyfriend, oh my god, he's so lame. She really knows how to pick 'em."

"My mother thinks she knows everything," Meredith said.

"If she knows everything, why are we still sitting in this apartment? If she's so smart?"

"She just thinks she's smart," Meredith said. "She actually knows literally nothing about anything."

"Mothers think they know things because guess what — they were our age once, too! My mother's always saying that to me. When she was my age my mother didn't even have a cell phone. Her internet only worked when it was plugged into the phone. A *landline.* But because she was once fourteen years old she thinks she knows everything about being fourteen years old."

"You know who else was fourteen years old once?" Meredith said. "Queen Elizabeth. And Jesus' mother. And Laura Ingalls Wilder."

Lisa laughed. "Who the hell is Laura Ingalls Wilder? Did you make that up?"

"No, I didn't make it up. She wrote all those *Little House on the Prairie* books."

"Oh, yeah — wait — that was a TV show, right?"

"Yeah," Meredith said. "The TV show was based on the books."

"I used to watch that when I was home sick from school. Oh my god, my mother *loved* that show."

"Laura and Mary and Pa and everything," Meredith said. "And something terrible always happened to somebody. There was always some fire or somebody was trampled by a horse or —"

"Who was the blind one? Mary? Oh my god, my mom loved Mary. She said if Mary could become a teacher then anything was possible. She talked about her like she was a real person."

"She was a real person," Meredith said.

"Right, okay, but whatever, you know what I mean. Like she was a *real* real person. She used to always say . . ." Lisa trailed off and looked past Meredith, looked right through the shower wall into her own living room, Meredith thought, the way she'd been able not so long ago to sit at the kitchen table and look through the fireplace and see her mother sitting in the living room on the other side.

"They think they're so smart," Meredith said. "Mothers. They think they can just . . . what's wrong?"

A thin line of blood was running from Lisa's left nostril. It dribbled over her lip and down her chin and onto her blouse. Meredith grabbed the roll of toilet paper, tore off a wad and passed it to Lisa. Lisa tilted her head back against the tile and held the toilet paper to her face.

"What's wrong?" Meredith asked.

"Don't know," Lisa said. She shifted to change her position and kicked Meredith hard in the ball of the ankle, at the point where her legs crossed. "Can you move over a little more?"

"There's no place to move," Meredith said. She started to get up. "You want —"

"No!" Lisa said. "Don't get out. Just, can you move like a tiny bit over that way? There. Okay. Just right there. That's good."

Lisa pressed the bloody wad of toilet paper against her nose. The toilet paper was the super-cheap kind, so thin you could literally see through it. It was already falling apart in Lisa's hand, pieces of it sticking to her upper lip.

"I think it's slowing down," she said.

It didn't look like it was slowing down.

"I think it's almost stopped."

Meredith was now sitting on her own feet. After about five minutes she couldn't even feel them anymore.

16

Claire's father called to say that he and Nancy wanted to come for Thanksgiving. He promised they wouldn't be in the way. They didn't require anything. They didn't even care if they were fed. They would fly in and stay at a nearby hotel (they always did), just for a couple days, but they'd been worried sick about everyone. They were trying not to intrude, but they wanted to see Meredith. They just wanted to put their eyes on her, her father said. Claire could understand that, couldn't she?

Yes, she could understand that.

An impossible amount of time had passed. Lisa Bellow was still missing. Meredith Oliver, also among the missing, though her body still occupied the bed down the hall. Leads in both disappearances had gone cold with the weather. Meredith had replaced her gladiator sandals with some equally awful boots that all those girls, Lisa's friends, wore, and every day Meredith walked out into the cold and Claire watched from the window until her daughter's body was out of sight.

She saw Colleen Bellow on television, on a national talk show. She wore a thin blouse and the hollow of her throat was a cavern, her shoulders knobs.

"Somebody has to know something," Colleen said. She must have said it ten times, facing the host, facing the camera, facing the studio audience. She said it like a plea, a prayer.

Yes, Claire thought. Colleen Bellow was right. Somebody knew something. Somebody had always known something. But clearly, six weeks in, that fact hadn't made any difference. Among those who knew something, choices had been made. Perhaps even promises. Secrets were deepening, taking root. Lives moved forward, days became nights became days, for anyone who knew, for one man, at least, and maybe for a tight web of people around him — a friend, a wife, a mother, a brother. Life continued for all of them, and every day the secret became more stitched in, inextricable — not comfortable, perhaps, but an increasingly acceptable level of discomfort. They did their jobs. They shopped for groceries. They went to the movies. It was life, again, still. So why tell now? Why risk everything? Why, in fact, risk anything? Maybe someone who knew had even watched Colleen Bellow on television, listened to her pleas, thought these things. It was not like telling could help. It was not like telling could bring the girl back. It was not like telling could change what, however regrettably, had happened to her.

Claire had not seen Colleen Bellow in person since that afternoon at her house. Meredith had been over there after school several times since, but Claire always asked Evan to fetch her. Evan excelled at awkward situations — he'd inherited this from his father, clearly, the ability to effortlessly put people at ease, set a comfortable tone. Good old whistling Evan, with his winning smile; one day he would make some woman the envy of her friends, make her miserable by being so perfect. Plus, the added bonus, the talent that set him a cut above even his father: Evan was good at rescuing Meredith.

Except. Except. Things had been oddly cool between her children for the last couple weeks. The deeper Evan folded himself back into baseball, the deeper Meredith folded herself . . . where? Somewhere Claire could not see. It was the new friends, yes, and it was Colleen Bellow, but there was somewhere else, too, somewhere else she was going in all that silence. Twice a week Meredith went to see Dr. Moon and came out looking tired and annoyed — though, to be fair, these days Meredith looked tired and annoyed no matter where she was. When Claire requested an update, Dr. Moon said, "She doesn't say a lot. But sometimes what she doesn't say is as important as what she does say," which sounded to Claire like a load of bullshit. She tried to imagine getting away with that degree of bullshit in her own treatment. How easy to be a therapist, the evidence of your failures always obscured! No rotting teeth, no abscess, no —

"Let's find a new doctor, then," Mark said. "There have to be good therapists in the world. They can't all be terrible."

"Fine," she said. "Ask around. Be my guest."

She knew he'd do nothing. Mark considered himself inept at such things, and so he was inept at such things. Give the man a shopping list and he'd make all your dreams come true. Ask him to find a new psychiatrist for your daughter and he'd dance around the edges of the job for a week before declaring himself unable to complete the task. It would fall to her. So why even waste the effort of pretending?

But the thought of finding a new therapist, all by herself, was exhausting. She needed to be patient, she reminded herself. It had only been six weeks. There was no magic wand, no miracle cure. Not to mention, she wouldn't expect Dr. Moon to know how to fill a tooth, so wasn't it gross arrogance to presume that she, only the mother, knew better than he how to counsel a trauma victim? She'd turned it over in her head a thousand times, and always wound up back at the same place: be patient. Let people do their jobs.

"I'm buying extra wine," Mark said. Yes, there he was at his kitchen table with his beloved list and his special list-making pen, his weapons of choice. "I'm buying wine for twelve."

She could not imagine drinking any wine. She hadn't had a drink since Halloween. Every day she did not drink made her a little less drunk in the minivan, a little less pathetic at the Deli Barn, a little less inappropriate standing at the foot of that stranger's porch with her broken phone and Logan Boone crawling through the grass looking for the lost battery. When Mark had asked her about it the next morning she had said, "It was fine. I was fine. Just *tired.*" He had nodded sympathetically, her faithful co-conspirator.

"It won't be for long," Mark said.

"What won't?"

"They're just coming for the day, right?"

"A flyby," she said. "On their way to Nancy's kids for the weekend. They don't want to intrude. I'm sure it was my father who insisted upon that. 'One day only. We shouldn't intrude. We don't want to add to their burden.' You know what he's like."

"Your mom was worse," Mark said.

"They were born that way," she said. "Both of them. Maybe that was what they had in common. A desire to not intrude. Maybe if you find someone who shares that desire then you never have to worry about intrusion again."

"Maybe. Though I guess it kind of depends on what your definition of intrusion is. If intrusion is just showing up . . ."

"Get like six bags of stuffing mix," she said, peering over his shoulder at the list. "Evan can eat four by himself."

"Got it," he said. He wrote "x6" after "stuffing."

She heard a thud on the roof, like a very heavy bird falling from a tree.

"What was that?" she asked.

"He's out there playing," Mark said. "Our stuffing man."

"What? On the roof?"

Another thud. She was already at the back door, her hand on the knob.

"Stop. Jesus, of course he's not on the roof. Jesus, Claire. He's throwing a ball onto the roof and letting it roll off. That's all."

Thud.

"He's throwing a ball onto the roof?"

"He's practicing. He throws it up there with some spin on it so he doesn't —"

"I don't care," she said. "I really don't care about the details. I could not care less about —"

Thud. A new addition to the baseball symphony.

"You were right about the pop-ups," Mark said. "They're killing him. They're impossible. And I don't think it's getting any better. He's trying all sorts of drills, making them up as he goes. I don't know . . . maybe it's a little better. But only a little."

"Think about the number of things he could do," she said. "Sports, I mean. I'm not trying to be a bitch about this, okay? I know everybody thinks I'm the world's biggest killjoy, but good god. He could swim or run or play soccer, even. Don't you think he could play soccer?"

Thud.

"Do you remember him playing soccer? Do you remember how terrible he was?"

"He was nine years old," she said. "He was —"

"Exactly," he said. "And now he's seventeen. *Seventeen.* He's a baseball player, Claire. He's been a baseball player for ten years. He can't just learn to be a soccer player now. That's not how it works. It's not what he does. It's not who he is."

"Baseball is not *who he is,*" she said. "He's lots of things. He's smart. He's funny. He could do a thousand different things really well if he put his mind to it. It's not like all his windows of opportunity have closed. He might be great at something else and not even know it yet."

Thud.

"But this is who he is right now," Mark said. "I mean, you can take it or leave it. But I don't think there's anything you can do about it."

Evan came into the kitchen and laid his mitt on the counter. His cheeks and hands were pink. The lenses of his glasses were thick with steam and he took them off and wiped them with his shirt.

"How's it going?" Mark said.

"Good," he said. "Better. Better every

day." He smiled at his mother, his face naked, open, vulnerable. Oh, she had been astonished, completely staggered, holding him in her arms for the first time. She had not been herself at all, not the Claire she'd known her whole life, pressing him against her chest, holding him for dear life, that newborn boy. She did not even recognize herself as a mother. In a two-year period her own mother had died and she had nearly left her husband and now here was this impossible thing, this *life,* all packed into this tee-ny-tiny body no bigger than a throw pillow. And so she had held him and held him and held him, through babyhood and toddlerhood and beyond, long after it was necessary, carried him to bed, carried him through supermarkets and malls and airports, carried him from the car to the house lest his toddler feet falter, and then one day — maybe he was six? maybe seven? — she had put her little boy down and never picked him up again. If only she had known that day, that time, that it was the last time. But by then she had another little life she carried around (though not in the same way, if she was being honest, never with exactly the same fervor), and one day when that life, her little girl, was six or seven she put her down and never picked her up again either. Would it be better to know that moment was *that* moment? Or was it better not knowing? Better to know, as she lowered her boy onto his SpongeBob SquarePants sheets, that she would never lift him again? Better to know, when she and her mother talked idly about the coffee they always stopped for at that diner on I-35, that it was the last conversation they would ever have?

Her father and Nancy flew in late the night before Thanksgiving and came over early in the day on Thursday. Meredith was still in bed and Evan was out for a run when Claire answered the door. They had skipped their normal June trip west — the summer had been consumed by Evan's surgeries — so she had not seen her father since the Christmas before, and watching him and Nancy slip off their winter coats in the front hall she felt it had been years, that she had lived a whole life since seeing them last, and she felt some emotion in her break ranks for a moment, as if this father might be a father to whom she could say, "Daddy, oh my god, you can't believe what I've been through . . ." But, instead, there were the typical exchanges and predictable expressions of support, her father with his one-armed hug for all and then Nancy, the stupendously loving Nancy, who surely would have hugged everyone with eight arms if only she had been born an octopus.

There was endless fussing over Evan when he returned from his run. How wonderful he looked! How handsome! The glasses were so becoming! Had he grown another six inches since they'd last seen him? Did the girls ever stop calling? He fielded the questions with ease. He seemed happy to discuss anything and everything with his grandfather and Nancy. His grandparents. They were indeed the children's grandparents and to pretend otherwise, Claire knew, was unfair to everyone involved. Nancy and her father were already married by the time Evan was born. The children called them Grandma and Grandpa, and she did not move to correct them, because there was no correction that made sense.

The hardest part was that her children, when they were young, did not understand that Nancy was not her mother, that there had been another woman, a mother, who had raised her into adulthood but died before she could meet them. The number of times she had this conversation with both children, looking at the photo album: "Who's that?" "That's my mother." "I thought Grandma was your mother." And then she would have to tell them, yet again, break the awful news of her mother's death to her children for the fiftieth time. They still forgot occasionally, even as teenagers, and sometimes asked Nancy questions about their mother as a child, and Nancy would cheerfully say, "You'll have to ask your grandfather," and Claire would mentally add, *"because your mother was raised by another woman who died before you were born, and who was not afforded the immense pleasure of knowing you, her beautiful grandchildren, whom she would have utterly cherished."*

God, she thought, death was complicated. And exhausting. And apparently it just kept on being complicated and exhausting forever, probably until you yourself died and became an exhausting complication that someone else had to constantly negotiate.

Maybe, Claire decided, standing at her kitchen counter over the dead turkey, it was possible that she was a tiny bit depressed.

"It's like my brain just *knows*," Evan said to her father at the dining-room table. He held a fist out in front of him, representing the ball. "I've done it so many times that it's hardwired. Catching's harder than hitting, but —"

"You'll get there," her father said, a medical pronouncement based on absolutely nothing of fact, because her father had never been overly concerned with facts. "It'll just take time. Like riding a bike."

Mark looked across the table at her, the merest shade of a wry smile on his lips. Even he — even *Mark* — knew that catching a baseball half-blind was absolutely nothing like riding a bike.

"When does the season start?" Nancy said. "I want to plan our trip now."

"There are some preseason games in February," Evan said.

"Baseball in the snow!" her father exclaimed. "This stuffing is tremendous."

"May I be excused?" Meredith asked flatly. She had disposed of much pretense of politeness over the last couple weeks, although the level of sourness displayed today, especially in front of her visiting grandparents, was something of a new low. She'd hardly said a word throughout the meal.

"Don't you want seconds?" Mark asked. "There's more of everything. There's loads of stuffing."

"I'm really tired," Meredith said.

"It's been a long day," Nancy said, nodding. "Full of excitement."

It had not been a long day, Claire thought,

and there had been no excitement.

"Yeah," Meredith said. "I mean, yeah. I'll be back, okay? I'm just going to lie down for like ten minutes."

She scooted her chair out and left the room, and the table fell silent, everyone slipping seamlessly into the we're-not-talking-because-we're-too-busy-eating charade. *Well,* Claire thought. *Now you've seen her. Now you've put your eyes on her. Now you know.*

"I think she looks terrific," Nancy said after a minute. "Considering everything."

"There are good days and bad days," Mark said, pouring himself another glass of wine. Claire wondered if he really thought this was true or if this was just the white-washed in-law version of things. Since it was Mark, it was entirely possible he had talked himself into believing that there were good days. She wondered which days, specifically, he had in mind.

"The poor girl," Nancy said. "The other one, I mean. What's her name?"

"Lisa," Evan said.

"Lisa. It's terrible to think what might have happened to Lisa."

"Theirs not to reason why . . ." her father said earnestly. Her father, now retired from teaching for ten-plus years, always had a line of poetry at the ready when he was without something of his own to say. She'd noticed that it had gotten worse since retirement, but he'd done it before, too. This particular "theirs not to reason why" had always been one of his go-to sentiments, an easy fallback, close enough to be relevant in most situations. Had he said it to her mother twenty years ago, after her cancer diagnosis?

"Really?" Claire said. "That's all you've got?" She made sure she was smiling when she said it so that everyone would know she was not having a nervous breakdown but was merely being funny. "Already trotting out the Longfellow? It's only six o'clock."

"It's Tennyson," Evan said with his mouth full.

"That's my boy," her father said. He pointed his fork at her. "It is Tennyson. He's been listening in class."

"See?" Claire said to Mark. "Poetry — yet another talent. Maybe he could be an English major."

When she'd finished putting away the leftovers — a job she happily accepted — Claire glanced into the living room. Mark and Evan and her father were watching a football game. Where was Nancy? She went upstairs to Meredith's room. The door was two-thirds closed but she could see Nancy in there, sitting on the corner of Meredith's bed petting the tolerant cat. Claire backed herself against the wall so she could listen without being seen.

"You're lucky to have a sweet kitty," Nancy said.

"Yeah," Meredith said. Claire could only see Meredith's feet, or the shape of them, under her blanket.

"I had a sweet kitty a long time ago, when the boys were still at home. Long, long ago. She was sweet but such a pest."

"Yeah," Meredith said.

"Once she spent the night in the car. She slipped in while we were taking out grocery bags and no one saw her. She tore up the backseat with her claws. You would have thought there was a bear in there."

"Wow," Meredith said.

A for effort, Claire thought. *Just sit on the corner of that bed forever talking about your sweet kitty. Be my guest, Grandma. Just see how far you get.* She knocked lightly on the door and stuck her head into the room.

"Anyone for pie?" she asked.

"When did you learn to cook like this?" her father asked, admiring the bite on his fork.

"My god. This pie is extraordinary."

"It's from the bakery," Claire said.

"Ah," her father said.

"Someone call the baker," Evan said. "Tell him Grandpa likes the pie."

It was silent for a moment, until Nancy said, "I always say, why spend hours and hours baking a pie when you can get something everyone loves at a bakery."

"No argument from me," Mark said.

Claire was acutely aware that Nancy had spent the last eighteen years trying to make things up to her. She could not recall a single instance in the almost two decades where this woman across the table in her festive holiday sweater had been anything but supportive and friendly, about everything from childrearing to pie buying. It seemed to Claire now that their relationship had been one long, sustained apology, which was made doubly awful by the fact that they both knew very well that there was nothing to apologize for.

"And what are you all doing tomorrow?" Nancy asked.

"I'm going shopping with my friends," Meredith said.

"You are?" Claire said. "With who?"

"With Becca."

"Becca who?"

"Becca my friend Becca. Becca Nichols. You don't need to quiz me. You just say yes." Meredith smiled tightly, to indicate that she might be cleverly playing the role of the obnoxious teenager or she might actually be the obnoxious teenager. The line between the two, the role and the reality, was no longer visible. "No questioning necessary. Just a simple yes will do."

The table was silent until Evan dramatically cleared his throat. "Let me just say, as the elder child: that's probably not the best way to get the result you want."

"I don't even know this Becca," Claire said. "I've never met her."

Meredith glared at her. "She was at Lisa's house the day you were there, so technically, yes, you have met her."

She was emboldened somehow. Could this have been brought on by her grandparents? What exactly about her father and Nancy was emboldening? Had their empty, grandparent-ly platitudes, their kitty stories and their assurances — *just like riding a bike!* — given her some kind of bizarre confidence?

"We can talk about it later," she said. "I don't think this is the time."

"Speaking of time," Nancy said. "We have had a lo-o-o-ong day. But we'll see you in the morning? I hope?"

"Probably not me," Evan said. "I'll be at the gym."

"Well, I'm not going to be the person who stands between you and your workout," her father said, standing. He shook Evan's hand, as if Evan were a man who was now making manly decisions. *Why don't you ask him about college?* Claire thought. *Why don't you ask him if he's filled out any applications? Why don't you suggest that instead of rolling a ball off the roof he spend a bit of time working on his personal statement?*

After they'd gathered their coats and left, Claire went back into the kitchen and found Evan and Meredith still sitting at the dining-room table, Evan eating pie straight from the serving plate, Meredith making designs in the remnants of her dessert with the tines of her fork.

"Well, that was embarrassing," Claire said.

"Agreed," Meredith said, not looking up from the table.

"I hear that you're angry," Claire said, bracing herself against one of the dining-room chairs for support. "Okay? I hear that. What I don't understand is why you're so angry at *me*. You talk as if —"

"I have a life, okay?" Meredith said. "I have friends. I have things to do. I have plans. I don't know why you can't accept that."

"I don't know why you think I can't accept that. All I said was that I didn't know a certain person and —"

"Becca. Her name is Becca. Becca Nichols. She's my best friend."

"Since when?" Evan asked, finishing the last bite of pie.

"Since now," Meredith said. "Since right this second. Since —"

"That's fine," Claire said. "I'm happy she's your friend. I just don't know why you —"

"Hey, let's all cool down," Mark said. He'd come in behind her and she sensed he was about to put a reassuring hand on her shoulder, so she quickly took two steps to the right. "Let's all just —"

"I don't need to cool down," she said. "I asked a perfectly reasonable question. I asked, 'With who?' I don't think that's an extraordinary thing to want to know. It's just simple common sense that —"

"Common sense!" Meredith said, slamming her fork to the table. "Like the common sense you used on Halloween when you drove drunk to pick me up?"

Claire could tell she'd been saving this up, this hoarded trump card, now so triumphantly revealed for all to see.

Meredith turned to Mark. "Did you know that, Dad? Did you know she drove drunk?"

"Your mother was not drunk," Mark said, shaking his head. "I saw her before she left. She was absolutely not drunk."

"Really? Then why was she hitting on a high school guy at the party?"

Evan laughed a bark of a laugh, so absurd was the accusation.

"For god's sake, Meredith," Claire said. "I dropped my phone. He found my battery in the dark yard."

"Well, I've never heard it called *that* before," Evan said.

Meredith turned to Evan. "It's true," she said bitterly. "It was that Logan guy. From your class. He said he knew you."

"Logan *Boone*?" Evan asked. "Ha! Mom, remember that guy? He was such a dick in grade school. Then finally somebody knocked some sense into him."

"I knocked some sense into him," Claire said. "*I* knocked some sense into him." She laughed out loud in her dining room. God, she *hated* the dining room. Once they had laid wooden train track across this table, and then they had sorted baseball cards, and then later it had been a bead-making factory, but after that . . . what? What was there to spread out, after the days of train tracks and baseball cards and plastic beads? Tax forms. Suspect books. Living wills.

"You want to go shopping?" she said to Meredith. "Go shopping. I wasn't even going to say no. That's what's so funny. Everyone always thinks I'm going to say no. Sometimes I just want to ask questions before I say yes. That's all."

"But then all the answers to your questions are no," Evan said. "So it's kind of hard to tell what you're after."

"What I'm *after*?" This was infuriating, coming from Evan of all people. "I'm not *after* anything. I have no agenda. I have no plan." She turned to Mark. "I have no *goal of the day.*"

Which was absolutely true, and now the full weight of it struck her. Was there something horribly wrong with her? Was it possible that, as it seemed in this moment, she had never actually made a decision to do anything in her life? Here, in the dining room, her daughter with the accusatory fork, her son and husband witnesses for the prosecution. The charge, simply this: she had always always always let everything be decided for her. Her only decisions, her only moments of taking charge, were spontaneous and terrible. Starting up with that man when her mother was sick. Hurting a young boy, a future finder of phones. Driving to pick up Meredith at the party when she was still drunk.

"What do you want from me?" she asked Evan. "What do you expect me to —"

"I think you're doing fine," Mark said, touching her elbow.

"Shut up," she said, yanking her arm away. "This isn't about you."

"Don't talk to him that way," Meredith said. "He hasn't done anything wrong."

"What have *I* done wrong?" she asked her daughter. "You tell me. You tell me what I've done wrong. You tell me what I'm supposed to do. You tell me how I'm supposed to make this better. Any of this. You tell me and I'll do it."

Meredith stared at her from across the table. Determination. Detachment. Silence. Claire stared back. Their game faces were set. Maybe, Claire thought, they were set for good.

"I'm sorry," Mark said to her later, in bed. "I know you're getting the brunt of this. I know she's taking it out on you."

"I can't stand to get up tomorrow and drive my father to the airport," she said. "That'll be the last straw. I just can't stand it. I'm going to tell them I'm sick and they have to take a cab."

"That's pretty harsh," he said. "They're only here for thirty-six hours."

"That's their doing," she said. "Not mine."

"I think they wanted to see Mer in the morning. You know. Breakfast or something before the plane."

"I can't stand it," she said. "I can't stand to look at their —"

"I'd do it," he said. "I'd take them. But I have Hillsboro tomorrow."

Hillsboro. Their geriatric dentistry. Last Friday of the month. It was his turn.

"I'll trade you," she said impulsively.

"That bad, huh?"

"Honestly, I swear to god, I just can't sit through that drive with the three of them. I can't do it. I'll go to Hillsboro. I don't mind. It's fine."

"Okay," he said. "If you're sure."

"I'm sure," she said. "Tell them we got our signals crossed. Make it sound like you —"

"Give me a break, kid," he said, turning off the light. "I know how to lie to your father."

17

Meredith awoke to her father gently poking her shoulder.

"Come to the airport with me?" he said. "I have to take your grandparents."

"Can I sleep? I never get to sleep in on Fridays."

"There's breakfast in it for you," he said. "Pancakes. Keep me company?"

It was not company he wanted, she knew. Her mother was already at work and Evan was probably already somewhere not catching baseballs, maybe dropped from a cliff or a helicopter or something. Her father did not want to leave her alone.

"I'll be fine here," she said. "Please."

"It would mean a lot to them," he said. "I know they'd like to spend a little more time with you."

"Then why aren't they staying for longer?"

He sat down on the edge of her bed. "They don't want to *intrude*," he said, drawing out the *ooooo* to absurd lengths.

Well, that she could appreciate. All hail to Grandma and Grandpa, who seemed to understand that all they had to do to outstay their welcome was to arrive.

Ashamed by the thought, she rolled over so she was facing away from her father. What was wrong with her? She imagined Lisa slashing another green BITCH tally up on the shower wall. But the fact was that she didn't particularly want her grandparents around. It was nothing personal. What did she want? To be left alone. To be left in her bed. To be left in her head. She might have stayed there all weekend except that, if she tried, surely everyone would decide there was really something wrong with her. So she would get up. She would eat pancakes with her grandparents and drop them off at the airport and then drive home with her father. At least there was this: after the scene last night, at least she wouldn't have to drive with her mother. She probably wouldn't even have to see her, at least until the evening. That was one thing to be thankful for on the day after Thanksgiving.

"And another," Lisa said, marking the wall. Blood had been trickling from her nose for hours, days . . . or could it even be weeks now? The rim of the bathtub was lined with wads of soggy, pink toilet paper, the small bathroom wastebasket long overflowed, its contents spilled onto the floor. Why wasn't anyone emptying the trash? Where was the man? How long had it been since they'd seen him? How long since Lisa had eaten? Or peed? Or slept?

"Can you be ready in ten minutes?" her father asked.

"Sure," she said.

"*Maybe* we'll see you at Christmas," her grandmother said.

"If not, we'll talk on the phone," her grandfather said.

They stood beside the car, shivering, while her father pulled their luggage from the back of the van.

"You take care of yourself," her grandmother said. She gathered her in for a hug and held it until Meredith felt dizzy and gently twisted free.

"See you around like a doughnut," her grandfather said. He gave her a one-armed hug. This was his specialty, the old one-armer — she and Evan had often laughed over this — as if every person he loved was a high school chum. "Tell your mom we said good-bye."

"I will," she said. She wondered why her mother wasn't here. Sometimes she felt like her mother would be happier if there were no actual people in her life, but rather just a series of tasks to complete, a checklist of root canals. This thought didn't even make her angry; it just made her feel heavy now, the weight of its sadness draped over her like one of the x-ray blankets. Alien Examination. Evan with his giant lamp. Her father wheeling down the corridor on his stool. Her mother . . . where?

She sat silently in the car with her father. They watched her grandparents negotiate the revolving doors with their rolling bags and then they were gone.

"Are we going for Christmas?" she asked.

"I don't know," he said. "You wanna go?"

She imagined the drive, her safe place, her middle seat, her brother with his iPhone, the box of car stuff, the sound of her parents' voices in the front seat. She imagined them in the van in the dark, the lights splashing on the windows. It made her feel hollow inside, the thought of all that time, all those miles, with her family.

"Not really," she said.

"I guess we'll see," he said. "I guess we'll see where everybody is. I guess we can decide at the last minute if we have to."

Her phone buzzed in her purse. A text from Becca: *r u coming? were here.*

She looked at the text for a moment, then out the window. She watched a plane's steep ascent, imagined the strangers inside, gazing down on their tiny van.

Can't come, she replied. *Family thing.*

K. I'll txt later

"What's up?" her father said. "Big plans?"

"I guess I'm just going home," she said.

"No shopping?"

"Nah. Something came up with them. I think I'm just going to crash."

"You need anything?"

"Not for crashing, no."

"Then home we go."

He turned up the radio and she knew she was safe. She trusted his silence. Unlike with her mother, there was nothing lurking under her father's silence. Sometimes Meredith wondered why they'd ever gotten married, and sometimes she wondered why they stayed married. It was two different questions, with two different answers. Or maybe two hundred different answers. How could you share your life with someone, forever, especially someone who was so different from you? If two became one, like the cheesy songs always said, what happened to what was left over?

■ ■ ■ ■

"I'm cold," Lisa said.

The skin around her eyes was pasty, and the space between her top lip and her nose was raw from the rough toilet paper. How many rolls of toilet paper remained? At some point they would surely run through it all, and then what? Meredith stood up.

"Wait," Lisa said, but not very convincingly. Meredith's knees cracked as she stretched and stepped out of the tub. She swung open the door of the cabinet below the sink. It was empty but for the crumpled corpse of a daddy longlegs. She closed the cabinet and opened the medicine chest. There were a few cellophaned Pepto-Bismol tablets and a flat tube of travel-sized toothpaste.

"I'm *freezing,*" Lisa said.

There was a single hand towel, dingy, stained, probably once yellow. Meredith pulled it off the towel rack and draped it over Lisa's middle. Even Lisa smiled at this.

"Thanks," she said. "Much better."

"Take my sweater," Meredith said.

"It's okay."

"No, really." Meredith pulled her sweater over her head and laid it across Lisa, spreading the arms carefully over Lisa's bare shoulders. Now she stood in her bra by the tub. She had nothing else to offer and Lisa's teeth were chattering.

"This is dumb," Meredith said. "I'm going to go get a blanket."

"Where?"

"Out there. On the couch."

Lisa shook her head. "No. There's not one there. I'm pretty sure."

Meredith couldn't remember. She could hardly conjure the couch in her mind. She realized that she couldn't recall the last time either she or Lisa had left the bathroom.

"It's okay," Lisa said. "Really. I'll be all right."

Meredith bent down and put her lips on Lisa's forehead. This was what her mother had always done to test for fever when she was younger. Her mother claimed the hand was a poor indicator, that only the lips could tell for sure. She and Evan had spent much of their childhood illnesses swatting their mother away. "Get a thermometer," they always said. "Please. A thermometer." And eventually she had.

"You're burning up," she told Lisa, standing. "Seriously. I'm going to get a blanket."

"Are you sure?"

"Yeah. It'll just take a sec. I'll be right back."

"Meredith?"

"What?"

"Be careful."

"He's not even out there," Meredith said. "When's the last time you heard him?"

Lisa shook her head. "I don't remember."

"Me neither," Meredith said. Still, she turned the knob quietly and eased the door open.

"Meredith?"

She turned back, exasperated. "What?"

Lisa wiped the blood from under her nose. "Thanks."

"Sure," Meredith said. "I'll be right back. It's gonna be okay."

The apartment was dark and quiet. What time was it? She couldn't see any light behind the living room curtains, so it must have been nighttime. She didn't think he was home, but to be safe she felt quietly around the couch in the dark, not wanting to turn on any lights. She recalled the blanket that was piled on Lisa's lap their first morning in the apartment. Where had that blanket gone? What had that blanket even looked like?

Well, it was obvious where she could find a blanket, even if it wasn't that one. She went back to the little hall. The bedroom door was a few inches ajar, as usual. She crept to it and pushed it open slowly. She had never been in the bedroom before, never seen more than just a slice of it.

There was a figure in the bed. She could not see it well, but there was a little light from the parking lot, and as her eyes adjusted she could see that the figure was the man. He was asleep on his back. His mouth was open. He was shirtless, and Meredith remembered that she, too, was shirtless, and as soon as she remembered this goose bumps ran across her stomach and down her arms. There was only one blanket on the bed — a royal-blue fleecy thing — and it was on the man, though only up to his waist, and thrown over him haphazardly as if by someone else. It was not tucked in. One swipe and it was hers. One swipe and she could be back in the bathroom and Lisa could be warm.

She lifted a corner of the blanket. No, not a swipe. Surely that would wake him. Gradual was better. Gradual and he wouldn't even know it. Then she could return it later, in a few hours, before he woke up.

She took a step backward and the blanket slid a few inches below his waist. He was wearing underwear, the black boxers Meredith had seen before. She stood still for a moment, then she took another step backward, then another. Every small step drew the blanket down a few more inches: past his thighs, then his knees, then his hairy blank shins. Finally, with a little lift, it was over his toes.

The man lay motionless in the bed. Maybe he was passed out drunk. Maybe that was why he was so still.

Meredith backed all the way into the hall, dragging the blue blanket, then gathered it into a soft bundle in her arms and turned to the bathroom. The door was closed.

She did not recall closing it.

She put her right hand on the doorknob and turned. The knob turned one inch and stopped. The door was locked.

"Lisa," she whispered.

No sound came from inside the bathroom. There had never been a quieter place than this apartment. It was as if the whole thing was frozen in time, a tomb, a relic. Meredith looked back into the bedroom. The feet, unmoving.

"Lisa," she said, a little bit louder. She tapped as quietly as she could with the tip of her index finger, not daring to make a fist, not daring to knock.

"Lisa. Come on."

Lisa was sick. She had lost a lot of blood. So now maybe she was unconscious, lying there in the tub, unable to move. But if that were the case, then who had locked the door?

Meredith tried the door again. Maybe it wasn't locked. Maybe it was just stuck. She gave it a shake. It rattled against its frame. Still the knob did not turn. She checked the bedroom. The feet, unmoving.

"Lisa," she said.

She shivered, pressed the blanket to her bare stomach. The apartment was as cold as a cave. She made a fist. She knocked.

"Please. Come on, Lisa. It's me."

Dinner was what her mother always called catch-as-catch-can, leftovers heaped on a plate and each person's individually microwaved. You were responsible for your own meal. They ate at the kitchen table. Meredith thought her mother looked horrendous. She looked like she'd wandered from the wreckage of a plane or something. Was this the result of last night's blowup? Where had her mother been all day anyway? Right, she remembered, the old folks' home, whatever it was called. Probably not a very happy place. But her mother didn't just look sad; she looked sick.

"Can I please spend the night at Becca's?" Meredith asked, sliding in the "please" as a favor, a peace offering, even.

"Who?" her mother asked, squinting slightly.

"Becca Nichols," Meredith said, annoyed. How was it even possible, after last night, that her mother had forgotten Becca again?

"They were supposed to go shopping," her father explained quickly. "But it didn't work out."

"Yeah," Meredith said. "So she wondered if we could do a sleepover instead."

"Maybe she could come over here," her father said.

"She invited me over there," Meredith said. "There might be other people, too."

This part was a lie. When she'd texted, Becca hadn't said anything about other people. But who knew? It was always possible there might be other people. She hadn't said there *wouldn't* be other people.

"Hey, is that Amy Nichols's sister?" Evan asked.

"Yeah," Meredith said, too late realizing why he'd asked, then trying to backtrack. "I mean, maybe. I don't know."

"She almost had her baby in the library on Wednesday. No joke. Somebody ran for the nurse. But it was a false alarm."

"Her sister's pregnant?" her father asked. "How old is she?"

"Her sister's not my friend," Meredith said. "She doesn't even really like her sister. I don't even know if that's her sister. It's a common last name."

Her parents exchanged looks across the table. Now it would come, she thought. Now it would come. *Bring it on,* she thought. *Try to tell me what I can't do. Try to tell me you know anything about me. You don't know where I spend my days. You don't want to know where I spend my days. Tell me I can't go and I'll tell you that it could have been me, should have been me, was me. Tell me I can't go and I'll tell you what he did to Lisa. Bring it.* She looked at her mother. *Bring it.*

"Fine," her mother said softly.

Her father turned to her mother, surprised. "Are you sure? We could —"

"It's fine," her mother said.

"I —" Meredith started.

"Go," her mother said, looking at her squarely. There was something wrong with her mother's eyes. It was like her mother had seen something terrible, and it had actually done something to her eyes. Suddenly Meredith wasn't sure what she should do, if she should even go to Becca's. She recalled that night after Evan's second surgery, her mother crying in the kitchen, alone. And then, unexpectedly, she pictured Lisa, shivering in the bathroom, alone.

"I don't —" she started.

Her mother looked away and shook her head. "Please," she said. "Just go."

Meredith could not stop looking at Amy Nichols's belly. She had never been so close to someone so pregnant before. It was ridiculous. It was like she was pretending to be pregnant and had stuffed a beach ball under her shirt. It didn't look like it could possibly be real, like a body could even *function* like that.

"It's kicking like crazy," she said to Meredith. "You wanna feel it?"

"I'm okay," Meredith said.

She and Becca were sitting on the couch and Amy was propped in a recliner.

"Really, it's totally cool. Come on. You should feel it."

"You should, Meredith," Becca said. "It's super weird." Her phone buzzed and she took it off the arm of the couch, glanced at it, and laid it back down.

Meredith had never felt a baby kick before. She got up and put her hand as lightly as she could on the peak of Amy's stomach. Amy grabbed her hand and moved it down six inches and Meredith felt a little thump. There was no mistaking that something was in there. In truth, it made her feel a little bit like throwing up.

"Wild, right?" Amy said. "Sometimes she turns around and you can feel her little butt. So weird."

"You know it's a girl?"

"Yeah. We've already done up her room and everything. It's really cute."

"You wanna see?" Becca asked. "Let's go see it."

"I'm not going," Amy said. "I'm not moving."

Meredith followed Becca upstairs to the nursery. There was a crib and a chair and the white walls were painted with pink and purple clouds. She stood in the dark with Becca. Becca's phone buzzed again but she didn't look at it.

"It's cute," Meredith said.

"My mom says it will be less cute when there's something crying in it. She said it's all great until there's a baby, and then it becomes a horror show."

"Is your sister staying in school?"

Becca shrugged. "She says she is. I guess there's a whole group of them. They have like a little club. They do their homework while they breastfeed or whatever."

"I guess that's nice," Meredith said. "Who keeps texting you?"

"Oh, it's Lisa's mom," Becca said. "She keeps asking me to come over for hot chocolate. She texts me like five times every night. Sometimes I go. It's only like two blocks from here. But sometimes I pretend I didn't get the text. I know — I'm shit."

"She texts you every night?"

"Well, lots of nights. I go over there and just talk for like a half hour and then I say I have homework or whatever. Which is true."

"What do you talk about?"

"She asks me about school and friends and stuff," Becca said. "Sometimes we talk about Lisa, but mostly about other people, like who's going out with who or whatever."

"Maybe we should go," Meredith said. She pictured Mrs. Bellow's hopeful smile from the car window, imagined her at the kitchen table with her phone, texting Becca, then texting her again, then again. "It's okay with me."

"Are you sure?"

"Sure," Meredith said. "I don't mind."

Mrs. Bellow met them at the door with the mugs of hot chocolate. They sat at the kitchen table and talked about Thanksgiving. There was a fire crackling in the fireplace, and the dogs were splayed on their sides in the open space under the fireplace, the tunnel that connected the living room to the kitchen. It was the perfect little cave, and Meredith knew Lisa must have spent countless hours under there when she was little. If she'd been Lisa's friend they would have had a fort there and draped blankets over the side so the adults couldn't see in.

"The kids were here," Mrs. Bellow said. "With Peter. All they ate was mashed potatoes. We have so much turkey left. Do you guys want turkey?"

"No thanks," Meredith said. "I actually just had some earlier."

"We ordered way too much," Mrs. Bellow said. "I'm just going to freeze it and save it for Christmas."

"That makes sense," Becca said.

There was snow falling outside. It was bitter cold. Winter had arrived abruptly — but didn't it always seem that way, like one day it was just suddenly winter? Because it was, Meredith thought. Because there wasn't supposed to be any space between one thing and the thing that was next to it.

"You want to go up to Lisa's room?" Mrs. Bellow asked. "I don't mind if you do."

"That's okay," Becca said. "I told my mom we'd be back soon."

429

"You should just go up for a minute," she said. "I did a little work on it. A little redecorating. Got some cool frames. Put some pictures up. That kind of thing."

"Okay," Becca said. "Sure."

They went upstairs, leaving Mrs. Bellow in the kitchen. Lisa's room looked almost the same as the last time Meredith had seen it except that most of the pictures that had previously been Scotch taped to her mirror were now in sleek silver frames on the desk and the dresser. There was a framed photo that Mrs. Bellow had taken on her phone the afternoon Meredith had first come here, with all the other girls, the day her mother showed up. In the photo the four girls were sitting at the kitchen table and Amanda was absurdly making a peace sign. Then there was a framed photo collage with seven or eight pictures of friends and family, and included among the images was Meredith's seventh-grade school photo which she could only imagine Mrs. Bellow had photocopied from the yearbook, because there was no reason why Lisa would ever have had a picture of her.

"Maybe we should call somebody," Becca whispered. "Like one of her friends."

"Is your mom her friend?"

"Not really. I mean, she knows her. But I

wouldn't say she's really her friend. But this is weird." She nodded to the xeroxed photo of Meredith in the photo collage. "No offense, but you know, that's just weird. Like if Lisa ever came back to this room, she'd be like, *Who the fuck is that?*"

Mrs. Bellow appeared in the doorway. "What d'ya girls think?"

"It's great," Meredith said.

"Yeah," Becca said. "I love it."

Mrs. Bellow looked at her phone. "It's pretty late," she said. "And it's snowing. Why don't you guys stay here? I could call your mom, Becca, and just tell her you're staying over."

"Oh, that's okay," Becca said. "It's not snowing that hard."

Mrs. Bellow came in and sat down on Lisa's bed. "Plenty of room," she said. "It's really no problem."

"My mom said we have to come back," Becca said, although Meredith knew Becca's mother had said nothing of the sort. They hadn't even seen her mother, in fact. "She's expecting us. My sister, you know. The baby is —"

"I'll stay," Meredith said suddenly. She wasn't even sure why she'd said it. But she didn't want to leave Mrs. Bellow alone.

Becca looked at her.

"It's fine," Meredith said. "I'll stay and you go. I'll just . . . I'll come back in the morning."

"She'll come back in the morning, Bec," Mrs. Bellow said. "That sounds okay, I think. Don't you think?"

"Okay," Becca said. "If you're sure. But all your stuff's —"

"It's fine," Mrs. Bellow said. "She can borrow something to wear. And I always have extra toothbrushes. I buy them at CVS when they go on sale."

"That's smart," Meredith said, smiling at Mrs. Bellow.

"Well, you never know, right?" Mrs. Bellow said. "You never know what's going to happen."

Becca looked at Meredith.

"It's fine," Meredith said. "It's all good."

What she thought was: *Go away, go away, go away.*

She changed into Lisa's pajamas — a sleeveless purple top and black bottoms that tied at the waist — and sat down on the edge of Lisa's bed. Mrs. Bellow came in with a glass of water.

"Do you like water in the middle of the night?" she asked. "Sometimes Lisa likes water in the middle of the night and then she's always so annoyed that she has to go down to the kitchen and find a cup. So I try to remember to bring her one."

"Sure," Meredith said, setting the cup on the nightstand, next to a little bobble-head dog.

"It's nice having you here," Mrs. Bellow said, sitting down beside her on the bed. "I know how it seems." She looked away, embarrassed. "How *I* seem. It's just nice to have company . . . like, your age company, I mean."

"Sure," Meredith said. "I understand."

"Sometimes I talk to her," Mrs. Bellow said. "I tell her things. I know I'm talking to myself but I do it anyway. Like I'll be watching TV and I'll say, 'Can you believe that?' Or I'll be looking in the fridge and I'll say, 'Do I want orange juice or cranberry juice?' Little things. Dumb things. Those are the things you miss. The dumb things. The things you thought didn't mean anything."

For a moment Meredith thought Mrs. Bellow was going to cry, and she prayed this would not happen. Mrs. Bellow seemed to recognize the precipice as well. She took a deep breath and steadied herself, then patted Meredith on the hand and stood up.

"Anyway," she said. "It's nice to have

someone to talk to who's really here."

"I know," Meredith said. "I mean —" *I mean I know,* she thought. She slipped her feet under the covers. She thought that the last time someone had lain under these covers was the night before the Deli Barn, when Lisa had lain down and her mother had come with a glass of water and Lisa had gone to sleep, thinking . . . thinking what? Not thinking that tomorrow everything would change, forever. Maybe thinking she was going to break up with her lax bro. Maybe thinking that she was going to take his picture from the door inside her locker. Maybe thinking that she would do it when that loser Meredith Oliver wasn't standing there gawking.

"Call me if you need anything," Mrs. Bellow said. "Okay? I'm right next door."

"Okay," Meredith said. Mrs. Bellow shut off the light, but there was a streetlight outside so Meredith could still see the room. She could see the photo collage on Lisa's dresser, which was only a few feet from the bed. Lisa and Becca at Six Flags. Lisa and her mother sitting on a stone wall with a waterfall behind them. Lisa and Becca and Abby and Amanda somewhere — maybe a concert? Lisa at five or six, wearing a Villanova cheerleading outfit and waving blue and white pom-poms over her head. Then the outlier, the sore thumb — and yet among them, connected by a common frame: the picture of her from last year's yearbook. God, she hated that picture. She looked terrible, her mouth somewhere in between a —

The yearbook. The *yearbook.*

She sat up in the bed and squinted across the room at Lisa's bookshelf. Some of the books she could recognize from their spines, even if she couldn't make out the words: a few books they'd read in English in seventh grade, two Harry Potters, *Twilight,* a popular horse series they'd all devoured in elementary school, with the telltale fancy cursive titles with swishy horse tails. None of these was what she was looking for. But there, on the end of the bottom shelf, was a tall red book that from afar looked for all the world like —

I took the yearbook. It's on my bookshelf and she's never even noticed it.

Meredith got out of bed and walked across the room to the bookshelf, then sat cross-legged on the floor in front of it and carefully slid the tall book from its place. She set it face up on her lap before she looked down.

Meredith gently opened the book, turned its pages as if they were thin sheets of glass. She found the section for the senior class. "Jazz Band!" "Girls Volleyball!" *The Music Man!"* Then finally the class photos. Abrams through Ashley, Atwood through Bart, Bashor through — and there she was. Colleen Bellow, eighteen years old, smiling brightly into her daughter's dark bedroom, no earthly idea of what her life would be beyond the moment when she blinked away the photographer's flash, no notion that fifteen years later a girl named Meredith Oliver would be dressed in her missing daughter's pajamas and looking back at her.

There were about a dozen men pictured on the page. They were boys, really, exactly Evan's age, as stupid and lost as he was. Beck. Birch. Bolton. Was one of them the man that Lisa's grandfather had pointed to, had said, "That's your father? Sssssshhhhh-hhh." Which one was it? Did Gregory Bond have Lisa's eyes? Did Brian Bosley have her smile?

"Why would I want to look him up? It's not like he ever looked me up."

The yearbook was here on the bookshelf, precisely where Lisa had said it would be, exactly where Lisa told her it was. Lisa had *told* her this. There was no other way she could have known it. And if that were true, it meant the apartment and the bathtub and the BITCH tally and the bloody toilet paper and the soft blue blanket, all of it, it was real. And it meant something else, too. It meant Lisa was still alive.

But something was nagging at her, tugging on the leg of Lisa's black pajama bottoms. Maybe she *had* seen the yearbook before. Maybe that's why it looked so familiar. Maybe she had seen it here some other day, noticed it when she was in Lisa's room that first afternoon with Becca and Abby and Amanda, talking about the charity bracelets. Maybe even one of the girls had slid it from its place, said, "What's this?" and she had spotted the cover from where she was sitting at Lisa's desk. Maybe one of them had said, "It's her mom's old yearbook." Maybe one of them, one of Lisa's real friends, had said, "Remember Lisa showed us that last year?"

Maybe. Or maybe not. Or maybe. Or maybe not.

She was shaking. She slid the yearbook back into its spot on the shelf. She climbed into Lisa's bed. Something was wrong with her legs. They were shaking from the inside, like when she was in the car with the man, with the man and Lisa, the Deli Barn a tiny spot behind them. "You *suck,*" Lisa was saying. She leaned forward until she was practically right behind the driver's right ear. "Do you hear me?" She was screeching. "You *suck.* You asshole!" Meredith grabbed for her and knocked the glass of water off the nightstand. Something was wrong with her. Something was crushing her chest; something had fallen on top of her. She was having a heart attack. She was thirteen years old and she was having a heart attack. It happened. Things happened. Things you couldn't believe. Things that couldn't be explained. Inconceivable things. They happened.

"Lisa," she said. She was pounding on the bathroom door now. The feet, unmoving. "Lisa, it's me. Open the door."

The overhead light came on and Mrs. Bellow was in the doorway.

"Meredith?" she said. "Hon, what is it?"

She couldn't say anything. Her tongue was a dry lump in her mouth. A dog was whimpering. Annie the dog was outside the front door whimpering in the snow. She had been put outside and then forgotten, and she was cold and standing by the flowerpot with the cigarette butts and she was not dead but had just run off, run off in the night and gotten lost and couldn't find her way back because all the apartments looked exactly alike and she was just a stupid dog. A stupid freezing dog.

"Let her in," she whispered.

"What?"

Her face was wet. Was she crying? Had she thrown up? Was she bleeding? Was her *nose* bleeding? She was putting her hands all over her face trying to find the source of the moisture.

"Hey, girl. Hey there, girl." Mrs. Bellow was beside the bed. "Stop," she said, putting her hand on her shoulder. "I'm here. It's okay. I'm here."

"Would your parents know?"

"Know what?"

"If you didn't come home after school. Would they know it was something bad?"

"They would know," she said to Mrs. Bellow. "I think they would know. I think they would know."

"Shhhh," Mrs. Bellow said. She left the room and came back a minute later with something in her hand.

"Take this," she said. "Okay? It helps me. It'll help. It'll help you sleep."

Meredith was sitting up. A small purple pill was in her right hand and a glass of water was in her left hand. She closed her fist around the pill. Her knuckles ached from knocking. She opened her hand and swallowed the pill. Mrs. Bellow fluffed her pillow and tucked her in. Then she lay down beside her, on top of the covers, and took hold of her hand. She rubbed Meredith's wrist. She was rubbing the watch away. She was smudging the watch drawn by Steven Overbeck and it would not be 2:15 anymore, ever. Soon there would only be a green stain where the bracelet had been.

"Okay," Mrs. Bellow said. "You're all right now. I've got you."

Sleep or something like it came over her, and for a little while she was happily suspended and it was not 2:15 but it was not any other time either — *what time isn't it?* — and her face dried and her parents knew everything and Evan was catching the ball every try and she had leaped up right away, just as the car was driving out of the Deli Barn parking lot, and she had taken a picture of the license plate with her phone and then she had called the police, the car still in her sights.

"Can you please sit on the middle of your

chair so your butt's not hanging over the side?"

The car, still in her sights. The license plate. The numbers. She spoke them clearly to the dispatcher.

"This is the best day of my whole summer."

She woke with a jolt and time started and it was 2:15 and she was late for algebra.

Vertical Asymptote: $x=2$
Horizontal Asymptote: $y=1$

Meredith sat up in Lisa's bed. "I have to go," she said.

"You can't go, hon," Mrs. Bellow said. She was still lying in the bed, over the covers, and she talked as if she were sleeping. "Not now. It's the middle of the night."

"I have to," Meredith said. She stood up. "I just . . . I just have to go to the bathroom. And I need a pen."

She was looking all over Lisa's desk, pushing aside the frames and opening all the little drawers. Something fell on the floor, then something else. Finally she found a Magic Marker, one of those smelly ones that everyone got in fifth grade. It might work.

She stumbled out of Lisa's room and into the hall. She was looking for the bathroom.

She had to finish her graph. Where was the bathroom? She just had to get to the bathroom.

18

Well, she had made the deal, hadn't she? Traded the airport trip for geriatric dentistry. It sounded like a joke, but she knew she'd gotten the better end of the bargain, driving the little car twenty minutes out to Hillsboro, the two cases in the trunk with all she would need for her work today. It felt like a clean getaway, like winning the avoidance lottery, not like killing two birds with one stone but more like killing *eight* birds — dishes, shopping, Evan, Meredith, Mark, her father, and Nancy. She counted them as she sped down the highway. Okay, seven. Seven birds dead for the day, and no great loss among them.

How far could one woman get, exactly, with a freshly serviced Audi and two satchels full of dental tools? Across the state line? Into another time zone? Into another time? She turned up the radio. She didn't know the song that was playing and she didn't care. Mark and Meredith had still been asleep when she'd left, Evan in the garage, *ping*ing. She had left earlier than necessary, slipped out when she realized he was coming to the end of his swings. She could sit in the car with her coffee. She could sit there for hours, happily, in the Hillsboro parking lot, irresponsibly plowing through her tank of gas to keep the car warm, until her father was airborne, Mark at the office, her children . . . where? It was Black Friday. Maybe they would shop, or go to the movies, or eat out with their friends. Maybe they would lie in their beds and think thoughts she could not imagine, devise plans she was not privy to, make decisions they would soon regret.

They were gone, her children, to wherever children went when they left. Had she gone so far away, when she was thirteen, or fifteen, or seventeen? She supposed she must have, but she could not recall now with any clarity or certainty what it had felt like to be that age. It was as if those years — not what had occurred externally, but what had occurred internally — had just been wiped away; the only person who'd played a part in those years that she still had any regular contact with was her father, and "regular contact" was just a nice way of saying that they were not estranged. Maybe who you were didn't really start, didn't really *count,* until you found the majority of people you were going to spend your life with. Maybe the rest was too easily lost, because there was no one there to keep reminding you of who you used to be.

But these were only Black Friday, early morning, coffee-in-the-parking-lot-of-Hillsboro-Home thoughts. Ever since the argument in the dining room, she felt as if she'd been cut loose and was floating. It was neither a good nor bad feeling, though if pressed she'd have to say the primary emotion that accompanied it seemed to be relief.

There were far worse places in the world than Hillsboro Home, a fact Claire often had to remind herself of when she felt especially crushed by the weight of its collective despair. There was the clinic in Honduras where her in-laws extracted children's teeth that had been rotted black by malnutrition. There were hospitals in war-torn countries where the elderly — yes, someone's grandmother, yes, someone's grandfather — slept on a hard floor for days waiting to see a doctor. The patients at the Hillsboro Home (they were supposed to be called residents, but by this point, honestly, they were patients) were well cared for. It was not an inexpensive facility, so either the patient himself or someone in the family had the necessary resources to provide. It was clean and well staffed and there were people in the kitchen with chef hats. There were daily events posted on a board in the front lobby: Humphrey Bogart Movie Night, Poker Tournament, Wii Bowling, Life Collage Workshop. And yet despite all this it was awful. Maybe it was made more awful because apparently this was the very best you could hope for after you got too ill or too feeble for non-assisted living. Clean. Well staffed. Cable TV. Dental care.

The mobile dentistry practice consisted primarily of routine cleanings. Almost all the residents of Hillsboro Home were wheelchair bound, and many entirely bed-ridden, and so only for a true emergency would a patient be put through the stress of an ambulance trip to a dentist's office. Better, in the final months and years, to stave off infection, reduce as much pain as possible, focus on preventive dentistry so that there could be one less thing to worry about as multiple other systems began to break down. Patients were seen every six months, which meant that often Claire and Mark saw each person just once — by the time the next appointment rolled around, chances were fifty/fifty that the patient was dead. There was heavy turnover at Hillsboro Home. It was, Mark had once commented, like the trenches in Belgium, except that there was no floss in the trenches.

Ninety-four-year-old Mr. Mitchum had clearly not paid attention to the attrition statistics; Claire recalled seeing him at least twice before, although Mr. Mitchum certainly did not recall her and lay still in his bed staring up at the ceiling, his jaw dangling open like a broken marionette. Often it was utterly silent, this particular dentistry, more like the operating room Claire had once imagined than her regular office ever would be. She knew Mark talked to these people, some of whom did not, could not even, talk back, and some days she made an effort to do so as well. But today she could not bring herself to say these kinds of things: "It's getting chilly out there!" "What wonderful holiday decorations!" "That's a very handsome sweater!"

There was a new woman, Mrs. Ogles, who was chatty and smiley and referred several times to "when I move back in with my daughter." There were three others, standard cleanings, then a filling at the end of the day. The fillings had to be done in a special exam room at the end of the hallway, a cold place that doubled as medical storage and had shelves lined with gauze and rubber gloves, patient gowns, sheets, towels. Mark hated "the closet," as he called it, but today Claire preferred it to the patients' rooms because at least inside the closet there were no reminders that the mouth she was inside belonged to an actual person, no mementos, no photos of happier days, no needlepoint pillows, no proof of life.

She inserted the novocaine needle into the gum.

"Where's Thomas?" the mouth said.

"I'm the dentist," Claire said. "I'm going to fill your tooth."

"But where's Thomas?" the mouth said.

"It will only take a couple minutes. I'll have you right out."

She filled the tooth and wheeled the wheelchair back into the hallway. It was almost lunchtime and the wheelchairs were lined up along the wall.

A hand reached out from the wheelchair and grabbed her lab coat.

"Thomas? Tommy?"

Claire removed the hand from her coat and walked down the corridor. This was where it ended for you, she thought, and you could pretend all you wanted, but the chairs that lined these halls waiting for lunch were where you were headed. Maybe you were lucky to be Lisa Bellow, struck down at your most ignorant, never to know the pain of lost parents and lost children and lost lives. But that wasn't fair — even Lisa Bellow, at fourteen, knew what it was to lose a parent, or to never have one, which was in many ways the same thing. And yet there were so many agonies she would never encounter, never have to face, chief among them the realization that every day had the potential to be its own little individual agony because you never knew what the hell you were doing, or why you were doing it, or what was going to happen to you or the people you loved. Perhaps life itself was no great loss, depending on the life you led. Perhaps Colleen Bellow, having lost her only child, would be better off with no life at all than the one that awaited her.

Grief and hope were cruel bedfellows, incompatible. There was no chance that grief would ever run its course, Claire knew from experience, and thus in cases of the missing there should be a statute of limitation on hope. It was only fair, only just, that after one year or three years or five years you could wake up on the assigned date and know, with absolute certainty, that the waiting was over, that the window of possibility had closed, that there was no chance your lost girl would return. What horrible stories, those few miracles of women kicking through doors into the sunlit neighborhoods they'd only ever seen from nailed-shut windows. Better for those stories to be kept secret, for the tales of joyous homecomings to be censored. How cruel that such a statute did not exist, that fifty years from now Colleen Bellow could be sitting in a wheelchair in this stuffy hall waiting to have her tooth filled, could hear footsteps approaching and believe, if only for a moment, that the footsteps belonged not to the mobile dentist but to her beloved daughter. It was not right and it was not fair and Claire resented the system of inequalities that existed, dictating who would be waiting forever for the chosen footsteps and who would be rewarded on Sunday afternoons with their sound. Here was her darling Evan! Here was her clever Meredith! Better if no one's children came. Better if all were equally lost. Better if you knew well in advance that the footsteps you heard would never be the footsteps you were waiting for.

"Can I please go to Becca's for a sleepover?" Meredith asked.

They were eating Thanksgiving leftovers.

There was talking. Evan said something. Mark said something. They were all talking at once. Meredith was scowling. As a baby she'd scowled all the time. Hoarded her best smiles for Evan, given them out sparingly, grudgingly, to everyone else. Of course she was just a baby, so it was absurd to assume she had done this consciously, with hostile intent, though maybe it was even worse if it hadn't been deliberate but genuinely the way she'd felt.

The turkey on Claire's plate was dry. Had it been dry yesterday and she just hadn't noticed? Had she overcooked it? She had forgotten to be thankful, was the thing. She had broken the Thanksgiving rule and not taken a minute out of her day to be thankful, not for a single thing. And now it was the day after Thanksgiving and obviously too late for anything like thankfulness.

"Fine," she said. "It's fine."

They were looking at her. Mark said something. Meredith said something, probably something snotty, but Claire couldn't be sure because she had stopped listening.

"Go," Claire said. "Please. Just go."

Meredith got up from the table. The food on her plate was hardly touched.

"Mom," Evan said. "Are you okay?"

It wasn't a joke, the way he said it, her

half-blind boy. She couldn't think of how to respond. She couldn't even imagine the words.

She woke Saturday morning to the phone ringing, the landline, which almost never rang anymore. She looked at the clock. It was 7:25. The bed was empty beside her. She picked up the phone and said hello.

"Mrs. Oliver?"

"Yes?" She sat up. She felt hungover, or like she'd been asleep for eighteen hours, her senses simultaneously sharp and dull.

"Is Meredith there?"

She thought for a moment, then remembered. "No," she said. "She's spending the night at a friend's house."

"This is the friend." A pause. "This is Becca. Becca Nichols."

Claire swung her legs out of the bed. The carpet was cold under her bare feet. For a moment she couldn't even remember what month it was.

"What is it?" she asked. "What's wrong?"

"I don't know," the girl on the phone said. "I . . . she spent the night somewhere else."

Claire stood up. The phone felt strange and bulky against her ear. Why did news so often come this way, plastic boxes pressed against our temples? Half the things that mattered in her life had come through this box. Why was she never where the thing was happening?

"She what?"

"It's okay," the friend said. "It's . . . I just . . . I'm sure she's fine. She spent the night at Lisa's house. We went over there for a while last night and then I came home and she stayed."

Claire's racing heart slowed. Meredith was in a known location. She was in a house. An adult was present. "Why did she stay?" she asked.

"Mrs. Bellow wanted us to. Both of us. She said it was because it was snowing, but I think she was just lonely. She was acting kind of weird. I tried to get Meredith to leave but Meredith said she wanted to stay. I think she was just trying to be nice. But I wanted to let you know and —"

"Thank you," Claire said. "You were right to let me know. Thank you."

"I think she was just trying to be nice," Becca said again. "I think Mrs. Bellow just really needed someone to talk to, you know."

"Of course," she said. "Thank you for telling me. I'm sure it's fine. I'll have Meredith let you know when she gets home. I'll text her right now."

"I already texted her and she didn't

answer," Becca said. "That was kinda why I called."

"Okay," Claire said. "Okay. I'm sure it's fine. I'm certain it's fine."

She hung up the phone and immediately tried Meredith's cell. She was bumped to voice mail before the first ring, which meant the phone was dead, which only meant it had gone uncharged, which only meant Meredith had forgotten to take the charger, which happened all the time. She found the Bellows' number on her own cell and called their house phone. It rang four times before the machine picked up. It was a girl's voice on the machine — Lisa's voice, she assumed:

"Hey there! Nobody's home right now, but —"

She hung up and got out of bed and walked into the hall. Evan's door was open, his room empty but for the intolerant cat sleeping on his pillow. She went downstairs. The house was silent. They were gone. Where were they? She found a note, scrawled from Mark, on the kitchen table:

at the park

The park, yes. The baseball field at the park, the rocky, uneven diamond where

Evan and his friends had played as little kids, before it really mattered, before it meant anything. Mark was hitting him pop flies. Evan needed them off the bat, was what he'd said, she remembered now. Not tossed from his own hand or rolled off the roof. He needed them off the bat. The bat was unpredictable. Sometimes a ball off a bat went in a straight line, as evidenced by the dark lens of his glasses. But more often the connection of ball and bat created something unpredictable, unique. Every time was different. Every single time, a new line.

She tried Evan's cell. Evan should definitely be the one to go get Meredith. If she was upset, if Colleen Bellow was upset . . . Evan could handle it. This was his specialty, rescuing sisters. He and Mark could swing by there on their way home from the park. Mark could stay in the van and Evan could just go to the door and say —

"Hey, it's Evan. Leave me a message."

She frowned, picturing the phone sitting on the weathered bench beside the rocky field, its buzzing unheard or ignored.

"Evan," she said. "Evan, I need you to go get your sister. Please." She was struck by the pointless urgency of an unheard message, the way it lay in the box like every other message, carrying no extra weight until it was heard. "Evan. Call me as soon as you get this."

She hung up. She stood for a moment in the kitchen. The intolerant cat, apparently roused by her visit to Evan's room, was standing at the back door.

"What?" she asked it. "What do you want?"

She did not like the sound of her voice in the empty house. Her voice, alone, was a hollow thing, as pointless as the message she'd just left for her son. She was not going to wait around for him to pick up his voicemail. She went to get dressed.

In the Bellows' neighborhood only a few dog walkers were out, and even the dogs looked sleepy. It was a cold morning and the holiday was over and the shopping day was over and, miraculously, it was still the beginning of the weekend, and most of the world was celebrating this fact by staying in bed. Which was where she should be, and really where everyone in her family should be, relishing the sleep. But Meredith was in another girl's bed in another family's house.

She thought she understood why Meredith had stayed at the Bellows' while the friend — Becca, it was — had left. She was even a little bit proud of Meredith, or impressed by her, or both. Meredith felt bad that Lisa's bed was empty, and she saw herself as a body who could fill it. Claire might have even approved the choice, given the chance. If Meredith had called and asked her advice (as if!), she might have said yes, stay there, sleep in her bed, wear her pajamas, if it will allow her mother one moment of peace, one moment of relief, we can take that hit, we can give you to her for a night, for a day and night, every so often, if that helps even the score, if that helps balance the loss. Not share you, no, but let that mother have a share *in* you. She deserves that; it's fairer than the all or nothing we are left with, the all of you and the nothing of Lisa, the all of our family and the nothing of hers. Give her that: sleep in her daughter's bed, eat her daughter's cereal, use her daughter's hairbrush. If it helps. If it helps, we can give her that. We can give her you.

She pulled into the driveway but did not shut off the engine. What was it but a sleepover, really? Maybe she shouldn't even go knock. Maybe she should wait a few minutes and see if Meredith emerged, headed back to Becca's house, or if Evan called the cell. But who knew when he would call? She imagined them on that chilly field, Mark trying to hit the ball straight up, missing half the time, connecting, and then the ball dropping just out of Evan's reach. Who knew how long they would be? They might be there forever trying to get it right. They might be there forever and *never* get it right, but stay anyway.

She got out of the car and walked to the front door, then gave a tentative, light knock. The dogs inside exploded into fits of barking. Well, so much for the quiet knock, the gentle awakening. The dogs were right on the other side of the door, whimpering, their tails slapping the wall. She prepared her apology face.

But no one opened the door. Had they really slept through the barking? Maybe Becca was wrong. Maybe Meredith had not spent the night here. Maybe Colleen Bellow was at her boyfriend's house . . . but if this was the case, then where was Meredith?

She rang the bell, propelling the dogs into further hysterics. Then she pounded on the door, first with her knuckles and then, in some imperceptible shift caused by the lack of response, as seconds passed, with the side of her closed fist. Probably she was waking up a neighbor. Probably she —

The door opened, leaving her fist suspended, almost comically, mid-pound. Colleen Bellow stood there in black sweatpants and a gray American Eagle T-shirt, her face expressionless, her eyes heavy with sleep. Or with something. She stared at Claire for a moment as if she didn't recognize her.

"Is Meredith here?" Claire blurted out.

"Meredith?" Colleen said sleepily. "Um . . ."

Claire pushed past the dogs and into the living room. One of the dogs bolted out the door and sprinted across the front lawn.

"Shit," Colleen said.

"Where is she? Is she here?"

"What? Who?"

"Meredith," Claire said. "Is Meredith here?" Then she called to the house, in a voice she did not recognize, "Meredith?"

"She's in the bathtub," Colleen said.

Claire turned. "What?"

"She's . . . she's in the bathtub. I'm sorry."

Claire saw her then, her little girl. She saw the unseeable image on the other side of the door. The door opened and the sight of her dead daughter came at her with the rush of water, a wave that was remarkable mostly for its *sound* as it crashed over her and she could hear nothing, not the dogs nor Colleen nor the sound of her own feet pounding up the carpeted stairs to the hallway that seemed to have a thousand different doors, opening the door first to a bedroom, then spinning and opening another to a towel-packed closet, then spinning again and opening finally to a sink and mirrortooth-brushsoapdish, knowing already what she would see in the next moment, what she had lost sometime in the night as she slept unaware, what she had already, already, already, already, impossibly, impossibly lost.

Meredith was asleep in the bathtub. There was no water in the bathtub. The sound of the wave ceased and Claire felt her legs give out under her and she was kneeling beside the tub and her hands were shaking.

"Meredith," she said. "Meredith . . ."

And now again a moment, when she did not stir — but no, she was breathing, her chest rising and falling under the unfamiliar pajamas. On the tile wall above her daughter were criss-crossed lines drawn in red marker.

"She's asleep," Colleen said.

Claire turned.

"She's sleeping," Colleen said. "I gave her something to sleep."

Claire stood up, still trembling. "You what?"

"I gave her something to help her sleep. She was upset. I —"

"What did you give her?"

"Just what they gave to me," she said. "The same thing I take."

"How many?"

"What?"

Claire could have shaken her, struck her. "How many did you give her?"

"Just one," Colleen said. "That's what I —"

"Are you sure it was just one?"

"Of course I'm sure." She was angry now. "What do you think I am? I'm not crazy."

"How long has —"

"She was upset and I wanted to help. But then afterward she came in here and I thought she was just going to the bathroom but then I came in and she was like this. I woke her up and asked if she wanted to get into bed but she said she just wanted to stay here. But she was okay. She is okay. She's just . . . sleepy."

"Meredith," Claire said. She crouched down and put her hand on her daughter's arm. "Meredith, wake up."

A small stir.

"What exactly did you give her?" she asked Colleen. "And when? What time?"

Colleen took a pill bottle from the pocket of her sweat pants. Claire snatched it from her hand and looked at it.

"Meredith," she said firmly.

Meredith opened her eyes for a moment, then closed them again.

"I just thought it would help her sleep," Colleen said. "It helps me. She was upset."

"Of course she was upset," Claire said.

"I just —"

"This is wrong," Claire said, standing, turning to face her fully. In her sweats and T-shirt Colleen looked somehow tinier than ever, so slim and fragile and young, not like a parent at all. "You have to see that. You have to know this is not okay."

"She said it —"

"No," Claire said. "She's a child. She's just a child."

"Lisa was a child," Colleen said.

"Yes," Claire said. "Yes. I know. She was."

Claire crouched down again. "Meredith," she said. She looked once more at the red lines on the tile wall. Was it a graph? Some kind of math problem? There were dots, marking a curve.

"We're going to stand up now," Claire said. "I'm going to take you home."

Meredith opened her eyes. "What?" she said.

"We're going to go home," Claire said. "I'm going to take you home."

"No," Meredith said.

And there was a moment, even then, assessing the momentous task that lay in the tub before her, when Claire thought maybe it would make sense, right now, to leave her daughter where she was, just for a little while longer, to let her sleep it off, to sit downstairs with a cup of coffee and come back up in a couple hours with reinforcements — the brother whom she worshipped, the father who could lighten the mood — come back when Meredith could stand without assistance, when both she and Colleen had overcome their sedation, to heed her disoriented child's simple request, her dazed "no," to let her make this decision for herself. Meredith was not going to die in this bathtub. She was not going to be abducted from it. She was in no imminent peril. She was, Claire thought, in no greater danger than the danger posed by a mother who would make the choice, for whatever reason, to not carry her daughter to safety.

She slid one arm under Meredith's shoulders and another under her thighs.

"You can't lift her," Colleen said.

Claire half-lifted, half-slid Meredith from the confines of the bathtub, then fell backward onto the bathroom floor with Meredith sideways across her lap. Something rolled from Meredith's hand onto the bathroom floor, an uncapped Magic Marker.

"Come on, sweetheart," she said. "We have to go home."

"You can't carry her," Colleen said.

Meredith opened her eyes again. "Mom," she said.

Claire got her feet under her. She stood slowly, her knees shaking, her daughter draped across her arms. She took one step. She took another.

19

This is me. This is my real life.

The toilet flushed but she did not break eye contact with her reflection.

This is me. This is really me.

It was the Friday before Christmas break and Meredith did not want to go to school. It wasn't even a real school day. They'd watch movies in half their classes, and there was some assembly where the sixth-graders were putting on a holiday play and of course it was going to be awful. She would have to decide who to sit with and that part would be awful, too. Mostly now at school she wanted to sit alone — in classes and in the library and especially at lunch. It was easier that way, and not nearly as lonely or lame as it sounded. She appreciated the quiet, the way the world spun while she stood off to the side. She watched without caring, or caring only in fragments, a moment here or there.

Like yesterday, she had wound up by accident walking into the locker room at the same time as Kristy, and so wound up changing beside her, and so wound up basically inadvertently being her changing shield. And that had been fine, if a little weird, because Kristy kept looking at her sideways like she didn't quite trust her to hold up her end of the bargain. But then before Kristy went out into the gym, and Meredith was still tying her sneakers, Kristy said, "I hate volleyball," and Meredith said, "Me, too." And so there was that.

She slipped the cracked phone into her purse without looking at it, brushed her hair, put on her watch. Her father had given her the watch last week, claimed he'd seen it in a shop window, though she doubted this was true. It seemed like something he must've worked hard to find. Instead of whole numbers, the watch had equations around the dial, like instead of 3 it had 0.3*10. "That's right, Meredith," Evan had said earnestly, "this watch once belonged to Albert Einstein." She had shot him a look to shut him up, because she understood why her father had given her the watch, understood it was the grown-up version of comic books and Tater Tots, that there was practical value in this gift, that it could endure.

Evan knocked on her door and stuck his head in.

"Y'okay?"

She turned from the mirror. "Why?"

"Dunno. You look a little sketchy."

"It's dumb to even have school today," she said, sitting down on her bed. "It's all bullshit."

"Like most days," he said.

Was he a little less paunchy? Perhaps. He'd been in a hole and then he'd crawled out. It happened. You couldn't say why, but it happened. Last night she'd seen his catcher's mitt in the pile on the dining-room table, things they'd be taking with them on their trip. She had picked up the glove and smelled it, deeply, the way you'd smell a towel out of the laundry. It was the smell of Evan, not just the leather but the sweat and maybe something else, too. In a year he would be away at college, somewhere; the thought of that loss, coming so soon after everything else, was almost too much for her to bear, and she pushed it away.

"Hey, Evan," she said.

"What?"

"Nothing," she said.

He leaned against her door frame, took off his glasses and wiped them with the bottom of his oxford shirt. His face, without his glasses, was bare and unfamiliar, his left eye a stranger to her.

"So what do you want for Christmas?" he asked, looking up.

"I don't know," she said. "Nothing."

"Good. 'Cause I didn't get you anything."

"Get me a book," she said. "Get me one you haven't spoiled."

"Ha," he said. Then after a moment he said, "Thirteen sucks. For Christmas I'll get you fourteen."

"My birthday's not till March."

"I'm aware. You can have it early. You just can't use it."

"Thirteen didn't suck for you," she said. "Thirteen's when you got good at baseball. Thirteen's when you changed."

"Thirteen's when you changed, too," he said. "You know when else I changed?"

"When?"

"Fourteen." He put his glasses back on. "You know when else?"

"I get it," she said.

He winked. He wasn't blind when he winked his right eye, she reminded herself. His left eye had abilities. Movement. Shapes. Light.

A few minutes after Evan left for school her mother appeared at her bedroom doorway.

"You feel sick?"

"Sort of," she said.

"It's okay if you're late. I can write a note for you."

Meredith was sitting on the floor in the middle of her battling animals. Her mother came into the room and sat on the edge of her bed. The tolerant cat stood up and turned a half turn and lay down again.

"You missed goal of the day," her mother said.

"Bummer."

Her mother smiled. "Evan says you don't want to go to school."

"I don't know if I ever want to go to school," Meredith said.

"You'll have a long break," her mother said. "Almost two weeks. You might feel differently after. And if you don't, we can figure something out."

"Like what? Be an eighth-grade dropout?"

"Maybe you could go to a different school."

"You'd let me do that?"

"Meredith," her mother said. "We'll do whatever we need to do."

They had found her a new therapist, someone who was less useless than Dr. Moon. They took her and picked her up from school every day now, even when she said she wanted to walk. On an unseasonably warm day last week, her mother had come to pick her up but then left the Audi in the school parking lot and walked home with her — past the Deli Barn, down Chestnut Street, then left on Duncan, then the cut across the edge of the park, then the right on Glenside, up the lawn to their house. Was that crazy? It was a little crazy, yes. But her mother was insistent. Resolved.

Meredith picked up the battling tiger with the ax. His tail had been broken off for as long as she could remember — Evan had always claimed it was she who'd done it, chewed it off as a toddler, but she'd always suspected he was the guilty party. For one, there were no teeth marks.

"I used to talk to her," she said to her mother. "I mean, I used to pretend to talk to her. Do you think that's weird?"

She could tell her mother was surprised by this information, or at least by the sharing of this information, but she recovered quickly. "I don't think so," she said. "I think you do what you have to do."

Meredith twisted the ax in the tiger's paw. After a moment, her mother said, "Do you still do that? Talk to her?"

"Not really," Meredith said. "We . . . I don't know. We just . . ." She shook her head and lay the tiger gently on the floor. "Not really."

Sometimes she imagined herself back into the bathroom in the apartment. Sometimes she stood at the sink and looked into the mirror. Sometimes she could see Lisa in the reflection, stretched out in the tub, unobstructed. Sometimes Lisa was sleeping, her breaths deep and even. But sometimes Lisa was looking at her, and their eyes locked in the mirror, but Meredith did not get in the tub, and Lisa did not ask her to.

"It must be strange," her mother said. "I don't mean *weird* . . . just it must be strange, talking to someone you didn't really know that well."

"We were friends in fourth grade," Meredith said.

"Were you? I didn't realize that."

"For a little while," she said. She did not say, "for an afternoon." "I don't think she was really all that different than she was then. She was just, you know . . . she was just what she had to be. She was just what she was, what the world made her, like everybody."

"She had a mother who loved her. And friends who loved her."

"Yeah," Meredith said.

Here was something she knew. She knew

that Lisa's words — the things Lisa had told her at the apartment — weren't really Lisa's words. She knew those were words she had given to Lisa, guesses, maybe good guesses, but guesses. She knew that Lisa's only words to her, maybe since that day in the cafeteria when Lisa had told her she had a big butt, were the ones Lisa had said on the floor in the Deli Barn. She had been holding onto those words, selfishly, desperately, for months. They were probably the words that had made all the other words happen.

"I need to go to the Bellows'," she said, looking up at her mother. "I need to talk to Mrs. Bellow. I need to tell her something."

"What is it?"

"It's something," Meredith said. She considered before going forward. "It's something private."

She was fairly certain this would not fly with her mother, not after everything that had happened. She had not been back to the Bellows' house or seen Mrs. Bellow since her mother had come for her that morning, although she knew that Mrs. Bellow sometimes called, and that her mother sometimes talked with her.

"Are you sure?" her mother said.

"Sure that it's private or sure that I need to tell her?"

"Both, I guess."

"I'm sure."

"Then it sounds like you should do it. I could take you there after school."

"Do I have to go to school?"

"Yeah," her mother said. "I think so."

Meredith walked through the falling snow up to the Bellows' front door. It was one of those light, powdery snows that melted almost as soon as it landed, the kind of snow that parents loved and kids hated. The stone path to the Bellows' door was dusted white. Meredith rang the doorbell and a moment later a man answered. Meredith had never seen him before, but she assumed this was Mrs. Bellow's boyfriend, the one Lisa had called lame. He was balding and wore a sweater with a Christmas tree on it. It was a lame sweater to be sure.

"Is Mrs. Bellow here?" she asked.

"She is," he said. "Just a sec."

He left her standing on the porch, which was fine with her. After a moment a little girl, maybe eight years old, ran past the storm door and stopped when she saw a person on the other side. The girl had a long ponytail and wore a black T-shirt that said "Oh No You Didn't!" that Meredith was 99 percent sure had once belonged to Lisa. The girl looked left and right and then, apparently confident she would not be seen, did a little hula dance, pushing out boobs she did not have, and then laughed and ran off. A moment later Mrs. Bellow came to the door and opened it.

"Meredith, come in! I can't believe he left you in the cold."

"It's fine," she said. "I'm just here for a minute."

She did not want to go into the house. She knew that for sure. She saw Mrs. Bellow realize this, but Mrs. Bellow didn't have any shoes on so she slid on the man's brown loafers that were beside the door and stepped out onto the porch. She was coatless and crossed her arms against the chill.

"How are you?" she asked.

"I'm fine," Meredith said.

"Haven't seen you in a while," Mrs. Bellow said. "I've been —"

"I've been really busy," Meredith said. "And we're getting ready to go away for Christmas tomorrow, to my grandparents'."

"Oh, that sounds nice. Where are they?"

"Kansas City," Meredith said. She felt her nerves crumbling. It had been a mistake, coming here. It was not too late to back out, to say Merry Christmas, to keep her treasure to herself.

"That's a long trip," Mrs. Bellow said. "You guys don't drive?"

"We do," Meredith said. "Always. We always drive."

"That must take —"

"I have to tell you something," Meredith said. The words tumbled out before she could stop them. "I mean, I wanted to tell you something. I wanted to come today so I could tell you something."

"I'm sorry about that night," Mrs. Bellow said. "I tried to call afterward but —"

"It's not about that," Meredith said. "It's about Lisa."

Mrs. Bellow pressed her lips together. It was probably the wrong thing to say. "It's about Lisa." How could anything good ever follow those words again? The next time Mrs. Bellow heard those words would probably be from a policeman, and his face would be stone and his hand would be on her arm.

"It's about that day," she said. "The day it happened. I wanted to tell you something because I didn't tell you before. I didn't tell anybody. It's just a little thing but I kept it to myself because . . . I don't know why. I just —"

"What is it?" Mrs. Bellow asked.

The man appeared behind her at the door,

then moved away.

"At first," Meredith said. "When it first happened, Lisa was really scared. She was crying. I wasn't scared at all. I mean, I guess I was, but I was in shock or whatever, so I didn't actually feel scared. I was just kind of in a daze or something."

She looked up. Mrs. Bellow was just staring at her, waiting for her to go on.

"But then I got scared. I got really scared because I thought he was going to shoot me. I was sure of it, actually. But then Lisa stopped being scared."

"Why?" Mrs. Bellow asked.

"I don't know," Meredith said. "But I could tell she wasn't scared anymore. I was looking right at her. She was like six inches from me. She stopped crying and she looked just like herself, just like always. We were just lying there and I was so scared and she wasn't, not anymore. And then she said something. She told me it was going to be okay. She said, 'It's okay Meredith. It's going to be okay.' That was what she said to me. She almost smiled, even. And then right after that was when . . . was when she had to leave."

"That was the last thing?" Mrs. Bellow said.

"Yeah," Meredith said. "That was the last thing."

A gust of wind sent snowflakes swirling against the storm door. The door was warm from the heat of the house, and the flakes vanished on contact.

"I wanted you to know she said that," Meredith said. "I think about it a lot, but I didn't ever tell anybody. I didn't think it would make any difference. But I wanted to tell you now. Because I think she would want me to tell you." She paused. The neighborhood was silent in the snow. "Actually, I know she would want me to tell you," she added quickly.

"Yeah," Mrs. Bellow said. Her voice was thin as a breath. "Why do you think . . . why do you think she said that?"

"I don't know," Meredith said. "I really don't." She could see Lisa clearly, standing at the counter, glancing up, meeting her eyes through the glass door of the Deli Barn. "I think maybe she was just being nice," she said.

"Yeah," Mrs. Bellow said. "Maybe . . . maybe so."

"I hope you have a good Christmas," Meredith said. "I mean . . ."

"Thank you," Mrs. Bellow said quickly. "And same to you."

Meredith turned and walked across the Bellows' front yard toward the minivan. Through the drifting snow she could see her mother, who looked for all the world to be sound asleep in the driver's seat. Her eyes were closed, her head tilted back, her chin pointed forward. She looked, Meredith thought, almost absurdly relaxed, like she was on a beach instead of in a minivan. It was weird to be so comfortable — wasn't it? — in a van, of all things, a van, a big blue metal box with wheels, a suburban cliché held together with screws and rods and whatever else held cars together. There was nothing at all special about their minivan. There were parking lots full of them, exactly identical to theirs. This wasn't the kind of vehicle you remembered when you got old. It was just a thing that took you places with your family. It was just a way to get where you were going.

But maybe . . . maybe her mother loved the van as much as she did. Maybe there was no place else she would rather be. Maybe that was why she had made the decision that they would drive west for Christmas. And right now, maybe she was imagining what it would be like when they headed out first thing tomorrow morning, the smell of coffee, the glare off the windshield, the click of the blinker, the hum of the tires, the entrance ramp, the van full, the day, the night, the road, the miles, the parents, the children, the journey.

Just as she reached for the door handle her mother opened her eyes and turned to her, startled. The look on her face was something like surprise. It was almost as if her mother was not expecting her. Meredith opened the door and slid into the passenger's seat.

"Okay," she said.

"Okay what?" her mother said.

"I'm ready," Meredith said.

ACKNOWLEDGMENTS

Thanks to Brady Chilson for recognizing the poignancy of asymptotes and patiently explaining them to me. Thanks to Dr. Donald Oliver for dental expertise. Thanks to Officer Tim Lively for help on police procedure. Thanks to Ellie Park for fashion insights. And huge, profound thanks to Kirk Robinson for impeccably detailed, plot-altering information about the effects of catastrophic eye injuries. Thanks also to friends too numerous to name — but you know who you are — who saved me with a crucial detail here and there.

Thanks to my BFF&N Mary Beth Baken for great advice and confidence early in the game, and to Marion Winik for great advice and confidence late in the game.

Thanks to Dickinson College for continued support, especially for the unexpected riches of *Norwich*. Thanks to my Dickinson colleagues and students, especially the students who shared the adventure of Norwich with us. Thanks to my friends in Norwich and Carlisle who supported me — often in ways they didn't even realize — while I wrote this novel.

Thanks to my editor, Marysue Rucci, who is equal parts brilliant and patient. It has been my great honor and pleasure to collaborate with her for the last twenty years. Thanks to Zack Knoll for answering my emails, especially the weird, frantic ones, and to all the people at Simon & Schuster who do their jobs so well and have always been such a joy to work with. Thanks to the remarkable Molly Friedrich for breaking her own rules and taking a chance on me, and to everyone at the Friedrich Agency for enthusiastically leaping on board when I needed them most.

Thanks to Chase Perabo and Brady Chilson for making me laugh every single day, and for amazing me every single day. Thanks to my sister Betsy, and to my mother and father, for being smart and funny and believing in me and always being the people I want to tell good news to immediately.

Finally, most importantly, thanks to Sha'an Chilson for eating Waitrose hummus and crackers with me, in the living room on Unthank Road, during my short lunch breaks. I know you lost me for a while in this novel, both in the UK and the US. Thanks for letting me go, and for picking up the slack — in every way possible — in my absence. I could not have written this book without you.

ABOUT THE AUTHOR

Susan Perabo is Writer in Residence and Professor of English and Creative Writing at Dickinson College in Carlisle, Pennsylvania. She is the author of two collections of short stories, *Who I Was Supposed to Be* and *Why They Run the Way They Do,* and the novels *The Broken Places* and *The Fall of Lisa Bellow.* Her fiction has been anthologized in *Best American Short Stories, Pushcart Prize Stories,* and *New Stories from the South.* She holds an MFA from the University of Arkansas, Fayetteville and is on the faculty of the Queens University low-residency MFA program.